Bloodsworn II

Linked by Blood

by

Kathy Lane

Bloodsworn II: Linked by Blood

Contact Information: info@thewildrosepress.com

Cover Art by *Tamra Westberry*

The Wild Rose Press
PO Box 708
Adams Basin, NY 14410-0706
Visit us at www.thewildrosepress.com

Publishing History
First Faery Rose Edition, 2011
Print ISBN 1-60154-946-6

Published in the United States of America

"You want me," she whispered, aware her voice trembled with wondrous discovery.

"Forgive me," he said, averting his eyes and pulling away from her. Even without his touch, his guilt assailed her, the emotion strong, but not enough to overpower that yearning desire. "I never meant to frighten you. I only sought to keep you from injuring yourself. I'll leave—"

She grabbed his retreating hand. Not even with Sayjan had she felt such breathtaking desire. Sayjan had loved her. But her senses had not blossomed under her late husband's touch. Not like this. Compared to what she sensed now, she'd been blind before.

With her shield half up, and only Bracca close enough to sense, she found the invading emotions easily bearable. More than bearable. Intoxicating.

"Bracca..." She reached up to touch his face. He stilled instantly. Pressing her hand firmly to his cheek, she said, "I feel you."

He swallowed hard. "How can you even bear to touch me?"

She didn't understand his question. Not bear to touch him because he was a Blade? Or because she'd swore never to get involved with a Blade again? How could he know? Not even Karess knew of her vow. At the moment, she had trouble even remembering why she'd made it.

Slowly he raised his hand and traced the edge of her face with calloused fingers. Wonder and longing swirled through the desire with a poignant sweetness that brought tears to her eyes.

"You are so beautiful," he whispered. Head bending, he leaned closer.

Praise for
BOUND BY MAGIC: Bloodsworn, Book One

"A great story about what happens when magic meets science. Anyone interested in a solid romance with a lot of action should read this book."
~*ROMFan Reviews*

"[*BOUND BY MAGIC*] has everything you want in a book—action, sexy men, romance, adventure to other worlds, and a great plot which brings it all together in one fantastic story!"
~*Rite of Romance Reviews*

Dedication

To all of my Guardian Angels in Heaven, but especially to:

My mother, who always encouraged me to do my best and to follow my heart. I'm glad you got to read the whole Bloodsworn story before you had to go.

My best friend and sister-of-my-heart, Sue, who always gave me her unconditional love and support, and who loved reading my stories.

And my husband, John, who didn't mind when I talked about my dream of writing, even when we were fishing. You took part of my heart with you when you left, sweetheart. Keep it safe for me.

Acknowledgement

Again I have to say thanks to my editor, Frances, for all her patience and for her efforts to keep me focused, which is a full-time job in itself. And thanks, too, to the ladies of Romantic Hearts and Sexy Tarts for all the tips, tricks, and most especially, encouragement. You ladies rock!

Notes from the
Because-I-Now-Live-On-Another-Planet Dictionary compiled by Avera St. John

Akelia Wine: A powerful aphrodisiac distilled from the Akelia flower. *(Decreases inhibitions, impairs judgment, and generally makes you horny as hell. ASJ)*

Avatar: Sometimes referred to as a 'Regent', an Avatar is a person who embodies the magic of their home world. *(I've yet to meet Avalyr's Avatar, but I'm told her name is Luma and she's definitely not a lanky blue giant. ASJ)*

Blade: An inhabitant of Avalyr who cannot absorb Avalyr's magic on his own. A Blade must blood-link with a Bloodsworn who then provides the magic essence to them through their mental link.

Blade-illness: The affliction that makes it impossible for someone born on Avalyr to touch the planet's magic. Historically occurs only in males between the ages of 15 and 25. *(Sadly, this is changing, and no one knows why. ASJ)*

Blood-Link or Link: The mental connection between a Bloodsworn and a Blade.

Bloodsworn: A person on Avalyr who can mentally touch the veil of magic surrounding the planet. They can blood-link with others and feed them Avalyr's magical essence through a mind-link. *(Previously indigenous only to the planet Avalyr, all Bloodsworn used to be male. Since I'm now Bloodsworn that makes me a freaking anomaly. Go figure. ASJ)*

Bloodsworn High Council: This council is made up of ten Bloodsworn whose job is to vet all new Bloodsworn as well as monitor every Bloodsworn on Avalyr.

The *Calling* or being *Called*: Refers to when a blade-sick man feels drawn to a Bloodsworn before they are even linked. Legend states such a pairing is destined by the gods. Prevalent in ages past, the Calling is believed not to exist anymore.

Concourse: Made up of Avatars of all the magic-based worlds the Concourse's main duty is to monitor and control contact between magical and non-magical worlds. *(Think police force on steroids. Devlin worries they have too much power. ASJ)*

Ellerad: A realm of Avalyr located on the far western coast. *(Bloodsworn Hall is located in this realm. ASJ)*

Feyune: A race of people on Avalyr. *(There are other races, but I haven't met any of them yet. ASJ)*

First Bloodsworn: A Bloodsworn appointed by Luma who is responsible for carrying out the orders of the Bloodsworn High Council.

Gate: A magical portal. There are two types. See Inner Gate and Outer Gate. *(I love these magical short cuts. Can't wait until I'm able to call up one on my own. ASJ)*

Hedaud: A Realm of Avalyr located east of Illian.

Illian: A realm of Avalyr, ruled by clan Tragar.

Inner Decca: An elite group of ten Blades who are the personal bodyguards of a Bloodsworn.

Inner Gate: A Gate between two places on the same world.

Karia: Old Feyunish for *heart*.

Malimes: Old Feyunish for *little knife*. Used as an insult to imply a Blade is untrained or ineffectual.

Me`surrasie: Old Feyunish for *my beloved*, or in some dialects, *my darling one*.

Moiwie City: Capital city of Illian.

Mystia: A northern realm of Avalyr.

Outer Decca: The next closest group of ten Blades to a Bloodsworn. Few Bloodsworn have more than twenty Blades.

Outer gate: A Gate between worlds.

Pakell: Old Feyunish for *brother*.

Savames: Old Feyunish for *old knife* or *worn-out knife*. Used as a Blade insult.

Senyah: An island realm situated far off the western coast.

Shetha: A cast of Feyune women who see to a Blade's or Bloodsworn's lust after a deep healing. *(The term prostitute would be incorrect as shetha don't charge for their services. They also seldom bed a man who is not a Blade or Bloodsworn. Shetha are highly sought after as wives due to their level of expertise in bed. Talk about different cultures. ASJ)*

Solace: Voluntary ritual death—usually requested by a man with the blade-illness who does not want to become a Blade. Solace can also be requested by someone already dying or fatally ill.

Sorlina: Old Feyunish for *sister*.

Suterra: A Realm of Avalyr located between realms Illian and Hedaud.

The Tragar: Title of respect for the leader of Clan Tragar. *(Similar to Scottish Clan tradition. ASJ)*

Tu-kai: An insult from one Blade to another implying the one insulted isn't worthy of having a Bloodsworn.

Vet: Feyune swear word. *(No one will tell me what it means, but usage indicates it might replace 'shit'. ASJ)*

Devlin Tragar's Inner Decca:

1 Fate An-Derrith	6 Shan Ga-Linnian
2 Karess Si-Faderan	7 Valcon Fe-Linnian
3 Strum Ko-Varaith	8 Dune Tu-Annun
4 Judan Si-Atorus	9 Gideon Tu-Annun
5 Sarreth Te-Allian	10 Thern Li-Erano

Chapter One

Bracca Cu-Laurian paused at the entrance to the training grounds. Directly above the western battlements, Avalyr's two moons hung like a pair of ghostly eyes, the pale, thick crescents squinting against the rising sun. Despite the early hour, the huge outer courtyard held at least three decca of Silver Blade warriors. Thirty men, all with good reason to hate a former Black Blade.

He'd had a taste of their dislike over the past two days, contemptuous looks, sly verbal insults—minor annoyances designed to prod his temper and tempt him into striking the first blow. He didn't count the two warriors in the deserted hallway last night. The pair were staggering drunk and probably would have picked a fight with anyone who happened to cross their path. He'd knocked them both out before reporting their whereabouts to their leader, Fate An-Derrith. With the rank of First Blade, Fate was Captain of the Silver Blades, and thus responsible for their behavior. He had not been pleased. Whether his displeasure was because the two Silver Blades had tried to attack Bracca or because they'd been bested so easily was debatable.

Sooner or later, he and Fate would have to come to an understanding, but it probably wouldn't be today.

Bracca stepped out onto the packed sand. The Silver Blades' training grounds were extensive, occupying an entire outer bailey. The surrounding palace, home of Prince Devlin Tragar, ruler of Realm Illian, was as big as a thriving village. It

1

encompassed numerous wings of rooms, several towers, a multitude of smaller courtyards, and countless hallways. He had yet to explore a quarter of his new home, something he needed to remedy as soon as possible.

He glanced around, noting the placement of exits, weapon racks, benches. A picturesque well hid in one corner shaded by a lush tree. His gaze moved up as he crossed the open yard, checking the balconies and roofs of the surrounding buildings.

An uneasy silence descended over the courtyard. He shot a quick glance at the crowd of warriors who'd stopped whatever they were doing to watch him with narrowed eyes. He didn't need the empathic talents that only the females of his world possessed to know he wasn't welcome. Their tensed jaws and clenched fists spoke far louder than words.

Bracca ignored them all. He'd held his own in the midst of a hundred *Black* Blades. Damn if he would flinch for thirty *Silver*. He made his way toward a rack of practice swords on the far side of the huge yard. Murmurs rose behind him. He caught the words "Camarie's Black Blade" more than once, usually coupled with a curse. He fought back the urge to forcefully remind them the sword at his side was no longer black.

The link with his former Bloodsworn had produced a sword as black as sin and twice as cold, just like Camarie's soul. The sword Bracca now possessed could not be more different. Golden amber in color, the gracefully curved weapon at his waist reminded Bracca of a slice of sunlight, warm, bright, and as beautiful as the woman it represented.

A woman. A female Bloodsworn!

Throughout history, only men had been chosen by Avalyr's magic to become conduits for the planet's magic. But Avera St. John proved that nothing was ever written in stone. Born on Earth, she knew nothing about Avalyr or Bloodsworn or Blades. Yet the instant he saw her, Bracca had known she was the Bloodsworn he was destined to serve. A woman he would die to protect.

That Avera now had another, far more powerful protector, did not faze Bracca in the least. He knew she belonged heart and soul to Prince Devlin, Bloodsworn to the Silver Blades. She was the prince's prophecy bride, the woman Lord Devlin had traveled to Earth to claim. And if that wasn't enough to bind them together, she was also his Starmate, the other half of his soul. Interfering with a Starmate bond would be as suicidal as taking on thirty armed men at once.

Knowing all this, Bracca was still determined to do his duty as Avera's First Blade. He would protect her to his last breath. If that meant putting up with her Starmate's jealousy and his warriors' less than welcoming attitudes, then so be it.

A cynical smile touched his lips. Perhaps, instead of fighting them, he should teach the Silver Blades a few new phrases for cursing Black Blades. He'd spent the last ten years of his life among the ranks of Camarie's damned warriors, cursing himself and Camarie, too, more times than he could count.

"Are you ready to die?"

He recognized the voice despite the deep pitch, so he took his time selecting a practice sword. If Karess Si-Faderan wanted him dead, he would not stoop to back-stabbing. "I am honored you would take the time to kill me yourself, Si-Faderan. Surely Lord Devlin's Second Blade has more important things to do than slaughter a poor Amber Blade?"

The blonde-haired warrior grinned at him, a challenge flashing in his gray eyes. "*Are* you a poor Blade? I would have thought anyone who survived numerous years as one of Camarie's bunch would have learned a thing or two about staying alive. Come, Amber Blade, show me your legendary skills. Prove to me you are worthy of the title of Lady Avera's First Blade."

Bracca rotated his wrist and shoulder, loosening the muscles. *Lady Avera's First Blade.* Spoken aloud, the words still had the power to amaze him. His memory flashed back to his brief sojourn on Earth, to the exact moment he realized his sword was the color of warm amber instead of chilling black.

Camarie had sent him to Earth to kill Avera in order to prevent the Seventh Prophecy from coming true. But the moment he saw her, he knew he couldn't do it. Somehow, he'd sensed she was Bloodsworn. *His* Bloodsworn. Instead of killing her, he broke his sword, severing his link with Camarie in order to protect her, knowing it would mean his death.

But Avera refused to let him die. Whether by chance or by the grace of the gods, she'd snatched him from death by forming a blood-link with him. No one was more surprised by his new status as an Amber Blade than he was. Or more grateful.

Needless to say, her Starmate felt just the opposite.

Bracca inclined his head and followed Karess out onto the sands, wondering if the challenge was Karess' idea or Devlin Tragar's.

****

Sheren Ni-Annun welcomed the heat of the rising sun as she climbed down from the wagon. She paused in her survey of the stable yard to stretch a kink from her back. The two hour ride from Villa Porenmagie to the Tragar's palace had never seemed so long. Honesty made her admit it might have had something to do with the way she'd held herself stiffly on the wagon's seat the entire time, trying to avoid accidentally brushing against Nerrilik.

Her gaze slid to where the warrior stood giving instructions to a stable boy. Nerrilik had been close friends with her late husband. Since Sayjan's death, he'd appointed himself her protector and lately was pushing her for something more.

Lifting her basket from the wagon's bed, she quickly headed for the door to the kitchens, hoping to avoid another uncomfortable scene. Nerrilik was a Silver Blade. That alone made it impossible for her to accept his suit.

"Sheren!"

Not quick enough.

"I'm not sure how long I'll be," she said as she faced him, hoping to head off his usual interrogation. He was obsessed with keeping an eye on her when they were away from the villa, as if afraid someone might steal her. "I have several errands to complete this trip."

"I'll accompany you." His hand slid down her arm to shackle her wrist in a possessive hold.

"That won't be necessary. I'm perfectly capable of finding my own way. You don't need to neglect your Blade duties for me." She twisted her wrist, trying to break free gently, but his hand tightened.

"I know what you're thinking," he said, his voice lowering as he moved closer. "You know I'm not like Sayjan, Sheren. You can trust me." His other hand stroked her check. She barely kept herself from flinching. "I would never ignore you like he did, *me`surrasie*."

She did flinch then. No one but her Sayjan had ever called her his *beloved*. "Nerrilik, please, let me go. You know I don't feel that way about you."

"You could," he said, his voice dipping to an urgent whisper. "You could if you would just let go of the past. If you let go of your memory of Sayjan before he became a Blade."

She'd heard all of this before. Different words,

same argument. She was getting tired of fending off Nerrilik's attentions.

"I know how he treated you," he said. "We argued about it the night he was killed. I promised him I would look after you if anything happened to him. Would you have me foresworn?"

"How can you be foresworn? You protect me every day by helping to protect the villa where I live and work. I am always grateful for the presence of you and the other Silver Blades."

His eyes tightened at her words. He'd been captured the same night Sayjan had been killed. By the time he was rescued, the injury to his leg was beyond repair, even by a deep-healing. He'd been retired from the Tragar's personal guard and put in charge of security at Villa Porenmagie. A position Nerrilik seemed to embrace and hate at the same time. She'd come to believe it was only her presence at the villa keeping him from requesting a different assignment.

"I'm grateful for your vigilance in keeping us all safe, Nerrilik." She stepped back as far as his grip on her wrist allowed. "But I can't offer you more."

The skin along his jaw whitened. For a moment, she thought she felt a wisp of anger seep through her shields, though it had to be her imagination. Her empathic gift wasn't strong enough for her to identify emotions.

"There you are, Nerrilik. Come, I have that new mare you ordered."

Sheren smiled at the stable master as he approached. With a final squeeze of his hand, Nerrilik released her and turned to face the older man.

She used the interruption to slip away, conscious of Nerrilik's gaze tracking her to the kitchen door. This could not go on. There had to be some way for her to convince Nerrilik to look elsewhere for a wife—some way that didn't involve her going to Prince Tragar and risking her position as chatelaine of the villa. If her marriage to Sayjan had taught her nothing else, she knew better than come between a Blade and his Bloodsworn.

Chapter Two

The clash of swords rang through the vast courtyard, echoing off the surrounding high walls. Bracca grunted as his own weapon clanged hard against Karess', the impact traveling up his arm. Karess retreated quickly only to return the next instant slicing the air in a deadly arc aimed right at Bracca's throat. He jerked back and brought his sword up in time to deflect the blow.

Barely.

Karess Si-Faderan was indeed skilled. But then, Bracca expected no less of the man who held the position of Second Blade in Lord Devlin's personal guard. The Silver Blades were known to be highly trained warriors. Their proficiency, coupled with a fierce loyalty to their Bloodsworn made them dangerous adversaries.

Bracca glowered at Karess as he met the next series of attacks. The blasted warrior definitely set his teeth on edge. Not because of the speed and skill with which he fought—things Bracca could understand and match—but because of the perpetual grin on the damned Blade's face. He wasn't used to seeing humor in his opponent's eyes. Usually all he saw was a thirst for his death.

The clear trill of feminine laughter drifting on the breeze startled him. Women nearby? Impossible. No female would dare enter the courtyard while warriors were engaged in battle, even mock battle. Male aggression had to be thick enough in the air to be painful to the empathic mind of a Feyune female unless she had very strong shields. He looked around quickly, certain he had to have imagined the provocative sound.

"No, you're not hearing things." Karess grinned wider, the amusement in his voice evident even over the noise around them. "Look up."

The ring of balconies hugging the tall walls of the surrounding buildings had been empty at sunrise. Now, several dozen women of varying ages, some maids, some ladies with the bottom half of their faces discreetly covered, littered the walkways. The attention of each woman seemed riveted on the training field, eyes full of curiosity and, in some cases, blatant admiration.

Their presence shocked Bracca, making him almost miss Karess' next attack.

"Ha, almost touched you that time, Cu-Laurian," Karess taunted. "Didn't anyone ever teach you to keep your mind on your work?"

Bracca scowled. Karess laughed outright and nodded toward the occupied balconies.

"Amazing how distracting they can be, isn't it? Don't feel bad. We Silver Blades have had years of practice ignoring them."

Distracting was an understatement, Bracca decided. Now that he knew the women were there, the urge to look up at them lurked like a hungry beast in the back of his mind. He succeeded in ignoring their presence for all of a minute when motion on one of the walkways connecting two balconies demanded his attention more forcefully. He allowed himself a quick glance. Only another gawking woman.

Or perhaps not, he decided after a second glance. This female did not behave like the other women. She moved with purpose, seemingly oblivious to the courtyard's occupants. His curiosity stirred, followed immediately by a sense of frustration. With her face diverted, he couldn't see her features very well. All he could tell was that she wore a blue gown the color of the morning sky and had pale blonde hair plaited into a long thick braid trailing down her trim back.

He continued to watch her from the corner of his eye until she opened a door and stepped out of sight. A sense of loss came out of nowhere, making him wonder if some of Karess' blows hadn't addled his brain.

He tried to put her out of his mind, but found his curiosity wouldn't allow it. Who was she? Why did she act differently from the others? Was she so jaded, so used to the sweating, half-naked bodies of the men below her that she no longer paid them any attention? Did that mean she was old instead of young, her hair silver gray instead of white blonde as he first thought? For some reason, that possibility annoyed him even more than Karess did.

With a quick shake of his head, he wrestled his wayward mind back to the business of sword-work. It wasn't easy, and he blamed his lapse of discipline on the enigma of the woman. She had no business being so close to the training yard. But then, none of the women did.

"Do they do this often?" he asked between blows, irritation spiking when he caught himself shifting in order to scan the balconies for the mysterious woman.

"Do what, watch us?" Karess asked, his brows rising. Gray eyes full of appreciation sent a quick glance at their audience. "Every blessed day."

Bracca wondered at the audacity of the people he found himself among. The women, as well as the men who should be watching out for them.

"The Tragar allows this?"

"Gods, yes." Karess flashed his annoying grin and danced back, just out of Bracca's reach. He gestured to the side with his sword. "Nothing like a female audience to encourage the novices to perform their best."

Bracca's gaze followed Karess' gesture, noting the pair of young warriors battling furiously nearby. His peripheral vision caught Karess lunging from a relaxed stance. Bracca sidestepped, captured the sword thrust at him with his own blade, and shoved the Silver Blade back.

Karess laughed and moved out of reach once more, nodding in appreciation of Bracca's quick reflexes. "Not to mention, their presence clearly demonstrates to even the most thick-headed warrior the importance of keeping his attention on his adversary."

As if to demonstrate, another round of giggling laughter cascaded over the balcony rail. Most of the older, seasoned warriors, ignored the sound. The heads of others not so disciplined jerked up as if pulled by strings. More than one sword found its mark on an inattentive Blade. An effective lesson, indeed.

Bracca focused his attention on Karess for the next few minutes. He tried his best to ignore the unusual audience, but for all his years of experience, he couldn't entirely keep from glancing up now and again. The situation was too novel, too...surreal.

The sword-dance shifted, became more demanding. He and Karess exchanged places, once, twice. The third time, he ducked, rolled beneath Karess' next attack, and caught a flash of sky-blue skirts as he came smoothly to his feet. Without pausing to think why, he broke the pattern of the training routine, forcing Karess to switch places with him a fourth time. His mysterious lady stood facing the courtyard, deep in discussion with another woman. The morning sunlight caught her face perfectly.

Not old. Smooth, high cheeks, rose-tinted lips,

finely arched brows over eyes he swore were the color of a lavender sunset. Gods above, she was beautiful. He had to get a closer look.

Once again he broke out of the training pattern, forcing Karess back with several hard blows. Perhaps the sudden heavy clash of swords reached her ears, for she glanced down. The impact of her startled gaze meeting his drove every thought from his head. A long heartbeat of time passed. Bracca felt something move inside his mind, light, fleeting, like the touch of a butterfly.

He blinked, his awareness returning in time to notice Karess' sword speeding toward him in an unfamiliar move. Swearing, he threw up a hasty guard. Karess' sword twisted and slipped free, the blunted tip catching Bracca just above his left eye. Karess gave a triumphant shout.

Knowing he couldn't allow the Silver Blade to wallow in his success, Bracca sternly brought his concentration back to the moment at hand. Swiping at the blood pouring down his face, he launched an attack of his own. A dozen strokes later, he slashed the dulled edge of his sword across Karess' belly.

Karess jerked back, eyes wide in surprise and renewed respect. "A killing move. One I've not seen before. You are full of surprises, my new friend. Show me the move again." He motioned with his practice sword and flowed into a defensive stance.

Bracca hesitated. Before meeting Avera and becoming her Amber Blade, he would never have thought to share his fighting secrets with anyone. They were the only things that had kept him alive, even from his own blade-brothers. Especially from them. The concepts of trust and friendship were foreign among the ranks of Black Blades. He had learned quickly to depend only on himself.

Before he could convince himself such survival instincts were no longer needed, Karess straightened and signaled an end to their match. "Perhaps another time." The Silver Blade shrugged, his eyes holding more understanding than Bracca was willing to acknowledge. "No doubt you're ready for a break."

Bracca snorted and relaxed slowly, too used to sneak attacks to let his guard down entirely. "It will take more than sparring with a grinning idiot to tire me, Silver Blade."

The ridiculous grin widened, mischief dancing back into gray eyes as Karess waved a water-boy forward. "Then we'll have to see what we can do about that. A word of advice, however, one warrior to another..." He paused, giving Bracca time to refuse the offer. Surprised by the gesture, Bracca inclined his head for Karess to continue.

"Don't let Fate hear you say you're not tired after a sparring match. He'll consider it more of a challenge than I do, and you don't want to fight him yet. He may not show it, but he's still not happy with you."

Bracca glanced over to where the Tragar's First Blade, Fate An-Derrith, was engaged in a sparring match with the young Blade, Kiel Na-Turesh. Both men were of a similar build, tall and lean, though Fate's body spoke of a hardness Kiel's had yet to attain. They whirled in a graceful sword-dance, weapons flashing, Kiel's pale limbs moving in response to Fate's darker ones. To the untrained eye, they would appear evenly matched, but Bracca knew better. He'd seen the deadly First Blade in real battle.

During the fight on Earth, the warrior took on four men at once and came out of the conflict un-scathed. Only when twice that number attacked him did Bracca decide to go to his aid. An act that had earned Bracca a cracked skull along with Fate's eternal resentment.

Karess tossed him a dry cloth. "See if you can get that wound to stop bleeding before we start again. I wouldn't want to be accused of taking unfair advantage when I beat you." He walked away before Bracca could respond to the taunt.

Bracca wiped the blood off his face, then pressed the cloth to his forehead, thinking that if he wasn't careful, Karess' boast about beating him just might come true. If not for the woman in blue, the Silver Blade never would have touched him. He knew better than to let himself get distracted.

"Excuse me?"

The soft, female voice was barely audible above the din overflowing the courtyard. An odd awareness filled him. Somehow he knew, even before he turned, who the voice belonged to. His lady in blue stood just inside one of the archways leading to the courtyard. And she was even more lovely up close.

Tendrils of her pale blonde hair had come loose from her braid and curled around a face dominated by the most vivid lavender eyes he'd ever seen. Darker blonde brows arched gracefully over those striking eyes, matching the thick lashes. An elegant nose swept down between high cheeks to a pair of full, luscious lips. Her chin was small, but firm, hinting at a strength belied by her fragile appearance. He imagined her with that wealth of silky hair unbound, curling like a lover's hands around her slender body, and the word ethereal came to his mind.

Giving himself a mental shake—such thoughts could only get him into trouble—he met her determined gaze as he approached, stopping a few feet away when he saw her body tense. He bowed respectfully, never taking his eyes off her. "How may I serve you, my lady?"

She seemed to gather herself before taking a step toward him and holding out her hand. "I saw what happened. This ointment will stop the bleeding and seal the wound." Despite the offer of aid, her words sounded clipped, her expression heavy with disapproval. Strange. It almost felt as if her disapproval was directed at herself more than him.

He bowed again. The wound above his eye was small and would, no doubt, stop bleeding on its own, shortly. He didn't really need the ointment. Still, he could not very well refuse her generous offer. "Thank you for your kindness, my lady." He reached for the small jar she held, his finger tips brushing her palm as he scooped it up. He froze when her body jerked slightly. She sucked in a breath, and her beautiful lavender eyes grew wide, her face suddenly as pale as snow. She swayed.

Bracca dropped the cloth and jar, reaching out to steady her. "Are you all right, my lady?"

For a moment, she didn't answer. Then she blinked, long lashes fanning the curve of her cheeks. "I'm not... Yes, I-I'm fine." Her gaze dropped down for just an instant then shot back to his face. A touch of panic joined the stunned expression in her eyes. "Release me."

He found himself extremely reluctant to do as she demanded. He didn't want to let her go. Ever. That emphatic thought shocked him into looking away from her distressed face. His gaze snagged on a smear of bright red against pale white skin. With a silent oath, he snatched his hands away, a rush of self-disgust filling him at the sight of his blood smeared on her arms.

"Forgive me." He bent and retrieved the jar and cloth from the courtyard sands. When he stood again, all he saw of her was a swish of blue skirt disappearing around the corner of the short hallway. He took a step to go after her, shame washing through him, followed by anger. This is what comes of allowing females near warriors during training. If not for the Tragar's idiocy, Bracca would not now be feeling as if he needed to track her down and fall on his knees begging her forgiveness.

"Cu-Laurian?"

Bracca turned at Karess' sharp call. For once, the warrior's grin was absent. He wasn't scowling exactly, but the slightly drawn brows over hard gray eyes communicated his displeasure.

"What did you say to Sheren?"

Sheren. So that was her name. It sounded as lovely as she looked.

"Nothing. I—"

A shout rose from a corner of the practice yard. Sparring warriors disengaged and moved quickly toward the corner, taking up defensive positions. Bracca could just see the glowing edges of a magic gate over the tops of their heads.

"Visitors," Karess murmured into the wary silence filling the courtyard.

Bracca's gaze swept across the line of tense backs and shoulders between him and the gate. "Unexpected visitors, I take it." The glow of the gate vanished as he spoke.

"Definitely unexpected. Devlin lets us know when a fellow Bloodsworn plans to visit. Less chance of a misunderstanding between Blades. Come, let's see who our guests are."

Chapter Three

Sheren didn't stop running until she reached a small inner courtyard with a bubbling fountain. Thankfully, no one else was there. She immediately dampened the hem of her gown and scrubbed the blood off her arms. Despite her first impression, there wasn't much, just a few smears here and there. When she was done, she leaned against the fountain's edge, struggling to make sense of the last few minutes.

Looking down into the training yard was her first mistake. Though she might be forgiven considering the man who drew her attention. For just a moment, the vision of him exchanging blows with Karess flashed into her mind. The way he moved had mesmerized her, drawing her eyes to the bunch and flex of muscles beneath his gleaming, sun-kissed skin. She would have had to be dead not to notice him.

Her second mistake was meeting his eyes. His dark, intense gaze had captured hers, making it impossible for her to look away. Her only consolation was that she sensed he was just as captivated. She should have realized then that something was happening to her. *She'd sensed his emotions!* She'd never been able to do that before. She might have come to her senses eventually, but then Karess drew the warrior's blood. All sane thought and common sense left her in a rush of breathless concern.

Going down to the courtyard was her third mistake. She simply hadn't been able to stop herself. All that blood! For some reason, she had to see him.

She had to make sure the injury wasn't as bad as it looked.

Offering the ointment was mistake number four, this one beyond foolish. Though she didn't recognize him, the warrior had to be a Blade. Only Blades practiced in that courtyard. His Bloodsworn could heal almost any injury he incurred short of death. Yet again, something inside her compelled her past sanity or self preservation to offer the ointment. Guilt maybe? He *had* been looking up at her when he'd caught that glancing blow from Karess' sword.

Then he touched her. In that instant, her mental shield, the one that had served her quite well for years, collapsed. No, vanished would be a better word. Years of adequate protection wiped out by a fleeting brush of calloused fingers against her palm.

The rush of emotions sweeping into her unprotected mind had been overwhelming. Never had she felt anything so strong. And she *knew* each emotion. The bursts of anger, frustration, surprise, and satisfaction coming from the sparring warriors were easily recognizable. But none of those emotions were as strong as the admiration and concern coming from the injured warrior.

His emotions had over-shadowed everything else, as if his feelings alone were important. The possibility frightened her. All she could think was that his touch, his blood, had somehow created a link between them, opening a door to her mind. Maybe even to her soul.

So she'd run. And Luma help her, she swore never to set foot near the training courtyard again. She would go back to Villa Porenmagie, and he would stay at the palace and serve his Bloodsworn. They could never meet again.

A small part of her rebelled at the thought. Just the memory of how his admiration touched her stroked a neglected place inside her that she hadn't been aware of and sent flutters through her stomach.

With an effort of will, she forced the memory away. She wasn't a shy, innocent girl to be dazzled by a warrior's attentions. She was a widowed matron. A mother. She had her son to think of now. Admiration wasn't nearly enough for her to risk getting involved with a Blade again.

Blades *always* put their Bloodsworn first.

****

Bracca followed Karess through the crowd of warriors to the clearing in the corner of the courtyard. Five men, Blades from the look of them, stood in a loose semi-circle around a sixth man who had to be their Bloodsworn. None were men Bracca had ever seen before.

The young Bloodsworn took a step forward, his face clearly unhappy behind the lines of a neatly trimmed beard and mustache. "Where is Devlin?"

Fate An-Derrith did not appear to be impressed. "Our Bloodsworn is unavailable at present. I will tell him of your need to see him as soon as possible."

"I'm not here to play diplomatic games with you, Fate. I don't like it any more than you do, but this is Council business." He pulled three scrolls from a belt pouch. Selecting one, he held it up. "This is a summons for a female named Avera St. John, demanding she submit herself at once to the Council so they may determine whether or not she is actually Bloodsworn. A ridiculous notion, I grant you, but the Council deems the charge serious enough to investigate."

He added a second scroll. "This one is addressed to the First Bloodsworn of Avalyr, instructing him to see that Avera St. John presents herself with all speed. And this," he held up the third scroll. "This scroll is for the arrest of a Black Blade named Bracca Cu-Laurian."

Cold seeped into Bracca's veins as the strange Bloodsworn leaned closer to the Tragar's First Blade. "I told my grandfather and the other Council Elders that Devlin Tragar would never harbor a Black Blade, Fate. Tell me I did not lie."

Bracca felt a host of eyes settle on him—hostile, aggressive, resentful. He expected any moment to hear someone call him to the Bloodsworn's attention. No Blade alive on Avalyr had any reason to protect a former Black Blade. Especially not at the risk of his own Bloodsworn.

Before Fate could answer, Karess' laugh shattered the tense stillness. "You will be happy to know your honor remains unsullied, my Lord Jerran. I assure you, no Black Blades are hiding here. Considering Devlin's animosity toward his uncle, you and I know a Black Blade would have to be a grinning idiot to even set foot inside these walls."

The reference to his earlier taunt was not lost on Bracca. A smile curled his lips despite the seriousness of the situation. Was Si-Faderan's lunacy catching?

"There is, however, an Amber Blade here."

Bracca swore to himself. He couldn't tell who had spoken up, but someone evidently did not intend for him to go completely un-noticed.

The Bloodsworn's dark brows drew together. "An Amber Blade? I don't think I know which Bloodsworn—"

"You wouldn't," Karess said, his smile fairly cracking his face in two. "You haven't met her yet."

The Bloodsworn's eyes flew wide then narrowed. Not in suspicion or disapproval, but, if Bracca read them correctly, in interest.

Bowing to the inevitable, Bracca stepped forward. The five visiting Blades immediately came to attention, hands hovering near swords. One went so far as to close on a hilt and lift the sword slightly to show a hint of sapphire metal.

Bits and pieces of information he'd heard over the years came together, and Bracca realized the Bloodsworn's identity. Jerran Ti-Peregrine, head of Clan Peregrine, was known to be a close friend of Devlin Tragar's. His unhappiness at having to deliver such messages was now clear.

Bracca stopped at Fate's side, a subtle reminder of their equal status, and bowed respectfully. "My lord Ti-Peregrine. It is a pleasure to meet you. I am Bracca Cu-Laurian, First Amber Blade to Bloodsworn Avera St. John."

Lord Peregrine stared at him a long moment, then sighed. The scrolls crinkled in his clenched hand. "Of course you are." He turned to Fate. "I don't care what Devlin's doing, if he's not dead or dying, get him down here."

Chapter Four

Devlin felt as if he were drowning. Not that he cared. There were worse ways to die than drowning in lust for one's Starmate. Ignoring his need for air, he deepened the kiss, pulling Avera closer until every naked inch of her pressed tightly against him. Finally, after a torturous week of courting, of traveling back and forth between his world and hers, he had her where he wanted her—on his planet and, more importantly, in his bed.

Two weeks ago, he'd been dreading the thought of being forced to take a prophecy bride. Then the Oracle revealed his destined bride was also his Starmate, the other half of his soul. Not even the fact that she was from another world mattered then. He'd gone to Earth, met her, wooed her, and nearly lost her to assassins more times than he cared to recall. Now she was safe. Now she was his. The warrior inside him roared a triumphant victory cry. *Mine!*

Slim-fingered hands dragged slowly through his hair. The scrape of her nails against his scalp sent erotic tingles all the way down his spine. Avera's hips moved languidly against him. She sighed into their kiss. The soft sound shot like an arrow straight to his groin while at the same time stirring his conscience. She sounded tired.

Shame washed through him as he admitted he was responsible for her exhaustion. He hadn't been able to keep his hands off her for more than a few minutes at a time since yesterday afternoon. From the moment she accepted him, agreeing to be his

Starmate, his bride, *his*, the need to touch and taste her, be inside of her, was all consuming. He doubted she'd had more than a couple of hours sleep the entire night.

Not even a full day into their Starmate-bond and he'd already committed the sin of not seeing to her welfare. He should let her rest.

He started to pull back just as her body undulated beneath him more forcefully. The invitation was blatant, as was the need he glimpsed in her partially closed eyes. She might be tired, but the magic of the Starmate-bond ran through her veins just as fiercely as his. Capturing one of her nipples in his mouth, he sent his hand sliding down her body toward the junction of her legs. He would be a poor mate indeed to ignore her need. Once more, he decided, one more taste of her, one more trip into the realm of mutual pleasure, and then he'd insist she rest.

A sharp tugging sensation shot though his mind. He didn't even have to shuffle through his many mental links to identify which of his Blades was requesting his attention. He opened the link long enough to growl, *Not now, Fate*, before slamming it closed again. Another tug surprised him. Fate was usually wise enough to know better. Barely controlling the irritation boiling up inside him at the interruption, Devlin snapped the link open. *What?*

Lord Jerran Ti-Peregrine has just arrived—

Tell him to come back later.

He comes as Herald bearing a summons from the Bloodsworn High Council.

A few silent curses ran through Devlin's mind. Caveon, the leader of the Council, probably wanted his help tracking down Camarie. The dark Bloodsworn's attempt to kill Avera had certainly earned him the death sentence as far as Devlin was concerned, but running his infamous uncle to ground would have to wait.

Tell him I will attend the Council in a few hours. Inform him of the circumstances. He didn't bother explaining those circumstances. Fate would know by the hot rush of desire he couldn't keep from spilling into the open link. Lust ran unchecked through his blood, building with each kiss, each touch of skin against skin. Luma's tears, he wasn't going to be able to wait much longer. He wanted to hear her cry out his name again, hear her call him *me'surrasie*, her beloved.

Forgive me, my Bloodsworn, Fate said, his tone both urgent and apologetic. *But the summons is not for you, but for Lady St. John.*

He paused in his exploration of the soft skin beneath his lips. Impatience shifted to concern. *They have summoned Avera?* He'd hoped to give her more time to acclimate to her new life before subjecting her to the Council's scrutiny. She'd had too many things thrown at her in the space of a few days. Chased by Camarie's Black Blades, learning the man she loved was from another planet, being dragged to that very planet against her will and told she could never return to Earth. And, oh, yes, becoming Bloodsworn. Luma forbid he leave that one out. How could he ask her to endure more?

Yes, my lord. She is commanded to appear before the High Council immediately to prove her Bloodsworn status. He carries a second letter addressed to the First Bloodsworn, commanding him to compel her cooperation if necessary. He also has an arrest order for Cu-Laurian.

Devlin gave a mental snort as he brushed Avera's raven black hair back from her beautiful face to kiss her temple. *They're leaving nothing to chance, are they, my friend?*

As the Prince of Illian, he might get away with ignoring an immediate summons. Avalyr's First

Bloodsworn could not. He wondered how they had found out about Avera so soon. No doubt, news of the first female Bloodsworn in Avalyr's history was already spreading, but she'd only arrived on planet two nights ago. Bloodsworn Hall was a continent away. Only another Bloodsworn could have sent the news so quickly. The question was, who?

"Devlin?"

He raised his head to find his Starmate gazing at him, the hunger simmering in the depths of her dark green eyes overshadowed by confusion. A slight frown wrinkled her perfect brow.

"What is it?" she asked. "You stopped kissing me, and you look upset. Is something wrong?"

He heaved a mental sigh, hating that he couldn't finish what he'd just started. "Forgive me, Avera. It is not that something is wrong so much as inconvenient. Fate tells me a messenger has arrived. Apparently, your Bloodsworn status is being called into question by the Council. They are demanding your immediate presence."

She stiffened, her frown deepening. "What council?"

"The Bloodsworn High Council. Its members are responsible for overseeing every Bloodsworn on Avalyr."

She pulled back from him, suspicion replacing the desire in her eyes. He let her sit up, but didn't release her entirely. He wasn't about to let the damn Council come between them. "Oversees them how?" she asked, her tone wary.

"Nothing very intrusive, as a rule. The Council keeps track of the number of Bloodsworn, and tries to make sure their distribution is fairly even across Avalyr."

"You said, as a rule?"

"Yes. They only interfere when necessary. When a Bloodsworn cannot or will not control his powers.

Most Bloodsworn see their status as a sacred commission, a responsibility to others. Abuse of the magic granted them is rare." He silently cursed his outlaw uncle at her sudden look of skepticism. "Camarie is truly an exception, Avera, and he will be punished, I swear it. The day he sent his warriors to Earth to kill you, is the day he sealed his fate. Before, the Council only tried to rein him in, hoping a milder punishment would make him see reason. Now he lies under a death sentence."

She gave an emphatic nod. "Good. Because anyone who treats people like he treats his Blades doesn't deserve to live. You don't know what he's done, what he's capable of." Her gaze slid away from his. A small shudder shook her body.

He pulled her back into the shelter of his arms, tucking her head beneath his chin. He would have given anything, done anything, to keep her from knowing the depth of Camarie's depravity. Unfortunately, he hadn't been on Earth when she'd blood-linked with the dark Bloodsworn's Black Blade. If he had, he would have killed the warrior called Bracca Cu-Laurian before he could link, mind-to-mind, Blade to Bloodsworn, with Avera.

The only reason he didn't take the man's head now was because Cu-Laurian had saved Avera's life on more than one occasion. That and the fact his prophecy bride would probably never forgive him. Avera took her new Bloodsworn duties very seriously.

My Bloodsworn? Fate's call reminded Devlin of his own duties.

Tell Jerran I'll meet him in my study. Devlin closed the link and eased his tight hold on his Starmate reluctantly. "The Council's Herald awaits us, beloved."

"All right." The frustration in her voice echoed his own, allowing him to find the strength to let her slip entirely from his arms. She stood beside the bed, gloriously naked, and indulged in a slow, luxurious stretch. He let his gaze run over her bare back and firm bottom, admiring the shift and ripple of feminine muscles. The way her night-black hair fell like a stormy cloud across her soft shoulders.

She walked around the bed, turning her head from side to side, as if looking for something. When she bent down to look under the bed, the sight of her shapely bottom sticking up in the air almost made him swallow his tongue. He snapped his eyes closed and ran both hands over his face. Judging by the demanding ache in his groin, the next few hours were going to be a living hell.

"Devlin?"

He opened his eyes, immediately forcing his gaze to her face and not her delectable body. A small smile played about her lips. She held her arms out to her sides and looked at him expectantly.

He had to clear his throat before he could speak. "Yes, my love?"

Her brows rose in question. "You magicked my clothes away yesterday, remember? How about using some of that cool magic of yours and wishing me up some more?"

Yes, he remembered banishing her clothes, but he couldn't for the moment recall where he'd sent them. He hadn't been thinking of anything other than getting his hands on her bare skin. Most likely they were back in her room on the other side of the palace. When one didn't firmly direct the magic, it had a tendency to take the most logical route.

"The nature of Avalyr's magic doesn't allow us to create or destroy things," he explained, rising from the bed. "We can only move them or change their appearance. Your clothing is probably in your room in the Ladies' Wing. I can call a gate for you, or I can change something of mine into suitable clothing." He drew her into a loose embrace, marveling anew at how perfectly she fit. He kissed the tip of her nose. "The choice is yours, but I advise you to make it quickly."

She smiled and kissed his chin. "Do I have time for a bath?"

"Absolutely. I will meet with the Herald and come for you in an hour." A kiss to her temple this time, his lips lingering.

Her breathing quickened. "Then I would like one of your magic short-cuts, please, before things get out of hand again. I wouldn't want to keep your precious Council waiting."

Damn the Council, he thought. But he sighed, released her, and called a gate to her room with a flick of his hand. The look of wonder on her face made him feel as if he'd just worked some monumental bit of magic instead of a simple, everyday task.

He let her step through the gate alone and forced himself to close the damn thing before he followed her. The thought of bathing with her made his already hard shaft jump eagerly. He looked down and stroked himself in sympathy. If he gave in to his desires now, it might be another day before he came to his senses again. With the Council breathing down their collective necks, he needed a clear head.

Damning the circumstances, he opened a gate to the spring-fed pond deep inside his private garden. Before he could change his mind, he stalked to the water's edge and launched himself into its freezing depths.

Luma's bloody hell!

****

An hour later, dry, dressed, and seething with anger at the Council and their secret informant, Devlin knocked on the door to Avera's room.

"Come in."

28

The voice was familiar, but not the one he expected. He opened the door to find his little sister, Gwenell, frowning mightily as she paced back and forth. Her face cleared the instant she saw him. She rushed toward him.

"Oh, Devlin, thank goodness. You have to reason with her. She won't listen to me."

"Reason with who, little *sorlina*?"

She made an exasperated noise. "With Avera, of course."

The door to the bathing chamber opened and the lady in question emerged. Devlin's gaze locked with hers. For a long moment her vivid green eyes were all he saw.

"You see," Gwenell moaned. "She can't possibly face the Council wearing those clothes."

His gaze moved down over the curves of Avera's body. He realized immediately that Gwenell was right. His Starmate could definitely not wear her Earth clothing to council. Not only would her tight pants—her jeans—call attention to the fact she was from another world, but he didn't like to think of the male attention they would call to her pert bottom. A concealing dress would definitely be better. Deep burgundy, he decided quickly, with gold trim and a gold chain belt to ride her hips. The image firmly in mind, he released his magic. He remembered her shoes this time, turning her sneakers into a matching pair of soft slippers.

Avera gasped and looked down at herself. Her hands tentatively touched the velvet material and brushed across the links of the belt. She lifted the skirt and held out a foot, turning it from side to side. She looked at him quizzically. "Not that I don't appreciate the new wardrobe, but why the change of clothes? My jeans not good enough for a meeting with your Council?"

He prudentially shooed Gwenell out and closed

the door before answering, all the while thanking the gods for his years of practice at diplomatic tact. "This is an important meeting, Avera. The High Council has the power to deny a person Bloodsworn status if they deem them unfit. The fact you are female will be hard enough for them to accept. It is best if you do not appear any more different than you already are."

"How can they deny that I'm a Bloodsworn if I already have two Blades?"

"They can't. But they can decide that you aren't capable of handling the magic. If they do, they have the power to take your Blades from you." He braced himself for her reaction and wasn't disappointed. Her eyes hardened to green crystals.

"I'd like to see them try."

He ran his hands up her arms to her shoulders and looked deep into her eyes. "No, you would not, and neither would I. With only two Blades, your access to magic is extremely limited. Even if you knew how to wield it, you wouldn't be able to fight them. If the Council judges you unable to bear this burden, they'll pin you and Cu-Laurian down and break his sword without the slightest effort. Then they'll send someone to do the same with Tyr."

That someone would be him, though he hoped she wouldn't make that connection. As First Bloodsworn, he was responsible for enforcing the Council's rulings.

She shook her head emphatically, and tried to shrug out of his hold. "Then I won't go. I refuse to even risk putting Bracca and Tyr in that position."

He subdued her easily, pulling her against him, knowing he was going to have to damn himself. "Stop struggling and listen to me. You have no choice, Avera, and neither does Cu-Laurian. If both of you do not answer their summons, the Council has ordered the First Bloodsworn of Avalyr to bring you to them."

She stilled, her angry gaze shooting up to him. "You said *you* were First Bloodsworn."

He nodded, hating the shadow of fear springing to life in her eyes.

"You'd do that?" she whispered. "You'd drag me and Bracca to them in chains?"

He shook his head and smiled slightly, hoping to divert some of her fear with humor. "What is this fascination you have with chains, *me`surrasie*? First you accuse Fate of wanting to use them, and now, myself. You must know I would never bind you in chains." He paused and leaned down to whisper in her ear. "Not unless you ask me to."

Heat flashed in her eyes before her brows lowered in disapproval. "I can't believe you're teasing me at a time like this. You just got through agreeing with me yesterday that there has to be a reason why I'm a Bloodsworn, why I can smell scents during a linking when no one else can. How are we going to figure out what that means if this council of yours decides I'm not good enough to join their ranks?"

He took her face in his hands, and gazed intently into her eyes, willing her to understand. "You are good enough, Avera, never doubt that. But you must promise me you'll abide by the Council's ruling. We will figure everything else out later, I swear. Just promise me you will not fight them." Or me, he added silently.

Chapter Five

Sheren hurried down the palace corridor, anxious to complete her tasks so she could return home. There was still the possibility, however slight, that she could run into the strange warrior again. She wasn't sure what she should do if that happened. Pretend this morning's meeting never occurred? If only that were possible.

"Sheren, wait."

Nerrilik's impatient voice only caused her to want to quicken her pace. A futile gesture. There seemed to be no getting away from him today despite his limp. A hand closed around her arm just as she came to a stop. She smothered her irritation. Losing her temper with him only made things worse.

"I told you to wait for me before leaving the servants' wing, Sheren. Why did you diso...disregard my request?"

She tried not to notice how he'd switched *disobey* to disregard. Sometimes things ran smoother when she pretended a little ignorance.

"I'm sorry, Nerrilik, but I have an appointment to see Lady Patria. Her time is not ours to waste, and if I'd waited for you I would be late. I still might be if you do not release me. It is best not to incur her displeasure when I am seeking favors for the villa."

He moved until only the wicker basket over her arm separated them, his frown turning angry. "You still should have waited. Whether you agree or not, you are mine to protect, Sheren. I swore it on Sayjan's grave, and nothing you say or do will change that."

Sheren fought back a shiver of alarm. The words she'd heard before, but this time his tone bordered on menacing. This obsession of his was getting out of hand.

"Nerrilik?"

The masculine call came from down the hall. Nerrilik straightened, released her, and took a step back. Her arm throbbed, her hand tingling as blood surged back into place. Nerrilik turned, deliberately keeping his body between her and the approaching men.

With a sense of relief, she recognized Karess Si-Faderan, Second Blade to Prince Devlin Tragar. Then she saw the man with him. Panic locked her limbs as she recognized the injured warrior from the training grounds. His intense gaze swept over her, causing her breath to catch in her throat. Looking away from him seemed a monumental task. With something close to desperation, she wrenched her gaze away and focused on the pale hair and gray eyes of Karess Si-Faderan.

"Yes, Second Blade?" Nerrilik stepped forward. "You wished to speak with me?" His attempt to draw attention to himself and away from her was obvious. Nor could it have failed more completely. Karess nodded, but his gaze rested on Sheren with obvious pleasure.

"Sheren. It is good to see you. I trust you are well? Seth thrives? The villa prospers?"

The questions were lightly asked, but she sensed a deeper undercurrent in his voice. He'd seen the slight bruising on her arm from Nerrilik's tight grip. She smiled to reassure him. While she welcomed his interruption, she was not ready to place herself in another Blade's hands. Not even Karess', who she knew to be an honorable man. "Both I and my son are well, Second Blade. Thank you for inquiring. Villa Porenmagie does indeed prosper."

His head tilted to one side, a chiding smile curving his lips. "Second Blade, Sheren?"

She felt the blush creep up her cheeks. Karess had been Sayjan's mentor when her husband first entered the ranks of the Tragar's Blades. Her resentment that he had not been able to keep her reckless husband from taking one too many risks suddenly seemed a petty thing behind which to hide. Especially after four long years.

"Forgive my teasing, my lady," Karess apologized before she could form an answer to his gentle scold. The absence of humor in his voice—something she'd come to recognize as essential to Karess Si-Faderan's existence—struck her as wrong. She held out a hand. A tightness inside her eased as he took it.

"A well-earned scold between friends doesn't warrant my forgiveness, Karess. I am the one who should be asking forgiveness of you for holding you at arm's length for so long. Sayjan would be ashamed of me."

Smiling in clear relief, his lips brushed the back of her hand. "Forgiven, Sheren. We shall not speak of it further." He straightened and indicated the man beside him. "I don't believe my friend introduced himself earlier. This is Bracca Cu-Laurian, First Blade to Lady Avera St. John, our beloved prince's Starmate. Bracca, this is Sheren Ni-Annun."

Bracca Cu-Laurian. The name ran through her head several times as she murmured a polite greeting. She was afraid to touch him again, but not offering her hand would be an insult. She willed her muscles not to shake as he took her hand.

As before, her empathic senses surged to full and powerful life, treating her shield as if it wasn't even there. Curiosity slammed into her first. Her mind "tasted" the emotion and immediately labeled it Bracca's. So was the rush of warm admiration that followed.

His lips brushed her hand.

Nothing about his respectful expression prepared her for the hot lick of lust that curled around her mind like a hungry cat. Her body reacted, stomach and thighs tightening, breasts throbbing. She fought back a shudder. *Such a powerful emotion.* She broke the contact with him as quickly as she could, desperate to rebuild her shield.

Nerrilik growled a question, his words unintelligible, meaningless sounds as she fought her internal battle. Darker emotions—contempt, disgust, loathing—surged against her mind, threatening to drown her. She bit back a frightened whimper.

This should not be happening. Even a child had better control than she did. She struggled to breathe evenly, terrified the three men might discover her plight. She had no wish to be poked and prodded by the mind-healers.

Karess spoke, his tone sharp, and a wave of acceptance laced heavily with trust covered the harsh emotions in a calming blanket.

Nerrilik said something else, and Sheren felt herself jerk slightly as the darkness threatened to engulf her once more.

Without conscious thought, she reached for Bracca's emotions as if they were a life line. For a heartbeat, she was free, safe, wrapped in a longing so strong it brought tears to her eyes. Luma help her, if she didn't get things under control soon, she would find herself in a weeping puddle on the floor.

She wondered how the men didn't already know something was wrong. She'd never been good at dissembling. Her face had to be either drained white with shock or flushed with fear. Maybe both, considering the way Bracca suddenly stepped away from her. A shaft of disappointment, bright as a silver sword, stabbed through the tangled swirl of emotions. She bit her tongue to keep from crying out, not sure in that moment if the disappointment was his, or hers.

It wasn't until Nerrilik laid a possessive hand on her arm that she understood her senses had returned to normal—at least, normal for her. Two measured breaths, and she was able to fumble her usual shield back into place. She could only pray it held this time.

"Forgive our haste, Second Blade," Nerrilik said. "I am escorting Sheren to her meeting with Lady Patria. Perhaps we could speak another time as she does not wish to keep her ladyship waiting."

"I see," Karess said, his tone thoughtful.

"I'm sorry we can't visit longer, Karess," she said, amazed at how normal she sounded. "Perhaps you could ride over to the villa soon. Seth would love to see you."

He smiled warmly. "I'll do that, Sheren, thank you for the invitation. Forgive me, however, for disturbing your plans further." He turned to Nerrilik. "The Tragar's schedule, and thus mine, has changed. This is the only time I have to take your report, and the meeting will have to be brief. We should get started right away."

Nerrilik threw a glance at her, his displeasure with the order evident. He might not want to leave, but Sheren knew as well as he that he had no choice. As Second Blade, Karess oversaw any guards stationed outside the palace, including those at the Tragar's villa.

In truth, Nerrilik's absence would be a blessing. She needed time to compose herself before her meeting with Lady Patria.

"Perhaps," Nerrilik began, "I could make my report another day, Second Blade. Sheren should not go un-escorted."

Karess stared at Nerrilik a moment, considering the request. Then his eyes brightened. "No need to worry, my friend. I'm sure Bracca would be delighted to escort Sheren to the Ladies' Wing while you give your report."

"No," Nerrilik said, his hand moving to the hilt of his sword. "I'll not have—"

"Second guessing my orders again, Nerrilik," Karess said softly. "One would think you'd learn from your mistakes."

Nerrilik's mouth snapped shut. His knuckles turned white around the sword's hilt before his fist slowly opened. "You trust him?"

Karess held Nerrilik's angry stare and said nothing. Even she knew the fact he'd suggested Bracca at all was answer enough. Finally, Nerrilik looked away.

Karess nodded once. "Bracca?"

Bracca stepped forward and inclined his head toward her. "I would be honored to escort you, Lady Sheren."

"Thank you, Bracca," she said, working to keep the dismay from her voice. She wasn't sure being alone with him was a good idea. He'd done something to her empathic abilities. Until she figured out what, she had to make sure they didn't touch again. "But it's just Sheren. I have no claim to the title of Lady."

"Wonderful." Karess clapped a hand to Nerrilik's shoulder. "Now that we're all friends, come, Nerrilik, time passes. My lady." He winked at her, turned to leave, then paused and snapped his fingers. "Ah, yes, Bracca, do remember you have an appointment of your own. Devlin and Fate both will be extremely disappointed if they miss you."

"Disappointing your Bloodsworn and his First Blade," Bracca said with one dark brow arched in disdain, "is not high on my list of concerns.

Disappointing *my* Lady Bloodsworn, however, is something I plan to avoid at all costs. I will be on time."

Karess chuckled. "Fair enough." Sheren watched him leave, one hand still on Nerrilik's shoulder as if to hurry him along. She waited until they'd turned a corner before facing the man beside her. For a moment, his dark eyes seemed to burn with some emotion she couldn't name. Then they cooled dramatically.

"Shall we go, my lady?"

She opened her mouth to remind him of her lack of title, only to decide against it. Perhaps the less said between them the better. Surely she could get through a handful of minutes in his presence without getting caught up in another maelstrom of emotions.

She started down the hall, deliberately setting a brisk pace. He fell in behind her, staying a proper two steps back. Again, a courtesy more befitting a lady than a mere chatelaine, even a chatelaine in charge of so large a household as Villa Porenmagie. The distance between them, however, allowed her to concentrate on restoring her calm and strengthening her shield. By the time the double doors to the Ladies' Wing loomed before them with their attendant doormen, she was able to face him with at least some measure of equanimity. That, and the hope she would not embarrass herself if he took her hand again.

She lifted her eyes to his, proud of the fact she could offer him a serene smile. "I thank you for your time, Amber Blade."

He did not smile in return. Instead, he bowed, one hand pressed to his chest. "You are most welcome, my lady."

Then he turned around and walked away.

Sheren stared after him, stunned by his abrupt

departure. Surely a man who had looked at her with such interest on the training grounds and again in the hallway earlier, would have found a reason to linger a moment. Her curiosity piqued, she created a slit in her shield and waited to see what might come through from the retreating warrior.

A sense of longing swept in, deep and heartbreakingly wistful. Sheren pressed a hand to her chest just as a blanket of stern pride ruthlessly covered the terrible yearning. She shook her head, amazed at the clarity of the mental image. The mantling emotion sparkled, fresh-made in the middle, but had dark, tattered edges, as if worn away by years of insults and degradation. Part of her ached to reach out and help mend such wounded pride.

Before she did something stupid, the prominent emotion shifted again with a sense of urgency. She identified the strong emotion as protectiveness, though it also had a possessive quality to it that seemed almost child-like in nature. *Mine*, it said.

A burst of anticipation tinged with worry flashed, followed by appreciation. Then, one after another, separate emotions began to stream in— remorse, guilt, envy, love, jealousy, regret. Wonder bled into the mix, fresh by the taste of it.

Sheren firmly closed the slit before she became overwhelmed. So that was how a Blade felt about the person responsible for his very existence. She'd forgotten Bracca's appointment with his Bloodsworn. That must be why he'd hurried away.

Mystery solved to her satisfaction, Sheren glanced down to check her dress for wrinkles and stains, though it was too late now to do anything about either. Then she turned and nodded to the doormen. Mentally, she slipped into that narrow niche between servant and lady that she occupied when dealing with the Tragar's mother. Lady Patria demanded respect, but respected strength, a narrow path to walk indeed.

Gods, the things she had to do for a few bottles of scented soap and bath salts.

****

Bracca congratulated himself. He'd carried out the favor Karess asked without once giving in to the unwise urge to touch the woman again. She'd made her opinion of him plain by cringing when Nerrilik accused him of still being a Black Blade. Even though Karess corrected Nerrilik, the look on Lady Sheren's face made Bracca feel as if he'd sullied her soul just by being in her presence.

A woman so pure and beautiful was not for the likes of a former Black Blade, no matter how much he might wish otherwise.

He forced such useless longing aside, replacing it with the knowledge that he had worth to at least one female. His Bloodsworn, Avera St. John, considered him her friend. Or she had.

Bracca drew his brows together as a worrisome thought occurred to him. Her friendship may have altered after the deep-healing she'd performed on him. When her healing magic flooded him, he hadn't been able to keep the powerful lust it created completely to himself. He'd tried, gods, he'd tried. He hadn't wanted to frighten or disgust her. He hadn't wanted to damage the trust she had in him. If the Tragar had not arrived...

Ah, but he had. Nor had the powerful Bloodsworn wasted time in whisking his Starmate away, effectively protecting her from Bracca's baser instincts. He'd been relieved, of course. How could he not be? Protecting Avera was Bracca's only desire now. Seeing them together, however, had sparked a tiny bit of jealous envy deep within him. Not of Lord Devlin's place in Avera's heart, but for what they had together. To have a woman of his own, a wife, a mate, was a possibility he'd never allowed himself to think about. Not when he'd been a Black Blade.

As an Amber Blade?

Well, memories were long, as Nerrilik pointed out so forcefully. A *shetha*—one of the cast of women who saw to the physical needs of Blades—might talk with him, laugh with him, accept him into her bed in exchange for the pleasure of his deep-healing lust. But he would never be acceptable on any terms by a woman like Sheren Ni-Annun. He'd do well to remember that in the future.

Chapter Six

Bracca had never been inside the Bloodsworn Hall before. Camarie's break with the Council occurred several years prior to Bracca becoming his Blade. By then, the only Black Blades to walk these hallways were ones in chains. Pity. He found the tapestries and painted murals lining the walls of the main corridor fascinating. He would have enjoyed being able to study them at length. As it was, he barely had time to glance at each one as he walked past. Partly due to the brisk pace set by the two people walking ahead of him and partly because he was trying to figure out what was wrong with them.

Though his Lady Bloodsworn and her Starmate walked side-by-side, there was a distance between them wider than the hallway they traversed. He found it hard to believe the two lovers could be at odds so soon. But then, considering what he'd learned of Avera through their link, he shouldn't be surprised. She was nothing if not strong-willed. And independent. Having to justify her Bloodsworn status to the council would be just the thing to set her back up.

They came to the end of the corridor where a brace of huge doors, easily as tall as three men, formed a large rectangle in the wall. Lord Devlin lifted his hand, palm out. Slowly, the doors moved, swinging open to reveal that not only were they overly large, but overly thick as well. When they came to a stop, Lord Devlin took Avera's hand.

"Wait here, I will speak to the Council first." His gaze went to Bracca, delivering a command impossible to miss.

"She will be safe in my care," Bracca assured him, irritated he should have to put into words something so obvious.

Lord Devlin nodded, kissed her hand, and marched into the council chamber. The five Silver Blades who'd accompanied them filed in after him. The doors swung ponderously closed. They met with a muted boom, leaving Bracca and Avera standing alone in the empty hall.

Bracca glanced at his Bloodsworn, trying to gauge her mood. She stood by his side, arms crossed, a look of aggravation on her open face.

"This is ridiculous," she muttered.

"I agree, my lady."

She swung around to face him, hands going to her hips. "Those are the first words you've spoken to me all morning. I was beginning to worry I'd done something to your vocal cords the other night when I healed your head wound."

He bowed stiffly. Of course her thoughts were on that night. How could they not be? "Forgive me, my Bloodsworn. It is not my intention to cause you worry."

"Oh, knock that off. You know I don't like all the bowing stuff." She sighed deeply. "Look, one of the first things I learned as a research chemist is to not make the same mistake twice. When something doesn't turn out right the first time, you need to find out why so it doesn't happen again. So while I wouldn't usually pursue a subject that obviously makes you uncomfortable, I can't apologize unless I know what I did wrong."

Amazement froze his tongue. She wanted to apologize to him?

"Well?"

"Why would you feel the need to apologize, my lady? It is I who should beg your forgiveness."

Her eyes widened in genuine surprise. "For what?"

"When you deep-healed me with your magic..." He paused, feeling an unaccustomed flush warm his face. There was no easy way to discuss this with a female. "I felt your fear when my lust rolled back to you through our link. You cringed away from it, from me, yet you kept the link open until I was fully healed. I could feel what it was doing to you. I..." He looked away from her, shaking his head. "I never worried about such things before. With Camarie, it was not a concern."

Avera's cheeks colored, but she waved a dismissing hand. "Yes, well, just because I'm a woman doesn't mean I don't know what lust is or how to handle it. Not that I'd like to experience what happened on a daily basis, mind you, but it's not enough to put me off being your Bloodsworn."

Her expression clouded with an unaccustomed hesitancy. "Unless you're saying the situation is too uncomfortable for you?"

He started to reassure her that wasn't the case, but she hurried on, pacing nervously now as she spoke.

"Heck, there aren't that many men in my own culture who'd be comfortable depending on a woman for their existence. If that's the problem, I completely understand. Devlin told me one Bloodsworn can bequeath their links to another. If there's someone else you'd prefer to be linked to, we could give that a try. I mean, it's not like you had much of a choice when you broke your link with Camarie."

He stopped her with a touch on her shoulder. She looked at him, her distress at the thought of breaking their link plain on her face. He was sure it mirrored his own. "My lady, believe me. There is no other Bloodsworn for me. Your goodness, the very purity of your essence, *Called* to me the moment I set foot on Earth. When I saw you, I knew, one way or another, my days with Camarie were over. I rejoiced in that knowledge. As a Black Blade, I merely existed. As your Amber Blade, I have a chance to live. But not at the price of your trust."

"I trust you, Bracca. I don't see how anything could possibly change that. And if you want proof," she said gently, "just open your side of our link. Let me show you why I think we can make this Bloodsworn-Blade thing work." She stepped closer and reached up to curl her hand around his neck.

With a sense of wonder, Bracca let her pull his head down until his forehead rested against hers. He took a deep breath. He was almost afraid to look beyond his own mind. What if she was wrong, and her fear and disgust of him was simply pushed deep into her subconscious? He'd break his own link if that were the case, he decided.

He placed his hands lightly over her shoulders. Then he opened his side of their link. Her acceptance of him hit with the force of a blow, leaving no room for doubt. Amazement filled him as her thoughts flowed into him freely. She *knew* him. All his black deeds, the terrible things he'd been forced to do as Camarie's Blade. Yet, what she focused on were the instances where he'd secretly tried to undo some of the damage wrought in Camarie's name. He'd thought them mere acts of futility. Nothing he did could wipe away years of shameful acts. The weight of his sins was too great. The weight of his guilt and remorse even greater.

She acknowledged his thoughts, and wrapped him in her approval anyway. Then she drew him deeper into their link. What he found there humbled him beyond belief. The thought of giving up their link bothered her more than she was willing to admit.

Yes, she said, the shyness in her mental voice touching his heart. *When we formed this link, I saw your whole life, Bracca, and I know you saw mine. That it all happened in the flash of a few vision-filled minutes doesn't matter. Severing this...connection, would be like cutting myself off from someone I'd known all my life. I'd rather that didn't happen again anytime soon.*

He glimpsed the lingering pain from the disappearance of her father before she quickly tucked it away. As she did, another thought of hers slipped out of hiding. Bracca froze.

You think of me as...family?

Embarrassment colored her thoughts. *Yeah. Sorry if that bothers you.*

He wasn't sure it did. At least, not in the way she meant. It had been a long time indeed since he'd had any contact with his family. The blade-illness came upon him when he was barely into adolescence. Bound to Camarie, he'd been cut off from his parents and younger siblings for a very long time. And there was no such thing as camaraderie in the ranks of the Black Blades, much less any feelings of friendship or family.

Gods, to have a family once again.

I know, she whispered softly. And he realized she did know. Not just because she was his Bloodsworn, but because she had experienced the same aloneness. Not for as long as he had, but certainly with as much intensity.

Bracca pulled her into a tight hug. *You honor me beyond all words, my lady.* Her tears wet his tunic. To distract her, he pictured the Tragar's face when he found out Bracca had taken up the role of her brother. Her laughter rippled through his mind. She stretched up and kissed his cheek.

You two are just going to have to learn to get along, she said firmly. *I'm not giving either of you up.*

He swallowed around the lump in his throat. From the moment he'd seen her in that shadowed warehouse back on Earth he'd known she was special. Something in him recognized her, answered the call of her Bloodsworn magic. But he'd never for one moment imagined he could actually become her Blade much less her friend. Even after their remarkable linking, he'd never expected their relationship to be more than servant and lady. Never even thought to hope for anything more.

Now, for her to see him as a *pakell*, a brother, instead of a servant, or worse, a mere duty, was nothing short of a miracle. Tears pricked his eyes, gratitude filling his heart to overflowing.

The sound of a throat clearing startled them both. He looked up to see the big doors to the council chamber standing wide open. The room beyond seemed stuffed full of men with hostile faces, all staring at him and Avera with expressions ranging from disapproval to disgust. He knew immediately the weight of their judgment was not just because Avera was Bloodsworn, but because of the tight embrace they shared. *Vet!* They'd probably even seen her kiss his cheek.

He knew the moment she realized her sisterly hug had been misconstrued as something much more intimate. Her body stiffened, her mind drawing back from his. He had to fight his protective instincts when she took a step away from him. Her embarrassment and uncertainty made him want to shield her from those accusing eyes. Even her Starmate, the one man who should have known she would never betray him with another stared at her coldly. Outrage made his fingers itch for his sword. How dare they judge her?

They're like a bunch of gossipy old ladies jumping to conclusions, she said, her mental voice

47

suddenly filling with indignation. He watched her straighten her spine and lift her chin. *Don't worry about it. We weren't doing anything wrong. A sister can hug her brother if she wants to.*

They do not see a sister and brother, only a Bloodsworn and Blade.

That's their problem, not mine. I'm not going to let them make me feel like a teenager caught necking in the school hallway when we're completely innocent.

Pride swelled in his chest as he watched her march into the council chamber with the bearing of a true princess. He felt her resolve falter as she joined her Starmate. Bracca wanted to crush the man, smash his fist into the emotionless mask he'd donned, and shatter the cold blue orbs of his eyes. Devlin Tragar was hurting Bracca's *sorlina*, the sister of his heart, and Bracca wanted his blood.

It's all right, I'm fine.

But it wasn't all right, and he knew it. She wasn't blocking her emotions from him. He could feel her hurt, her disappointment. He ached to comfort her, but didn't know how or what to say. All he could do was let her feel the depth of his own love and devotion.

And maybe plan the beating of a certain idiot Bloodsworn if he didn't come to his senses.

Chapter Seven

Devlin burned. The fire in the pit of his stomach flared to life with searing intensity the instant the doors opened wide enough to reveal Avera and Cu-Laurian lost in each other's embrace. Rage consumed him, causing his magic to buck and thrash, begging to be released.

A restraining hand touched his arm. Someone cleared their throat. His Starmate, *his wife in all ways save one*, raised her head from another man's shoulder and gazed at him without the slightest remorse in her beautiful green eyes. A deep cold settled over him, snuffing out the burning rage and leaving behind the bitter ashes of betrayal.

They'd bonded as Starmates. They'd risen from hours of making love only a short while ago. He'd almost died protecting her. How could she do this? Here he'd been pleading her case to the Council, trying to convince them to acknowledge her and accept her as one of them despite the fact she was a woman, and all the while she'd been in the hall in the arms of her damned Blade. He couldn't even look at Cu-Laurian. If he did, he'd kill the warrior right where he stood and consequences be damned. How dare the conniving male touch what was his!

Why, in the name of Luma's everlasting hell, did Avera choose this moment to shove her desire for her Blade in his face? Why couldn't she have waited until they were alone? He would have listened to her, he would have—

What?

Tracked down Cu-Laurian and shattered that

amber sword of his without mercy before going a step further and shattering the man's very bones. He still might. Even if Avera were not his Starmate, already bound to him by the magic veiling his world, sharing her with another was not something he was capable of doing.

With the measured tread worthy of a ruling monarch, Avera advanced down the wide aisle. The burgundy velvet dress clung to her at each seductive step, the heavy gold girdle riding low on her hips, trailing links swaying side to side.

Devlin swallowed. He'd seen women so gowned thousands of times, yet he couldn't take his eyes from the V of the girdle resting just above the junction of her legs. Memory stirred, and so did his body. Cursing silently, he shifted his stance. Always before, his desires followed his dictates and had been under his complete control. It was a decidedly uncomfortable feeling to find just the sight of Avera affected him this much. Uncomfortable, because the possibility that she'd been playing him for a fool last night and this morning was too real for him to ignore. He would have sworn he knew her heart and soul after their bonding. But then, she was an Earth female. Perhaps they had ways of hiding things he knew nothing about.

He dragged his gaze back to her face. Her tongue darted out, moistening her lips. More heat flooded him, and he felt himself grow harder. Luma's bloody hell! He had to be seven kinds of a fool to want her now, fresh from her Blade's arms. But want her he did.

She walked straight to him, her head high, not sparing the men waiting behind him a single glance. He'd meant to walk by her side down the wide aisle, a show of support so she wouldn't be afraid. Now he wasn't sure what he wanted to do. Leave her to face the Council alone? Laugh in her face to show her treachery meant nothing to him? Drag her into his arms and kiss her? Take her until she cried out his name?

With effort, he gathered his scattered wits and forced his mixed emotions aside. He would have to work through them later. Then he would confront her about her behavior. For the sake of the damned Seventh Prophecy, he was still willing to formalize their mate-bond, but she would have to realize what that meant if she expected any kind of peaceful existence with him. He had no intention of sharing her with her Blade or anyone else. He had seen that type of behavior destroy his parents' marriage— though it had been his father who had strayed and not his mother. He had no plans to repeat their mistakes.

Saying nothing, he acknowledged his lady with a stiff bending of his head before offering her his arm. He turned to lead her up the aisle. They had not gone three steps before he surprised himself by whispering. "You play a dangerous game, my lady."

So much for waiting to confront her.

****

"What game would that be?" Avera whispered back.

"You know what game. Flaunting your affection for Cu-Laurian in front of the Council could get him killed and you banished."

Avera looked up at Devlin sharply, the fist of hurt around her heart squeezing, making it ache. Did he really think so little of her? Did he really think she was the kind of woman who went from one man's arms to another's like a buzzing bee in a field of flowers? Anger blossomed inside her. "You know, my father used to tell me that jumping to conclusions can land you in a world of trouble. Pity no one ever told you that."

She faced forward again, trying to get herself

under control. How could things go to hell so quickly? They'd spent the night in each other's arms making love so sweet she'd cried. She'd told him she loved him. Didn't that mean anything in his world?

A painful realization struck her. He'd said something in his vows about pledging his love to her, but he'd never actually *told* her he loved her. Not once. A cold, sick feeling spiraled through her. He'd never said the words. Not even while they were making love. She would have remembered. Why hadn't she realized that sooner?

Because she'd been blinded by mind-blowing sex, that's why. And the sad truth was, great sex wasn't a substitute for love.

Tears burned her eyes. She blinked them back. Not for all the magic in the world would she reveal how much it hurt to think he could believe she'd betray him. They might not know each other very well, but he should at least have sensed that much about her. Shouldn't he?

Her heart heavy, she forced her attention back to the Bloodsworn Council chamber.

A domed ceiling held up by massive columns capped the huge, oblong room. Tiered seating, like a mini stadium, lined a wide center aisle. At the far end of the room, more tiered platforms rose, curved into a half circle from one side of the room to the other. Ten heavy wooden chairs perched on the curved tiers in a haphazard pattern. One man occupied each chair while five others clustered behind it. All of them watched her approach intently.

Devlin brought her to a stop under the stares of the sixty men. She couldn't help a nervous glance at him and inwardly cringed when he didn't so much as acknowledge her look. His face might as well have been set in stone for all the emotion he showed.

Fine, she snarled, removing her arm from his

and taking a step away from him. If he insisted on being a judgmental idiot, let him. It had been a long time since she'd needed anyone's support or approval. She would face whatever the Bloodsworn Council had to throw at her alone, just like she faced everything else.

Except, maybe she wasn't as alone as she thought. Her link with Bracca suddenly flooded with warmth. *You are not alone in this, Avera St. John.*

Thanks, Bracca. She flashed him a brief smile.

Devlin suddenly grabbed her hand and gave a sharp tug. He took a few steps forward, all but dragging her with him. She followed, trying to reclaim her hand without causing a scene. She wasn't a child who needed her hand held to keep her out of trouble.

Devlin obviously thought otherwise since, instead of releasing her, his fingers tightened. He stopped walking and pulled her up even with him. His deep voice rang out clear and strong in the chamber. "Members of the Bloodsworn High Council, I present to you Lady Avera St. John, late of Earth, newly made Bloodsworn of Avalyr, and my Starmate."

The men in the chairs stirred, as if uneasy with the introduction. The white haired man sitting in the middle of the top tier harrumphed. "In light of your connection to this...Bloodsworn..." Avera bristled over his hesitation. "We wonder, Tragar, if you should step down from your position as First Bloodsworn in this instance."

"That, I cannot do, Caveon," Devlin said. "Though I may not always agree with the importance of the ancient Prophecies, it is my duty as First Bloodsworn of Avalyr to see they are fulfilled. Banishing Lady St. John from Avalyr would endanger the Seventh Prophecy. Camarie has already tried to kill her before she left Earth, and will no doubt try again before our union is formalized. You will understand why her safety is my primary concern. Regardless of whether or not she retains her Bloodsworn status, she must remain here on Avalyr under my protection. That is not negotiable."

"Now see here," another Bloodsworn sputtered. "You have no evidence at all that Camarie was even on Earth much less that he attacked this woman."

Avera felt Bracca's aversion. *Do you know him?* She asked.

Yes. His name is Kapatree Du-Farishi. I saw him once with Camarie. The two behind him look familiar as well, but I do not know their names.

"His Blades were seen," Devlin said. "My Silver Blades killed some of them. I killed one myself before he could take her life."

"Yet you could produce no bodies, no blood evidence."

"True, but we have something almost as condemning." Devlin pointed to Bracca. "Camarie's Blade, Bracca Cu-Laurian, now First Blade to Lady St. John. Ask him about Camarie's involvement."

Kapatree sat back, lips lifting into a sneer. "A renegade and betrayer. Why should we believe anything he has to say?"

Devlin shrugged. Avera got the impression he hadn't really expected them to question Bracca. "I will not argue the point with you. The Concourse has our statements and is looking into ways to determine whether Camarie is using illegal gates. If they find he is, they may not only sanction him, but the rest of us as well."

Several of the men sitting in the chairs started talking at once. A couple of them jumped to their feet. The noise level rose, along with the tension in the room. Every Blade suddenly looked on edge, ready to draw his sword.

When it didn't look like they were going to calm down any time soon, Avera shook her head in disgust. What she wouldn't give for a good loud whistle. Almost at once, a loud, piercing whistle came from beside her. She grinned. Bracca must have picked up what she wanted through their link.

The room immediately fell into a shocked silence. "Thank you, Bracca." she said calmly, sweeping the room with her gaze. "Now, if you *gentlemen* are quite through throwing your tantrums, I would appreciate it if we could get on with this meeting."

A couple of the men sputtered, but quieted as Caveon stood. Everyone else went back to their places.

"A bit blunt, but well put, my dear," Caveon said. "We shall deal with the Concourse at another time. For now, we have other business to discuss. Lady St. John, are you aware of the reason you are here?"

Avera shrugged. Their rude stares earlier had wiped away any intentions she had of playing nice with this pious group. "I gather you and your fellow club members think you have the right to decide whether or not I remain a Bloodsworn. Personally, I think all of this is just an excuse for you males to throw your weight around and beat your chests. Just to let you know, that doesn't impress me."

"Avera—" Devlin began, no doubt intending to scold her for her flippant attitude. Before he could say more, Caveon waved him to silence with a hint of a smile on his face.

"The lady's honest speech is refreshing, Tragar. Too many have stood in her place and spouted what they thought we wanted to hear. Take your seat, please, First Bloodsworn, and we shall endeavor to conduct ourselves in a more impressive manner."

Avera glanced at Devlin, suddenly nervous. She

might be angry with him for doubting her, but his presence at her side made her feel safe. As if sensing her distress, he reached out and squeezed her hand before moving off to the side to sit in an empty chair she hadn't noticed before. Fate and the others went with him, leaving her and Bracca to stand alone.

Caveon sat back down and regarded her seriously. "Lady St. John," he began formally. "This Council has been given to understand you claim a blood-link with the man standing beside you, thereby granting you Bloodsworn status. Is this true?"

Chapter Eight

Bracca watched Avera calmly fold her hands in front of her. "That is correct," she said, her voice exquisitely polite. Only he knew her calm reached no further than her appearance. She was genuinely worried.

Caveon raised a brow. "Do you have any idea how anomalous such a claim is?"

"I believe I do."

Kapatree snorted. "Impossible. You can know nothing of our customs or traditions. You are an Earthling and a female."

"Neither of which is synonymous with stupid, I assure you," she said sharply. Then she took a deep breath. He could feel her trying to rein in her irritation. "Look, I'll admit, a week ago I'd never even heard about Bloodsworns or Blades. Heck, I'd never even heard of Avalyr. But I can tell you right now that I have a mental connection with this man." She laid a hand on his arm. "I can hear him in my head. And I can feel this...vast ocean of magical power pressing in on my mind." She raised both hands to her head briefly before throwing them up in the air. "You think you're amazed that I'm a Bloodsworn? Imagine how I feel."

"And still you have no explanation for just how such a miracle came to pass?" a man sitting up near Caveon asked.

She shrugged. "Through the same method many things happen. Necessity. I already had a load of questions about Avalyr by the time Devlin's Blades showed up at my office." She waved a hand in Lord

Devlin's direction. "He'd been sending me presents and little notes all week, and they were driving me crazy.

"When Bracca showed up and didn't try to kill me right away like the other Black Blades, I started asking him questions. He told me about how the blood-link worked between Bloodsworn and Blades, and how it's formed. He even said something about me being a Bloodsworn. Not that I believed him, mind you. I'm used to compiling a few facts before giving credence to an outlandish hypothesis." She paused and glanced at him, her voice roughening slightly. "But when he broke his link with Camarie, I didn't have a choice. He was dying. Since he'd saved my life earlier, I thought the least I could do was give the blood-link thing a try. Believe me," she said emphatically, "no one was more surprised than I was when it worked. I didn't even know real magic existed."

This earned her an indulgent smile from the elder Bloodsworn. "We were told of the Tragar's search for you. How his Blades found you and protected you. They described your apparent linking ceremony with Cu-Laurian—"

"Which we find as hard to believe as their story that you killed two men," Kapatree snapped. "Females are not strong enough mentally to handle the emotional backlash of killing someone much less a linking."

Avera's frustration seeped into their link. He could almost hear her teeth grind together. He caught her intent an instant too late to stop her. She grinned and crooked her finger.

"Why don't you come down here and see for yourself whether or not I can handle a little violence. You and me, one on one, Kapatree, what do you say?"

Bracca tensed. *My lady, this is not wise.*

Don't worry, she told him. *Years of self-defense lessons with my father have to count for something. Besides, he's sure to underestimate me because I'm a woman. There's a good chance I can take him. That'll wipe the sneer off his face.*

Kapatree leaned forward and leered at her. "Why Lady St. John, I had no idea Earth females were so aggressive. I swear, even with your Starmate in the same room, you tempt me. But then, considering your public embrace of your Blade, perhaps you enjoy an audience."

Rage suffused Bracca. No one was allowed to insult his heart-sister. Before he could recall the foolishness of challenging a Bloodsworn, his sword was in his hand. He stepped protectively in front of Avera. She grabbed his arm just as a strangled sound came from Kapatree. The man sat rigid in his chair, eyes wide, mouth open and gasping. One hand came up to grab at his throat as a look of terror formed on his face. His Blades suddenly jumped forward, only to freeze like statues around him.

Bracca wasn't sure what was going on until Lord Devlin growled. "You have a right to question her, Kapatree, not insult her. Do so again, and you and I will have more than words."

Bracca shot a glance over at Avera's Starmate. The barely controlled rage on his face soothed Bracca's own anger.

"Tragar! Release him immediately," Caveon ordered.

Several heartbeats passed before Kapatree slumped back in his seat, coughing and gasping for breath. His men, also released from Lord Devlin's hold, drew their swords and surrounded their Bloodsworn protectively, their angry glares split between Bracca and the Tragar. Tension in the room spiked.

Bracca cursed silently as other Blades drew

their weapons as well, increasing the possibility of violence. He could almost see the bloodbath coming. *And Avera will be caught in the middle of it!*

On the top tier, Caveon rose, a look of disgust on his face. He swept an impatient hand through the air from one side of the room to the other. Immediately Bracca felt magic pass over him in a tingling wave. As the wave receded, so did his aggression, leaving a strange calmness in its wake. Some of the men blinked at their drawn swords in confusion. Her hand on his back, he felt Avera shiver.

Have to give the man credit, she said. *That's pretty impressive magic. He just sucked the adrenalin right out of everyone. I bet he's great at controlling riots.*

Bracca nodded. The impetus of his anger might be gone, but he still wanted Kapatree's blood.

Avera moved up beside him. *Forget it, Bracca, he's not worth it.* She sounded distracted.

He glanced at her to find her focused intently on the raised tiers. He followed her gaze. It took him a moment to follow her thoughts and notice the same things she did. The warriors standing uneasily behind the chairs, the men whose job it was to guard their Bloodsworn, they gave the most away. It was interesting to see who watched who. He took special note of which ones focused on Devlin Tragar and his men.

"Don't you just love politics," she muttered under her breath.

Bracca grunted in agreement as he sheathed his sword.

"Kapatree, control your Blades," Caveon ordered sharply. "And yourself, if you please. I will not have this meeting disrupted a second time. Tragar, I remind you that your presence on this Council is one of strict impartiality."

"You and I both know that is impossible in this case."

"Apparently. However, if you cannot control your temper—"

Devlin held up a hand in surrender before settling back in his chair. "As long as Kapatree, and everyone else, is civil to my Starmate, I promise to behave."

"I see no reason for insults," Caveon agreed, his stern gaze going to Kapatree until the man nodded once. When he turned back to Avera, he inclined his head. "Please accept our apologies, Lady St. John."

"You aren't the one who needs to apologize." Bracca noted she made a point of *not* looking in Kapatree's direction. "But for the sake of expediency, consider it accepted."

"Well enough," Caveon said. "Now, back to the matter at hand. We have two questions before this council. The first is whether or not you actually have a blood-link with this man."

"And just how am I supposed to prove that?" Avera asked.

"Believe it or not, young lady," Caveon said dryly, "we do have procedures for such things." His gaze shifted, fastening on Bracca. "Bracca Cu-Laurian, stand forth and present your sword."

Bracca took a step forward and drew his amber sword again. Murmurs drifted down from the tiers, along with a few snickers. He ignored the derisive comments, struggling to keep his smile hidden as Avera's outrage flooded their link.

I care not what they think, he told her. *And neither should you. They are blind fools. Your sword is a reflection of your physical beauty, the strength of your spirit, and the purity of your heart. I would have no other.*

Her boiling outrage faded to a slow simmer.

"Lay the weapon on the table," Caveon ordered.

Bracca approached the long table situated a dozen feet from the lowest tier. Reverently he laid his sword on the blood-red cloth covering the table before returning to Avera's side.

Lord Devlin's friend, Lord Peregrine, rose from his seat and jumped down off the tier.

"Platkus. Akrinon." Caveon called out the two names and a moment later a Blade from two separate groups joined Lord Peregrine. The Tragar's friend gestured, and a small pile of folded cloth appeared on one end of the table. He shook out each piece, revealing two strips of cloth and two thickly woven hoods.

Bracca's stomach clenched. He knew what they were about to do. This type of test was painful, not only to the Blade, but the Bloodsworn as well. He couldn't even try to shield Avera. Their link had to remain wide open if she was to prove her Bloodsworn status.

Lord Peregrine wasted no time in using one of the cloths to gag Bracca. Then he slipped one of the hoods over Bracca's head.

Dread began to seep into his link with Avera.

"What's going on?" she asked.

He couldn't think how to answer her. How did he tell her that in the next few moments she would be assaulted by pain, *his* pain?

"A true Blade can sense when his sword is in the hands of another," Lord Peregrine explained. "It causes a mental pain that eats away at his mind until the sword is once again in his hands. A true Bloodsworn feels this same pain, though to a lesser degree. What we do here is but a test to make sure you are both what you say you are."

Bracca felt her hesitate. She reached out to him. *It should be brief,* he assured her. *The Tragar will not allow the test to go on longer than necessary.* Or so he told himself. Avera must have caught that wisp of doubt because she huffed in his mental ear.

Maybe that was true an hour ago, but I'm not sure of anything right now. Why didn't he tell me about this?

Probably because of his position as First Bloodsworn. He is supposed to be impartial. Had he warned you, the other Bloodsworn may have seen it as tampering. They might have decided not to test you at all.

Arrogant bastards.

He gave in to the urge to smile around the gag while he had the chance. Soon, there would be nothing at all to smile about.

"Lady St. John?"

"All right," Avera snapped.

He heard the rustle of cloth.

"This is to keep you from calling out any verbal cues to Cu-Laurian." Despite Lord Peregrine's reassuring explanation, little spurts of panic shot into the link from Avera. Bracca tensed.

My lady?

She didn't answer at first. He heard more cloth rustling, the hood going over her head. The spurts of panic became a tightly clenched stream.

Avera!

It's okay, it's okay, she repeated over and over. *I can do this, Bracca, don't worry, I can do this.*

No, something is wrong. He lifted his hands to his mask. *I will have them stop—*

No, she said sharply, her order freezing him in place, fingers just shy of touching cloth. He heard her draw in a deep breath. *No,* she repeated more calmly. *Let's just do this and get it over with, all right? I can handle it if it doesn't take too long. You said it wouldn't take long, right? Please tell me you weren't exaggerating.*

He let his hands drop. *No, it should not take long.* He could still feel her panic, the wild urge to rip at the cloth keeping her from sucking in great gulps of air. But she controlled the fear. Her strength of will continued to amaze him.

He concentrated, trying to discern the reason behind her distress. As his mind sank deeper into the link he glimpsed images, bits and pieces of a memory so strong it still had the power to haunt her.

A man coming at her. Pain. Waking up to darkness. The feeling of being restrained. Of not being able to get enough air. The greedy touch of a grasping hand.

Impotent anger filled him. He hadn't been there to protect her. He couldn't even protect her now. Not only did she have to suffer through the Council's test, but the circumstances were forcing her to relive a moment in her past no woman should have to endure even once.

She gasped into his mind. *Talk to me Bracca. Give me something else to concentrate on. Tell me about your childhood. Where were you born?*

He responded quickly. Anything to help her. *I was born in Realm Hedaud—*

A discomfort close to pain rippled through him, cutting off his mental voice.

What is it? What's wrong?

Someone has picked up our sword.

He bit into the gag as the pain increased, fighting the instinct to shield her by closing the link. He had to stand by helplessly as increasingly powerful echoes of his discomfort trickled down to her. Between the pain and her panic, she was fast reaching her limit. He could hear her ragged breathing, feel her frantic need for air.

The pain flared, becoming sharp daggers cutting into his mind.

What the hell are they doing? she cried.

It's all right. I think they are merely testing the blade. At least he hoped that was all it was. He'd felt worse, but was certain Avera had not. If the damn Council did not stop the test soon, he would.

Then he felt something else. Something foreign, yet still familiar. Nebulous at first, the presence intensified until, with a rush, it surged into his mind, quickly forming a shield between him and the pain. The hastily erected barrier wasn't perfect. Some of the pain still got through. But enough was blocked that he could breath evenly again.

Bracca almost laughed aloud. The workings of Avera's strange, scientific mind were truly a wonder to behold. Unfortunately, now was not the time to hide behind shields. He sent a tendril of thought into the warmth, an urgent but gentle reminder that the pain was a necessary part of the test, something to be endured, not blocked.

Shock, chagrin, apology, and beneath those, a touch of outrage coupled with biting anger. One after another, the emotions flowed back to him in quick succession.

And none of them came from Avera.

The shield winked out of existence as that realization hit him. Before he had time to wonder just who had been in his mind, his link with Avera's sword jerked viciously.

Chapter Nine

Sheren gasped as Bracca's pain continued to assault her. Part of her wanted to cry, another wanted to scream in anger, and a third just wanted to shrink behind her personal shield as embarrassment and dismay washed over her. How could she have made such a stupid mistake?

Quite easily it seemed. The first, swift assault had exploded against her mental shield, scattering her senses. She'd cringed behind her flimsy barrier, prepared to pour her whole being into strengthening her protection. It took only a moment to realize she wasn't being attacked, that the pain she felt wasn't hers, but another's.

Bracca's.

Without conscious thought, she reached for the Amber Blade, instinctively shoving her mind between his and whatever was hurting him. It shouldn't have worked. For one thing, she wasn't a healer, for another, her powers were far too weak.

But it had worked.

And as a result, she'd almost cost Bracca his blood-link!

His message as he pushed her away had come through quite clearly. He didn't want her help. The pain was a test, a way to prove his connection to his Bloodsworn. A necessity.

Sheren shook her head, feeling sick at the thought of such calculated torture. Sicker at the thought of what she'd almost done. How he must hate her for her interference.

She wrapped her arms around herself, fighting

back tears and the constant shudders racking her body. Thank the gods she was alone in one of the many palace storerooms. She needed time to pull herself together, to remind herself of the consequences of having anything to do with a Blade.

The pain hovering just beyond her newly formed shield faded a moment later, leaving her feeling weak and lightheaded. A dull ache throbbed behind her eyes. Sighing deeply, she dried her face on her sleeve.

She had to do something. She had to break this link between her and Bracca Cu-Laurian before it was too late. Before she did something they would both regret.

****

Bracca!

Bracca drew in an unsteady breath between the waves of pain. Avera sounded very close to breaking.

Peace, little sister, it will be over soon.

But what if this isn't a test? What if they're trying to break your sword? Oh, God, Bracca, we're like a pair of stupid sitting ducks. These men can do anything they want, and we wouldn't have a clue until it was too late. If they break your sword, you'll die. We have to stop them!

He tried to reassure her, but her fear and panic washed over him in a wave powerful enough to drown out everything, even his pain. He staggered as her magic surged into him. Powerful magic. As powerful as any he'd ever felt from Camarie.

The room erupted with shouts and harsh cries. The hissing sound of drawn swords snaked down his spine, sending a burst of adrenaline through his veins. Standing blind was no longer an option.

Just as he reached up to jerk the cloth off, something warm and smooth slapped into his palm. Instinctively he closed his fingers, recognizing the feel of his sword.

Avera screamed.

Bracca had his hood off before the soul-rending sound ended. He paid scant attention to the circle of armed warriors surrounding him. His only concern right now was locating Avera in the sudden crowd. He spotted his lady Bloodsworn lying on the floor, Lord Devlin bent over her, and his heart stuttered. He jerked the gag from his mouth, snarling at the nearest warriors, and took a step toward them. A silver sword blocked his way.

"Stay where you are, Cu-Laurian."

Bracca looked from the sword to Fate's face. The man knew better than to try to keep a First Blade from his Bloodsworn. "She is mine to protect. If you do not move aside, I *will* kill you An-Derrith."

"There will be no killing in these chambers." Caveon's deep voice echoed un-naturally through the chamber. Almost immediately, the aggression running through Bracca's veins faded to something more manageable. Fate, too, seemed less tense, his sword slowly lowering.

Bracca dismissed the Silver Blade, his gaze seeking Avera once more. He tried to reach her through their link. Nothing. The link was open, but Avera's mind had retreated well beyond the subconscious level. A place even he couldn't reach.

Lord Devlin gathered Avera up in his arms. He took her to the table where Bracca had placed his sword, laying her down gently. He pinned Caveon with a black look that Bracca fully agreed with. "Are you satisfied?"

"That she is Bloodsworn? Yes. That she should remain so? That is another matter."

"She *Called* me!" Bracca slid his sword away and shouldered a path through Blades half stunned by his words. He reached the table and stopped at Lord Devlin's side. "No one is more worthy to be Bloodsworn than this woman."

"Impossible," Caveon said. "The *Calling* died out centuries ago. No Blade has been directed to their destined Bloodsworn by a *Calling* since before I was born."

"Nevertheless, I am telling you she *Called* me. How else can you explain the fact I *knew* she was Bloodsworn the moment I saw her? An-Derrith and the others did not know. They thought I was only trying to fool her. But she knew. She felt it, too. There was no other reason for her to want to keep me alive against the wishes of three Silver Blades. How else could she, a human female, have formed a blood-link with me if she was not meant to be Bloodsworn? *My Bloodsworn!*"

Caveon's gaze turned thoughtful for a moment, then he shook his head decisively. "Lady St. John has been chosen to play a pivotal role in Avalyr's future. She is the bride of Avalyr's First Bloodsworn, the caretaker of our Prophecies. As the Tragar has said, her presence here is not negotiable. It is my opinion that the Prophecy itself is working here and not a renewal of the *Calling*." Several of the Council nodded in agreement.

Of course they would think that. The fools. Lord Devlin caught his attention before he could muster another argument.

"You had an open link to her, Cu-Laurian. Do you have any idea what happened?"

He replayed the images that had flashed into his mind earlier. "I think so. I could tell she was upset as soon as Lord Jerran began putting the gag and blindfold on me. I thought it was anger at you to begin with, for not warning her of what to expect."

Lord Devlin gritted his teeth. "If I had warned her, the Council would have seen it as tampering."

True, thought Bracca. He could tell the decision to keep quiet weighed heavily on the powerful Bloodsworn. He watched Lord Devlin dab at the blood at the corner of Avera's mouth, then smooth her hair back from her still face. There was a sense of helplessness in the tender gestures. For once, Bracca realized, he and Devlin Tragar had something more in common than their hatred of Camarie. Not even with all the magic at his command had the other man been able to protect his beloved. He glanced up at Bracca, his gaze sharp and seeking.

"You said to begin with. What changed your mind?"

Bracca frowned, trying to recall the sequence of events. She'd been afraid the test was a trap, true, but that wasn't what had caused her initial panic. "There were images of a room deep with shadows. I could not see any details, just vague outlines, varying shades of darkness. One of the shadows moved, grew larger. Then came the emotions."

"What emotions?"

"Fear, anger, frustration, revulsion." Re-living the moment, Bracca once again found himself reaching for his sword to protect her. He stopped, and reached for Avera's hand instead as the images played out in his memory. Clamping his jaw over a roar of anger, he gently pushed the burgundy sleeve of her gown up her arm. Her golden skin was criss-crossed by many faint, white lines, a myriad patchwork of scars. "I think it had something to do with these."

There were a few gasps from those around them. Without a word, Lord Devlin firmly took possession of her arm, pushing Bracca aside, and tugged the sleeve back in place.

"Do you know what happened to her, Devlin?" Lord Jerran asked quietly.

"No more than what Cu-Laurian has said. I asked her, but she didn't want to talk about it. It's still too fresh in her mind."

"But the wounds are months old."

"Not so. One month, two at the most. I used magic yesterday morning to reduce the scarring. If a blindfold and gag were involved in her attack, it would explain her reaction to them here."

It would indeed, thought Bracca, feeling a fresh wave of anger toward her attacker. And the more he thought about what might have happened to her, the angrier he became.

A side door opened. One of Caveon's Blades entered, followed by a woman in a blue robe. Bracca recognized the healer who had come to the palace to tend Lord Devlin when he and Avera had been attacked by an assassin. It took a healer of exceptional skill and control to form the temporary bond necessary to heal a wounded Bloodsworn. Latessa was the senior healer for the Bloodsworn Hall.

"First Bloodsworn." Latessa inclined her head to Lord Devlin as she approached the table. She glanced at Bracca curiously, nodded once to him, then began examining Avera with quick, sure hands. After several long minutes, the healer placed a hand on Avera's forehead and leaned over her.

Bracca watched as the small wound at the corner of Avera's mouth healed. He heard Latessa murmur something, her words too low to make them out. The hairs on his arms stirred in the wake of what could only be a brush of powerful magic. Bracca suppressed a shiver. Magic was not something he was used to feeling outside of a blood-link.

The healer stepped back. "She will awaken in a moment."

"Thank you, Latessa," Devlin said.

"My thanks also," Bracca said, bowing his head in respect.

She responded with a smile. "You are welcome,

First Bloodsworn, First Blade. It is my pleasure to serve." Nodding once to Caveon, she slipped away quietly.

Avera moaned softly. Her eyelids fluttered and her brow creased. She raised a shaking hand to her temple. When her fingers curled into a fist in her hair, Bracca reached for her wrist, afraid she would hurt herself more. Devlin knocked his hand back, and gently ensnared Avera's wrist himself. Bracca had no time to be offended.

Her eyes still closed, Avera's other hand shot out, dealing a glancing blow to Lord Devlin's cheek before he captured that wrist as well. Avera began to struggle in earnest, whispering words that tore at Bracca's heart. "No, no, not again. Not again!"

Lord Devlin caught both wrists in one hand and touched her face. "Avera, it's all right. You are safe. Open your eyes, *me`surrasie*."

Bracca reached out to her confused mind. *You are safe, little sister. Your Starmate holds you. He hovers over you like a fierce hen protecting her chick. It would help sooth his ruffled feathers, I think, if you opened your eyes.*

Her struggles halted abruptly. Her eyes snapped open, dark with confusion and traces of fear. "Devlin?"

Lord Devlin wrapped his arms around her shoulders and pulled her close. "You are safe," he repeated.

Bracca watched patiently as she took a deep, shuddering breath. When she lifted her head from Lord Devlin's chest, he was relieved to see her brilliant green eyes were clear and alert. She reached a hand up to her Starmate's face. The powerful Bloodsworn swallowed hard and turned his face to kiss her palm. For a moment, it was as if they were the only ones in the room.

Mentally, Bracca cleared his throat. Avera's

gaze slid over to him, a faint blush staining her cheeks. She extended a hand to him.

"Are you all right?"

Her question seemed ridiculous to him. She was the one who had collapsed. But he couldn't deny her concern.

"I am now that you are awake." He thought about kissing her palm, as the Tragar had, but kissed the back of her hand instead. Baiting Devlin Tragar, who was sometimes referred to as the Tiger of Illian, would only distress Avera right now. She was upset enough, he decided, feeling her embarrassment rise as she focused on the dozens of men around her. Moaning, she dropped her face into her hands.

"This isn't happening. Someone please tell me this is a bad dream."

Lord Devlin smiled and rubbed her back gently. "No dream I'm afraid, bad or otherwise."

She made a noise, something like laughter, but not quite. Lifting her head, she pushed her hair back. "Ah, well. At least tell me that Bracca and I passed the stupid test."

"Indeed, my lady." Smiling ruefully, Lord Jerran fingered the back of his head. "When it became clear you were in distress, I tried to help remove your hood. As soon as I touched you, your magic sent me skidding across the floor. You are, without doubt, the strongest new Bloodsworn I have ever encountered. To have only two new Blades and still be able to tap into the power you just displayed is unheard of."

"Not completely unheard of," Caveon corrected, "but certainly unusual. And disturbing."

"What do you mean, disturbing?" Avera swung her legs over the side of the table. Bracca stepped back as Lord Devlin helped her stand so she could face the elder Bloodsworn.

"Sometimes," he began, "those called to serve as

Bloodsworn cannot control Avalyr's magic."

She nodded. "Devlin told me about that."

Caveon's gaze shot to him in apparent surprise. "Did he indeed?"

Lord Devlin raised a brow. "Did you really think I would keep something so important from her?"

Caveon cleared his throat. "Yes, well, what he may not have told you is that the magic succeeds in breaking the minds of such individuals. They become drunk with power, uncontrollable, and uncaring of the damage they cause. They fall into fits, flinging magic around chaotically, often killing anyone nearby. We call it bloodrage."

Avera paled. "Are you saying I just killed someone?"

No! Bracca said at the same time as Lord Devlin.

"Of course you didn't," Lord Devlin assured her. "Caveon, you heard Cu-Laurian's explanation. You cannot truly believe what just happened to Avera was bloodrage."

"Despite what might have precipitated her actions, what else are we to believe," Kapatree said with far too much satisfaction. "She's had her two Blades less than a week. The strongest Bloodsworn on Avalyr are in this room. Can anyone here say they could have duplicated Lady St. John's actions? Could you, Tragar, who are the strongest of us all? Why, she even took control of her sword and sent it back into Cu-Laurian's hand in the middle of her bloodrage fit.

"It was not bloodrage," Devlin ground out. "No one was killed."

Bracca fixed his gaze on Kapatree. Only the table separating them prevented him from slitting the man's throat when he called out, "Akrinon, how many of your Blade's ribs did you say are broken?"

"Three," Akrinon replied from where he tended

his Blade. "But they are only fractured, not broken."

"Only fractured," Kapatree repeated, cutting his eyes at Avera. "I don't believe Platkus' Blade got off quite so easy. His shoulder broke when he hit the column you threw him into."

The blood drained from Avera's face. "What? Devlin, what is he saying?"

Instead of answering her, Lord Devlin said, "Tell us what you were thinking just before you tried to remove your blindfold."

Her gaze shot to Bracca.

Why is he asking this? What did you tell him?

He needed to know why you reacted as you did. As your Starmate, he has that right. I told him what I saw and felt through our link concerning your attack.

Her green eyes darkened. He sensed her disapproval, but she sighed. *Okay, maybe he did need to know. That wasn't what started everything though.*

No, and Bracca hadn't had time to correct her wrong assumption about the test. If he knew nothing else about Devlin Tragar, he knew the man would not stoop to subterfuge if he wanted Bracca's link severed.

"Avera?"

"All right," she said calmly, though impatience and embarrassment swirled through their link. "If you must know, I got worried that maybe this whole thing was a set up."

"A set up?"

Her chagrin deepened, tinged with a bit of anger. "A trap, okay. I thought you'd rigged this up so you...they...somebody, could get Bracca's sword away from him and break it." She grimaced. "I thought maybe you were trying to break my link with him."

Lord Devlin's head jerked back as if she struck

him. He tossed an angry glance at Bracca before meeting Avera's gaze. "If I wanted to sever your link with Cu-Laurian, I would not use deception. I would simply take his damn sword from him and break it myself."

"You could try," Bracca said evenly, meaning every word. He would enjoy taking the Tragar's measure in a purely physical fight. No magic, just swords backed by a warrior's cunning.

Caveon cleared his throat in warning. Apparently the elder Bloodsworn was tired of quelling fights. "I think we need to get back to the subject at hand. As I said before, the Council recognizes the blood-link between Lady Avera St. John and the warrior, Bracca Cu-Laurian. Unless someone has an objection, I hereby confirm Lady St. John's Bloodsworn status." He paused.

Bracca wasn't surprised when the rat-faced Bloodsworn, Kapatree, stepped forward with a look of false worry. "I must disagree. By your own words, Caveon, you have acknowledged Lady St. John's importance to the Prophecies. Can we then, in good conscious, allow her to risk her life by serving as a Bloodsworn?"

"That's my choice to make, not yours," Avera shot back.

"I must disagree, again. The fulfillment of the Prophecies is paramount. I do not believe there is anything in the Seventh Prophecy requiring your Bloodsworn status. If the Council deems your life is endangered by your blood-links, it is our duty to see those links are severed with all speed."

"Now you listen here—"

"Avera," Lord Devlin said placing a calming hand on her.

"No, Devlin, this is wrong. Forming the blood-links didn't hurt me. I'll admit the magic felt a little overwhelming at first, but I'm used to it now. I can handle it. Don't let them do this."

Bracca stood by quietly as a long look passed between Avera and her Starmate. The conflict was easy to read on Lord Devlin's face. The temptation to side with the Council was great, yet if he did so, Avera might find it impossible to forgive him. And Bracca felt no give in the strength of Avera's convictions. She wasn't just fighting for herself, she fought for him and for Tyr.

Lord Jerran spoke into the strained silence. "I disagree with Kapatree. Lady St. John has shown great restraint and courage. She walked into this Council chamber and was forced by sixty strangers into a stressful situation. Our *test*, tested more than just her link to Cu-Laurian. We tested her trust and her patience. She was well within her rights to protect herself and her Blade when she felt threatened. Furthermore, her actions were not those of a Bloodsworn overwhelmed by magic, but someone in precise control. No one was attacked other than those she perceived as a threat. By that evidence alone, she is more than capable of handling her magic. I vote to allow her to keep her Bloodsworn status."

Several Bloodsworn shifted, moving through the crowd to form a circle around Caveon. Low murmurs passed back and forth. Finally, Caveon held up a hand, and a white ball of magic formed over his head. Each of the Council members formed a smaller ball and sent it flying to join Caveon's.

What are they doing? Avera asked.

Casting votes. Bracca watched with interest as each small ball of magic was absorbed by Caveon's larger one. He'd heard of this, but never seen it done. Camarie rarely dealt with other Bloodsworn. When he did, he made sure his vote was the only one that counted.

When all the Council had voted, The large

sphere split into ten separate balls, each one flying back to a Bloodsworn. Another moment passed as the Council members absorbed the voting results. Caveon nodded his head several times, his brows rising and falling as if in response to the votes he mentally counted.

"Lord Jerran has made a valid point. The Council has voted seven to three to recognize Lady St. John's Bloodsworn status and allow her to keep the two links she has already formed."

Relief spun through Bracca as Avera flashed him a smile. He wasn't sure what he would have done had they decided to sever his link. He was certain Avera would have fought them. The only way for Bracca to protect her would be for him to obey the Council and break his own sword. Again. Not a pleasant prospect.

"However," Caveon continued. "Lord Kapatree also raises a valid concern. As honored as we are to have a female Bloodsworn in our midst, we feel there must be a stipulation to her status."

"What kind of stipulation?" Lord Devlin asked before Avera could. Bracca moved closer to her. He had a feeling she was not going to like what Caveon had to say.

"It is the opinion of this Council that it is too dangerous for Lady St. John to take on the responsibility of any more Blades. While she seems able to control what she now has access to, it would be foolish indeed to expose her to more of Avalyr's wild magic."

Bracca saw Avera stiffen. He also saw Lord Devlin's shoulders relax slightly.

"Can they do that?" Avera demanded of Lord Devlin.

"They can," he assured her. "As I told you before, the Bloodsworn Council is the ruling body for all Bloodsworn on Avalyr. Their word is law."

She turned back to Caveon. "And just how long is this outrageous stipulation supposed to last?"

"Perhaps indefinitely, my dear," Caveon said gently. "You must realize how unusual you are, how unique your position. It requires we take special precautions, especially since you are the prophecy bride of our First Bloodsworn and play such an important part in the fulfillment of the Seventh Prophecy. It would be terrible indeed if you were somehow...injured while trying to provide for those afflicted with the blade-illness. Especially when there are so many of us who are more than capable of fulfilling that role."

She didn't make a sound for several heartbeats. Bracca's nerves sprang to attention when her hands went to her hips.

"What I realize," she said slowly, her words dripping contempt, "is that Avalyr's males can be just as chauvinistic as their Earthling counterparts. Here you all are," she paused and waved a hand across the room causing every man there to flinch, "the Loyal Order of the Water Buffalo Club afraid to let a woman enter your hallowed halls. Talk about a double standard. And you," she said swinging around to face Lord Devlin. "Don't think I didn't see that smile on your face when you heard that chauvinistic drivel. You're just as bad as they are. No, you're worse. If I'm going to be your wife, you should be on my side, not theirs."

She stopped speaking, her eyes accusing her mate of something Bracca knew he couldn't even deny.

"I will not lie to you," Lord Devlin said cupping Avera's face in his palm. "Allowing you to form more blood-links goes against every protective instinct within me. I know you believe you are Bloodsworn for a reason, but for once, Kapatree is right. The Seventh Prophecy says nothing about my bride being

Bloodsworn."

Avera's bitter disappointment and sadness flooded Bracca just before she slammed the door closed on their link. He took a deep breath to still his own howling emotions. He wanted to comfort her, but wasn't sure how. Even he understood Lord Devlin's decision. What sane man would want his mate mind-linked to another?

Avera lowered her head, the glimmer of tears in her eyes. Without another word she pushed past them both.

"Avera—" She twisted away, dodging Lord Devlin's outstretched hand.

"Leave me alone. I'm leaving." She blindly waved a hand in her Starmate's direction. It was almost funny how quickly an empty path formed between them as grown men backed away warily. Almost.

Bracca slipped his way around the group of warriors as Avera continued her rant.

"You and the Grand Poobah work out all the details of my life you want. It's not like I have any rights any more anyway."

****

Frustration seethed through Devlin as he watched Avera march past the knot of Blades. When one hand lifted to her face in a quick wiping gesture, he started after her, but stopped when he saw Cu-Laurian swing into step beside her. He knew she was too angry to accept his presence right now, but—and the truth of it bothered him more than he wanted to admit—she would accept her Blade's. The warrior would keep her safe until Devlin himself could join her. There were a few things he needed to discuss with the Council before he could leave.

A hand touched his shoulder. Turning, he found Jerran shaking his head, a sympathetic look on his face. Then his friend spoiled the effect by grinning.

"Devlin, my friend, I am sincerely glad I'm not you."

Devlin turned back to watch Avera stalk away, her hips swaying in burgundy velvet. The sight summoned memories of their heated night together, those same hips held firmly in his hands while the luscious globes of her backside kissed his crotch again and again as they pleasured one another. The love of Starmates bound them together as one. He had to believe that nothing, not hurt or anger, not even his own infernal jealousy, could keep them apart for long. And when they reconciled...

Devlin's lips stretched into a wicked grin of anticipation. "Jerran, my friend, I am glad you are not me, too."

Chapter Ten

As soon as the gate closed behind them his Bloodsworn separated herself from the Silver Blades and their Bloodsworn. Bracca stayed close to her side. Even with their link closed, he could still feel her pain and anger.

When she spoke, her words held a hurt impossible to miss. "I would appreciate it if someone could show me the way back to my room in the Ladies' Wing. I haven't been here long enough to know my way around yet."

The Silver Blades hesitated, but after one look at their Bloodsworn, they quickly left the courtyard without a word. Devlin Tragar turned his gaze on Bracca, no doubt willing him away as well. Bracca smiled slightly and remained where he was. No one but Avera commanded him. The prince stiffened, but said nothing to Bracca, choosing to address his lady instead.

"You have a new room, Avera. One I will be happy to escort you to since I am going there myself." He bowed her ahead of him. Avera didn't move.

"By that I'm assuming you mean your room?"

A muscle ticked in the prince's jaw. "*Our* room."

"I see."

Their link popped open. *Bracca, would you please wait in the hallway over there? I think his lordship and I need to get a few things straight.*

As you wish, my lady. He bowed, shot Devlin Tragar a warning look, and marched over to the arched opening. He stopped just out of sight, unwilling to leave her entirely.

"Don't go making presumptions," Avera said. "I may have accepted you as my husband—"

"Starmate."

"Whatever. That doesn't mean you get to rule every aspect of my life. If we're going to make this relationship work, I have to be able to make my own decisions."

"I never said you could not."

Her laugh was bitter. "You just did. You let those men back there make a decision that should have been mine."

"That was different. Even I have to abide by the Council's ruling in regards to Bloodsworn duties."

"Then prove to me I have rights outside their influence."

"How?"

"I need some space to work through this. I want a separate room. One that isn't in the Ladies' Wing. I want it somewhere Bracca has access to."

A long silent moment passed. Then Bracca heard the Tragar's voice, calm, polite, carefully controlled.

"I advise you not to push me too far, Avera. Not if you value the life of your Blade as much as you profess."

"That sounds suspiciously like a threat."

Bracca snorted softly, his hand curling around the hilt of his amber sword. Of course it was a threat.

"It is a promise." The Tragar's next words came so low Bracca had to strain to hear them. "If I *ever* catch him in your bed—"

"Stop it!" Avera shouted. Her outrage joined Bracca's, forcing him back toward the courtyard. He stopped just as the arguing pair came into view. Despite the Tragar's threatening pose—looming over her, one hand wrapped around her neck, the other around her waist—Bracca sensed no fear coming from Avera.

"What is the matter with you?" she demanded, pushing against him with no results. "I swear you really have to work on getting this jealousy thing under control, Devlin. How could you even think such a thing?"

Bracca knew how. He'd seen jealousy turn perfectly sane men into raving idiots before.

"Look," she said, stopping her struggles long enough to poke Lord Devlin hard in the chest. "Last night and this morning aside, you obviously don't know me very well. I don't sleep around, buster, so you can just keep your dirty little assumptions to yourself. That's not what I meant when I said I wanted him to have access to my rooms. I don't think about him like that. Bracca is my friend, Devlin. He's my Blade, not my lover. I would no more sleep with him than you would with Fate."

Some of the tension left Lord Devlin's body. His hands moved to frame her face in a gentle hold. "Point taken," he said quietly. "As long as you admit there is no going back, Avera. As of yesterday, you are mine in all ways save one, and that merely awaits the coming solstic. I warn you now, I have no intention of ever sharing you with anyone."

"That's good, because I don't intend to share you either." She rose up on her toes and closed the small distance between them. The kiss was a slow meeting of mouths, a perfect seal to the simple statements that held the flavor of vows.

Bracca moved quietly back into the shadows of the hallway, away from the poignant moment. Bits and pieces of Avera's emotions spilled over into their link. He closed his eyes and leaned against the wall, trying to separate himself from the emotions without success. Her pain seared him. Her confusion battered him. Her longing for her mate, for the closeness they'd shared before the Council's interference, made him ache for her. As softly as possible, he shut his door to their link.

Then his mind caught up with his ears.

"Devlin, your men don't like Bracca. I know you don't like him either, but you can't deny he saved my life. Where I come from, that means something. I'm not asking you to throw him a party or hand him the keys to the palace. All I want is a place where he can relax and not have to worry about watching his back. And all he wants is to protect me. I swear to you that he doesn't have any designs on me, not for himself, or Camarie, or anyone else. You of all people should understand how I know this."

Bracca wanted to hug her all over again. No one had ever thought of his comfort before. No one.

The Tragar's voice, when it came, was filled with resignation. "I am trying very hard to understand, Avera, to give you time, but you... Circumstances make it difficult."

"I think you can handle a little difficulty, Devlin. My father always said easy is for wimps and wusses, and you don't strike me as being either one. You are right though, I do need time. A lot has happened in the past couple of days. If you can give me some space, let me get a handle on things, I think we'll be all right."

Bracca spent the next several heartbeats willing the Tragar to give Avera what she needed. More than anything, he wanted his new heart-sister to be happy.

"Very well. I will have your things moved into the suite down the hall from mine. It is the best I can do. You have only to let the servants know if you need anything further."

"And Bracca?"

A hard edge crept back into his voice. "There is a room across the hall from yours suitable for your

Blade."

"Thank you," she said.

"If you wait here, I'll send a servant to show you the way."

Bracca moved to the edge of the hallway once more. Devlin Tragar raised her hand and rubbed the back of it against his check. Then he turned it over and planted a kiss firmly in the center of her palm. Without another word, he left, walking quickly across the courtyard to another archway. Avera stared after him, her fingers curled into a tight fist, as if she held something extremely precious.

The servant arrived a moment later and led them both to their new quarters. After inspecting all the rooms, Bracca sought Avera, and found her standing by the large bed in her suite. On the golden comforter lay a pair of dark blue pants, the kind Avera had been wearing the first time he'd seen her. Jeans, she'd called them. A white blouse with long, narrow sleeves lay next to the jeans. She sighed, fingering the soft material of the blouse.

"From the Tragar?" Bracca guessed.

She nodded. "Oh, Bracca. How am I supposed to stay mad at someone so thoughtful?"

He put an arm around her shoulders, and bent to place a kiss on the top of her head. "Give him time, little sister. The rift between you is not very wide. You will soon find your way back to each other."

She sniffed. "I hope you're right, Bracca. Because I don't think I could stand living without him." She sniffed again.

"You're tired, my lady Bloodsworn. Why not lay down and rest?"

She smiled and wiped a quick hand across her cheeks. "I'd love to, but I was raised by a man who insisted on polite manners, even when it came to his enemies. Since I'm moving out of the Ladies' Wing, I need to track down Devlin's mother and thank her for her hospitality."

"You consider Lady Patria your enemy?"

She grimaced. "Maybe. Our first meeting didn't go so well. She threatened to chain me to Devlin's bed, and I kind of inferred she was a bitch and ordered her out of my room."

Bracca chuckled. "A most unfortunate beginning indeed. I would have enjoyed seeing it."

"You're not helping. I'm trying to be good here. For Devlin's sake, you know. The least I can do is mend a fence or two."

"That would be very diplomatic of you."

"Yeah," she said. She ran her fingers slowly across the dark blue pants. When she looked up at him, mischief glittered in her green eyes. "I think I'll change clothes first, though."

Chapter Eleven

Sheren tipped the ladle of scented soap into the delicate glass bottle, careful not to spill a drop. When she'd requested soap for the villa, she had no idea Lady Patria had none prepared. Usually there was an abundance of extra bottles to choose from in various fragrances.

"I am trying a new procedure," Lady Patria told her. "It takes more time, but I believe the results will be worth it. Several batches will not be ready until next week. Fortunately, two kettles started earlier should be done today. Come by the stillroom after the noon meal. If I deem them ready, you may fill the bottles you need. A decca of each should last the villa until the rest are prepared."

Sheren could hardly believe the generous offer. She'd always wanted to visit Lady Patria's famed stillroom. The prince's mother was known throughout Illian for her scented soaps and oils. Sheren had no idea, however, that filling the small bottles would take so long—or require such skill.

She slowly poured another ladle-full of thick, opalescent liquid into the bottle, stopping as the level reached the point Lady Patria had indicated. With a sigh of relief, she set the bottle in the holding tray next to the other nine already filled. Half way done. If the other ten bottles went as quickly, she might have a few minutes to look around before Lady Patria returned.

The second pot of soap stood cooling on another table. Sheren replaced the lid on the first pot and hurried to get started on filling the second rack of bottles. She was just topping off the first one when she realized she wasn't alone.

Sheren glanced up and almost dropped the bottle she held. Never had she seen a female dressed so. Instead of a skirt, the woman wore a pair of dark blue trousers just like a man. The sight was very strange, but as a woman used to hard work, Sheren immediately recognized the potential benefits. No hem to drag the ground, getting soaked or dirty when mopping or gardening. No layers of cloth to wrap around her ankles and trip her when she hurried up and down stairs. The very practicality of the strange attire made her wonder why she'd never thought of wearing trousers before.

"Excuse me," the woman said.

Sheren hurriedly set the bottle and ladle aside. "May I help you?"

The woman smiled hesitantly. "I hope so. My name is Avera. I didn't mean to bother you, but I'm looking for Lady Patria. Someone said I'd find her in here."

Shock ran through Sheren. Avera? As in Lady Avera St. John?

"You're Bracca's Bloodsworn?" Heat scalded her cheeks the instant the question popped out of her mouth. Not only was her tone rudely incredulous, but her use of Bracca Cu-Laurian's first name without the formal family-clan reference hinted at a personal connection that wasn't there. She bowed her head. "Forgive me, I meant no disrespect, my lady."

"That's all right. You're not the first to be surprised by my Bloodsworn status. I just left a whole room full of skeptics." She nodded toward Sheren, her gaze turning speculative. "You surprised me a bit, too. I didn't think anyone here knew Bracca."

Something close to panic rushed through

Sheren's veins. "I don't."

Lady St. John's eyes widened at the forceful denial. Sheren groaned to herself. What was wrong with her? Why couldn't she control her tongue?

Fear, probably. The possibility that Lady St. John was here in search of her didn't escape Sheren. Assuming he recognized her touch, Bracca would have told his Bloodsworn of Sheren's earlier interference. She would be angry, and rightly so.

Sheren began straightening the already straight line of bottles on the table. "I'm sorry, I don't mean to sound rude. I meant that I just met Bracca Cu-Laurian today. I don't know him. We don't know each other at all." *No matter how much it might feel otherwise.*

The memory of those brief, but eventful meetings rose, taunting her, causing her heart to race. Out of fear, she told herself, because she didn't understand what he did to her empathic abilities. Not because she was attracted to him. She couldn't afford to let herself be attracted to him.

"I see," Lady St. John said. "I'm sorry, I don't usually jump to conclusions like that. I didn't mean to upset you."

A warmth that had nothing to do with her embarrassment leaked past Sheren's shield. Astonished, she met Lady St. John's sincere gaze. This woman was nothing like she'd imagined a female Bloodsworn to be. Soft-spoken, kind, her expression gentle, Lady Avera St. John was a far cry from some cold, hard warrior woman. Sheren liked her, even though she found the woman's friendly attitude disconcerting. Was Lady St. John not used to dealing with servants on her world?

"No apology necessary, my lady. My name is Sheren Ni-Annun. I am chatelaine of one of Lord Tragar's holdings. Lady Patria was here, but she stepped out into the garden for a moment. Would you like me to take you to her or let her know you are here?" She waited for some sign of recognition at her name, a flash of anger in those brilliant green eyes or a tightening of lips in disapproval.

Lady St. John smiled easily. "No, that's okay. If she's coming back, I'll wait for her." She moved closer, her interested gaze resting on the simmering pot of soap. She sniffed. "Mind if I ask what you're cooking? It smells wonderful, like fresh peach preserves."

Sheren laughed before she caught herself. Lady St. John's fault, she decided. The woman made herself far too approachable. "I doubt you would find the taste as appealing as the smell. This is scented soap for bathing."

Green eyes lit up with excitement. "Homemade soap? Really? What do you use as a base? How do you infuse the scent into the mixture? Do you extract the oils by expression or distillation?"

Sheren blinked at the rapid fire questions. She held up a hand. "Forgive me. I did not mean to mislead you. This is Lady Patria's stillroom. She makes the soap, not I. I'm afraid you will have to wait and ask her your questions."

Lady St. John's brows arched. "Lady Patria made this? Devlin's mother? Are you sure?"

"Yes. Lady Patria is quite well-known throughout the realm for her scented soaps, lotions, and oils. She has been making them for years."

Lady St. John looked around the room, her gaze lingering on the line of tables where pots and glass jars simmered and perked in various stages of Lady Patria's new process. She shook her head, her expression one of bemused shock. "Who would have thought the queen bitch and I would have anything in common?" she murmured.

Startled, Sheren dropped her head to hide her smile, certain she'd not been meant to hear that last remark. Still, she couldn't keep quiet. "Do not be too concerned, my lady. I understand two people must have several things in common before being considered anything alike." She picked up the ladle again and another bottle to fill. She glanced at Lady St. John and found the woman grinning.

"You really shouldn't encourage me. I promised myself I would be on my best behavior. You see, my first meeting with Devlin's mother didn't go very well at all. I wouldn't be surprised if she didn't try to stuff me into one of her pots."

"Oh, she would never do that," Sheren assured her, barely managing to keep the smile from her face. She wondered at her own audacity in daring to joke with a noblewoman who was also Bloodsworn. Normally, she would never be so bold. This was a day for craziness. "I'm not sure, but I don't think essence of Bloodsworn is a scent she would wish for her soaps."

Lady St. John laughed. "No, I suppose not. As for what we have in common, I was referring to the fact that what she's doing here is a form of chemistry, which is my field of expertise." Her brow furrowed. "Or was. Not sure what my field is now." Her eyes mirrored the sadness in her voice, making Sheren want to reach out to her.

"You are Bloodsworn," she reminded gently. "Would not magic be your field of expertise now?"

"Such an assumption would be incorrect."

They both started at the sound of Lady Patria's stern voice. A sick feeling settled in Sheren's stomach. How much of their conversation had Lady Patria overheard? She faced the formidable woman and bobbed a curtsey. "I did not mean to assume, my lady."

Lady St. John stepped up beside her. "You didn't. You asked a question. Big difference. Wouldn't you say so, Lady Patria?"

"Indeed." Lady Patria passed them, her attention on the pots and bottles on the table as she spoke. "However, my admonition was a reminder for you, not Sheren. Your position as my son's wife is far more important than your status as Bloodsworn."

The stern pronouncement did not seem to quell Lady St. John in the least. She didn't bow her head in acceptance or even lower her eyes. Instead, she met Lady Patria head on. "That depends on who you talk to," she said evenly. "I know a couple of people who would disagree with you."

Lady Patria's head snapped up. Sheren held her breath as sharp, blue-gray eyes clashed with brilliant green ones. A long moment passed before Lady Patria said, "I'm sure you do."

Sheren choked back a laugh. She didn't think anyone had ever challenged Lady Patria face-to-face before. Her son, perhaps, but never another female. She schooled her features and checked her shields as Lady Patria turned her attention on her.

"You're doing well here, Sheren. When you are finished, feel free to explore the stillroom until I return. I have several new plantings along the south wall that I think you might be interested in. We can discuss cuttings and seedlings while I show you how to seal and pack the bottles."

Sheren could hardly believe her ears. Lady Patria Kel-Tragar was offering some of her stillroom plants for the villa? She hated the villa. Sheren had always felt like a beggar on a queen's doorstep when she came to ask for supplies. "Thank you, my lady. Such an offer is extremely generous."

A graceful hand waved in her direction. "Yes, yes, we'll talk later. Come," she said to Lady St. John. "Join me on the terrace. I think it time you and I became better acquainted. There is much you need to learn about your new position."

"All right," Lady St. John said. "After you." She

held a hand out and waited until Lady Patria sailed past her. Then she turned to Sheren, rolled her eyes, and grinned.

Sheren forced herself to smile in return to keep her worry from showing. Lady Patria Kel-Tragar was a law unto herself, her word second only to her son's. Her disapproval of her daughter-in-law was plain. So was her intention to force Lady St. John into the role of dutiful wife and princess, no matter the cost.

****

"Your stillroom is beautiful." Moving onto the curved terrace, Avera glanced back at the huge room. Circular in shape, it had numerous glass doors, many of which opened onto the terrace. Pots of plants, most with exotic blooms, graced every shelf and crowded nearly every table. Baskets of live plants hung from the open rafters, vying for space with tied bundles of dried herbs and grasses.

Avera drew in a deep breath. A veritable scented smorgasbord hung in the air. Rose, jasmine, and lavender mixed with the sharper, spicier scents of sandalwood and patchouli, cedar and cinnamon.

"Thank you." Lady Patria stopped at a table. Her disapproving gaze moved over Avera before she waved her to one of the two chairs. "One of the first things we must discuss is your attire. The Princess of Illian does not wear trousers."

Betrayed or not, Avera decided she owed Devlin a kiss. The look on his mother's face was priceless. The woman had burned the jeans Avera had arrived from Earth in, deeming them unsuitable. Avera might have been madder about their loss if Devlin hadn't gone to Earth and brought everything she owned back to Avalyr. He'd done it in an effort to make her feel more at home. The frustratingly thoughtful man had even brought her the carpet off the apartment floor.

And then he goes and spoils everything by siding with the Council.

The painful reminder tempered some of Avera's pleasure at Lady Patria's pursed lips, and helped her recall the reason she was there in the first place. *Manners, Avera, remember your manners.*

She decided to ignore the remark about her clothes. "I saw a distillation unit on one of the tables as I came in. Is that what you normally use to extract the essential oils you use to scent your soaps?"

Lady Patria's brows rose a fraction. "It depends on what I'm working with. Sometimes expression is the most efficient method, though distillation seems to concentrate the scents so they last longer."

"Have you tried adding a bit of vetiver when combining the oil and soap? The bonding process wouldn't take nearly as long, and the color and fragrance should last longer, too."

Lady Patria sat forward, her gaze intent. "How do you know about vetiver oil?"

Avera shrugged. "I'm a chemist. I know all about compounds and elements, suspension fluids and fixatives. Vetiver oil is used all the time in the perfume industry back on Earth."

Devlin's mother leaned back in her chair again. She waved a hand toward a servant Avera hadn't noticed before. The woman came forward with a tray laden with refreshments. Avera stayed quiet as plates of small cakes and cups were set out. Lady Patria remained quiet, too, her expression thoughtful. The servant poured hot tea into the cups before retreating.

"I have found," Lady Patria said, not looking at Avera as she added cream and sugar to her tea, "that vetiver tends to overpower the more delicate scents."

"It can," Avera conceded. She added cream and

sugar to her cup, too. Normally she didn't drink hot tea, but was willing to give it a try. "A lot depends on where and how it's grown. Climate and soil can affect its essence. Some varieties also lean more toward a floral quality while others have a smokier scent. There's even a difference between the wild variety and the cultivated kind, but don't ask me why."

"Can you identify the different varieties on sight?"

"Maybe. It's been a while since I did that particular research."

Devlin's mother didn't seem to be disappointed. If anything, she looked more animated, more...human.

Avera smiled to herself. Lady Patria, human? Perish the thought.

The woman in question dabbed her lips with a napkin that she then folded and laid on the table. "I admit to being surprised. I did not think to find a common ground with you so soon. You are an unusual young woman, Lady St. John."

Avera almost snorted her next sip of tea. A brittle laugh slipped out. Unusual. Yeah, that was her.

Lady Patria's brows rose, and Avera quickly held up a hand. "Sorry, I'm not laughing at you, just your choice of words. You're not the first person to call me unusual today."

"I take it you refer to the Bloodsworn Council. Your interview with them did not go well?"

"Depends on who you talk to."

"But you retain your Bloodsworn status, do you not?" Distaste colored the cultured voice. Avera wasn't surprised Devlin's mother already knew the Council's decision. She was a powerful woman. She would have her sources of information.

"Yes, and if you know that, you also know

they've forbidden me to link with any more Blades."

Blatant satisfaction crossed Lady Patria's stern face. "One of the few edicts handed down by that body I agree with."

"Really? I find that rather strange. You don't strike me as a woman who would approve of men over-riding the rights of women. Especially men who seem bent on protecting their elitist little club."

Lady Patria inclined her head slightly. "While some of your perceptions may be correct, your understanding of the Bloodsworn Council is in error. The role of Bloodsworn has fallen to the males of our world more out of necessity than covetousness. The very nature of their sometimes violent duties places the status of Bloodsworn outside the realm of possibility as far as women are concerned. It is a position we Feyune females do not covet."

"I'm not Feyune."

"But you *are* female. If you were to ask, I am sure most, if not all, of the council members would say their decision was based on protecting you, not their so-called vaulted positions. More, you are Starmate to one of the most powerful men on Avalyr."

Avera frowned. They were back to the subject of her dual roles. Maybe she needed to hear what Lady Patria had to say. At least that way she'd know how to deal with the situation. "What does being Devlin's Starmate have to do with me being Bloodsworn?"

"My son has many responsibilities," Devlin's mother said. "He is the Tragar, the head of our clan. He is also the ruler of Illian, the realm in which we live." She sighed. "And he is Bloodsworn to one hundred and seventeen Blades."

Avera blinked. One hundred and seventeen? She couldn't have heard right.

"Did you say one hundred?"

Lady Patria nodded. "And seventeen, at last

count."

Avera sat back in her chair, completely stunned. Devlin had one hundred and seventeen men dependent on him for their very lives? One hundred and seventeen *links*? Merciful heavens, how did he do it? She was freaked just being responsible for two lives. And while she resented the Bloodsworn Council forbidding her any more, if she was truthful with herself, the thought of having more than two Blades scared her...a lot.

Not that she would turn her back on anyone if they came to her like Bracca and Tyr did. She wasn't a coward. But heavens, just the thought of what one hundred and seventeen links would feel like in her mind made Avera shudder. Something like that would be enough to drive a person crazy, wouldn't it? Yet Devlin Tragar appeared sane enough, at least what she'd seen of him. Maybe it got easier with time.

"Umm, just out of curiosity, how long has Devlin been a Bloodsworn?"

Lady Patria rose and walked to the edge of the terrace. Avera followed, still a bit bemused by what she'd learned. Below the terrace was a huge garden. Flower beds and hedges lined the walkways. Trees shaded benches. The sound of water trickling from at least a dozen fountains drifted up to them.

"My son became Bloodsworn six months after his seventeenth birthday. The same year his father died. That was twelve years ago. He was chosen as First Bloodsworn three years later. As you may imagine, his life has been quite full, the demands on his time great. With the last three prophecies left to be fulfilled, those demands will only increase." She looked at Avera pointedly. "My son does not need more problems to deal with, particularly in his own house."

"And you think I'll cause him problems."

"You cannot help but do so. Feyune women are trained from birth to know and understand their place in our society and to be a comfort to their husbands when they marry. It was my hope that when the Oracle finally named his bride, Devlin would at last have a source of peacefulness in his life. Someone he could turn to when the demands on him became too much of a burden. Instead, you know nothing of how the wife of a man in Devlin's position is expected to behave. Add to that your Bloodsworn status, and the situation becomes intolerable."

Avera gazed out at the garden without seeing its beauty. She knew of a few societies on Earth where the women were still raised to believe their whole purpose in life was to be at the beck and call of their men. A situation completely foreign to what she envisioned a marriage should be. In fact, she was so far from what Devlin's mother expected of her son's wife that it wasn't funny. No wonder the woman resented her.

A sense of hopelessness welled up inside her. What if Devlin felt the same?

He had to realize there was no possible way she could ever be content to live in his shadow. And yes, she could see now how her being Bloodsworn only made things worse, emphasizing her difference just that much more. With a sinking heart she realized her links with Bracca and Tyr would always be a point of conflict between them. She thought she understood a little, now, why Devlin sided with the Council.

"If I'm so wrong for him," she said softly, "why did he come after me in the first place?"

"Because of the Seventh Prophecy, of course."

Her matter-of-fact tone jerked Avera out of her misery. She made it sound so ridiculously obvious. But it wasn't obvious to her. "Couldn't the prophecy be wrong? I mean, it would have to be wouldn't it, if I'm so bad for him."

A shadow streaked across her eyes as Lady Patria's lips twisted into a brief grimace. "Unfortunately, the Oracle is never wrong."

The other woman's sour expression felt like a blow. Avera wasn't used to being on the receiving end of so much animosity. It grated on nerves already strung tight. "I'll tell you what," she said hurriedly. "You figure out a way to get around this prophecy thing, and I'll gladly step aside so Devlin can marry some nice Feyune girl."

Liar! She didn't want to give Devlin up. Ever! But what if all his sweet words and hot kisses were just because of a stupid prophecy?

No, she wouldn't believe that. She *felt* his love every time he touched her, looked at her. It was real, it had to be.

"Impossible," Lady Patria said, thankfully discarding Avera's stupid offer to throw away the best thing in her life. "The Oracle named you specifically. Neither I nor Devlin will do anything to thwart it."

And that was what really bothered her, Avera decided. It sounded like, if he wanted to, Devlin had the power to say no, but what she wanted didn't count. Never mind that she had no intention of leaving him. That option for her was never on the table from the beginning. She wasn't an equal partner.

Avera ran a hand through her hair, just barely keeping from pulling it out in frustration. "You know, I really don't understand you. Why would you risk your own son's happiness on the words of a prophecy written Lord only knows how many centuries ago?"

"Happiness does not matter. The fulfillment of the prophecies is all that is important."

"Not in my book. I'm not willing to risk being miserable for the rest of my life just because some silly Oracle says so." She turned and started walking away. She'd had enough of Oracle and Prophecy talk for the day. A strong hand on her arm pulled her to a stop.

Lady Patria gazed at her sternly. "What do you mean?"

"I mean, Devlin has agreed to give me time, time for us to get to know each other better. He and I have come to an understanding of sorts, one that doesn't include any mention of a prophecy. Between you and me, I hope things work out."

"And if it does not?"

"Then I guess I'll be looking for another place to live. Speaking of which, thank you for your hospitality, but I'm leaving the Ladies' Wing and moving to new quarters. If you'll excuse me?"

****

Sheren hid behind a table loaded with several tall pots of rosemary just as Lady St. John marched into the stillroom. She knew she shouldn't have eavesdropped, but hadn't been able to help herself. She'd been worried. Though after a few moments of listening, she realized Lady St. John could more than hold her own.

Slipping behind another row of tables, she hurried to the far side of the stillroom. It would not do for Lady Patria to catch her lingering near any of the open doors. She paused to check the bottles she'd hastily filled to make sure Lady Patria could find no fault, then moved on quickly. She was examining a bush of miniature yellow roses when she caught sight of clan Tragar's matriarch.

Lady Patria moved gracefully through the room, sweeping around tables and low hanging baskets with the ease of long practice. She stopped at a cabinet set snug into a small alcove Sheren hadn't noticed before. Taking a key from the pocket of her dress, she unlocked its doors and pulled them open. Sheren only had to move a little to see inside. Rows of sealed boxes and bottles lined the shelves along with several bound scrolls and books.

Reaching up, Lady Patria removed a tall, thin bottle from the top shelf, then closed and locked the doors. Moving to one of the stillroom's glass doors, she held the bottle up to the light, turning it back and forth as if checking the contents. After a moment, she nodded, and slipped the bottle into the pocket of her dress.

Her heart pounding, Sheren ducked down again, and moved to a table of lilies two rows over. She bent over a stalk of buds and tried to slow her breathing. She wasn't sure why, but the sight of Lady Patria with that bottle sent chill bumps down her arms. She had no idea what it contained. Nor did she have any reason to believe it had anything to do with Lady St. John.

Yet she couldn't shake the suspicion that whatever was in that bottle did not bode well for Bracca's Bloodsworn.

Chapter Twelve

Devlin regretted agreeing to Avera's requests as soon as they parted company. She was his Starmate, his other half, their bond sealed by Avalyr's magic. She belonged with him. In his rooms, in his arms, and most certainly in his bed. She'd already wormed her way so deep into his heart and mind nothing could get her out. The only thing preventing him from rescinding his agreement and locking her in his room was the fear of further breaking her trust in him. Love could not thrive without trust, and he wanted her love more than anything.

So time and space she would have—even if it killed him.

He tracked down his chamberlain and informed him of the change concerning Avera's living quarters. Then he headed for the public wing where meetings with visiting officials were held. He needed a distraction to get his mind off his willful mate for a while.

"My Lord Tragar."

Devlin looked up at the call to see a man running toward him. He recognized one of the regular palace guards.

"My Lord," the man said. "Captain Vargis requests your presence. One of Lord Churian's guards has returned."

Distraction indeed. It was about time Churian sent another message. But why use one of his guards and not a hired runner? He nodded and waved the man ahead of him, impatient to hear his brother's latest excuse for not returning home.

He wasn't overly worried when the guard led him to the Healers' rooms instead of the guard's barracks. Not until he stepped inside and smelled blood coupled with the cloying odor of rot.

****

An hour later, Devlin sat in his study awaiting the arrival of his Inner Decca, still fighting not to believe what he'd learned. His brother was blade-sick. Worse, Churian was blade-sick in another realm where Devlin couldn't reach him. Even if he were to use gates to sneak into Realm Hedaud, he might already be too late.

The guard had rambled in his report, delirious from a fever caused by an infected wound. But there had been lucidity in his gaze at one point. Lucidity and fear.

"Camarie searches for your brother, my Lord... Black Blades are everywhere. I didn't want to leave. You must believe me. Lord Churian...he ordered me to go. The other two runners...we waited, but you never came. They must have been captured."

Devlin's hands fisted where they rested on the desk top. He'd all but cursed Churian these past two months, thinking him a selfish bastard for not returning home. He never once imagined his brother might be fighting for his life, trying to stay out of their uncle's hands. The young fool. There were several honorable Bloodsworn in Hedaud. Why hadn't he gone straight to one of them?

He shifted in his chair. The idea of someone else holding his brother's life in their hands did not sit well, but at least he would have been safe from Camarie's black link. Instead, the possibility Churian might already be bound to their demented uncle was far too real.

A sharp rap on his door.

"Come."

Fate entered, followed by the rest of his Inner

Decca, all except for Karess. Fate bowed respectfully. "You sent for us, my Bloodsworn?"

"Yes. We'll wait a moment for Karess—"

"Who has arrived," Karess announced. He waltzed into the room, a smile playing with his lips. *You should have warned them,* he sent.

Perhaps, thought Devlin, sensing the tension in the room spike as Bracca Cu-Laurian followed Karess inside. The Amber Blade moved no further into the room, choosing instead to lean against the wall near the closed door. He struck a relaxed pose, though Devlin could see the tension in his eyes. Dark eyes that noted every movement in the room as more than one warrior shifted to put himself in a position between Devlin and Cu-Laurian.

"Stand down," Devlin ordered, aloud and mentally. "Cu-Laurian is here at my request."

"Does this have anything to do with Churian's guard in the Healers' room?" Karess asked.

Devlin nodded, his gaze skipping around the room, not surprised to see that knowledge reflected in each man's face. His Blades had their own ways of keeping up with what went on in the palace.

"He says Churian is in Realm Hedaud. Blade-sick."

From the murmurs, that was something they hadn't known. Nor would anyone else, since Devlin had sworn the healers to secrecy. That kind of knowledge was dangerous.

"That information does not leave this room." He waited until he had an acknowledgement from each man. Then he locked gazes with Cu-Laurian until the Amber Blade nodded in agreement.

"Camarie knows," Fate said, astute as always.

"Yes."

More murmuring, this time peppered with several curses.

"According to the guard, Camarie's Black Blades

have been chasing Churian for weeks." He blew out a frustrated breath and shoved to his feet. "He may already be caught."

"Just one more reason to find Camarie and kill him." Strum grinned nastily and popped his knuckles. "I don't think it will bother Churian to have to change Bloodsworns. He'd love the chance to order you around like the rest of us do."

A smile flickered over Devlin's lips. He could imagine Churian's delight in the role reversal. He'd always been the protector, watching over his younger sister and brother. Perhaps more than he should in his brother's case. It hadn't escaped him that this trip of Churian's had been a way to get out from under his older brother's watchful eye. The idiot had even refused to take one of Devlin's Blades along.

"Shan, Valcon." He pointed to the cousins, his Sixth and Seventh Blades, one fair haired, the other dark. "You two will be in charge. Each of you pick nine men and meet me in the practice courtyard in one hour. I'll gate you to Hedaud. The guard said Churian was hiding north of the town of Kardnya when he left. That's not far from the border. Enough time has passed that Churian could be anywhere in between. Shan, you'll start your search at Kardnya. Valcon, you and your men will start near the border."

"Hedaud is two realms away," Karess pointed out. "Communication is going to be a problem."

Devlin thought a moment. "Bloodsworn Robist Du-Vrain lives just over the border in Realm Suterra. We'll stop there first and ask for the loan of two of his Blades. One will go with each decca. I want daily reports sent to Du-Vrain through his Blades."

"Can we trust him?" Strum asked. "One word to Prince Ahvemet about Silver Blades running loose in

Hedaud could spark the blaze between your two realms that you've been trying to avoid."

Devlin snorted. His relations with Realm Hedaud and its volatile ruler was the least of his worries right now. "Black Blades aren't known for their subtly. If they have been after Churian as long as the guard said, Ahvemet probably has his hands full trying to forestall widespread panic. Besides, Robist has two younger brothers of his own and no love for Ahvemet or Camarie. He'll keep his mouth shut and contact me as needed."

He approached Cu-Laurian. "I understand you grew up in Realm Hedaud. I'd like you to go with Shan's group."

Steel glittered in dark eyes gone suddenly flat. "While I appreciate your trust, you must know my answer has to be no, Lord Tragar."

Devlin had expected as much. What First Blade worth his sword would leave his Bloodsworn in the hands of others? Still, the denial grated on nerves already strung tight. Magic tripped like dancing feet across his skin, begging to be released, to force Cu-Laurian's cooperation. Devlin swallowed the urge just as the Amber Blade inclined his head.

"I will, however, share what knowledge I have with your men. It's been a few years since I was anywhere near Kardnya, but I doubt much has changed. If you show me what maps you have, I can point out the check points that were in place the last time I was there. I can also give you the names of a few people you can trust to approach for information."

"How do you know they can be trusted?"

"Because I know what Ahvemet cost them. As long as you do not mention my name when you ask about Camarie, they should be willing to help you."

"Not very popular back home?" Valcon's taunt lacked the usual bite his men were wont to toss in

Cu-Laurian's direction.

"A Black Blade is not popular anywhere," Cu-Laurian said. "Least of all his home. Those who remember me would have to see my amber sword for themselves to believe I have changed."

"This might be a good time to show them," Shan said.

Devlin shook his head. "No, Cu-Laurian's right. His place is with his Bloodsworn. The offer of his knowledge is enough." He moved to stand in front of Shan and Valcon, placing a hand on each of them. "Find my brother, but stay safe. If you need me, have the Blade Robist sends with you hold your sword for a time. I'll feel it and gate to you as soon as possible."

"Yes, my Bloodsworn," both men said. They bowed before slipping quickly out of the room. Cu-Laurian bowed also, though not as low, and left with them.

Devlin closed his eyes for a moment, letting Shan's and Valcon's determination and loyalty flowing back to him through their links, spread like a balm over his anxiety. They would find Churian for him. At the very least, they would learn his fate. Of that he was certain.

"Have you told Lady Patria?"

He opened his eyes at Karess' question. For once, his friend's face held no hint of humor. He crossed to the small side table holding an array of decanters and crystal glasses. "No, I have not, nor do I intend to. At least, not yet."

He poured a glass of his favorite Talla wine. Swirling the dark blue liquid in his glass, he stepped back and gestured for his men to help themselves.

"She will be upset enough when she learns Churian is a Blade," he continued. "I would prefer not to have to tell her his sword is Black, or worse, that he is dead."

"From the little I've gotten out of Cu-Laurian, I'm not so sure that shouldn't be the other way around." Karess poured his own glass of blue wine and handed the bottle to Strum.

Devlin paused with his glass halfway to his mouth. He would have agreed with that assessment a few days ago. And not just because of the degradations Black Blades were rumored to endure. Up until he met Cu-Laurian, he'd been sure no man could hold to his honor while tied to a mind as twisted as Camarie's. The realization he was wrong was both a relief and a burden. If Cu-Laurian could be saved, were there others? Men who clung to the light of their souls while surrounded by pure darkness? Men wanting, *needing*, to be rescued? The possibility was staggering.

"No, Karess, death is worse. Its sentence is final. We now know becoming a Black Blade is not."

"True enough," Strum said stroking his sword hilt. "If Camarie succeeds in capturing Lord Churian, we will simply take him back." The other Blades murmured quick agreements.

Devlin welcomed their enthusiasm. He'd refrained from hunting his uncle in the past out of respect for the Council's wishes. They were still of the ridiculous notion he could be reasoned with. Devlin knew better. Nor would he stand by any longer while Camarie threatened his family. First Avera, now Churian. Such madness had to be stopped.

He lifted his glass, and took a small sip of wine. The spicy flavor nipped pleasantly at his tongue before sliding warmly down his throat. He started to take another swallow only to stop as a faint, sweet taste bloomed at the back of his throat. Strange. Perhaps a barrel was tapped prematurely. He raised his glass to taste again to be sure.

"Devlin, stop!"

Karess reached him in two strides and knocked the glass from his hand.

"*Vet* and hell," Strum exclaimed spitting blue wine back into his glass.

"What is it?" Fate demanded. "Poison?"

A cold rage bled into Devlin's mind, fed by the anger and fear coming from his men. Had he been poisoned? Was that the odd flavor he'd detected? If so, it was truly insidious. The sweet, seductive taste was like warm honey on his tongue. Even now he craved another swallow.

"It might as well be poison," Strum said. He stomped to the fireplace and tossed his wine into the small blaze, muttering the entire time. Karess followed, waiting for the flames to die down before emptying his glass as well. The fire flared high, curling up to lick hungrily at the top of the fireplace.

Karess pointed at the other Blades who'd chosen drinks other than the blue Talla wine. "Do any of you detect a sweet, honeyed aftertaste? We need to know how many bottles are affected."

"Affected by what?"

"Akelia wine, thrice damned stuff." Strum looked ready to spit on the floor. He pointed to a bottle of dark brown whiskey. "Anyone know if this is safe?"

"Yes." Judan, Devlin's Fifth Blade, held up his glass. "At least I think so. No sweet aftertaste that I can detect. What is Akelia wine?

Devlin knew. He'd heard of Akelia wine before. Distilled from the rare Akelia flower, it wasn't actually a wine, but an elixir. One prized among the more hedonistic of his acquaintances. It was also extremely rare and expensive. He'd never tried the stuff personally, though apparently Karess and Strum had.

"It's an aphrodisiac," Karess said. "Very potent. How much did you drink, Devlin?"

Enough to heat his blood and make him want more. "Only one sip."

"Good. A sip isn't enough to send you running to the *shethas*." Strum took a large drink of whiskey and swished it around in his mouth before swallowing.

"Why in the name of Blood and Blade would he seek a *shetha*?" Judan asked, sounding offended. "Our Bloodsworn is newly mated, Strum, or have you forgotten?"

"No, we haven't forgotten," Karess said, helping himself to a drink of whisky from Judan's glass. "But Akelia is worse than the worse deep-healing lust you've ever been through. Someone under its influence only seeks pleasure for themselves, not their partners."

Devlin ignored the concerned gazes of his men as he dropped into one of the chairs near the fireplace. They knew him well. He would never treat Avera with so little respect. Nor would he ever dishonor her by seeking another. This night was going to be hell.

Strum picked up the bottle of Talla wine and walked to the fireplace.

"I wouldn't," Karess cautioned. "Not unless you want the hairs singed from your face."

Strum held the bottle up, measuring its contents. "You're probably right. I'll dispose of this later." He set it gingerly on the mantel.

"What we need to discover," Fate said coming to stand behind the second chair, "is who put it into our Bloodsworn's private wine and why?"

Devlin almost laughed aloud. He already knew who the culprit was. He just wasn't sure of her motive.

"Who would even have the opportunity?" Karess asked. "Not just anyone can walk in here past the guards."

"My mother can."

He glanced at the faces of his men, watched their expressions transform from stunned surprise to disgust. They'd been on the receiving end of his mother's haughty tongue too many times to like her. Respect her, yes. They all knew the ruthless streak that ran hand-in-hand with her determination. Some, like Karess, had been around long enough to know she always did what she felt had to be done regardless of the consequences.

Karess flopped into the chair opposite Devlin. "Is she out of her mind? Doesn't she know what Akelia wine does? It makes whoever takes it insatiable." He leaned forward, elbows on knees, as serious as Devlin had ever seen him. "You know me, Devlin. I'll try anything once. Usually I have no regrets. But that damn stuff gave me the best and worst hard-on I've ever had. Took me days and a horde of women to get over it. And the honey taste is not something I'm going to forget for at least a dozen lifetimes. Why do you think I never touch real honey anymore?"

"A horde of women?" Gideon Tu-Annun grinned and nudged his twin brother, Dunn. "Maybe we should have a drink of that before they get rid of it."

"No!" Strum and Karess said together.

Devlin waved them to silence and turned to his ninth and eighth Blades. It was unusual enough to have cousins serve the same Bloodsworn. To have brothers was almost unheard of. Too much conflict in regards to loyalty for one thing. Devlin had been called a fool on more than one occasion for accepting the twins. More than a fool for allowing them to serve together in his Inner Decca. Yet he knew the hearts of these two. Each would give not only his life, but the life of his brother to protect him. A choice he hoped never to force them to make.

"Strum and Karess are right. The elixir made

from akelia flowers is very potent. A single drop in a cup of wine will enhance a man's sexual prowess and keep him hard a full night. From what I've been told, the amount in that bottle will completely subvert a person's inhibitions. Instinct, reason, emotions, everything disappears in a haze of need so desperate the person will do anything to gain relief. Anything." He closed his eyes and wiped a hand across his face. Neither motion dispelled the painful image his words had conjured. Avera, her body battered and abused, the trust in her beautiful green eyes shattered beyond redemption—by him! Gods, what had his mother been thinking?

"She was counting on your mate-bond to hold you in check," Fate said.

Karess and Strum exchanged a glance. Karess nodded. "It might have. But why would she do such a thing in the first place? You and Lady Avera are already bound by the magic of the Starmate bond. What possible result could your mother expect by forcing you to your mate's bed?"

Anger began to flood Devlin's veins with heat. Of course that was just the result his mother expected. She was ever impatient in regards to the damn prophecies. "She knows Avera and I quarreled. She knows Avera has refused to move into my rooms. As usual, she's trying to force things into what she perceives is the proper path to the fulfillment of the Prophecy. In short, she wants us in the same bed." As did he. But never at the price of Avera's trust. He would get Avera back in his bed, but it would be on his terms, not his mother's.

"You know she's just going to keep interfering, don't you?"

He met Fate's solemn gaze. Bitterness rose to join his anger. Of course she would.

"Don't let her," Karess said urgently. "Don't let her ruin this for you, Devlin. You've got enough to contend with without worrying about what she'll do next. It may not be you she tries to manipulate next time, but Lady Avera."

The possibility sent a red haze over Devlin's eyesight. He would not have Avera's trust abused further. Not by anyone.

Chapter Thirteen

Sheren stared at the door in front of her. It had taken her a long time just to work up the courage to ask the whereabouts of Lady St. John's room. Now that she was here, she couldn't believe what she was about to do. She had no proof. None. Just a nagging, uncomfortable feeling that refused to go away.

What if she was wrong? What if she actually accused the mother of the Prince of Illian of plotting against her daughter-in-law and nothing happened?

What if Lady Patria found out?

Sheren licked lips gone suddenly dry. If she was imprisoned, who would care for her son? If she was simply dismissed from her position, where would they go? How would they live? She was a widow with a small child and no other family. She had to be mad to even think of putting herself at risk for a virtual stranger.

She turned away from the door just as it opened. Startled, she swung around, stumbling back when she saw the tall warrior filling the doorway. Bracca Cu-Laurian's large hand shot out to curl around her arm to steady her. Afraid for her shield, Sheren gasped and jerked her arm. "Let go!"

He released her instantly. Emotion swept through his dark eyes, gone before she could tell what it was. His gaze went flat. "Lady Sheren. How may I serve you?"

She held back a shiver at the cold, impersonal tone. "I..." What did she do now? How did she explain her presence without compromising her position?

His dark eyes went suddenly wide, then narrowed angrily. "It was you."

The words sounded like an accusation. Sheren had the feeling that until that moment, he hadn't known she was the one who'd mistakenly tried to help him earlier. If she'd simply stayed away, she could have remained anonymous, safe. From the look on his face, she was safe no longer.

His hands flexed, turning into fists. "Why?" he growled, his tone no longer cold, but scalding hot. "Why would you take such a risk?"

His anger seeped around the edges of her shield like dark smoke. She didn't try to push it back. What was the use? It would just seep in again no matter how thick her shield. Instead, she allowed his anger to spark her own.

"I meant no harm," she hissed back at him. "I felt your pain and reacted just as any other empath would. How was I to know it was a test?"

"That is not what I am referring to."

She blinked. It wasn't?

"Any other female would know better than to risk her mind by stretching it across three realms."

His words sucked her anger out of her in a rush, leaving her feeling confused. What was he saying? "What do you mean across three realms? You were here. You escorted me to the Ladies' Wing." She was sure the test had taken place somewhere inside the palace. The intensity of the pain, the sureness of the touch of his mind, the way he'd communicated, everything pointed to close proximity.

"Lady Avera and I were summoned this morning to the Bloodsworn Hall to face the Council's test. After I left you, the Tragar gated us to the Hall in Realm Ellerad."

Sheren's blood turned to ice. Realm Ellerad was on the far western edge of the continent, leagues and leagues away. Not even Bloodsworn could touch the mind of one of their Blades that far away. What she'd done should have been impossible.

"Sheren?"

His voice jerked her back to awareness. He started to reach for her, but dropped his hand. "Are you all right?"

"Yes, I'm fine." Scared, but otherwise fine. Or maybe not. It was looking more and more as if a trip to the mind-healers was inevitable.

"Bracca?"

Sheren almost groaned aloud when she heard Lady St. John's voice. Things were getting far too complicated.

"Who is—oh." The lady's sharp gaze darted to Bracca before returning to Sheren. There was no mistaking the rampant speculation in her green eyes. Or the warmth in her smile.

"Hello, Sheren. Nice of you to visit." A slight pause, barely noticeable, coupled with another swift glance at her Blade. "Yes, Bracca, Sheren and I have already met." Green eyes twinkled with amusement when she looked at Sheren again. "All things considered, I think she and I are going to be good friends." She held out her hand in welcome.

Sheren's heart danced a rapid pace. Friends? This noblewoman wanted to be her friend?

When Sheren didn't immediately take her hand, Lady St. John lowered hers. "Or maybe not," she said doubtfully, her expression turning serious. "Is something wrong, Sheren?"

Bracca shifted slightly, placing himself a little in front of his Bloodsworn. One dark eyebrow rose slowly.

A dare?

Did he think her too cowardly to befriend a woman from another world? Or was he warning her away? Either way, she had no intention of letting him intimidate her.

Squaring her shoulders, Sheren turned back to Lady St. John and held out her hand. "No, my lady, nothing is wrong. I would be honored to be your friend."

Lady St. John smiled in relief. "Good. I can use all the new friends I can get. Come inside and let's chat. Did you get all your bottles filled?"

Sheren allowed herself to be pulled into the room. Bracca dipped his head as she passed him. His face remained unreadable, but his approval brushed against her shield like a contented cat. An approval that made Sheren uncomfortable.

Her decision to remain silent about Lady Patria's bottle was based on Lady St. John being a stranger. Unless she was lying to everyone, including herself, about her wish to be Lady St. John's friend, that reasoning no longer applied. Friends did not let one another walk into danger unknowingly.

Even the possibility of danger.

Freeing her hand, Sheren stopped in the middle of the room. Taking the deepest breath of her life, she spilled the words out in a rush so her sense of survival had no chance of calling them back.

"Before we go any further, I need to speak with you on a matter of grave importance concerning Lady Patria."

****

Devlin faced his mother across the expanse of her sitting room. He didn't trust himself anywhere near her right now. Pacing by the door seemed wiser. If his anger got the better of him, he could at least put a door between them before he said or did something he would later regret.

He swayed a little and reached out to lay a hand on the back of a nearby chair. Last night had not been pretty. After gating his men to Realm Hedaud, he'd taken Fate, Strum, and Karess with him to one of his remote holdings. Diluting that damn sip of Akelia wine with whiskey had seemed like a good idea at the time. Both Strum and Karess had agreed. Together, the three of them had drunk themselves into oblivion, leaving Fate to watch over them. Waking late this morning with a pounding head and an ache in his groin, had not improved his mood from yesterday.

He'd thought seriously about summoning his mother to the throne room. The formal setting— ruler to subject—would have guaranteed her some protection. He was glad he'd dismissed the idea. Especially since his mother still refused to see the damage she'd caused by her help.

"Do not make the mistake of interfering again, Mother. I promise you, you won't like the consequences."

For the first time in his life he didn't try to hide the violence of his emotions in the presence of a female. Not even the tightening around his mother's mouth, indicating she felt at least some part of his displeasure—such a mild word for what he felt— didn't cause him to relent.

His mother shifted in her chair. "Threaten me all you like, it will not change the facts. You and I both know the foolishness of allowing your Starmate to put distance between you. If she were Avalyran, it might be another matter, but she is not. Nor is she some frightened, biddable young innocent. She is an obstinate, strong-willed Earth female with a completely different belief system and no suitable training for her position. The Prophecies mean nothing to her despite the fact she is essential to the future of our world. Instead of indulging her whims, you should be tying her to you in every conceivable way. I only helped you bridge the gap she forced between you in the quickest manner possible."

"I could have hurt her. Badly. Did you think of

that at all?" Just the possibility had him swallowing back bile.

"It is not like you to be so dramatic, Devlin," Lady Patria said calmly. "Akelia wine does not make one violent. It merely enhances sexual pleasure and need by evoking and strengthening memories of past encounters. Since you've already bedded Lady St. John once, the urge to do so again would have simply driven you past whatever ridiculous barriers you allowed her to place between you. As your Starmate, she was never in any danger. The mate-bond would never allow you to harm her."

He clenched the back of a chair, this time to keep his hands from shaking with the rage building inside him. "First, you're guessing about the Starmate-bond. Ours is only the third mate-bond in a hundred years. You have no proof, no solid evidence of how strong such a bond is or what it means. Basing the outcome of the Seventh Prophecy on a *guess* is not like you, mother. It reeks of desperation.

"Second, your information on Akelia wine leaves much to be desired. I was informed by both Strum and Karess that the amount you put into the bottle of Talla wine was enough to drive a decca of men mad with lust. Mad, mother. Completely uncaring of what damage they inflicted while sating their hungers. Is that what you wanted for Avera? To have me take her like an unfeeling animal, like a beast? Have you forgotten what that's like?"

Her face paled. She raised a trembling hand to her throat. "No, they have to be wrong. I only put a little into the wine. Half what your father—" She broke off, shaking her head as her blue eyes became shadowed by dark memories.

Devlin hated himself for dredging up those memories for her. His father had been a sick bastard who enjoyed forcing women, his wife included. How she survived her years as Gabrin Tragar's prophecy bride, Devlin would never know. Her stricken expression touched his heart, almost silencing him. For all her faults, he loved her. She'd done her best to protect him and his brother and sister from their father's less than paternal attentions. Normally he would never willingly cause her pain.

But he couldn't stop now. He had to make her realize what she'd done, had to make sure she'd never do anything similar in the future. He turned and reached for the door knob, pausing with it slightly open to look back at her.

"Congratulations, Mother. You finally found a way to turn me into the same kind of monster Father was." He carefully closed the door. If this did not bring her to her senses, he would have to think of something else. Banishment seemed the only other option. The thought was enough to sober him so that he made his way out of the Ladies' Wing and all the way to Avera's suite without staggering once.

He knew her rooms were empty the moment he opened her door. Still, he checked every one, even the bath chamber. Then he checked Cu-Laurian's room, not surprised to find it empty as well. He stared at the Blade's neat, wrinkle-free bed a long moment, comparing it to Avera's, which was thoroughly rumpled. He pushed the resulting image away before his mind had a chance to latch onto it. Avera had assured him she had no interest in her First Blade. He had to trust her. How else could he expect her to trust him?

Frustration warmed his blood as he left Cu-Laurian's room. Trusting Avera still did not tell him her location. He'd been a fool not to set another guard outside her door. Was she trying to avoid him?

The hunter in him roused at the possibility. In this, he would not give her a choice. He needed to be with her in order to begin rebuilding the bridge between them. Finding her was only a matter of time. Lips pressed into a tight smile, he set off in the direction of the Ladies' Wing again. Perhaps she was with Gwenell.

Before he even reached the end of the hallway, sharp tugs came from several of his links at once. Impatience thinned his lips as he clenched his jaw tight. He didn't want to get side-tracked by some Blade dispute. He wanted, needed, to locate Avera. He opened Fate's and Karess' links at the same time to tell them to handle whatever crisis had arisen.

Your Starmate is here, both men said, Fate's tone thick with disapproval, Karess' laced, as usual, with amusement.

Devlin jerked to a stop. His warriors were in the Blade's courtyard this time of morning, finishing a round of sparring. *You mean she's on the balconies? Which one?* He called his magic, holding it in check as he waited for a reply. Gating to her would be far faster than traversing half the width of the palace.

No, Fate said. *She is not on the balconies. She is here, on the grounds.*

Devlin snapped the gate open, barely waiting for it to enlarge before diving through. His anxious gaze scanned the courtyard, searching for a feminine figure among the dozens of warriors—warriors who weren't sparring, he noticed. Every single man stood still, his attention fixed on the opposite side of the courtyard from where Devlin had gated in. Karess' chuckle rumbled in his mind. *Don't worry, Dev, she appears to be just passing through. Someone told her this was a short-cut to the stables. She's smiling and asking for you, by the way. Are you sure you two fought yesterday?*

Devlin stopped where he was, hidden in the shadow cast by a balcony. Something inside him, a tension he hadn't even been aware of, eased at Karess' words. Avera was smiling. She was asking for him.

Blood and Blade!

Karess' sharp curse snapped him to attention. *What?*

Amusement colored Karess' voice. *Kiel just braved Bracca's glower and offered to show your lady to the stables. Impudent lad. Don't kill him, Dev, but he's even offered her his arm. You should see Strum's face. I think he's convinced his precious protégé has gone mad. Ah, they're leaving now. If you hurry, you can get to the stable ahead of them. I'll round up Fate and a decca or so others and meet you there. Don't leave the palace without us.*

Devlin couldn't keep from grinning as Karess' tone changed from playful to serious. He might not have Fate's constant intensity, but Karess was just as serious when it came to Devlin's safety. *Fine, but don't dawdle. When Avera is ready to leave, we leave.*

He closed his links on two different indignant replies, and opened a gate to the stables, trying not to let relief get the upper hand. The fact Avera was smiling and looking for him this morning didn't mean everything was all right. They still needed to talk without their anger getting in the way. And he knew just where he wanted such a conversation to take place.

****

The dirt road curved ahead, leading to another hill. Avera sat back, slowing her racing mare down to a canter. Devlin slowed his horse as well, so that they took the hill side by side. They pulled the blowing horses to a walk at the top.

Avera glanced around at the rolling green hills. "I can't believe how beautiful it is here. The countryside is simply gorgeous." She drew in a deep breath and let it out slowly. Things didn't seem nearly as hopeless this morning as they had last night. What with missing Devlin and worrying about his mother's possible plotting, Avera hadn't gotten much sleep. And she still hadn't decided whether or not to confide Sheren's suspicion to Devlin. She hated opening up another can of worms when she was already hip deep in problems.

"So," she said, trying to think of a topic that wouldn't immediately set them at odds. She didn't want to spoil the beautiful morning with an argument. "Tell me about this whole magic thing. How does it work? Better yet, where does the magic come from? Is the source infinite or finite? It felt infinite when I touched it, but that's a perception not a fact. Does the magic regenerate as it's used?" Avera realized she was babbling but couldn't help it.

Devlin arched a brow. Thankfully, he chose to address her questions rather than tease her. "Many scholars," he began, "have pondered the origins of magic over the years. Most agree a planet's magic is conceived with the birth of the planet itself, and that it grows with the passage of time."

"Then why doesn't every planet have magic?"

"They do."

She shook her head. "Earth doesn't. At least, nothing like I can feel up here." She tapped her temple.

"Ah, but Earth is a young planet. Its magic is no more than a slumbering child, which, believe me, is best for now. Were the magic to awaken before it matured, it would be wild, un-disciplined. Even sleeping, it can cause problems, creating legends, myths, and other unexplainable phenomenon."

"Legends and myths?" The idea was too intriguing. "Are you saying things like our Loch Ness monster and Big Foot might really exist?"

"If those are strange creatures for which your science has no explanation, then yes, it is quite possible. Earth's magic could have brought them to life in a moment when its consciousness came close to waking and brushed the edge of Earth's present reality."

That wasn't a very comforting thought. It was a little scary to think a thirty-foot sea monster could be a manifestation from some magic child's dream world. "Makes you worry about what might pop up next, doesn't it?"

Devlin started to answer, but stopped. He looked around at the meadow through which they were riding, smiled, and reined in his horse.

"What?" she asked. What had put that pleased smile on his face?

"Come," he said. "I have something to show you." He dismounted, tossing the reins to one of his men. Avera started to dismount, and found herself swept out of the saddle by a pair of strong arms.

"Devlin!"

He chuckled.

"Impatient much," she said as he set her on her feet.

"Sometimes." Grinning, he took her hand and led her into the meadow of lush grass. Avera laughed at his evident excitement. He stopped just as the land started to rise, and faced her.

"You asked where the magic comes from. The answer is all around us. Avalyr is the only planet whose magic can actually be seen from space. It is a physical veil encircling the planet like a vast ocean. Its waves wash over us, become a part of us even before we are born. He held up a hand. "A wave is passing over us now. Can you feel it?"

Despite the look of anticipation on his face, Avera suppressed a shudder of unease. She hadn't consciously tried to touch that ocean of power since two nights ago when she'd linked with Tyr. Truth be told, she was afraid to. Now, at the encouragement in Devlin's gaze, she closed her eyes and held her hand out near his. At first, she felt nothing unusual.

Just the heat from the sun and the caress of a breeze on her skin.

She heard Devlin move but kept her eyes closed. He stopped behind her, his hands settling on her waist. Warm lips pressed against her temple. "Feel with your heart and soul, Avera, feel with your mind. Avalyr's magic is the essence of life. You've touched it already. It is there, waiting, wanting you to reach for it. You are not Feyune, but you *are* Bloodsworn. You should be able to feel the essence without even trying. All you have to do is open yourself to its presence."

Goose bumps ran down her arms. She wasn't sure if they were from his warm breath brushing her skin or the fact he wanted her to open herself up to that vast well of magic. If she did that, she'd be vulnerable, unprotected. Anything might happen. Anything at all.

As if reading her thoughts, he whispered, "Don't be afraid. I won't let anything harm you. I'll protect you." His words fell hot against her ear as he leaned over her, surrounding her, protecting her.

As soon as she focused on his voice, some of the tension in her muscles eased. This should be easy. She'd done it before. All she had to do was repeat the process. Devlin wouldn't let her get in over her head.

Picturing her barriers, she slowly started taking them down one by one. She braced herself when the last wall fell. Instead of a tidal wave rushing in to drown her, she felt a tingle at her fingertips. The tingle waned, then grew stronger, and waned again, like waves of ocean water lapping at her toes. Inside, she felt a swelling, a filling of a slight emptiness she hadn't been aware of before.

"Devlin, I feel it," she said, her voice hushed in awe. "I feel the magic." And it wasn't scary this time. It was...intoxicating.

She opened her eyes to find him standing right

in front of her again, watching her avidly, hungrily, as if just the sight of her touching Avalyr's magic did something to him. Her heart turned over. She would have plastered herself against him right there if one of the men waiting patiently with the horses hadn't coughed, reminding her they weren't alone. With a smile that told her he knew the color in her cheeks wasn't just from the sun, Devlin reached out and took her hand, tucking it through his arm. Instead of walking her back to the horses, he started up the hill.

She searched for something to cover up her embarrassment, picking a question she'd been meaning to ask for a while.

"Devlin, why are there Blades? Why can't they touch the magic like everyone else?"

"No one really knows. There are only vague clues in the Prophecies. Did you read the first prophecy I sent you?"

"Yes, but I don't remember very much of it. Something about a precipitate birth and a violation of some kind?"

"'A violation wrought by the hand of an impetuous child'," he quoted. "And from the violation, whatever it was, the blade-illness was born. Only when the ten successfully stand as one will the essence return to its rightful purpose. The assumption is that when ten Prophecies are successfully fulfilled, the illness will be cured by the healing of the essence. Until then, there is no predicting who will develop the blade-illness. It does not follow family lines. We only know that when the illness strikes, the man must seek out a Bloodsworn to link with, to get the essence from, or his mind and body both fail."

Her gaze touched on Bracca, pacing them a few yards away. She made sure their link was firmly closed. He wouldn't want her pity any more than the rest of the warriors she'd met would. "It must be very hard for these men to go from being so self-sufficient to being totally dependent on someone else."

"It is. That is why the defense of their Bloodsworn is so important to them. In some small measure, they are fighting for their own lives, controlling their own destiny."

"Tell me about Camarie. What does he have against you?"

Devlin's face twisted in distaste. "Camarie is the antithesis to what a true Bloodsworn should be. He uses the blood-link to bind as many Blades to him as possible, not to help them, but for the sake of power. The more Blades a Bloodsworn is linked to, the more magic he can access. Camarie uses that magic for his own evil purposes."

He glanced at her, his expression wary. She waited, wondering at the shadow of pain in his eyes.

"There is something you should know," he said finally. "Camarie is my uncle."

Shock washed through her, making her stumble. He caught her immediately, steadying her until she had her feet working again. She could feel his cool gaze on her while she walked, measuring her reaction.

"Your uncle wants me dead?"

"He wants us both dead. You, so the Seventh Prophecy will fail, and me, so he can claim my throne."

She narrowed her eyes on his calm face. This was the first she'd heard about him being in danger. "Maybe you'd better start at the beginning."

Devlin inclined his head. "Fair enough. Camarie is my father's older brother, or half-brother, I should say. Still, he has always claimed Illian's throne should be his, even before my father's death. He was of the opinion that only a powerful Bloodsworn was worthy to rule."

"You're father wasn't a Bloodsworn?"

"No."

"But you are."

He glanced meaningfully at the warriors around them and smiled.

She made a face at him. "My point is that you're a Bloodsworn, so what's your uncle's excuse now?"

"Simply put, I am not him. He believes he should be the one to rule Illian."

"Greedy bastard." The words slipped out before she knew it. She slapped a hand over her mouth. Devlin chuckled.

"Actually, he is."

"Is what?" she asked. "Greedy?"

"That too, but the bastard part is true as well."

She started to ask what he meant, but at that moment they came to the top of the hill. Avera's breath caught. Below them stretched a patch-work quilt of a beautiful valley. The mostly green palette was dotted here and there with splashes of color. Houses, she realized.

Avera drank in the sight, her gaze eventually moving to the hillside just below them. There, nestled in a vast garden like a prized Easter egg, sat the most beautiful house she'd ever seen. Dark, orange roof tiles gleamed in the afternoon sun. Golden cream walls peeked through the green riot of the gardens that were more managed than manicured.

The whole idyllic scene brought a pang of homesickness to Avera. She and her father had spent some time in Italy shortly before he'd disappeared. She'd fallen in love with the Tuscan landscape and spent hours exploring, basking in the warm sunshine. Her father had laughed and called her his changeling sun-child. She'd laughed, too, and promised their next vacation could be somewhere cold. Raphael St. John loved snow. *Had* loved snow.

Tucking away the bittersweet memory, she sighed. "This is just so beautiful."

"Do you like it?"

"What's not to like?" She waved a hand to include the whole valley. "Honestly, Devlin, if I didn't know we were on another planet I'd think we were in a place back home called Tuscany."

A frown flitted across his face, there and gone again. Before she could wonder why, he smiled and held out a hand. "Would you like to get a closer look?"

Startled, she pointed at the lovely house and asked, "Do you mean go down there? We can do that? You know the owner?"

"I do. So, yes, we can."

He had their horses brought forward. The sprawling house wasn't that far away, but they had to go down the hill and around a perimeter wall in order to reach the long drive lined with tall, arrow-shaped trees. Once inside the main gate, Avera insisted on dismounting and walking the rest of the way. She didn't want to miss a single thing.

The flowers bordering the drive grew in abundance. Roses bloomed on bushes and trellised vines, their fragrance wafting in the breeze. Lilies nodded stately on their stalks in a myriad of shades, while clusters of moss roses carpeted winding beds. There were other flowers too, some she recognized but didn't know the names of, others she didn't recognize at all.

And fountains. Fountains were everywhere, their sparkling, splashing water adding movement and sound to the picture postcard scene.

Avera knew she was behaving like a gawking tourist, swiveling her head from side to side, trying to take everything in at once. She didn't care. Every few feet something else demanded her attention, and she gave it gladly. So wrapped up was she in admiring the gardens that they'd almost reached the front steps before she realized she could feel the waves of Avalyr's magic much easier.

She turned to Devlin. "The magic is strong here."

He nodded. "This is a place of power, a place where several waves meet. My grandfather built this villa for my grandmother after my father was born."

"Why? Didn't she like living at the palace?" She looked up and to the west. Far in the distance, she could just see the immense, sand-colored palace where it sat overlooking the valley.

"No, she did not," Devlin said wryly. "Or it would be more truthful to say she did not care for living with my grandfather."

"Sounds like a difficult relationship. What happened?"

"My grandmother came from a wealthy family in another realm. Somehow she found out that part of the Fifth Prophecy included her marriage to my grandfather. She was in love with another man, and the two of them ran away together. By the time my grandfather tracked them down, she was already carrying Camarie. Quite a scandal at the time, though it was quickly hushed up."

"What did your grandfather do?"

Devlin's voice took on a hard note. "What he thought he had to in order to fulfill the prophecy. He banished my grandmother's lover, took her back to the palace and locked her up until Camarie was born. Then he took her to his bed."

Harsh, Avera thought, though she didn't say anything. She had a feeling Devlin had more than one reason for telling her this story.

"My grandmother never forgave my grandfather. She demanded he build her this house after discovering the converging waves one day. Her intent was to try and change the Prophecy by raising my father in as powerful a place as possible."

"Change it how?"

"The Fifth Prophecy foretold that my father's reign would be short-lived. She hoped by living in an area so saturated with power, she could change that. Thank Luma and all the gods it didn't."

Such relief in that statement. She didn't know much about Devlin's father, but decided she probably needed to find out. But not today. "What about Camarie? Did he live here too?"

"No. When my father was born, my grandfather sent Camarie to his own father. He may have been trying to do the right thing for the child, but it is more likely he felt my grandmother would eventually come to accept her life with him if she did not have the boy as a reminder of her lover."

"She never did, did she?"

"No."

So much pain in such a little word. She had a feeling part of it came from the fear that his own prophecy marriage would turn out the same way. She went to him. Taking his hand, she kissed it. "We're not your grandparents."

He wrapped his arms around her, pulling her into a tight hug. "No, we are not." He kissed the top of her head, then released her. Taking her arm again, he led her up the wide terrace steps.

The front doors stood open, revealing an arched hallway. At the other end, Avera could see an open courtyard, a tall, sparkling fountain framed in the center. She hesitated, but Devlin bowed and held out a hand. "Please, it would be my pleasure to show you Villa Porenmagie."

"Porenmagie?"

Devlin smiled. "Roughly translated, Pure Magic."

Avera did a slow turn, raising her head to scan

the balconied second floor, then gazing out over the riotous gardens and their guardian trees. She closed her eyes as a wave of magic lapped over her, making her skin tingle. Pure magic indeed.

They entered the archway, their footfalls echoing loudly. The courtyard beyond was beautiful. Small trees, beds of flowers, and giant urns filled to overflowing with a variety of plants, were scattered throughout the large area. The perfume of flowers filled the air mingling with the clean smell of sun-baked stone. A vine-covered arbor sat in one corner, sheltering a swing complete with padded cushions.

Devlin steered her toward another corner where a pergola shaded a small table and two chairs. As they drew near, Avera noticed the table was already set. She stopped.

"Maybe we should leave. It looks like the owners are about to have lunch. I wouldn't want to bother them with an unexpected visit."

"Trust me, you're visit is neither a bother nor unexpected. The owner rarely lives here, but the villa is kept in constant readiness." He held out one hand to her and lifted the other toward the table. There was a teasing light in his deep blue eyes.

"In fact, as it is past noon, *me`surrasie*, would you care to join the villa's owner for lunch?"

Despite the mischief playing with his lips, she realized he was serious. Comprehension preceded a mental kick in the pants. Of course the villa was his. It had, after all, been his grandmother's.

Shaking her head at his joke, she smiled and put her hand in his. "Well, since you asked so nicely, I am a little hung—" Her words cut off abruptly as she glanced back at the table. Several dishes had joined the elegant place settings, some open and steaming, others covered. A small side table had also appeared. On it was an assortment of crystal carafes along with glasses and a small urn of ice.

Chapter Fourteen

Bracca snorted softly at the Tragar's blatant use of magic. *Showing off,* he thought, unaware he'd allowed the observation to slip into his link with Avera until her soft, mental laugh came back to him.

Yes, he is, and the poor little lady scientist is suitably impressed. Go find something to eat, Bracca, I'll be fine.

Are you sure? So far the Tragar had gone out of his way to be charming. That didn't mean he'd stay that way.

Yes. I promise to call if things get out of hand. The Tragar led her to her seat, lips brushing her hand before releasing her. Bracca could almost hear the increase of her heartbeat from where he stood. *That's out of hand in a bad way, not in a good way,* she added quickly.

He bit back a smile. *A good way, my lady?*

Well, yeah, you know. Even from across the courtyard, he caught the blush on her cheek. *I mean...*

He took pity on his heart-sister. *Peace, little sorlina. I am of an age to know what you mean.* He kept his mental tone solemn, but could do nothing about the amusement coloring each word.

She shot him a quelling glance. *Wretch. Just remember, paybacks are hell.*

Paybacks?

You'll be deep in conversation with a lady you wish to impress one day, and I swear I'll make you blush.

Smiling, he inclined his head to her. Far be it

from him to inform his Bloodsworn of the weightlessness of her threat. Since he deemed her the only female worth impressing, the circumstance she proposed seemed highly unlikely.

"Well, that's an improvement."

He turned to find Karess at his side, the man's gray eyes twinkling with amusement. Bracca raised a brow at the comment.

"The smile," Karess said, gesturing toward Bracca's face. "It's an improvement over the glare of daggers you've been throwing at Devlin all morning. For a while there I thought you were going to draw actual steel on him."

Bracca brushed past Karess, heading for the hallway his nose told him led to the kitchen. He checked the state of his link as he walked. He didn't want his anger leaking out and bothering Avera. He waited until he and Karess were out of sight of the courtyard before speaking, all but growling the words.

"He hurt her."

"He knows. Why do you think he brought her here? He's trying his best to make things right."

"He needs to try harder." Bracca started to turn away before he said something even more insulting, only to have Karess snag his arm. The Silver Blade's expression turned fierce.

"The entire Council plus their Blades saw you cuddling Lady Avera in your arms not two minutes after Devlin publicly claimed her as his Starmate. Such a thing would have sent a lesser man into a blind rage. You're lucky he didn't kill you where you stood. Hell, even I wanted to slit your throat. But he did nothing. He accepts that you and Tyr are a part of her life and thus a part of his. As for what she considers his betrayal, can you blame him for not wanting her to initiate any more links? You know the risks. As her First Blade, I would think you'd be grateful that he's trying to keep her safe."

"And so I am."

Karess jerked his head back, gray eyes narrowing. "Then why have you been staring at Devlin as if you'd love nothing better than to run him through? You've had Fate fingering his sword hilt all morning, and that's not something I've ever seen him do."

Bracca shrugged. "My concern is for Lady Avera's feelings, not the Tragar's. I understand his motives, but disagree with his actions. He hurt her. I should have beaten him to a bloody pulp right there in front of the Council."

Violence flitted through piercing gray eyes. "You could have tried, I suppose. Might have been fun watching you bleed. What held you back?"

"My Lady Bloodsworn is not one to condone rash behavior." He barely managed to get the words out with a straight face. Everyone knew Avera St. John had a tendency to act before thinking. Her impulsive actions linking them together as Blade and Bloodsworn, after he'd voluntarily sundered his link with Camarie, was the only reason Bracca himself was alive.

He held on to his solemn expression until he meet Karess' incredulous gaze. Then his lips twitched. Karess threw back his head, his laughter filling the hallway. Bracca joined in, his own laughter sounding quite strange in his ears.

Reminiscent of their first meeting, Karess threw an arm across his shoulders. Still chuckling, he said, "Come, Amber Blade, you and I will walk together, and I'll tell you a tale of a meddling mother's machinations."

Bracca tensed, wondering if Sheren's warning had substance after all. "Does your tale have anything to do with Lady Patria and a certain bottle?"

"How did you know?" A hint of wariness gleamed in Karess' eyes.

"Tell me your tale, and I'll tell you mine." Though he'd leave Sheren's name out of it. He'd take no chance of making her a target of Lady Patria Kel-Tragar's ire.

The Silver Blade tilted his head. "Fair enough."

They broke into a brisk walk—and slammed to a halt as a woman barreled into them out of a side corridor.

"Oh, excuse me." she said, her voice breathless.

Bracca's pulse kicked at the familiar voice. He hadn't expected to see Sheren Ni-Annun again so soon—if ever. True, Avera had claimed her friendship, but he'd already thought of several ways to absent himself if the two women chose to meet again.

The strange connection he felt to her was completely unacceptable, mainly because she played havoc with his concentration. As Avera's only fighting Blade, he needed to focus on her protection. He couldn't do that when Sheren was present. Her beauty was too compelling, too intoxicating. Just the brush of her long braid against his arm as he reached out to steady her sent a jolt of sexual awareness through him. He jerked his hands away.

A bundle she held in one arm fell as she struggled to keep the several bottles of wine in her other arm from coming to harm. Bracca tried to catch the bundle out of the air, but it was too loosely tied. He snatched at it, and the knot slipped open. A flood of palm-sized, round balls hit the floor, rolling merrily in their freedom.

Karess laughed. "Sheren, my lady, your captives seem to have escaped. Allow me to help."

Instead of bending to gather the small waxed balls of cheese, Karess began plucking bottles from her grasp. "These are for us, I take it?"

137

"They are," she said, a hint of laughter in her voice. She glanced at Bracca while clinging stubbornly to the last bottle. He wondered at the soft pink on her cheeks and decided it must be from exertion. She grasped the bottle tightly indeed.

Karess finally won the tug of war, and bowed his head to her before throwing Bracca a grin that could only be called conspiratorial. "We'll finish our talk later. I'll hurry these out to the men. Fate gets irritable when he's thirsty." He walked away with a jaunty step, working at a cork with his teeth.

Bracca could have cheerfully killed him.

Instead, he bent and picked up the square of cloth, catching up one round of cheese as it wobbled away slowly. Keeping his distance, he held the ball out to Sheren without meeting her gaze.

"If you will hold this, I'll tie the ends of the cloth." The quicker he helped her recover the cheese, the faster he could take himself from her presence.

When she didn't immediately hold out her hand, he glanced up at her.

Foolish move, Bracca.

That slight smile of hers he found so intriguing graced her lips, taking his breath. He felt his hands tremble with the ridiculous need to reach out and trace those lips with his finger. Exerting control, he gripped the cloth in one hand and shifted the cheese in the other. Holding the ball up at eye level, he raised his brows questioningly.

She dipped her head, the pink on her cheeks deepening. "Thank you." She reached out a hand. Soft fingers brushed against his calloused skin, the sensation shooting straight to his groin.

He pretended not to notice the way she jerked her hand back, almost dropping the round of cheese in her haste.

Twice a fool.

Knotting the cloth, he watched her from the

corner of his eye as she re-captured the runaway balls of cheese. He held the makeshift bag open, careful to keep his hands away from hers as she deposited her cache. Then he held the bag out to her.

"Perhaps you should carry that," she suggested, eyeing the bulging cloth warily. "I seem to be unable to hold onto things today."

He bowed slightly. "As you wish."

"The outer courtyard where the Blades take their meals is this way." She pointed in the direction Karess had disappeared earlier. Her shy smile flickered to life again. Breathlessly, he waved her ahead of him. He walked beside her, keeping the width of the hallway between them.

Other than jerking her hand away at his touch, she didn't seem to show any distress at being in the presence of a former Black Blade. A slight tightness to the shoulders, fingers laced together in front of her, but no disgust showed on her face when she turned to look up at him. Only…curiosity.

"I understand Lady St. John is your second Bloodsworn. Is your link with her very different from what you had before?"

Her question caught him off guard. Bracca opened his mouth and snapped it shut again. The difference between his links was so profound he didn't know where to begin.

Sheren turned her gaze to the floor and increased her pace. "I'm sorry. I shouldn't have asked something so personal."

"No," he said, reaching out a hand only to draw it back quickly when she flinched away.

Luma's bloody hell, when would he learn?

He stopped walking, relieved when she stopped, too. "Your question—I would answer it, but I don't think we have the time. The difference is too…vast."

"I suppose it would be, though I don't begin to understand the relationship between Blade and

139

Bloodsworn myself. My husband, Sayjan, had trouble putting it into words."

Cold flashed through him, draining the heat from his blood. *Her husband.* She was taken, already bound to another man.

"Your husband is a Blade?"

"*Was* a Blade. He died four years ago protecting his Bloodsworn, the Tragar."

He almost missed the bitterness in her words, too busy fighting back a powerful surge of relief. As if her marital status should mean—*could mean*—anything to him. "Forgive me. It was not my intention to bring up painful memories."

"Mama, mama!"

The child's cry raced down the hallway ahead of him, though not by much. Bringing his running feet to a stop beside Sheren, the small boy snagged a double handful of her skirt.

"Mama, there are Blades in the courtyard. Silver Blades. Lots of them. At least two decca." Excitement sparkled in the boy's dark brown eyes.

She had a child. Bracca didn't want to name the emotion that sank its claws all the way to his damaged soul. Jealousy, envy, either one was out of the question.

Sheren laid a calming hand on her son's head. "Yes, Seth, I know. The Tragar is here—"

"With his lady," Seth said. Bracca couldn't keep a smile from forming as words tumbled from the small mouth. "Lady Avera St. John. She's a Bloodsworn, too. Kiel said. I didn't know ladies could be Bloodsworn. I told Kiel I didn't believe him, but he said she has two Blades already, and one of them is here. Kiel said her swords are amber, not silver like the Tragar's. I've never seen an amber sword. Do you think her Blade will let me see his?"

"I..." Sheren's gaze shot to Bracca. He wondered at her indecision. Then the child followed his mother's gaze. The boy tipped his head to the side in a curious gesture. "I don't know you. Are you a new Silver Blade?"

Bracca bowed slightly. "Nay, young master, I am not." He did not mention his true status, reasoning that Sheren's hesitation was due to her not wanting her son to have anything to do with him. He did not blame her. Mothers had a right to protect their children from the Boogey-men of the world.

Her next words shocked him to stillness.

"Seth, this is Bracca Cu-Laurian, Lady St. John's First Blade."

Bracca waited for childish excitement to turn to fear. Instead, brown eyes rounded in what could only be called, awe. Apparently Seth had yet to learn the names of Black Blades.

"Her First Blade? Really? Can I see your sword? Is it really amber? I thought amber was a rock. If it's amber, won't it break when you fight with it?"

"So many questions," Sheren said, smiling, tugging the child to her. "Why don't we let Bracca eat first? His Bloodsworn may call for him at any moment."

"After he eats, then can I see his sword?"

"I would be honored to show you the sword of my Bloodsworn, Seth. If," he added in deference to a mother's authority, "your mother agrees."

The child gazed up at his mother who shook her head woefully at his pleading expression. "Incorrigible child."

Seth grinned. "I take after father, don't I?"

"Without a doubt," she said, bending down and kissing his forehead. Bracca's heart clenched at the tenderness of the gesture. His own mother had kissed him like that several lifetimes ago.

Seth grimaced. He started to wipe his forehead. At a look from his mother, he sighed, and let his hand drop. He turned to Bracca.

"Do you want me to show you where the Silver Blades are? You might want to hurry if you're hungry. They eat like a plague of locusts."

"Seth!"

The boy shrugged and reached for Bracca's hand. "Well, that's what you told Cook before they got here."

Bracca bit back a grin as Sheren's cheeks bloomed a bright rose. He searched her lovely face for any sign of dismay considering her son now clung to the hand of a former Black Blade. But—and he considered it a small miracle—he saw nothing other than embarrassment at her son's revelation. Seth took her hand, too, tugging impatiently until she fell into step with them.

They proceeded that way down the hall, Seth skipping between them, a happy, though oblivious, little buffer. It wasn't until they stepped into the open courtyard filled with Silver Blades and bustling servants that Bracca realized the picture they presented. More than one interested gaze turned their way.

From the corner of his eye, he saw Sheren start as she, too, realized the cozy tableau they made. Her hesitation was brief, covered by a smile down at her son.

The boy, blinded by the sweet innocence of youth, held tight to their hands until they came to a half-empty table.

Sheren excused herself, saying she needed to check on things in the kitchen. Bracca made a point of not watching her leave. He handed his bag of cheese to a hovering servant, then concentrated on filling his plate from the platters and bowls on the table. Oblivious to the speculative glances coming their way, little Seth scrambled into a seat next to him and began giving him advice on what was good and what—to his five-year-old-palate—was not.

Chapter Fifteen

Devlin watched Avera select a roll. She broke the bread open, spread butter on one half, and took a bite. Her eyes closed, a small moan of pleasure slipping past her lips. The sound rolled over him like a wave of magic, leaving his skin tingling.

"Mmm, this is so good. I love bread. It's my one weakness." Her tongue darted out to lick the tip of her finger.

Devlin shifted in his seat, searching for a more comfortable position. *Merciful Luma.* What should have been a quiet, relaxing lunch was fast turning into a very stimulating experience, at least for him.

"You're not eating." She looked at him over the rim of her glass of wine, eyes innocently wide. "Aren't you hungry?"

"Not very." At least, not for food. His present menu listed far different fare. Luscious lips, delectable neck, tender breasts... He could only be thankful the table shielded the evidence of his other appetite from her. Who would have thought the simple act of watching another person eat could be such a sensual experience?

He was relieved when a servant finally arrived with a small dessert tray, signaling the meal would soon be over. Without thinking, he chose a placket sweet and offered it to Avera. He chose a second one for himself, biting into the small, sugar coated pastry with relish. As soon as the heat of the spicy filling bit his tongue he knew he should warn her. "Avera—"

But it was too late.

He watched anxiously as she stopped chewing. Her eyes grew round in surprise and began to water. Devlin quickly shoved her wineglass into her hand.

"This will put the fire out."

She gulped the wine, quickly draining the glass. Then she grabbed Devlin's half-filled glass and drained it as well. She set the goblet down with a thump and glared at him.

"If I thought for one minute—"

"The combination of sweet and hot appeal to many Feyune palates," he interrupted her, trying his best to look innocent. "Even children love placket sweets, though theirs are usually milder."

Her glare diminished, but not by much. When she picked up a napkin to dab at her eyes, he cleared the table with a wave of magic, sending all the dishes except for their glasses back to the kitchen. He re-filled both goblets with chilled wine.

"Forgive me, Avera. I should have been quicker to warn you."

She shook her head. "It's all right. Believe it or not, it's not the first time I've scalded my taste buds with something a little too spicy. And it's a good lesson."

He frowned. How could she think such a thing? "It was not meant to be a lesson. You must know I would never willingly cause you pain of any kind."

"Not even to test my Bloodsworn status?"

He stiffened, her too accurate thrust piercing his conscience and hitting him right in his heart.

"I'm sorry," she said quickly. She reached across the table and pried his fingers from around his wine glass. "That was uncalled for. I understand you had no choice."

The pain in his heart lessened at her touch, though his conscience still burned with guilt. "You're wrong. I had a choice. I could have forbidden the test."

"Not without consequences, I bet."

"True. The Council would have denied your status and ordered me, as First Bloodsworn, to break your existing links."

"That," she said softly, "would have been a far worse pain."

He raised her hand to his mouth, brushing his lips over her knuckles. "So I deemed as well." He knew the pain of losing a Blade. It was not one he wished Avera to ever experience.

She squeezed his hand and sat back. He didn't try to hold on to her.

"When I said it was a lesson, I meant it was a reminder that I'm not on Earth anymore. Even though things might look familiar, they're not necessarily the same. You make it darn easy for me to forget that sometimes," she admitted, clearly uncomfortable with her confession.

Devlin felt just the opposite. If she could tell him this, feel this way about him even after the debacle at the council, then perhaps he had a chance to put things right between them.

He would, he decided, start the process by warning her about his mother. Not that he expected his mother to disobey him, but it never hurt to have all the cards turned face up on the table. He cleared his throat. "Avera, I need to tell you something."

She tilted her head to the side, considering him. "This sounds serious."

"It is."

"All right, I'm listening."

He took a deep breath and let it out slowly. "Avera, do you know what an aphrodisiac is?"

Her surprised look told him she did.

"Yes," she said slowly. "Why?"

"Last night I discovered an aphrodisiac called Akelia wine had been added to a bottle of Talla wine I keep in my study. Had not Karess and Strum been with me and sampled that same bottle, I would have consumed at least a glass full, possibly more."

"Someone tried to drug you with an aphrodisiac?" He caught the slight shiver that shook her body. Her eyes darkened, but with fear or arousal, he wasn't sure.

"Yes, my mother has a bad habit of interfering when it comes to the prophecies, and took exception to our...temporary estrangement. I confronted her this morning. She won't try that particular trick again. I cannot, however, guarantee she will stop her interference entirely." He grimaced. "She is nothing if not tenacious."

She surprised him by shrugging one shoulder. "So, your mother's a meddler. I already figured that out for myself. I also know she's worried about you. She might be autocratic, manipulative, and conniving, but her heart's in the right place. I promise not to hold her actions against you if she goes a little overboard now and then."

"You are far more understanding than she deserves," Devlin said, determined to point out the danger of his mother's interference. "You were already angry with me over the Council's ruling, Avera. Without Karess' and Strum's warning, I fear I would have done more than come begging at your door. I already crave you with every cell in my body. Add the Akelia wine and nothing would have kept you safe from me. Not myself, not my Blades, and most especially not your Blade. Nothing. I'd be no better than the man who gave you those scars." He waited for her fear.

She looked at him a long moment. Then she stood. He rose, too, and watched her walk around the small table to stand in front of him. She placed one hand flat against his chest and curled the other around his neck. Heat flooded him at her touch. He wanted to pull her close, fit her body to his the way it belonged. Instead, he placed his hands lightly on her waist to steady her as she rose on her toes. Her eyes drifted shut. She kissed him. He felt the sweet, feather soft touch of her lips right down to his soul. She pulled back before he could take charge of the kiss, leaving him desperate for more.

"I haven't forgiven you for siding with the Council," she said, her words like a dash of icy water. "That's something we still have to work through. But you're not scaring me away, Devlin. Not your mother, not you, not even you under the influence of a whole bottle of aphrodisiac. You are a lot of things, but a rapist isn't one of them. I should know. I've seen one of those up close."

He covered her hand on his chest with his, pressing it firmly over his heart, letting her feel how hard it was pounding. He had to know. "Did he...?"

Her cheeks burned red. She shook her head and tried to pull away. He refused to let her go this time. She'd made the first move. Time to let her know that not all of his impulses were driven by an aphrodisiac, deep-healing lust, or even a magical mate-bond. He scooped her into his arms. Her beautiful green eyes widened. "What are you—" He returned to his chair, positioning her so she sat sideways on his lap. Then he gripped her chin lightly and kissed her, slowly, deeply, with every ounce of need and craving he'd been holding back.

When he finally raised his head both of them were breathing hard. She glared at him, or at least tried to. The smile never left her eyes, and her lips finally gave in. "We're going to have to talk about this bossy streak of yours."

He kissed her again, nipping lightly at her bottom lip. "Feel free to try and reform me, my lady. I warn you however, I've been this way for years. It may take you a century or two to see results."

She chuckled softly, the sound sending shivers

through him. It seemed he responded to everything she did, however minor. "I think I have a century or two to spare," she murmured.

He kissed her hair. "About your attacker, are you telling me the truth?"

She tipped her head back to look at him, her brows sharply arched. "I'm not in the habit of lying. Especially about something as important to me as this."

He brought her hand to his lips and kissed her palm. "I did not think you were. But I foolishly thought perhaps you would not wish to tell me the truth knowing I would go back to Earth to hunt him down and kill him regardless of the Concourse's rules against such things." He could tell she didn't think he was serious. She patted his cheek.

"My very own knight in shining armor. Sorry, but you're a little late with the whole rescuing the damsel in distress thing."

"Not rescue, my lady, retribution. Your reaction at the Bloodsworn council was not merely fear for your link with Cu-Laurian. He told me he saw flashes of images, bits and pieces, but enough to know your reaction to the blindfold and gag had something to do with your scars." He couldn't help the anger growing in his voice. Someone had tied her up, held her bound and helpless. Hurt her.

She shook her head. "Let it go, Devlin. Just let it go. It's not like I'm ever going to have to see him again. True, I have a few scars, but thanks to you I'm coming to realize they're more proof of my ability to take care of myself than something to be ashamed of." She pushed her sleeves up, exposing her arms. "Besides, I think it's getting a little too warm to keep wearing long sleeves."

He released a whisper of his magic and her blouse was gone, replaced by a short, sleeveless tunic with a low scooped neckline. The soft material, shaded to match her green eyes, clung to her breasts in a way that made him hard just looking at her. He watched her closely as she surveyed her new attire. She ran a hand along her scars then let her arms fall. Her lips trembled. "This is going to take a little getting used to."

He didn't know if she was referring to his casual use of magic or her bare arms. Perhaps, she didn't know herself.

"You did say you had a century or two to spare," he reminded her.

"Yes, I did, didn't I?" She leaned toward him again, placing her arms around his neck. "So, tell me, how many bedrooms does this place have, and which one is yours?"

For a moment, he couldn't move, certain he'd misunderstood her meaning. Before he could decide how to answer her—turn to point out his room or simply sweep her into his arms and run up the stairs—she wiggled out of his lap.

"Not that you have to stay with me. I mean, I've enjoyed your company and all, but I know you must be pretty busy, right? You probably have another meeting to go to or something else important you should be doing."

She was babbling, nervous suddenly, and he found it utterly adorable.

"You are far more important than any meeting, Avera."

"Ah, yes, I'm part of your all important Prophecy, aren't I? I guess that does put me at the top of your to do list. Your mother told me you and I have to get married on your summer solstice in a few weeks. That doesn't give us much time to get to know each other, does it?" Her hesitant smile made him grind his teeth.

His mother again. Of course she would say just the wrong things. He knew enough about Avera to know she was a woman used to charting her own course, not having it laid out for her. Leave it to his mother to ignore Avera's independent spirit.

"Do you and your family stay here often?"

He welcomed her change of subject. "Gwenell and I do. She loves coming here just to get away from the palace. My brother, Churian, often joins her. My mother, however, flatly refuses."

Avera seemed taken aback. "But why? I know it has a sad history, but it's so beautiful, so peaceful. Who wouldn't want to live here?" Stepping out from under the pergola, she wound her way through the flower-filled urns until she reached the large central fountain.

Devlin followed, watching her, his thoughts suddenly spinning with a new plan.

"Would you?" he asked as they reached the central fountain.

"Would I what?"

"Would you like to live here?"

She froze, fingers dangling in the fountain's water, and blinked her eyes at him. "Did you just ask me if I'd like to live here?"

"Yes." He moved closer, brushed a wayward strand of dark hair from her face. "Would it make staying on Avalyr easier for you if you lived here, at Villa Porenmagie, instead of the palace?"

Her green eyes brightened, sparkling with delight in the afternoon sunlight. Her smile widened. "Oh, Devlin, yes," she said, throwing her arms around him. "I would very much like to live here."

Devlin held her tight, drinking in her scent and the feel of her body against his. The more he thought about it, the better he liked this new plan. It would effectively separate Avera from his mother's influence. Lady Patria vowed she would never set foot in the villa. He, on the other hand, could gate here anytime.

Avera stirred in his arms, pulling back much too soon for his liking. The joy on her face was a fair exchange. "I will see to it your things are moved immediately," he said, smiling at her obvious pleasure. "Would you like to see the rest of your new home?"

She looked up at him through her lashes. "Can we start with the bedrooms?"

****

Sheren did not re-appear until Bracca had cleaned his plate and pushed it aside. He leaned back in his chair, enjoying a second tankard of strong ale as he watched her move from table to table, directing the removal of dishes. Again, her behavior seemed unusual to him. She didn't laugh and banter with the warriors as most of the other females did. But neither was she rude. She responded to the occasional question, even smiled when appropriate. There was no doubt, however, that she intentionally kept a distance between herself and the Silver Blades.

Still, she didn't flinch when one touched her on the arm to get her attention, or when another turned suddenly, his hand coming into contact with hers. He didn't have to ask himself why she tolerated the touch from Silver Blades and not him. He found the knowledge disturbing that he could feel hurt over something so small.

"If you're finished eating, can I see your sword, now?"

Seth, impatient with Bracca's slow method of eating, had left the table earlier. He'd kept an eye on the boy, grinning to himself when Seth slipped between Kiel and Strum and stole Kiel's dessert while the young warrior wasn't looking. The ensuing argument between Kiel and Strum concerning the missing dessert went on a good five minutes. The blatantly mock quarrel puzzled Bracca until Kiel pretended to catch sight of Seth's grinning, pastry-smeared face.

The young warrior pounced on the pastry thief with a ferocity that had Bracca's muscles tensing until he heard the childish giggles. A tickle session ensued until Strum had called them to order. Seth's further punishment was a trip to the kitchen to secure a replacement dessert for Kiel. A chore the child embraced without the slightest demure, telling Bracca this was an act of thievery often perpetrated.

Seth stood now at his elbow, face clean, brown eyes wide with hopeful anticipation.

Without a word, Bracca sat his tankard on the table and stood. His sword slipped from its sheath with the barest whisper. He held it at Seth's eye-level. For a moment, the child was speechless. Then, "Luma's bloody hell," he said softly.

"Seth!"

The boy cringed.

Sheren marched toward them, her face stern. The situation was made worse by the hearty male laughter of the warriors lingering over their ale. Bracca struggled not to join them.

"Peace, Sheren." Karess, still laughing, moved to intercept her. "The boy can hardly be held responsible. He was overcome with awe by the sight of Bracca's mighty sword."

"Hardly a mighty sword," Kiel said derisively. His own sword hissed free, the silver weapon glinting in the dappled sunlight. "Now this is a mighty sword, Seth. A sword a warrior can be proud of. A sword enemies will fear. That fanciful piece of Cu-Laurian's is so scrolled and curved, an enemy will think it's a toy and fall down laughing."

Bracca ignored the taunt. It wasn't the first time Kiel Na-Turesh had insulted his sword. Most likely it would not be the last. The young Blade seemed determine to pick a fight with him. Perhaps a lesson on the training grounds was in order.

Seth's small face screwed up in concentration. His serious young gaze darted between the swords as if considering the merits of each. Finally he gave a decisive nod.

Seth reached out his hand. "I like this one."

Bracca jerked his sword back, but not before the tip of one small finger caressed the amber metal. His muscles tensed in expectation while his mind clamped down on his link in the hope of sparing Avera the results of his stupidity. Even the touch of a child could send pain crashing down on Blade and Bloodsworn both.

But what rippled through him was a far cry from the sharp sensation he'd experienced during the Bloodsworn Council's examination. The feeling wasn't comfortable, certainly, but neither was it so painful that he couldn't keep it out of his link with Avera with a little effort.

Sheren froze, staring at him, her eyes holding a mixture of horror and apology. She snatched Seth back, clutching him protectively in her arms. Her lips moved, quietly forming the words, "I'm sorry."

"It's all right," he said, his gaze moving to Seth's anxious face. "No harm done, Seth." He slid his sword home. The action seemed to free everyone else from their self-imposed paralysis.

Two tables over, Nerrilik snorted. "No one but a fool offers up his Bloodsworn's sword to another, not even a child. You never know who might be the enemy." Most of the warriors nodded in agreement.

Sheren's eyes flashed with anger. "Seth isn't anyone's enemy. He's a little boy, and little boys sometimes forget."

"I'm sorry. I'm sorry, Bracca," Seth said, tears starting down his cheeks. His little face was pale with fright. "I won't do it again, I promise. Please don't be angry."

Bracca glanced once at Sheren for permission, then placed a hand gently on the boy's shoulder.

"I'm not angry. The mistake was mine, Seth. I should have paid closer attention."

"Because I'm a enemy?"

"No, Seth!"

"No, Seth." He seconded Sheren's vehement denial. "You are not my enemy, nor the enemy of anyone here. Nerrilik didn't mean you, did you Nerrilik?" He fixed his gaze on the Silver Blade. If the man did not apologize to the child, bad leg or not, he would find himself challenged.

"Well, Nerrilik?" The threat in Karess' voice was thinly veiled.

Nerrilik grunted. "A misunderstanding. Seth knows I don't consider him the enemy. We've talked about it often enough. Ask him who the real enemy is. Ask him who killed his father."

"B-black Blades." Seth sniffed, running the back of his hand beneath his nose. "Camarie's Black Blades killed papa and hurt Nerrilik's leg."

Nerrilik nodded slowly, his eyes never leaving Bracca. "Black Blades are the enemy. They'll never be welcome—" Nerrilik blinked suddenly. Then he gasped, his face going dark with unconcealed rage. He slammed his mug of ale on the table. Glaring at Bracca, he rose from the table and limped stiffly from the courtyard.

Wondering at the warrior's odd behavior, Bracca almost missed Karess clearing his throat. The Silver Blade nudged Fate. "Do you want to tell him, or shall I?"

Fate stared hard at Bracca a long moment, then turned away without a word and quit the courtyard as well.

"What has happened," he demanded. He touched his link with Avera to assure himself of her wellbeing. The incandescent joy suffusing the link caught him off guard. Bemused, he staggered under Karess' slap to his back.

"Congratulations on your promotion, Amber Blade."

"Promotion?" He was already Avera's First Blade. For him, no status could be higher.

"Yes, the promotion that comes with the gift Devlin just gave his Starmate."

"What gift?" Bracca asked warily.

Karess held his arms out wide. "Why, Villa Porenmagie."

It took him a moment to realize Karess was serious. If Devlin Tragar had indeed given Villa Porenmagie to his Starmate, it would explain Fate's disapproval and Nerrilik's anger. As Avera's First Blade, the security of her residence fell to him. That meant any warriors assigned to the villa, including Silver Blades, were now under his command.

Bracca didn't know whether to cheer or curse.

Chapter Sixteen

Sheren hurried down a hallway, her arms full of linens and baskets, ticking off tasks in her head. The Tragar's chambers—now Lady St. John's chambers as well—had to be aired and freshened immediately. The evening's menu revised, along with those for the next few days. Maids to reassign, schedules to alter. So much to do.

To complicate matters, she also had to make arrangements to house Lady St. John's First Blade. Not that there wasn't room. The villa boasted several guest suites along with a full servant's wing and a separate Blade barracks near the stable. Assigning Bracca a room should be easy. The complicated part was the fact she had to assign him a room at all.

Sheren felt herself tremble just thinking about the darkly handsome warrior. His presence at the villa was so dangerous. Just the brush of his fingers against hers earlier had sent tremors through her shield-wall. How could she possibly avoid contact with him if he lived here? There were bound to be opportunities for an accidental touch.

Or a not so accidental touch, part of her whispered.

Curiosity. It had to be her lamentable curiosity. What else would cause her to even contemplate re-creating that rush of emotions she'd felt yesterday? Luma damn her for a fool for even thinking such a thing. Did she want to go mad? Not to mention he was a Blade! Attractive as he was, she could never allow herself to forget his status. Blades put their

Bloodsworns before everything. Even their families.

Sayjan had changed so much when he'd become a Blade. He'd still loved her and Seth. She'd never doubted that. But his thoughts no longer focused on his wife and son. It was as if the man she'd fallen in love with had truly died during his linking with the Tragar, and another man was born in his place. A man whose joy centered around his sword instead of his family. A man who thought nothing of taking chances with his life.

She refused to go through that again.

Entering the sitting room of the master suite, she crossed to the bedchamber. The sound of childish laughter brought her to a sudden stop. Looking around, she noted the half-open door to the rooftop garden. The familiar giggle came again. Sheren heaved a sigh. She'd sent Seth off to play after Karess' startling revelation, knowing she was going to be very busy. The last thing she expected was to find him in the roof-top garden off the master suite. He knew the second floor was off limits when any of the royal family was in residence.

Feeling a slight sense of urgency, she set her baskets of bath soaps and cleaning supplies on the floor and the fresh linens on a chair. She needed to get her boisterous child below stairs before he was discovered. Moving to the door, she pushed it open.

"Seth, you know better—" She stumbled to a halt, the bottom dropping from her stomach. Her son had already been well and truly discovered. She could see him running toward a group of potted trees, his progress also marked by the man and woman seated together on a long bench.

The Tragar, Prince of Illian, stood. "Ah, Sheren, just the lady we were speaking of." He smiled and beckoned her forward.

Her gaze left his to travel quickly to the lady still seated. Though Lady St. John announced their friendship yesterday in front of Bracca, Sheren wasn't exactly sure where she stood yet. She'd never been friends with a noblewoman before. Deciding to take the cautious approach, she curtsied deep. "My lady."

Lady St. John sighed, the sound one of long-suffering exasperation. "Devlin, honestly, is there any way I can get everyone to stop all the bowing and curtseying?"

Remarkably, he laughed. "I suppose you might ask, *me`surrasie*, but I rather doubt you will be successful. Such actions are signs of respect in our culture, manners taught from the cradle."

"Yes, well, we have cultures like that back on Earth, too, but mine wasn't one of them. Salutes, yes, bowing, no. I can't help it if it makes me uncomfortable." She rose gracefully, the impatience of her words at odds with the warm, teasing smile on her face. "Besides, Sheren and I are already friends, and friends don't bow to one another."

Lord Devlin chuckled. "Good luck getting that across. I've been trying to break Fate of the habit for years and it hasn't taken yet."

"Fate I can understand. I can't see him bending a rule, much less breaking it. We women know better." She winked at Sheren.

Put at ease by their banter, Sheren laughed lightly. "We do indeed, my lady."

Lady St. John pointed at her. "That's something else we're going to have to work on. My name's Avera. Feel free to use it."

"I found one!"

The call coming from behind the screen of trees in one corner spared Sheren an immediate answer. Not curtseying was one thing. Using Lady St. John's first name would take some consideration.

Seth pushed between two potted trees, nearly knocking one over in his haste, and sprinted toward them. "I found one," he repeated, his high voice, full of excited laughter.

To Sheren's surprise, Lady St. John turned and knelt on the hard tiles of the garden floor. Seth pattered up to her, eyes bright, hands loosely clasped together before him.

"See," he said, opening his hands slowly. Lady St. John leaned close, bending her head even closer, to see his prize.

"Wow, Seth, you're right. He's beautiful."

Sheren sent her puzzled glance to the Tragar.

Jade frog, he mouthed.

Her smile came automatically. Her son had a fondness for the jewel-bright amphibians. The smile vanished the next moment as Lady St. John fell back with a startled cry.

Seth giggled and clapped his hands. Sheren cringed. She didn't know Lady St. John well enough to judge what she might take offense to. "Seth, come here at once," she called, anxious to get him away.

"Wait, mama, I have to get the froggy off Lady Avera."

"Seth—"

Lady St. John laughed. She laughed and looked up from her un-graceful seat. "Yes, please let him get the froggy off Lady Avera," she said as Seth made a grab for the small spot of green on her shoulder.

Sheren could do nothing but stare in disbelief. The Tragar's Starmate—the highest ranking woman in the realm—sat on the ground with Seth all but in her lap, playing with a frog.

"Got him," Seth crowed.

Lady St. John steadied him as he got to his feet. "Well done, Seth. What are you going to do with him now?"

Sheren stepped protectively to her son's side as Lord Devlin helped his lady to her feet.

"I need to take him back to the tree where I found him," Seth said, looking to Sheren for approval. "Mama says it's all right to play with the froggies if I put them back when I'm done. That way they don't have so far to hop home."

"I think that's an excellent idea," Lady St. John agreed solemnly. "We wouldn't want to have a bunch of lost froggies hopping around."

Seth giggled.

"Come along then, Seth," the Tragar said, stepping forward. "You can show me where this little froggy lives in case Lady Avera decides to visit him again."

Watching the two of them walk away, Sheren felt herself adrift in a sea of bewilderment. Even before Sayjan had died, the few times she'd been in Lord Devlin's company she'd sensed he hovered on the edge of a vast and all consuming anger. This lighter side of the powerful Bloodsworn and ruler came as a complete shock to her.

"Your son is adorable."

Sheren started. Lady St. John stood at her side gazing fondly in the direction of man and child.

"Thank you. I...my apologies if he has disturbed you. He knows not to come upstairs when any of the royal family is here. I can't think how he could have forgotten."

Lady St. John smiled apologetically. "Oh, well, that's my fault, I'm afraid. Devlin and I ran into him downstairs. Somehow the conversation turned into a discussion about the bugs and other creepy-crawlies inhabiting the courtyard. Devlin mentioned Jade frogs and Seth said they were his favorite. I asked if he knew where one lived and, well," she waved a hand, "here we are. Please don't be angry with him."

Sheren stared at her a long moment. "You are very—"

"Please." With a pained expression, she held up

a hand. "Please don't say I'm *unusual*. The last person to call me that was Devlin's mother, and I still haven't gotten over it."

Sheren grinned. "I wasn't going to say you are unusual. I was going to say you're very kind. Not many noblewomen would deign to speak with a common clan-child, much less laugh with him over a frog." She tilted her head and, considering the things she'd seen and heard in the past few minutes, dared to point out something. "Though taking that into consideration, you have to admit that you are at least a little bit...unusual."

Lady St. John blinked several times before her lips curved into a wry smile. She nodded once. "Point taken. I'll try to remember that the next time someone tosses out that observation."

By the time Lord Devlin and Seth returned, Sheren felt, if not completely comfortable, then at least at ease standing next to the most powerful woman in the realm. It was as if they had found some common ground on which to stand. Woman to woman perhaps, for Sheren could think of no other.

She held her hand out to her son. "Come along, sweetling, back downstairs where you belong."

He skipped to her and slipped his smaller hand into hers. "Lady Avera says she has a new horse. Can I go see it?"

Sheren hesitated. Seth usually had the run of the villa, but with so many warriors around...

"My First Blade, Bracca, says he needs to check all the outbuildings. Perhaps Seth could be his guide," Lady Avera said.

Her son hopped up and down in place. "I can do that, I can show him. Please, Mama, please?" He gazed up at her hopefully.

"Would you like Kiel to go, too, Seth?" Lord Devlin asked. Sheren cast him a glance, wondering how he knew Kiel was one of the few Silver Blades she'd come to trust other than Karess.

Seth stopped hopping and nibbled his bottom lip. "Would I still be the guide?"

"Of course," the Tragar assured him. "Kiel can be your assistant."

That did it. Her child's face lit up, and Sheren knew she had no choice. To refuse would not only offend her employers, but send Seth into a case of the black dismals. She could never bear to see him so downcast.

She faced the Tragar, bobbed a curtsey. "Thank you, my lord."

Smiling gently, he inclined his head. "In case I've not told you before Sheren, thank you for your care of Villa Porenmagie. From everything I've seen it could not be in better hands."

Sheren felt her head spin from the compliment. "I...thank you, my lord." A different side of him indeed. She turned to the one no doubt responsible for such a remarkable change. "I'll return later to freshen the bedchamber." She hesitated, than added, "Lady Avera." It was the best she could do and still keep her heart from leaping into her throat in protest. Twenty-three years of manners were hard to set aside.

The other woman gave her a wide, pleased smile, and nodded. "Thank you, Sheren."

With a final curtsey she couldn't have stopped if she tried, Sheren turned and led her son back inside. No one knew better than her how hard it was to break old habits. But perhaps, with a little effort and the proper encouragement, there were some that could at least be bent.

Chapter Seventeen

Devlin didn't watch Sheren and Seth leave. He was too busy staring at Avera's lovely smile. Her eyes sparkled, and happiness radiated from her like light from the sun. She warmed him.

When she turned and reached for him, the last vestige of fear that his siding with the council had damned him forever in her eyes, burned away. Desire for her roared to unbearable life.

Meeting Seth had delayed their exploration of his bedchamber, a matter he intended to correct with all speed. He wanted her. Badly.

From the look in her eyes, she wanted him, too.

He reached to kiss her, but she leaned away, placing her fingers against his lips.

"I've decided I want to clear something up first," she said.

For a moment he struggled with the need to simply kiss her into submission. The trust in her eyes swayed him. He nodded. "You believe I betrayed you."

"And you think I betrayed you."

It galled him to admit his jealousy, but he did so. "Yes. The evidence was most convincing."

"Convincing," she agreed, "but only if taken out of context. If you'd bothered to ask, I would have told you that what you saw was Bracca and I coming to an understanding about our relationship."

Their relationship. Somehow, he kept his voice neutral. "And?"

"I grew up an only child, Devlin. An only child who was constantly uprooted and moved. It wasn't so bad when my dad was around, but when he wasn't, it was lonely." She smiled wistfully. "I often wished for a big brother."

Surprise shoved his eyebrows up as her words registered. "You think of Cu-Laurian as a brother?"

She nodded emphatically. "A big, scary, older brother who keeps me safe when you're not around."

He pretended to think about it while trying to hide how much her words pleased him. She'd been quite upset when he'd warned her what would happen if Cu-Laurian ever came near her bed. If she considered her Blade in the light of a brother, he now knew why. Family bonds were sacred. He let his lips curve into a slow smile.

"I see. Then you and your *brother* have my most abject apologies for misunderstanding your embrace, my lady."

Instead of returning his smile, she made a small grimace. "I'll accept your apology if you'll accept mine for not picking a better time to sort things out with Bracca. It wasn't my intention to embarrass you in front of the Council.

"I care not what the Council thinks. As long as you and I understand one another that is all that matters."

"Good." Her expression turned guarded. "That leaves just one more betrayal to explain."

Devlin felt his gut clench. There was no way he could explain his relief at the Council's edict without her thinking him petty and mean. A tyrant at the very least.

He sighed and ran a hand over his face while keeping his other arm snugly around her waist.

"I admit the extent of my…relief at the Council's edict was due in part to your embrace with Cu-Laurian. In short, I was jealous. I still am, even with your assurance that you see him only as a brother." He stopped her from speaking with a finger over her lips. "Jealous of your link, not of your relationship." He wrapped both arms tightly around her. "You are mine, Avera. My beloved. My Starmate. The other half of my soul. I have waited for you my entire life. Having to share you with your Blades..." He shook his head, trying to find words. "Cu-Laurian and Tyr are bad enough. The thought of more men sharing an intimate link to your mind had me grasping the Council's ruling like a drowning man."

She sighed, giving him a small smile. "I suppose my reaction to their test didn't help."

He snorted softly. "Definitely not. By then, all I wanted to do was gate you back home and lock you in the Ladies' Wing where you'd never encounter another male again. A foolish wish, I know." He kissed the tip of her nose. "You are not the kind of female to accept such restrictions."

"Thank God you realized that and didn't try locking me in the same wing as your mother. You might not have a palace left by now if you had. She and I don't exactly see eye to eye, you know."

"Another reason for you to live here at the villa. Having a small war break out in the palace halls would definitely hinder any future negotiations with other realms. My advisors tell me it is essential to at least appear to maintain peace in my own household."

She grinned, her hands, which had been flat against his chest, moved up and around his neck. "So you had an ulterior motive for bringing me here today."

"Not really. I wanted us to be able to talk in a place of light and beauty, and I could think of no place better than here. Offering the villa to you as your home was purely an inspiration of the moment."

One of her fingers circled his ear, playing with his hair, sending chills down his back. "An inspiration I truly appreciate. But Devlin, about my links. Maybe I don't see them as you do. To me, they're just a means of communication. Nothing more. Bracca and I can communicate a little better because we can sense each other's feelings, but that's all." She cupped his cheek in her palm. "Having him in my head doesn't come close to having you in my heart."

Something settled inside him. Without another word he leaned down to capture her mouth, drowning in a sudden rush of desire so strong he shook with it. His hands smoothed down her back to cup the firm cheeks of her backside, lifting her easily, urging her legs up and around his waist. Still kissing her, he walked the short distance to the bedchamber. Reaching the bed, he crawled onto it on his knees and leaned down, pressing her into the soft quilt. She broke their kiss, flinging her head back to gasp for air.

"Our clothes. Get rid of them."

"Soon," he murmured, sliding his mouth down her throat. He had no intention of rushing this time. There were things he'd been craving ever since their interrupted lovemaking yesterday morning. He wanted to touch her, taste her.

Her hips rubbed hard against him. "Now, damn it." Her rough demand vibrated through her throat and into his lips, making him want to bite her. But not here, not yet.

He kissed his way down her body. "Now, who is impatient?"

"I'll show you—"

Her words broke off in a gasp as his mouth settled over her breast. He bit down slightly on the firm nipple shielded only by thin material, drinking in her moan, loving the way her body arched, begging for more. To reward her, he removed her blouse with a stray thought. Hot flesh met his lips and tongue, and he set in to suckle in earnest, drawing deeply on the hard nub.

Nails dug through his shirt, into his shoulders. He switched to her other breast, taking his time bringing it to rosy attention as Avera's harsh breathing and needy moans filled the air—music to his ears. Her hands fisted in his collar and she tugged.

"Devlin, please. I need to touch you."

He pushed to his knees, bringing her up with him. He kissed her, whispered against her lips. "You want my shirt gone, remove it yourself."

The words had barely left his month when he felt her hands pulling eagerly at the hem. As soon as her fingers touched his skin, however, she paused. He held himself still by force of will while her hands traced hot trails from his back to his chest, down across the jumping muscles of his stomach, then around to his back again. Each stroke sent his desire spiraling higher. He was on the verge of getting rid of the damn shirt himself when she finally gathered two handfuls and pulled upward.

He had to release her in order to strip the shirt off. Then she was pressed against him, skin to luscious skin. He tried to hold her still a moment, just to drink in the sensation, but his Starmate had other ideas. She moved, sliding herself against him, her nipples teasing him as she nipped and licked his neck and throat. She bent down and lapped at one of his nipples, and he almost lost control.

Grabbing her by the waist, he pushed her back down onto the bed.

"No," she said, reaching for him.

He pressed a hand to her stomach, holding her down while he sent her jeans and undergarment the way of her blouse.

She lay back at once. "Yes," she whispered, her legs spreading for him.

He took her calves, ran his hands slowly up her legs, spreading her wider. Her dark thatch of hair glistened with moisture, beckoning, while at the same time hiding her most tender flesh from his hungry gaze. On impulse, he swept a hand over her mound, banishing the tight, black curls.

Avera gasped, her whole body jerking in reaction to the brush of his magic between her legs. She leveled herself up on her elbows, looking first at her smooth nether lips and then at him. "You have got to be kidding me."

He grinned and shrugged. "I wanted to see all of you."

She flopped back down and addressed the ceiling. "No more shaving or waxing. Dear Lord, I'm not on another planet, I'm in heaven."

Devlin wasted no more time. He bent down and spread her soft folds with eager fingers, feeling her thighs tense against his shoulders. She was beautiful, absolutely perfect. Pink and slick with her desire. A prime feast prepared just for him.

He leaned in and tasted.

"Devlin!" Her hands fisted tight in his hair, the small sting from her frantic tugs only adding to his pleasure. Holding her down with one arm across her bucking hips, he settled in to dine.

Each lick, each nibble, drew sounds from his lady love. Moans, gasps, even tiny whimpers, they all slammed into him with driving force, shooting straight to his groin. His shaft strained against his tight leathers, full to the point of pain.

He felt the moment she reached the edge of ecstasy. Every muscle in her body strained, seeking a release that only he could give her. He set his mouth around the bud of her sex and flicked it rapidly with his tongue. The moment she screamed his name he banished his leathers and rose over her. One smooth roll of his hips buried him deep inside her, exactly where he belonged.

Kissing her, he withdrew and pushed his way through her tight folds again, and again, her inner walls squeezing him endlessly. Even when he felt her body go limp he didn't slow his pace, but kept pushing, wanting to bring her to fulfillment again. Wanting to feel her come apart in his arms over and over. He would never get enough of her. Never.

By the time he brought her to the edge once more, Devlin was fighting back his own release, each stroke like a battering-ram against the walls of his control. He almost wept with relief when he felt the first tremor run through her. Growling softly, he slammed into her one last time before his body was racked with pleasure. Her shout of *"Me`surrasie!"* mixed with his as her rippling sheath squeezed his pulsing shaft over and over.

Joined as they were, Devlin didn't think he'd ever felt more complete in his life.

Chapter Eighteen

After leaving Lord Devlin and Lady Avera, Sheren and Seth found Bracca and Kiel waiting for them at the foot of the stairs. Seth fairly bounced down the steps, throwing himself into the role of guide with his usual enthusiasm.

"He'll be safe with us," Kiel said.

Sheren smiled. "I know he will." She glanced at Bracca. He inclined his head, the curve of his lips barely discernable. Did the man never smile?

Sheren stayed at the top of the stairs—well out of reach of temptation—until the three left, then returned to her list of chores.

An hour later, Sheren found herself outside the villa, trying to dispel a nagging feeling growing in the back of her mind. Something wasn't right. She glanced around, not sure where, or even what, the problem was. The entry to the gardens lay to her left, the stable in front of her, and the path to the paddocks and orchards on the right. Everything seemed fine.

Nibbling her bottom lip, she leaned against the villa's warm wall, trying to decide what to do. If she disturbed Lord Devlin and Lady Avera with nothing but her strange "feeling", they might think her mad. Perhaps she was. She'd never felt anything like this before.

You never felt a lot of things before touching Bracca Cu-Laurian.

As soon as she thought of him, her unease crystallized into full blown worry. Whatever she was feeling had something to do with Bracca.

And her son was with him.

Sheren pushed off the wall and started running toward the orchards, using the strange link between her and Bracca as a guide. A shout came from one of the paddocks, another from the Blade barracks. She saw people pointing. Her frantic gaze sought and found the thin stream of smoke rising above the trees. With a silent cry of anguish, Sheren ran faster.

****

Bracca stared at what was left of one of the villa's large storage sheds. The stone walls still stood, but the wooden door where the fire had started was gone. So was the roof. The entire thing had collapsed in the middle just after he'd managed to kick and claw a hole in the back wall big enough for him and Seth to crawl through.

Seth was fine, but understandably shaken. The parts of his face visible beneath the soot shown stark white even after his mother had snatched him out of Bracca's arms.

"How did it start?" Avera asked. "That's what I want to know."

So did he. The fact the only door had been fully engulfed before he or Seth had smelled the smoke seemed very suspicious.

Lord Devlin stood with his arms locked around Avera. "Fate found part of a crystal pitcher near the doorway. With the angle of the sun, it is possible the fire started by itself. Did you see anyone around before you and Seth went inside?"

Bracca shook his head. "I saw no one. Seth may have, but he didn't say anything earlier. I remember seeing the broken pitcher by the door when we went in." He'd almost picked it up. If he had, perhaps he could have spared Sheren's son the horror of almost burning alive.

"Someone probably left it there intending to put

it in the shed later," Nerrilik said as he approached. "Most of the things in that shed were broken or mismatched, no major loss to the villa."

"It was almost a very big loss," Avera snapped.

Nerrilik inclined his head. "Of course. We can be thankful Cu-Laurian found that weak spot in the wall."

"Seth told me where it was." Without the child's quick thinking, there would be human bones mixed in with the smoldering bones of discarded furniture.

"Kiel, where were you?" the Tragar asked.

The young Blade stepped forward, looking as shaken as Bracca felt. In his hand was a child's toy boat. He held it up. "Seth said he wanted his boat so he could show us how well it floated in the stream. I volunteered to fetch it for him. I'm sorry I was not with the boy as you ordered, my Bloodsworn."

"I doubt there was anything you could have done," the Tragar said.

"I could have stayed by the door. I could have put out the fire before it spread—"

"I could have decided the shed was not worth inspecting in the first place," Bracca pointed out. "Or whoever left the pitcher could have put it inside the shed instead of outside. We could sit here all day discussing what might have happened instead of dealing with what *has* happened."

"He's right, Kiel," the Tragar said, clapping a hand on his Blade's shoulder. "It's no use beating yourself over what-ifs. No lives were lost, that's the important thing."

On that, Bracca slightly disagreed. He wasn't convinced the fire had no help. True, the type of crystal used to make the pitcher refracted light very well, but the sun had been low in the sky, without much strength. Starting a fire in dry grass would have been hard enough. Starting one against a wooden door? Of that, he was far from convinced.

****

Sheren checked to make sure Seth was sleeping soundly before slipping out into the dark courtyard. She needed the comfort of fresh evening air. Despite giving her son a bath and washing his clothes, the smell of smoke lingered in their rooms. Each whiff sent her heart racing with remembered fear, bringing into sharp recall the moment she realized her child was in danger.

She didn't remember running through the orchard. All she saw when she closed her eyes was the building spouting smoke and flames high into the sky. She'd been so terrified she could hardly breathe. Too terrified to even call Seth's name.

And then, he was there, safe—her child wrapped in the protective arms of an Amber Blade Sheren should not have been so relieved to see—a man her thoughts seemed to conjure into reality as she rounded a tall urn of willowy plants.

He stood by the fountain, his head turned in her direction. He didn't seem startled by her arrival. Not surprising, since he was a Blade. He probably heard her the moment she'd stepped into the courtyard. If she had any sense she'd excuse herself immediately and return to her room.

He inclined his head. "Good evening, Lady Sheren. I hope Seth is well."

Apparently her common sense had gone begging tonight. "Good evening, Bracca" she said, advancing until she stopped opposite him at the central fountain. "Yes, thank you. He went to sleep a little while ago, right after telling me for the third time how you kicked down half a stone wall."

His smile was unexpected. "He exaggerates."

"Most children do. I...I want to thank you for saving him. He's all I have." She broke off when the tears threatened as they'd been doing off and on all evening.

Bracca took a step as if to circle the fountain to where she stood. She mirrored the movement. As long as she kept the fountain between them, she should be safe. After a few steps, he stopped. So did she. She thought he smiled again, but couldn't be sure because of the shadows.

"I've yet to ask," she said, "if your room is to your liking."

He inclined his head. "The room is more than acceptable, as is the location. I could not ask for better."

She glanced toward the back corner of the courtyard where the hidden staircase to the second floor began. His room sat opposite the landing. Placing him on the second floor itself had been out of the question, that level being reserved for guests of the villa. Not even in the loosest circles would a Blade be considered a guest. After careful thought, and consideration of his status, she'd deemed the Blade barracks and servant's quarters unsuitable as well. Both were situated too far from his Bloodsworn. The only option left had been the room next to hers.

She turned back to him. A small tremor ran through her at seeing him several steps closer. The man moved as quietly as a shadow.

"It seemed the most suitable location." She tried to put space between them again, but found it impossible. Every time she took a step, so did he. She felt pursued despite their slow, measured pace. And his strides were much longer than hers. By the time she forced herself to stop, only a quarter of the fountain separated them.

He reached behind his back and pulled out something flat and square. He held it up for her inspection. "I found a child's book behind the clothes press. Seth's?"

She started, feeling a flush of embarrassment.

174

She thought she'd checked the room thoroughly. "Yes. He sometimes plays in there." She didn't tell him she'd planned to move Seth into that very room in a month or two. What matter? The smaller storeroom on the other side of hers could be converted to a child's room with a little more effort.

He held out the book. Her heart pounded. Before she could stop herself, she took an involuntary step back. Her heel came down on the edge of an uneven stone, throwing her off balance. She felt herself falling.

Strong hands caught her, fingers closing over the bare skin on her arms.

"Are you all right?"

His concern washed through her shield as if it wasn't there. She gasped and sagged in his arms, her eyes squeezed tightly closed. A touch of fear added itself to the concern, the whole washed with a hint of panic.

"You need a healer—"

"No!" The panic was hers now. "No healers. Just...just give me a moment." There had to be some way to handle this flood, some way to dam the flow, or, at the very least, restrict it.

Breathing hard, she ran through the exercise to put her normal shield back into place, concentrating on making it stronger, denser. It appeared to be working until she became distracted by a new emotion winding sinuously over and around the half-formed shield. Desire.

Potent, all consuming, and definitely not hers.

She snapped her eyes open and caught the longing in Bracca's eyes an instant before he blinked it away.

"You want me," she whispered, aware her voice trembled with wondrous discovery.

"Forgive me," he said, averting his eyes and pulling away from her. Even without his touch his guilt assailed her, the emotion strong, but not enough to overpower that yearning desire. "I never meant to frighten you. I only sought to keep you from injuring yourself. I'll leave—"

She grabbed his retreating hand. Not even with Sayjan had she felt such breathtaking desire. Sayjan had loved her. But her senses had not blossomed under her late husband's touch. Not like this. Compared to what she sensed now, she'd been blind before.

With her shield half up and only Bracca close enough to sense, she found the invading emotions easily bearable. More than bearable. Intoxicating.

"Bracca..." She reached up to touch his face. He stilled instantly. Pressing her hand firmly to his cheek, she said, "I feel you."

He swallowed hard. "How can you even bear to touch me?"

She didn't understand his question. Not bear to touch him because he was a Blade? Or because she'd swore never to get involved with a Blade again? How could he know? Not even Karess knew of her vow. At the moment, she had trouble even remembering why she'd made it.

Slowly he raised his hand and traced the edge of her face with calloused fingers. Wonder and longing swirled through the desire with a poignant sweetness that brought tears to her eyes.

"You are so beautiful," he whispered. Head bending, he leaned closer.

Sheren knew she should stop him. Had to stop him. Yet the emotions pouring into her were like a heady draught of wine. She could no more stop drinking them in than she could stop breathing air. Merciful Luma, she wanted this.

The first touch of his lips went through her body like lightning. Her knees buckled. He caught her, one arm across her lower back, the other between her shoulders, his large hand cradling her head.

Sheren gazed up at him, clutching at his shoulders. Slowly, his gaze locked with hers, he lowered his head again, giving her every chance to turn away. She didn't.

His lips were firm and warm. Insistent. His tongue stroked firmly against her closed mouth, demanding she let him in. She surrendered with a moan. He kissed like a warrior, invading, conquering. Sweet pleasure laced with the bitterness of desperation crashed over her. His? Hers? She could no longer separate her own emotions from those she felt coming from Bracca. Nothing in her life had ever prepared her for this...fusion.

Their bodies shifted closer. He deepened the kiss. Her hands slipped up his strong arms, fingers sliding beneath the edges of his sleeveless tunic. The hard muscles of his shoulders shifted and bunched beneath her touch. So strong, so hot...

"Mama?"

She broke the kiss with a gasp.

"Shhh." Bracca touched a finger to her lips. "He stands at your door and cannot see us."

She nodded, not quite able to speak yet.

The mix of emotions shifted from pleasure to frustration. Regret and sadness flowed in, followed by more guilt.

Bracca dropped his hands and stepped away.

Sheren drew in a shuddering breath as the emotional sea in her head abruptly vanished. Strangely, it felt as if a piece of her went with it.

"Mama, where are you?"

The plaintive note in Seth's childish voice had her hurrying around the fountain. "Here I am, sweetling." She rushed across the courtyard. Bending down, she placed her hands on his small shoulders. "What is it, Seth? Does your tummy hurt?" She rubbed a soothing hand over his little belly. He nodded.

"Tummy's not happy. My head hurts, too." He raised a hand to his forehead. "Right here, mama."

She turned his face to the faint light of a nearby wall lamp. His cheeks looked flushed, yet when she laid her hand to his forehead his skin felt almost icy.

"Ah, sweetling, you're cold. Come, I'll tuck you back in bed." She gathered him into her arms and stood. His soft whimper sent a feeling of unease through her.

"Is he all right?"

She paused in the doorway, debated a moment, then turned to face Bracca. She didn't need the new senses his touch awakened to recognize the true concern on his face.

"I'm sure it's nothing. Just a childish malady. Probably too much excitement combined with an extra dessert I know he swiped from Kiel. He should be fine in the morning."

"Does Villa Porenmagie house a healer?"

"No. If we need a healer, a Silver Blade calls—"

She broke off at his raised hand. His expression hardened as he tilted his head to one side, as if listening for something. Sheren strained her ears, trying to discern what had caught his attention.

Suddenly he motioned her into her room. Leaning close, he whispered, "Lock the door. Do not come out until I return." Before she could ask why, he pulled the door closed.

"Sheren!" The low, urgent whisper through the door prodded her to action. She juggled Seth to her shoulder and reached to flip the lock.

The ringing of swords right outside her door made her jump. There was a shout, followed by more clashing swords and a heavy thud against her door.

Trembling, clutching her son tightly, Sheren backed away.

Luma help them, they were under attack.

Chapter Nineteen

Avera perched on a corner of the low wall of the rooftop garden outside her bedroom. From her cozy spot hidden behind the grouping of potted trees she could see out over the valley below. The dark landscape slept, its shadows gilded by the silvery light from two, half-full moons. She should be asleep, too, but knew it was hopeless. New surroundings, new bed.

She snorted softly. Who was she kidding? She was really waiting for Devlin. He'd had to leave after the fire was out, promising to return as soon as possible. His parting kiss had been filled with the promise of things to come.

Smiling at the expectant tingle in her stomach, Avera faced into the wind, inhaling the scents it brought her; the perfume of flowers, the smell of earth and rock and grass, the sharp scent of wood smoke mixed with the musk of horses. It surprised her how comforting the scents were. How at home they made her feel.

Not that she could ever mistake Avalyr for Earth. If the feel of magic in the air wasn't enough of a reminder, the two moons in the starry sky certainly were. "You're not in California anymore," she whispered into the breeze.

A tingle of awareness crept over the back of her neck, that feeling she was coming to recognize as the feel of magic being used. Specifically, gate-magic.

Feeling a little silly at the rush of anticipation running through her, she turned expectantly. Self-preservation kept her from running toward the gate.

It wouldn't do to let Devlin think she'd been mooning over him. Smiling at her poor pun, she glanced at the twin moons as she stepped to the edge of the trees.

And froze as three men she didn't recognize ghosted into the middle of the garden from the glowing oval. The gate closed silently behind them. Unease replaced anticipation. Then her breath caught as she recognized the glint of moonlight off the steel of two swords and one long, wickedly curved knife.

Not again, her mind screamed.

She slipped back behind thicker foliage, slowly, so as not to draw their attention. Taking a quiet breath that did nothing to calm her, she opened her link to Bracca. His answer came quickly, his tone sharp as he caught the taste of her fear.

What is wrong?

Three men just gated into the garden outside my rooms, and they don't look friendly.

Have they seen you? She got a sense of movement from him.

No, I'm in a corner behind some small trees, but if they search at all they'll find me.

Stay hidden, I am— His words broke off.

Avera got the impression of someone popping up in front of him before his link narrowed, telling her his concentration was elsewhere. The deadly clash of steel erupting into the night confirmed her fear. The three men in her garden were not the only intruders in the villa.

Two of the men slipped silently toward the door to her bedroom while the third began a survey of the rooftop garden. There weren't that many places to hide. Even with her dark colored clothing, he'd spot her in another moment. She had no choice but to run.

Flushed from her hiding place, Avera aimed for

the opposite corner where steps led down to a hidden alcove just off the courtyard.

"Here!" The man behind her shouted. One of the two men who'd gone into her bedroom came to the door, saw her, and darted quickly to cut her off. Skidding to a halt, Avera began backing away from both men. They came at her without a single hesitation.

The man who'd flushed her out of hiding got to her first. She tried dodging around him. The long knife in his hand flashed dangerously close, blocking her. He was fast, much faster than the man who'd attacked her in her apartment back on Earth. This man was thin and wiry, his movements quick and controlled. He handled the knife like a professional. Her only hope was that he probably thought her an easy target. Feyune women avoided violence. He wouldn't expect her to fight back.

Avera feinted, and then dove to the other side, sending out a foot to snap against the man's knee as she rolled. He swore, but she knew the blow was only a minor one.

Bracca! She screamed his name into their link. A sudden hot pain on her arm had her slamming her side of the link closed. Chagrin flooded her. He still had his hands full. If she distracted him again, it might cost him his life. She was going to have to deal with these guys on her own. Damn, what she wouldn't give for a decent pistol.

The first man came at her again before she even got her feet under her. He leaned over her, his knife slashing down toward her chest. She grabbed his wrist in both hands and shoved up, guiding the knife past her head and pulling him off balance. The blade screeched against slate tile. She planted her feet in his stomach, rolled backwards onto her shoulders, and propelled her attacker up and over. She didn't wait to see how he landed.

Scrambling to her feet, she grabbed a pair of potted plants from a small table as the second man ran at her. She threw the pots at his head one after the other. He dodged the first, but the second smashed into his forehead in a spray of dirt and broken pottery. He cursed, blinking dirt from his eyes, and kept coming. Avera dodged as his sword swept down. She upended the small table sending more pots scattering beneath his feet and ran for the other side of the rooftop. They were only one story up. She'd jump if she had to.

A third figure stepped from her bedroom and started running toward her.

Damn it, where was a friendly Blade when she needed one?

Avera changed directions again. The man behind her shouted. "Lady St. John!"

Recognizing the voice, Avera skid to a stop and whipped around. Before she could take even a single step toward Kiel, her first attacker cut her off, yet again. She dropped to the ground and somersaulted, rolling toward him instead of away. Coming out of the flip, she brought the heel of her foot slamming down into the man's groin. She felt a sharp sting on her calf as he doubled over, and she quickly rolled out of his reach.

Kiel grabbed her arm, pulled her up and shoved her toward her rooms. "Go!" he shouted.

She wasted no time obeying him. Behind her, swords met with a furious clash. She heard a grunt of pain and glanced over her shoulder to make sure it hadn't come from Kiel.

A low row of bushes in heavy clay pots waited in ambush. She stumbled over the first pot, tripped over the second, and fell on the third, biting back her own cry of pain when she felt the skin scrape from her knees and palms. Hissing at her stupidity, she sat up, only to find her second attacker coming at her again. Damn, these guys were persistent.

Panting, she leaned back on her elbows, waiting for him to get closer so she could take him down with a scissor kick. She could see the coldness of his eyes in the moonlight, anger twisting his pale face into a grotesque snarl. The sight made her shiver. Then those cold eyes slid up and over her. He stopped suddenly, even took a step back. Daring a glance behind her, Avera decided she didn't blame him.

Devlin stood in the doorway of her bedroom, blue eyes blazing with power. The look of anger on his face made her attacker's seem like mild annoyance in comparison. His open hand shot out then clenched into a fist. Avera heard a scream of pain and a clatter of metal on stone. She looked back at her attacker. His weapon lay at his feet, his body held immobile as if in a huge vice, arms clamped to his sides. Despite the look of pain and terror on his face Avera couldn't find it in herself to feel the least bit sorry for him.

She started to get up, and was suddenly engulfed by a pair of strong arms.

****

"Are you injured?"

Devlin tried to keep his voice calm as he picked Avera up. He didn't want to scare her with the rage seething inside him. How dare Camarie send assassins to attack her in the one place she should feel safe!

Hugging her tightly, he could feel every beat of her heart, its rapid pace no less frantic than his. He drew in a deep breath, nostrils flaring at the strong scent of fresh blood. All pretense at calmness vanished.

A low growl rose in his throat as he narrowed his eyes on the man who'd been chasing Avera. The assassin gasped, then began to squirm and whimper. His cries grew louder, punctuated by gasping pleas for mercy as the magical vice tightened inexorably around him.

Devlin's lips began to curl into a satisfied smile. "Devlin?"

His name, spoken in a husky female whisper, broke through his rage enough for Fate's practical question to register.

"Do you wish to question him, my lord?"

By Blood and Blade, no, he didn't want to question the man. He wanted to continue squeezing the life out of him. He wanted him dead for harming the precious woman in his arms. Painfully, brutally dead.

"I'm okay, Devlin. Just a few scratches."

He glanced down at her, expecting to see terror in her eyes, fear at the very least. Maybe fear of him. But her face, like her voice, was surprisingly calm. She still trembled, and her breathing still came too fast, but she didn't appear to be scared. It helped Devlin pull his anger back further.

Reluctantly, he recalled his magic. The assassin moaned and folded limply to the ground. "Take him," he said. "I will question him myself once I have seen to my Starmate." They would need information and if, as he suspected, the assassins were from Camarie, the Bloodsworn Council would want to question him as well. It didn't matter what they decided. If there was a way, Devlin was going to see that Camarie paid for his attempts on Avera's life in blood.

His arms tightened around her protectively as he carried her into her bedchamber and gently laid her on the bed. "Remove that," he ordered, nodding toward the dead body of one of the assassins lying near the foot of her bed. He activated a light globe and sent it hovering above the bed, then turned his attention back to Avera. "Where are you hurt?"

Her smile wobbled. "I think one of them nicked

my leg with his knife." She pointed to her right calf. His gaze never made it past the blood smeared across her palm. He didn't say anything, just took her hands and held them up to the light. Bad scrapes, not knife wounds as he had feared. Nevertheless, a tremor ran through him. The attack had been well planned. The timing for when he was away, the multiple groups of assassins designed to keep Cu-Laurian and the other warriors from getting to Avera.

He had come very close to losing her this night.

"It's okay, Devlin, they're not bad. I just fell and scraped my hands and knees. I don't think my leg is very bad either."

His jaw clenched. She should be screaming, crying hysterically, or at the very least, trembling from fear. He should be the one comforting her, not the other way around. She came closer than he wanted to think to being killed...again...and there wasn't even a tear in her eye.

Devlin touched her beloved face, tracing the curve of her cheek. She was so precious to him. He reached for her leg where blood stained the dark material of her flowing trousers even darker. He would see to her palms and knees in a moment. The fact she was hurt at all was unforgivable, but a knife wound could be serious.

He gently pushed the material up, revealing the injury. After examining the blood smeared area, Devlin breathed a little easier. Bloody, yes, but shallow. A deeper injury would have required the direction of magic into her body through a link or bond. Trained healers, those born with the gift of healing, could forge such links temporarily. Being a mere Bloodsworn, Devlin could only use magic to heal his Blades or the surface wounds of individuals he had no blood-link to.

He cupped a hand over the wound and called

forth the magical essence within himself, sending it through his hand even as his will directed what it was to do. Her leg jerked slightly at the brush of magic. His other hand tightened on her ankle, holding her still. When he was done with the cut, he moved to her knee, then did the same for her other knee. When he was through, he took her injured hands in his.

"They don't really hurt that much." Despite her brave words her voice wavered.

"Do they not?" He gently clasped his hands over her palms. He'd closed his eyes when he'd healed the injuries to her legs, but this time he kept his eyes open, locked with hers. Magic pulsed inside him, already primed and ready from his previous use of it. He let it flow to his hands and from them, into hers. He did it slowly, so she could feel what he was doing, so he could watch her eyes as his magic flowed into her skin. It wasn't a deep healing, but there was no denying what he was doing felt intimate, sensual. It soothed him and aroused him at the same time. Aroused him more as an answering heat kindled in her eyes.

When he was finished, he let one of her hands go, but retained the other. "Fate?"

"We count twelve assassins in all. Eleven are dead. Karess and the others are searching the grounds to make sure there are no more."

Devlin nodded grimly. *Good. Once the villa is secure, I will do what I should have done in the first place.* Self-disgust rose like bile in his throat. It was his fault this had happened. He'd known Camarie would try again to kill Avera. Until their formal union on the solstice, her death, or his, could still thwart the Seventh Prophecy. He should have thought to place a gate barrier around the villa. He'd been a fool, allowing himself to get distracted. First by Avera, then the fire, and then the messenger from the Concourse. He hadn't thought past leaving a physical guard. A nearly fatal mistake he couldn't afford to make again. "Where are the injured?"

"Thern and Carrik are in the courtyard. Their injuries are minor. We left Kiel outside." *Two of the villa's serving men were killed and another mortally injured. He will be dead before a healer can be summoned.* He slipped the report of the fatalities into Devlin's mind, unwilling, as Devlin read him, to upset his Bloodsworn's lady further. Devlin thanked him.

Avera sat up, her face showing her distress. "Kiel's hurt?" Her eyes suddenly went wide, one hand slapping against her other arm. "Bracca!" Her eyes lost focus, flickered, then she jerked free from Devlin and rolled off the bed on the other side. He caught her at the door to her sitting room.

"Where do you think you are going?"

"Let go! Bracca's hurt, I have to find him. He's out there roaming the gardens in the dark and refuses to come in."

"Then his injuries are nothing to worry about. He is a warrior, not a child, Avera. Let him do his job. You would only put yourself in more danger."

She glared at him, but stopped struggling. Her eyes lost focus once more. Her face scrunched up into a grimace. "Apparently he agrees with you." She took a deep breath and blew it out noisily. "How badly is Kiel hurt?"

Devlin went to query his Blade, and frowned when he couldn't find their link right away. When he did, and finally got Kiel to respond, he understood why the link seemed so elusive. Kiel was extremely upset with himself, his mind turned inward in disgust. Devlin shook his head at the depth of the young Blade's shame at being laid low. In truth, it rivaled his own, though his was for a different reason.

He had been the one to suggest Avera stay at the villa instead of his palace. He had failed her by leaving her vulnerable. Any shame, any reprisals, should fall on his head, not on a warrior who had risked his life and taken injury to keep her safe.

"Kiel took a sword through his shoulder." A sword that would have taken her life if not for the young warrior's swift actions. Her eyes widened in distress at his words. He rushed to reassure her. "He will be fine. Believe me, *me`surrasie*, he is more angry than hurt at the moment. The assassin got in a lucky strike which seems to have pricked his pride worse than his flesh."

She shoved at his chest. "What are you waiting for? Go heal him." She jerked her hands back, making a sound of disgust. Her palms were still covered in dried blood. Devlin took her chin and forced her to look up at him.

"I want you to stay here in your rooms, Avera."

"Yeah, you and Bracca both," she said in a petulant voice that had his lips wanting to smile. "Go on, don't worry about me. I need to get cleaned up anyway."

When she turned toward the door to the bathing room, Devlin caught her, pulled her back to him. He kissed her, his lips hard and demanding against hers. He didn't care how many others were in the room, he needed this, the sweetness of her lips, the heat of her body. He very much wanted to stay with her, comfort them both with an hour or more of touching, holding, tasting. Gods, he wanted to devour her.

But he couldn't. He needed to tend to his men. Nor would he be able to return later. When he broke the kiss and stepped back, he was pleased to see her eyes heavy with longing. Then she blinked and asked in a dazed voice. "What was that for?"

"A promise for tomorrow. I cannot return to you

tonight. I must see to my men."

"Oh," she said. "I guess it—" She broke off and frowned. "Wait a minute. If you're going to do a deep-healing, that means—"

She broke off a second time and pulled his head down until their breaths mingled. Her voice came out a fierce whisper. "I strongly suggest you come back here when you're done. The *shetha*s may be part of your culture, but I'll tell you the same thing you told me yesterday. I. Don't. Share."

Her possessive words had him instantly hard and sent his heart soaring. He grinned and touched her face lightly.

"I thank you for the warning, *me`surrasie*, and for your generous offer. But such a thing, I fear, would not be wise."

"Devlin."

He pulled her close and whispered in her ear. "I already want you so much I cannot imagine a deep-healing lust making that much difference. If I returned, it would be impossible for me not to spend the rest of the night savoring your body. As much as I want that, there are things I must do to see to your safety." He smoothed the worried lines from her forehead with his lips. "Be at ease, Avera. I assure you I have survived many such nights alone. I will survive this one as well."

He brushed his thumb once over her full lips, enjoying the catch in her breath, then forced himself to step away, turn, and leave without looking back. If he looked back and saw her standing in the middle of the room, alone, vulnerable, he wasn't sure he could leave her. And he had much to do.

Working the magic needed to form a gate barrier large enough and strong enough to protect the entire villa would take time as well as a vast amount of magic and physical energy. Lucky for him, deep-healing lust could easily be tapped for just such energy.

He would be exhausted afterward, and wished heartily that he might spend the coming day wrapped in the arms of his lovely mate. But no, the rest of her things were to be delivered at dawn. He would leave her to settle herself into her new home, and go to her at day's end. The knowledge she would welcome him with more than open arms sent a pleasurable rush of anticipation through him.

One thing at a time, he counseled, though his already stiff member proved his patience was still in short supply where Avera was concerned.

He knelt at Kiel's side. The young warrior's eyes opened, found him. His expression twisted in pain as he shifted. "Lady St. John..."

Devlin pressed a hand to Kiel's good shoulder. "Peace, my Blade, she is well. Your duty to my lady is done for the night. You have my eternal gratitude, Kiel. A hefty burden even for someone with two good shoulders. Lie still now, and we will see to your injury before more blood is lost."

He waited until Kiel closed his eyes and relaxed before closing his own. Deep inside his mind the magic stirred, eager to do his bidding.

Chapter Twenty

Despite a less than peaceful night, Avera rose early the next morning. The first thing she did was reach for her link with Bracca. She was getting better at sensing him—or rather his sword—even with their link closed. He was close. Her sitting room probably, and she opened the link with a sigh. His side was already open, and his mind greeted hers immediately. When he spoke, his mental voice sounded tired.

Good morning, my Bloodsworn. Did you sleep well?

Better than you, I imagine. You stayed awake all night again, didn't you? He didn't answer her, but sent her an unrepentant image of himself standing guard outside her door. *Go to bed, Bracca*, she told him firmly.

As soon as you are dressed and in the company of two Silver Blades, I will gladly obey.

Only two?

Since one of the two is not Kiel Na-Turesh, yes.

His answer startled her. *Did you just compliment a Silver Blade?*

He protected you when I could not reach you. She winced at the level of self-loathing in those words. Bracca had been on his way to her when he was ambushed by another group of assassins. By the time he'd finished them off, she would have been dead if not for Kiel. To say her Blade felt indebted to the young Silver Blade would have been putting it mildly.

Kiel has earned both my gratitude and respect.

He told her plainly. *We may not like each other, but I would not hesitate to trust him with your life.*

So until Kiel gets back, I'm stuck with two babysitters?

Unless you would like more, he teased. *The Tragar was most vocal on how you are to be guarded, and for once, I find myself in agreement with him.*

You barbarians always stick together, don't you? she grumbled. She didn't waste time arguing, though, but rose, washed, and dressed in a lovely split skirt and soft blouse that she knew had come from Devlin. He'd presented her with a similar outfit yesterday after the fire. A compromise, he'd suggested, between her jeans and what was considered proper attire for a princess. Lucky for him, she liked the feel of the soft material flowing around her legs.

Bracca was waiting for her when she opened her bedroom door, eyes sweeping over her as if to make sure she was all right. She obliged him by holding her hands out and turning in a circle.

"I'm fine, Bracca, all in one piece as you can see." She looked over at the other two men in the room. She recognized one of them and gave him a welcoming smile. "Good morning, Sarreth."

He sketched a bow. "My lady."

She looked to the other Silver Blade. He bowed as well. "I am Strum, my lady, Third Blade to his grace, the Tragar. A pleasure to serve you."

"Do all Blades have numbers?" she wondered aloud.

Strum's smile lit his dark brown eyes. He was a bear of a man with dark, reddish-brown hair. Easily as big as Sarreth though older, she guessed, but not by much. He had a pleasant smile. "Only those fortunate enough to hold rank in an Inner or Outer decca may claim such an honor. Counted positions are coveted and considered high status, though not being part of the twenty is not necessarily a measure of a Blade's skills. Not all men stricken by the blade-illness are meant to be warriors."

"I suppose that would stand to reason. So, if you two are my guards for the morning that means you..." she pointed at Bracca, "are relieved of duty as of now. Go to bed!" She glowered and pointed to the door.

He raised a brow at her, but bowed. "As my lady Bloodsworn commands, I obey."

"Only when it suits you." She smiled, watching him walk across the room and out the door.

Turning back to Sarreth and Strum, she was quiet a moment, thinking. The bright morning beckoned her outside. She was anxious to discover what kind of secrets the surrounding gardens held. The problem was whether or not it would be safe for her to wander the grounds, even accompanied by two warriors. She didn't want to run into any more assassins, but her nature rebelled at asking for permission. That was one reason she hadn't mentioned her plans to Bracca.

Better safe than sorry, she finally decided. "Do either of you see any problem with me exploring the villa's gardens this morning?" Worded that way, it sounded as if she was asking advice, not permission.

"If your concern is that more assassins might attack, you need not worry. The Tragar has taken steps to make sure that will not happen again."

She was going to ask what kind of steps, but her maid chose that moment to show up. The young girl, whose name she'd finally learned was Nori, was beside herself to find Avera had bathed and dressed without her assistance. She wrung her hands and looked as if she might break into tears any moment. Avera had to spend several minutes assuring her that her new mistress was more than used to looking after herself. By the time she had the girl calmed down Avera's empty stomach had made itself known, and she went in search of food.

After a quick breakfast, she steered a course toward the villa's front doors, pointedly ignoring her two shadows. The tug on her link with Bracca the moment her foot touched the garden path drew her exasperated sigh. It was a good thing she wasn't trying to slip away. An impossible task when one had an overprotective Blade sensing one's every move.

You're supposed to be sleeping, she reminded him pointedly. *I'm just taking a walk in the gardens. Strum and Sarreth are with me.*

You will leave our link open so I will know if you have need of me.

Exasperation moved toward irritation. *I don't need you to hover over me all the time, Bracca. I've taken care of myself for too long to give control over to someone else. You can leave your side open if you want, but I'm closing mine. I'll open it and call you if I need you. Now get some sleep and just let me roam a bit, will you.*

She let him feel her need for privacy, for a measure of the independence she was used to. In return, she felt the rumble of his discontent, but at least he didn't seem to be on the verge of charging after her. Closing her link, she congratulated herself on winning a small skirmish in her war for independence before beginning her exploration, guards in tow.

The gardens surrounding Villa Porenmagie were magnificent. Color was everywhere, including every shade of green imaginable. The various sections of garden were like a kaleidoscope of shapes, colors, and textures. Even the type and color of the pathway changed as it meandered from one section of garden into another. Gravel turned to field stone, which merged into slate, then cobbles, before the path devolved back to spongy grass.

Wandering through the half-wild gardens, Avera felt Bracca's sleepy touch several times as the morning progressed. After the first couple of times she became resigned, and made a point of answering each touch quickly. She didn't want him to get worried and track her down. Besides not getting the rest he needed, he would definitely insist on a much closer surveillance than Strum and Sarreth were providing. Though she knew the two Silver Blades were nearby, they did a very good job of staying out of her sight, which let her at least enjoy the semblance of being alone.

Walking by herself, she was surprised she didn't feel more nervous considering the recent attack. She thought about it as she enjoyed the morning and finally put her ease down to the fact she knew without a doubt that if it wasn't safe, she would have been confined to the villa. Neither Devlin nor Bracca would take chances with her life. Still, it felt a bit strange. Not once did she feel scared or threatened. Instead, she felt safe, at peace, but at the same time, excited. It confused her for a while until she felt a strong wave of magic roll over her, making her skin tingle.

Ah, the magic. Her sense of peace had to be a side effect of the magic. And the excitement, too. What else could it be?

After that first strong wave, Avera found that by concentrating she could feel other, more gentler waves, rolling lazily through the air. It became a game, trying to sense the waves before they reached her and turning into them so that they splashed against her face. She momentarily lost interest in the gardens in her quest to find the next wave, stopping suddenly, closing her eyes and turning in place, seeking the growing sensation of magic, before running to catch it. She laughed as it washed over her, then turning, moved with it, riding the power of it for several yards before it faded out or a garden wall stopped her. It took almost bumping into Sarreth to make her realize how strange her behavior probably seemed. Avera felt her cheeks flush as she took in the strange look on his face. He looked a bit flushed too, and she figured she'd led him and Strum a merry chase with all her running around. He cleared his throat, but his voice still came out a little huskier than she remembered.

"Are you well, my lady?"

"Yes, of course. I'm sorry, but the waves of magic are so strong here, and I've never felt anything like it before. It's a bit addicting, I'm afraid."

Longing filled his eyes. "You truly feel Avalyr's magic? Here?"

"Yes. Devlin told me that's why the villa was built here, because several different waves seem to converge on this spot."

"What does it feel like?"

His question made her pause and really think about it. "Like sparkling cool water splashing against hot skin." She ran a hand up her bare arm, conscious of his eyes following. "It makes you shiver, but it's a good shiver, and you can't wait to feel it again." She shrugged, suddenly a bit embarrassed. "Like I said, addicting."

"My lady?"

She and Sarreth started as Strum stepped out from behind a hedge. "Did you wish to return to the villa?"

"What? No, Strum, not yet, thank you. Just taking a break."

He inclined his head, gave Sarreth a hard look, and waited until the other man left the small garden area before disappearing once more behind the hedge, leaving Avera alone.

She let out a breath. Turning down a narrow

walkway, she tried to ignore the potent call of the magic waves. She didn't need to get pulled into acting like a child again.

Concentrating on the beautiful plants around her, it was a while before she realized she no longer wandered the gardens idly. Something had caught the attention of her mind, if not her awareness. She'd been taking paths leading back in the direction of the villa without realizing it.

She didn't think it had anything to do with the waves of magic. For one thing, this call felt different. For another, it was static, unmoving. Whatever it was, *she* was being summoned to *it*.

Avera stopped abruptly. Summoned. That had an ominous ring to it. Maybe it wasn't such a good idea to answer a summons on a world of magic. No telling what, or who, she might find waiting for her.

Then something moved inside her. The sensation of a fist closing and tugging felt both strange and familiar, and made her want to stomp her foot. *Crap, crap, crap!*

She glanced down at her body, turning her arms over, looking for signs of blood. How could this happen? She hadn't cut herself on anything. In fact, she made it a point to stay away from sharp, pointy things like knives, daggers, and swords. How could she have triggered her Bloodsworn magic?

A tug from Bracca's link jarred her from her shock. She ignored his query and forced herself back into motion before Sarreth and Strum became concerned. Walking slowly, she turned over her options.

Option one: ignore the pull.

She wrinkled her nose in distaste. Even if it were physically possible, ignoring a sick man when she had the means to help him just because she might get in trouble with the almighty Bloodsworn Council seemed cowardly. So, scratch option one.

Option two: call Devlin.

She snorted softly. Oh, yeah, that would work. He'd no doubt gate the unfortunate man away quicker than she could say Bloodsworn. Would he tell her if the man was able to link with another Bloodsworn or not? Of course he wouldn't. He'd want to spare her the guilt if the man died.

That left option three.

On the surface, the choice was not as easy as it appeared. She and Devlin were only now beginning to work things out between them. If she did this—took on the responsibility of another Blade in defiance of the Bloodsworn Council's edict—the consequences might very well destroy their relationship. Her future happiness weighed in the balance against an innocent man's life. What kind of choice was that?

No, option three wasn't a choice at all. It was a necessity.

Her mind set, she followed the lure to a large garden area surrounded by tall, lush hedges. The ground was carpeted in short, thick grass and shaded by several trees. The place seemed empty at first. Then she heard soft humming.

She walked forward a few more steps. When she saw Sheren seated on a long wicker bench, holding her son, Seth, Avera stopped and checked her inner compass. Yes, this was the place. So where was the blade-sick man?

"My lady?" Noticing her, Sheren shifted Seth in her arms, and started to stand. Avera waved at her to remain seated.

"Good morning, Sheren." She caught a glimpse of Seth's face as his head turned restlessly on his mother's shoulder. Eyes closed, his childish features were scrunched into a frown of pain. A shiver ran through his small body.

Avera suddenly felt sick to her stomach.

"He's not any better?" She'd asked Bracca to check on Sheren and Seth last night after the attack. He'd told her they were both safe, but that Seth wasn't feeling well.

Sheren shook her head slightly. "He should really be in bed, but he begged me to bring him to the garden. I thought the fresh air and sunshine might help." She rubbed her cheek against his hair. Her voice dropped to a whisper. "He is worse this morning. He complains of hunger, but can't keep anything down. I...do you know when the Tragar will return?"

"Probably not until tonight."

"Then may I borrow a carriage?"

"Of course. Mind if I ask where you want to go?"

"I think Seth should see the healers at the palace. He's rarely sick, you see, and I've tried all the usual remedies."

Avera sat beside her, never taking her eyes off Seth. She struggled to keep her growing concern from showing. This was not good. According to Devlin, children were immune to the blade-sickness. Yet, not only could she feel that same pulling sensation from when she'd first seen Tyr, she could feel little Seth's pain.

She raised a hand, needing to touch him. As soon as her fingers brushed his limp brown curls, it was as if she'd completed a live circuit. Seth jerked in his mother's arms and began whimpering. He pushed against her weakly. Sheren tried to hold him, sooth him, but with a cry he twisted free and dived toward Avera.

She caught him. As soon as she dragged him into her arms he wrapped himself around her with all his childish strength. Sheren stared at them with wide, worried eyes. She reached to pluck him back.

"I'm sorry, I don't understand why he would do such a thing." Tears swam in her eyes.

Avera captured one of Sheren's fluttering hands and squeezed gently. "Easy, it's all right. I won't hurt him, I promise." She turned her attention to the whimpering child in her arms. "Hush, baby, it's okay. Hush now." Seth took a shuddering breath. His small body suddenly relaxed, going very still and quiet.

The sharp tug on her link with Bracca demanded an immediate answer. Avera sighed quietly. The last thing she wanted was to involve him in her law-breaking. Unfortunately, she didn't think she had a choice here, either.

She opened her side of their link. *If you're not already on your way, I need you to find me.*

What's wrong? Are you in danger? His anxiety swelled into the link.

No, I'm not in any danger. I just...there's a problem.

What kind of problem? Why do I sense fear? Where are Strum and Sarreth?

She winced a little at the strength of his anger. *They're nearby. I'll explain about the fear when you get here. Can you find me, or do I need to send Sarreth to you?*

She heard him swear. *I do not need a Silver Blade to lead me to my own Bloodsworn. Stay where you are, I will be there in a moment.*

The child stirred in her arms. She rubbed his back, comforting both him and herself. She could probably count on one hand the times she'd held a child. Just like the other times, this one was a daunting experience. Unlike the other times, she couldn't just give him back to his mother and walk away. "It's all right, Seth," she murmured. "It's going to be all right." *Please, God, let me not be lying.*

****

Bracca sprinted into a large garden enclosed by tall hedges. He could feel Avera very near now, and slowed to a fast walk, every sense alert. He caught sight of her and Sheren just as Strum and Sarreth entered the garden from the opposite side. No doubt they'd heard him running. One look at his face and the naked sword in his hand, and they drew their own weapons.

"Wait," he said, holding up a hand to keep them from alerting their Bloodsworn. He approached the two women. Both looked worried, but unharmed. Seth appeared to be asleep in Avera's arms. He scanned the area in search of whatever might be causing the fear and unease coming from his Bloodsworn, but found nothing.

"What is it? What's wrong?" Strum asked gruffly.

"Nothing's wrong," Avera said. She met Bracca's gaze before glancing first at Sheren, then at the Silver Blades. *Put your sword away and send Sarreth and Strum back to the villa. I think the fewer people around when we do this, the better.*

Do what? He moved toward the two warriors. "You can return to the villa. Everything is fine. I'll remain to guard my Bloodsworn."

Both men hesitated. He saw Strum look pointedly at his amber sword. Bracca sheathed his weapon. "A misunderstanding," he assured them. "Lady St. John is still new to her links." He lowered his voice. "She is upset with herself for over-reacting. I ask that you not cause her further discomfort by lingering."

"Of course," Sarreth said.

Strum nodded, but from the look in his eyes, Bracca knew the warrior didn't believe him.

Here's a question for you, Avera sent to him as the Tragar's warriors left the garden. *Has any Bloodsworn ever blood-linked with a child?*

Her question had him whipping around. His gaze shot to Seth before locking with hers. *That is not possible. Children do not get blade-sick.*

Let's say one did. Would a blood-link work? Can a Bloodsworn provide the magic essence to a child?

Bracca frowned. Why was she pursuing this? *I see no reason why a link would not work once formed. But as I said, children do not get the blade-illness.*

Tell that to Seth.

He looked sharply at the child in her arms. The boy was ill, true, but blade-sick? It could not, *should not*, be possible. *Are you sure?*

Avera nodded slightly. *Don't ask me how or why, but I get the same feeling from him that I got from Tyr. Seth's mind is starving for magic.*

He approached them, his gaze going to Sheren. She sat very close to Avera, one hand on her son, her face a mixture of worry and fear. A sick feeling started in his stomach. *Does Sheren know?*

Not yet. I wanted you to be here when I told her. This isn't going to be easy for her to hear. She shifted Seth in her arms and held a hand out to Sheren.

"Sheren," she said, "I think I know what's wrong with Seth."

"You do? Is it something you've seen before? Can the healers help him?" The hope in her eyes tore at Bracca. He knelt in front of her, taking her other hand. She shuddered once, but didn't pull away.

"Don't worry," Avera said, her voice confident. "It won't be necessary to take him to the healers. You see, I've encountered this type of sickness before. Twice before, actually. Once when I linked with Bracca...and again when I linked with Tyr."

Sheren's hopeful expression changed to puzzlement. "I don't understand."

Bracca squeezed her hand. "I'm sorry, Sheren," he said. "There is nothing a healer can do for Seth because he is blade-sick."

Her eyes grew round. She snatched her hand

from his grasp and Avera's as well. "No. No, you're wrong. You have to be wrong. Children do not get blade-sick. Only men. Give me my son." She reached for Seth.

Bracca caught both her hands this time. She struggled. "Sheren, stop. Listen to me. Why would we lie about this? What reason could we possibly have to deceive you?"

"I don't know," she cried, tears spilling over. "But you have to be lying. He's only a child, Bracca. A baby!"

Feeling her pain as if it were his own, he cupped her face in his hands, willing her to listen. "You said last night that you can sense what I'm feeling." He ignored the sharp look from Avera. "Can you feel me now, Sheren? Can you sense any deceit in me at all?"

There was a long, frightened pause while he kept wild, lavender eyes locked with his. Then her eyes fluttered closed, her body wilting like a delicate flower in the sun. She drew in a deep, shuddering breath. "No. You're telling the truth."

Her pain ripped at him. All of his senses seemed attuned to this woman, plucked to a level of awareness he'd only felt once before—when the link between him and Avera was forged. He didn't want to stop and think what that might mean. Not now. Not when Sheren's world was crumbling all around her.

"I'm so sorry, Sheren," Avera said softly. "I know this is difficult for you to accept. Please, all I want to do is help."

Sheren's shoulders shook.

Bracca leaned forward and slowly drew her into his arms. She buried her face in his neck, her hot tears scalding his skin. After a few moments, she took a deep breath and raised her head. He could almost feel her sorrow shift to determination as she wiped the tears from her eyes. Her son was ill, and she would be strong for him. Admiration for her swelled in his heart.

Bracca had to force himself to release her as she sat back. Her shoulders squared. She reached over and laid a hand on her small son's back. "How long will it take the Tragar to arrive? I don't want Seth to suffer any longer than necessary."

Avera shook her head. "We don't need to call him. I was drawn to Seth, Sheren, just as I was drawn to Tyr. Forming a link with him is something I think I'm supposed to do."

Bracca frowned. He was concerned for Seth, wanted the child safe and well. But he was bound by his Blade oath to put his Bloodsworn's safety above all others. If Avera took Seth as her Blade, she would no longer be safe. "What about the edict?"

Not now.

"What edict," Sheren asked.

Bracca held Avera's gaze until she grimaced. "The Bloodsworn Council," she said finally, "has ordered me not to link with anymore blade-sick men. *Men*," she stressed. "Technically, I'm not going against that order. Seth isn't a man. Besides," she shrugged one shoulder. "I never agreed to anything.

"That said, there is also a chance, however slim, that if the link is successful and the Bloodsworn Council finds out about it, they might order all my links sundered." She turned to him, worry and indecision taking over their link. "What do you think, Bracca? Should I do this?" *You need to speak for Tyr, too. I hate putting you both at risk, but—*

Yes, my Lady Bloodsworn, he told her, nodding for Sheren's benefit. *If they dare censor you for saving the life of a child, I shall stand proudly at your side so we both may spit in the Council's collective eye.*

Her green eyes suddenly misted with tears as he felt her love flow to him through their link along with a whispered, *Thank you.*

He took Sheren's hand again, noticing that she didn't shudder this time. "If you agree, Sheren, Avera will attempt a blood-link with Seth. I promise you, she will do everything possible to help him, and so will I."

"If I can't link with him," Avera added, "then Bracca and I will go with you to see if Devlin can."

Sheren nodded once, but said, "How can he be a Blade? He cannot even protect himself."

"But I can protect him," Avera said.

"And I," Bracca said. "I'll not let him come to harm because of this, Sheren. I swear it." He wanted to take her back into his arms so badly he could barely restrain himself. Seeing the pain in her eyes was more than he could bear. Then she did something that caused him to think the world had come to an end. She pressed her soft hand against his cheek. Her eyes filled with more tears, each drop shredding his insides like a sharp claw.

"I know you will watch over him." A smile trembled across her lips, vanishing as she turned to Avera. "Very well. You have my permission to form a blood-link with my son."

Chapter Twenty-One

Avera felt her heart rate double as she looked at Bracca. She really was going to do this again. "What do we use?"

After a moment's hesitation, he drew a dagger from a sheath inside his boot and held it out to her. She shifted Seth until he sat sideways in her lap before taking the dagger. The boy raised his head just enough to look at her. Gazing into his hungry eyes, she cupped his small cheek.

"I'm going to try to help you, Seth. Do you understand?" She hoped he did. Hoped and prayed she was doing the right thing, that she wasn't about to make things worse. She didn't feel up to becoming a child's nightmare today.

She took the dagger and drew it quickly across her forearm. Scar number what? twenty-two, twenty-three? Could she really have lost count?

Ignoring the sting, she let the blade rest in the wound, hoping she was wrong. Hoping that what she felt was just her imagination. But it didn't take long for her to feel the now familiar drawing sensation deep inside. The magic in her mind pulsed in response. Powerful, so very powerful. Nodding, she met Bracca's gaze to let him know she felt the magic stir. A new chapter of the blade-illness was about to be written.

The dagger flared to life, glowing with a gold-tinted light. Sheren gasped. Avera took Seth's hand in hers, pausing to explain the next step to his mother. She didn't want the other woman to freak out when she drew Seth's blood.

Before she could even open her mouth, Seth reached out and grasped the double-edged blade with his hand. Sheren cried out this time, lurching forward just as Avera pried his small hand from the sharp steel. Bracca held Sheren back, and all three of them stared as lines of bright red blood appeared on Seth's palm and across his little fingers. A sob broke from Sheren. Bracca hauled her completely out of the seat and onto his lap, murmuring words of comfort.

Swallowing back the tightness in her throat at the sight of the blood, Avera placed Seth's hand on the dagger's hilt. Magic tagged her in a hot, giddy rush as soon as she closed his fingers into a fist. Fire raced through her body accompanied by blinding amber-colored lightning. She felt Seth stiffen in her arms. She wanted to let him know it was okay, but couldn't get her tongue to work. Speech, hearing, sight, all her normal senses were gone. Touch faded, too, as the intense conflagration centered with surprising swiftness on their joined hands. All that was left was her sense of smell.

She drew in a deep breath and almost choked on the strong scent of cloves. The sharp odor seeped into her very pores, dragging up memories of her own before the images of Seth's brief life wiped out everything else in her mind. Hardly daring to breath, she waited for the accompanying pain, heartsick for the child she held. Babies shouldn't have to suffer.

Scenes flashed past her mind's eye like bits and pieces from an old silent film. No pain or discomfort accompanied the flickering images. All she felt was breathless wonder and a child-like curiosity.

Maybe it was because she'd been bringing Bracca and Tyr back from the edge of death, or maybe it was because Seth was a total innocent, used to trusting blindly. Whatever the reason, she was thankful for the brief, intense spurts of emotion. She'd take that over pain any day.

The rush faded quickly, the whirlwind of Seth's emotions swirling and fleeing like dry leaves before a storm. The scent of cloves lingered. When the last echo of emotions had faded, she opened her eyes. Fresh wonder filled her. Clasped in their joined hands was a short but graceful, amber-colored dagger.

A dagger bathed in flickering fire.

It was apparent right away that Seth, like her, felt no pain or heat from the flames spilling over the dagger's guard onto their hands. In fact, the boy's face was a picture of pure delight. Reaching out his other hand before she could think to stop him, he ran one small finger through the flames, touching the warm metal.

"It tickles," Seth said, his childish laughter bubbling into the garden.

Avera shivered, not sure if the reaction came from that light touch on the blade or from the excitement and pure acceptance she felt coming from him. He wasn't afraid at all.

She felt the draw of magic through their link increase and let the essence flow. Seth giggled again and looked at her.

"That tickles, too."

"What tickles, sweetling?" Sheren whispered kneeling in front of them.

Seth looked at her and tapped his head. "Lady Avera is tickling me inside my head. It feels funny."

Startled, Avera and Sheren looked at each other then turned to Bracca. Smiling slightly, he shrugged.

"The sensation is different depending on how hungry I am. I cannot, however, recall a single instance when it *tickled*."

Avera felt Seth tug at her fingers still clasped

around his hand. "I want to hold it by myself."

Wary, she released her grip. Seth immediately held the dagger up and swished it through the air, drawing lines of amber flame. Gasping, she grabbed his arm lightly and looked at Bracca. "This might be a problem."

He arched a brow and gave her a look that asked, "You think so?" Then he squatted down next to Sheren. He reached toward the burning dagger. Sheren's hand shot out in alarm, wrapping around his wrist. From the look on her face, Avera wasn't sure who the woman was more worried for, her son, or Bracca. As the widow of a Blade, she had to know what happened when a Blade's sword was touched by someone else. But like Avera, she had no clue what the amber fire would do to Bracca.

"Trust me," he said, his eyes never leaving Sheren. *Trust me,* he said to Avera through their link.

Easier for me to do than her, she reminded him.

"It's okay, Sheren," she said. "Bracca would never do anything to hurt Seth."

Slowly, as if it was the last thing in the world she wanted to do, Sheren released Bracca's wrist. He reached for the dagger again, letting his palm hover near the happily burning flames a moment before closing his hand over Seth's small one on the hilt. The fire snuffed out.

Seth pouted.

"Peace, little brother," Bracca said, his tone solemn while a chuckle echoed in her head. "I will show you how to use your blade and teach you the proper time to release its fire."

Sheren moved onto the seat next to them. She looked dazed. "I cannot believe this is happening." Her voice hitched.

Seth scrambled out of Avera's lap and into his mother's. To her credit, Sheren neither cringed back nor pushed him away in fear, despite the naked dagger he clung to. Instead, she gathered her son in a fierce hug.

"It will be all right now, sweetling."

"I'm a Blade like papa now, aren't I mama."

Panic flashed into Sheren's eyes before she squeezed them shut.

"Not yet, Seth" Avera said quickly, patting the child on the back. "You have a lot of growing to do before you can fill your papa's shoes."

"But I'm you're Blade now, right?"

"Yes, but you can't tell anyone."

His forehead wrinkled. "Why not?"

"Because you're special. You're the only little boy Blade in the world, and we want to keep you a secret until just the right time." Whenever the hell that was. Right now, she had no clue. But she couldn't keep this from Devlin for long. Nor did she want to. She just needed some time to figure out a plan to counter the Bloodsworn Council's precious edict. Something that wouldn't cost her Blades their lives and separate her from the man she loved. If they sent her back to Earth without Devlin, she might as well be dead.

"You don't have to worry," Sheren said. "Seth is the best secret-keeper in the realm."

Seth bobbed his head up and down, gray eyes earnest. Avera smiled. Her link to Seth was wide open, and the love he had for his mother spilled back through it, bringing tears to her eyes. She narrowed their connection ever so gently, but didn't close it completely. His mind still craved the essence.

She looked at her First Blade. "I didn't think this through too well, did I?"

One side of his mouth kicked up, and he inclined his head. "That is part of your charm, my Lady Bloodsworn. Something I, for one, am very grateful for. Were you any different, I would not be here."

"True," she agreed with an answering grin.

Seth held his dagger up and was busy pointing out every detail of it to his mother while she made suitable replies. Avera couldn't help but note that Sheren didn't attempt to touch her child's new *toy*.

Avera rubbed her forehead. There were many things they would have to work out. Some aspects would require a little judicious experimentation. Well, most aspects, she amended. She was honest enough to admit she was probably breaking new ground here along with a fair number of rules. She didn't think it was every day a five-year-old Blade was born.

Seth finally climbed out of his mother's lap. He stood before Bracca with a serious face. "Mama says I have to keep my sword in a sheath. I don't have a sheath. Can you help me make one?"

"Of course. I would be honored to help you," Bracca said, equally serious.

Avera smiled at the sight of her big, bad Blade crouching down next to the little boy. When she turned to Sheren, she was surprised to see a single tear trailing down her cheek. The woman wiped the tear away quickly and smiled, her lips trembling.

"Thank you, Bloodsworn, thank you for the gift of my son's life."

Her gratitude made Avera very uncomfortable. She reached over and patted Sheren's hand. "I don't deserve your thanks. From what I understand it's a Bloodsworn's duty to provide for those who become blade-sick. As I see it, I'm just doing what I'm supposed to be doing."

"Not every Bloodsworn sees their duty as you do. Nor would they risk their power for the sake of a child they have no ties to."

"I would have done it regardless, but I think you're wrong about the no ties part." She slanted her gaze at Bracca before looking back at Sheren. The other woman blushed and ducked her head.

"Perhaps," she said shyly. "I have learned lately that many old habits can be broken with a little effort."

Together they watched Bracca pull his sword from its sheath to compare it with Seth's dagger. The rune-inscribed curved blades of both weapons gave off a subtle amber glow.

"Can I touch your sword now?" Seth asked in his little boy voice, his hand already reaching.

"Yes," said Bracca at the same time as Seth's small fingers slid along the smooth, amber metal.

Avera braced herself, expecting pain. But the slight tremor in Bracca's link was a far cry from what she'd experienced in the Bloodsworn council chamber. The strange feeling wasn't painful at all. She closed her eyes and tried to analyze exactly what she was feeling, to put a name to it. Just to make the task more difficult, she started getting something similar through Seth's link. It was almost like trying to listen to two different versions of the same song at the same time. Finally, she gave up and opened her eyes again.

Why doesn't it hurt when he touches your sword," she finally asked Bracca.

He looked up and met her gaze. *Because he is now my blade-brother, a part of our family.*

I guess that makes his mother part of our family, too, she said, keeping her tone innocent.

His reaction to her teasing was not what she expected. A trickle of pain ran through their link, quickly suppressed.

Bracca?

It is nothing, little sister. A minor insanity. He winked at her over Seth's head. *One not worth worrying about considering our current situation.*

Their current situation. What a prosaic way of describing her new outlaw status. Devlin was not going to be happy with her when she told him. And she had to tell him. He didn't strike her as someone who liked being kept in the dark.

True, Bracca agreed, evidently following her train of thought. *But perhaps we can delay a few days before informing your Starmate of your new link. At least until we have trained Seth to control his amber fire.* His chuckle spilled into her mind. *I most definitely want to be present at Bloodsworn Hall when that aspect of your link with the child is revealed. The Council will wet themselves.*

I take it the fire is something new?

Most definitely. At least, I have never heard of a Bloodsworn's sword burning before.

Devlin would probably know for sure, she mused. *He is First Bloodsworn, right?*

Yes, but asking him will undoubtedly raise his suspicions. No offense, my Lady Bloodsworn, but I cannot see even you holding out against an interrogation by the Tiger of Illian. He has been known to bite. And as Avalyr's First Bloodsworn it would be his duty to inform the Council of any breach of law. Your link with Seth lies within the spirit of the Council's ruling if not the words. Believe me, the Council takes such things very seriously.

His solemn tone worried her. *Do they really have the power to break our link?*

It is said that together, the Council can overcome any Bloodsworn except the Tragar, as he has the backing of Luma herself.

And yet you didn't try to stop me at all when I told you what I was going to do with Seth. There was no way she could have let mother and child walk away without helping them, and there was no way she could *not* have helped Seth when she knew what he needed. But it didn't make her feel any better knowing that by helping them, she'd leveled a sword right at Bracca's and Tyr's throats. And maybe even her own.

Bracca gave her a scolding look. *You are my Bloodsworn. My allegiance is to you, not the Bloodsworn Council.*

But what I do affects you and Tyr. And now, Seth, too. Damn it, Bracca, what are we going to do? I'm not worried about Sheren keeping this a secret, but Seth's just a child. He's bound to forget and say something, or worse, pull out that new toy of his at the wrong time. The second anyone sees that dagger...

Leave Seth to me. I am his mentor by default, so his conduct and training are my responsibility. He will not give himself away once he knows how important it is to keep his status a secret.

She could feel Bracca's confidence as well as hear it, but Avera couldn't help worrying. *I don't know, my friend. I think children are more prone to letting secrets slip than keeping them.*

Seth may be a child, but he is also a Blade now. Not a fighting Blade, true, but the instinct to protect his Bloodsworn should still be there. Once he knows he must keep the secret to protect you, not even the Tragar himself will be able to drag it from him. Trust me, we will contrive. His words held the flavor of a pledge as he brushed her arm reassuringly before moving toward Sheren and Seth.

Contrive. Avera wasn't sure she liked that word. It ranked right up there with plot and scheme. Arrange sounded better.

Seth giggled, and the dagger in his hand erupted into amber flames.

Yeah, this was going to take some arranging.

Chapter Twenty-Two

Pale, watery sunlight streaked the sky the next morning as Sheren watched Lady Avera, Lord Devlin, and several Silver Blades set off on horseback through the villa's main gate. She wondered if anyone else noticed that Avera's First Blade wasn't with them. To her, Bracca's absence was starkly obvious. But then, she knew why he'd chosen to stay behind.

"Feels like rain today."

She stifled her gasp and did her best not to jump guiltily at Nerrilik's pronouncement. So much for her hope of slipping away from the villa unseen. She swung around to face him, trying to keep her expression neutral. He hadn't bothered her since their trip to the palace. Hopefully, he'd finally accepted her refusal of his suit. "Good morning, Nerrilik. Yes, I noticed the heaviness in the air myself."

He stood in the doorway just behind her, a large and imposing warrior. She could barely detect how his stance placed most of his weight on his left leg, sparing the right. She made sure not to glance toward the spot where skin and muscle lay misshapen beneath his leathers, knowing how sensitive he was about his injury even after all this time. He motioned to the basket on her arm. "Going out to the gardens? You should hurry. You'll want to be finished before the rain sets in."

She flashed him what she hoped was a calm smile, though calm was far from what she was feeling. It was imperative Nerrilik not enter the gardens this morning. She patted the pair of pruning shears clearly visible in the bottom of the basket. "I know. I just want to gather a few fresh flowers for Lady Avera's room. I won't be going far." No farther than the secluded water garden where Seth waited with his new blade-brother and mentor, Bracca. The Amber Blade insisted on beginning Seth's training right away, hence Lady Avera's desire for a morning ride despite the impending weather. The fewer Blades at the villa, the less chance of one stumbling upon them during a morning walk.

She turned to leave, but stopped as Nerrilik's hand shot out, his thick fingers catching her bare wrist. Her breath lodged in her throat. She tensed, waiting for an onslaught of his emotions to crash through her barriers like they did when Bracca touched her. After several heartbeats of nothing, she began to relax in relief, only to stiffen again as Nerrilik stepped close enough for their bodies to touch. He reached out and trailed one finger along her jaw to beneath her chin. Even when he used that finger to tilt her head up, her barriers remained unbreached.

"Why do you continue to hold yourself apart from me, Sheren? You only punish us both."

She tried to focus on his words despite the confusion spinning through her mind. How could a single touch from Bracca shatter her mental walls with the strongest emotions she'd ever felt, yet Nerrilik's touch leave her feeling nothing?

She managed to snap herself back to the present just as he started to tip his head down to kiss her. "Please, Nerrilik, let me go." The fact he didn't cause her empathic abilities to flare out of control should have made her feel safe. Safer, at least, than kissing a man she'd known less than a handful of days who's slightest touch sent her senses reeling. But the thought of Nerrilik's lips on hers sent a shiver of distaste down her spine.

He paused, his gaze searching her face. Then something harsh flashed in his eyes and his lips firmed. He dipped his head closer.

"Don't." She leaned back, turning her head and twisting her hand in an effort to free herself. His fingers tightened, both on her chin and wrist. "Nerrilik, stop," she demanded, afraid she would actually have to fight him. Her heart pounded with a potent mix of outrage and fear. How dare he try to force her!

He might have continued if one of the maids had not entered the hall behind them. He released her, his expression dark with suppressed anger, and stepped back. The maid cast them a sidelong glance as she slipped past them, but kept walking. Sheren hurried to follow the girl into the openness of the side courtyard, conscious of Nerrilik following close behind her. He pulled her to a stop again just shy of the entrance to the gardens.

"You cannot lie to me any longer, Sheren," he said, his voice a harsh whisper "I felt you tremble at my touch. You desire me as much as I desire you. It is time to end whatever game you are playing and make our union official."

Others were in the courtyard now, giving her a sense of security. Still, when she swung around to face him, she kept her voice low and even, with no trace of the turmoil she was feeling. She knew Nerrilik wanted her, had known he'd admired her even before Sayjan's death. That was why she'd always been careful to keep him at arm's length while honoring his friendship with her husband. Now it appeared the time had come to increase the distance between them, perhaps sever the ties altogether.

"Nerrilik, I'm sorry, but you are wrong. I do not know how much plainer I can be. I have never desired anything more from you than friendship. I'm afraid if you continue in this vein, that friendship may be lost to us."

His grip on her wrist tightened to the point of pain. "You belong to me."

"No, I belong to myself."

"Mama!"

Sheren had never been happier to hear her son's sweet voice. She turned, looking for him just as he barreled out of the garden. He skidded to a stop between her and Nerrilik, snatching and pulling at the hand the warrior still held hostage.

"Mama, you have to come. I found a new froggy in the garden. Hurry before he hops away." He pulled on her hand until Nerrilik had no choice but to release her.

"All right," she said, letting him tug her out of the courtyard. "All right, sweetling, I'll come look at your froggy. And then you can help me pick some flowers for Lady Avera." She glanced back once to make sure Nerrilik wasn't following this time. He stood in the courtyard, the look on his face telling her their unpleasant conversation wasn't over, just postponed.

Apprehension wrapped itself around her as Seth led her deeper into the gardens. She hated the thought of a confrontation with Nerrilik. If she could not convince the warrior to turn his attentions elsewhere, she and Seth might have to leave the villa. Anxiety mixed with the apprehension, worry following hard on its heels. Far more worry than she thought the uncomfortable situation warranted. Then she and Seth passed into the next garden where Bracca waited. She realized with a burst of shock that some of the worry she felt was his.

She caught the concern on his face a second before he blanked his expression. The anxiety coming from him dropped dramatically upon seeing her. He took several steps toward her before stopping.

"Are you all right?"

"Yes," she said, but she wasn't really sure. She'd felt nothing from Nerrilik when he touched her a moment ago, yet now she could feel Bracca's emotions while they were yards apart. She concentrated on adding another layer to her shields. Before she could finish, she felt the roiling mass of emotions come to order, calmed and bound by what she sensed was tight control.

Why were her abilities suddenly so erratic? And why did they only flare when she was in Bracca's presence? She glanced at Seth, who skipped off after a yellow butterfly, then settled her gaze on the warrior. "Did you send Seth to me?" Even as she said the words, she knew she was right.

Bracca turned away to watch Seth. "He and I finished the sheath for his dagger. He wished to show it to you."

Not a lie, but not the whole truth either. She studied him a moment, feeling a spurt of frustration she knew was all hers, because his emotions were now bound so completely she could no longer read them. For just a second, she was tempted to lower her shield and reach out to him. "You're hiding something."

One dark brow arched while his lips twitched into that slight smile that never failed to surprise her. He reached behind his back and removed something from his waistband. "So I am." He held whatever it was behind his forearm and called to her son. "Seth."

She didn't have a chance to tell him that wasn't what she meant. As soon as Seth turned to them Bracca held up the object—the amber dagger snug in a new leather sheath—and her child's face transformed into an excited grin. He sprinted over to them.

She approved when Seth didn't reach for the dagger immediately. He stood in front of Bracca, hands clasped behind his back, body quivering with excitement, and waited until the warrior held the sheathed dagger out to him. Seth snatched the weapon and ran to her.

"See, Mama, see. Bracca cut the leather but I helped stitch it together. He's going to help me make a belt, too, so I can wear it under my tunic sometimes."

He held the leather encased weapon up for her inspection. Sheren leaned down a bit, making sure to keep her hands on the handle of her basket. She didn't want to inadvertently touch the dagger.

"That's lovely, Seth. You did a good job."

The child glanced over his shoulder at Bracca. The warrior nodded. Seth turned back to her and shoved the dagger closer. "You can hold it, Mama."

She jerked back. "No, Seth, you mustn't—"

"It's all right, Sheren," Bracca said. He stepped closer and placed a hand on Seth's shoulder. "Just hold the sheath without touching the dagger itself."

She stared at him in disbelief. Was he mad? Shaking her head, she backed away. She'd picked up Sayjan's sheathed sword to move it once. Only once. Her husband had come charging into the room in a rage and snatched it from her hands. The look on his face had terrified her.

"Bracca says you have to, Mama. It's important."

She raised her eyes to pin a glare on the warrior standing so confidently behind her son. For the first time she wanted to willingly touch someone in order to use her empathic ability to understand their motives. Why was he doing this? Why would he want her to cause her son pain?

"Seth," she said, forcing a smile. "Why don't you put your dagger in my basket while we walk to the water garden? You can run ahead while Bracca and I talk about this."

It bothered her that her son turned to Bracca for his approval before dropping the dagger in her basket and running off without a backward glance. She tried to remind herself that the warrior was now her son's teacher, so of course he would seek his mentor's approval. It didn't help much. She felt as if she were already starting to lose her child, just as she'd lost his father.

"Why?" she asked as soon as Seth was out of hearing. "Why would you want me to touch his dagger when you know what it will do to him?"

Bracca started walking, giving her no choice but to follow him. They paced along the path, close enough that if she wanted to act on her earlier impulse she could curl her bare fingers around his. She gripped the basket's handle, conscious that the temptation to do so wasn't just due to a wish to read his emotions. She didn't want to be drawn to him.

"The sooner he learns to deal with someone touching the physical aspect of his link with his Bloodsworn the better," Bracca said.

"He's only five."

"So he told me."

Anger surged. She hurried a step or two ahead and swung around, putting herself in his path, forcing him to stop and face her. "Then you know he is too young for this."

"His link is brand new, not yet as strong as it will one day be. An indirect touch now, most especially from someone who loves him and means him no harm, will evoke nothing more than a bit of discomfort. Easy enough for a boy his age to handle."

Her maternal instincts disagreed. "No, he is too young. He doesn't need to learn these things yet. I won't allow you to force him into growing up so fast that he misses out on being a child. He should be chasing butterflies and hunting for frogs, not playing with daggers and learning how to handle pain."

His placed his hands on her shoulders. The heat from his palms sank past the sleeves of her dress and into her skin. "Yes, he should," he agreed. "Unfortunately, the fates have decided otherwise. Sheren, your son has been burdened with a life that has sucked the will to live from grown men. Knowing that, I can already promise you that his future will be a brighter one than many children his age can hope for."

Tears pricked her eyes unexpectedly. If she'd learned nothing else over the past few years, she'd learned that it didn't matter how carefully you planned your future. Things happened that you couldn't possibly prepare for. "You can't know that."

"I can. I know it's true because I know the woman who has pledged her life to your son. Already Avera holds him in her heart and would give her life for his. As would I. I swear I will be there for him, training him, guiding him—"

"You are not his father."

She wished she had the words back the moment she spoke them. But it was too late. Bracca's face, so open and animated with emotion, changed, became blank, unreadable. His hands fell away and he stepped back. She had to force herself not to close the small distance between them that suddenly felt like a huge chasm.

"Bracca, I'm—"

He held up a staying hand. "Allow me to make my position clear. I am Seth's blade-brother. Just as I am blade-brother to Tyr and will be blade-brother to any other man fortunate enough to become linked with my Bloodsworn."

"You call becoming a Blade fortunate?"

"I call being linked with Avera St. John nothing less than a miracle. She is everything that is good and pure. The beauty of her heart and soul shines like a beacon in a world of constant darkness."

Sheren felt her chest grow tight as he spoke. She didn't know why until she realized what it was she heard in his voice. Love.

Again words slipped out of her mouth without thought. "You're in love with her." She looked away, feeling her face flush. Would she never learn to guard her tongue? It was no business of hers how he felt toward his Bloodsworn. They had kissed once, yes, but it was only a kiss. A kiss meant nothing. No matter how many times her wayward dreams had shown her what might have happened had Seth not interrupted them.

"Yes, I love her."

The tightness in her chest flared painfully.

"But as a sister only."

Shock spun her around to face him. "As a sister?"

He nodded, his gaze locked with hers. "Avera knew next to nothing about Bloodsworn and Blades when she initiated our blood-link. No one told her the relationship between us should be a formal bond between master and servant. She accepted the intimacy of another's mind linked to hers the only way she knew how. By claiming me as family." Pride shown in his eyes as he placed his palm flat against his chest. "I am the brother of her heart just as she is the sister of mine. She sees Tyr the same way."

Sheren had heard of Avera's Second Blade. The only son of the Tragar's stable master, Tyr An-Nazere was a mere youth who'd yet to see his fifteenth year. She, like everyone else had assumed he had contracted the blade-illness so young because he'd been weakened by years of a recurring illness. Only she, Bracca, and Avera now knew the terrible truth—that the blade-illness no longer restricted itself to young men between the age of fifteen and twenty-five. It now included boys, and, more horribly, even children as young as her Seth. She shuddered to think what would happen when that news became widespread.

"And how does she view Seth?"

He tilted his head to one side, the genuinely amused smile on his face making her forget for a moment that he was a lethal Blade. "I am not sure if she's made up her mind to see him as a much younger brother or a foster son. I sense part of her wanting to mother him, but she is fighting the urge. Out of fear of offending you, I think."

The memory of Lady Avera sitting on the ground with Seth in her lap, laughing over the Jade frog, had Sheren smiling softly. "You may tell her I have no objection to her practicing her mothering skills on my son."

"Thank you," he said, bowing slightly. "I will let her know." He held a hand out, indicating the path. "Shall we go? We might want to catch up to my youngest blade-brother before he gets into mischief. And I don't think the rain is going to hold off much longer."

She glanced up at the clouds beginning to scuttle across the sky. "Of course." As they walked, her gaze lit on the leather sheath in her basket. Again she noted its plain, utilitarian design. No ornate engraving or fancy stitching marred the smooth leather. Nothing to draw a second look or even hint at the special dagger it sheltered. "What else do you plan for this morning? Are you going to work on the belt Seth mentioned?"

He shook his head. "The belt is for later. Only when he has more control will I allow him to keep the dagger with him."

"Are you worried he'll pull it out in front of someone before Lady Avera reveals his status?"

"That is a consideration, but not the main

reason."

"The amber fire," she guessed.

"Yes. The flames appear almost as soon as he draws the dagger from the sheath. And they seem to be connected somehow to his emotions."

That was interesting. "How so?"

"He laughs, and the tongues of flame flicker and ripple as if laughing with him. It is early yet, but I'm beginning to believe they actually feed off his energy. This may be why he has been unable to extinguish them on command. The correct words come out of his mouth, but nothing happens."

"Of course not. Would you want to put the fire out if it were your sword wreathed in magic flames? He's already talking about flinging fireballs."

He glanced down at her, the twinkle in his eye catching her completely off guard. "Probably not. I am finding it difficult enough as it is to insist *he* do so."

"Whatever you do," she warned, "don't let him know that. You will never get him to listen to a word you say if he doesn't think you're serious."

They stopped by a tall hedge crawling with a heavily flowered vine. "Perhaps he has already discovered as much, in which case I am depending on you to back me up with the strength of your maternal authority."

Surprise widened her eyes. She had expected no more than to be allowed to sit off to one side while Bracca instructed her son. Present, but silent, without authority of any kind save to make sure her child was not put in harm's way. To be allowed to participate in Seth's training was something she hadn't even imagined.

"Do not look so shocked," Bracca said. "My experience with children is definitely lacking. Tyr is old enough that I need have no fear of finding a patch of common ground upon which to stand. He is far more mature than his years. But Seth is—"

A whoop followed by a splash and an infectious giggle came from the other side of the hedge. Sheren couldn't help but smile as the large man beside her shot a worried glance at the hedge before turning to her with raised brows.

"Need I say more?"

She tried not to laugh. From her experience, warriors, Blades in particular, did not appreciate being laughed at. But she couldn't help it. The first chuckle escaped her followed quickly by another. She was grateful to see he smiled with her. When she could finally catch her breath, she said, "I see your point. I would be honored to assist in any way I can. In fact, I advise that we see what Seth is up to without delay."

He caught several thick vines and pulled them aside, revealing the entrance to the water garden. "After you, my lady. Together we will endeavor to impress upon a child of five the necessity of restraint. Gods and Luma help us both."

She laughed again at his mock solemn expression and ducked through the opening.

****

Nerrilik watched Sheren and Bracca disappear behind the concealing vines from his hiding place. He hadn't been able to hear what they were saying, but seeing was enough. The branches of the hedge he held aside shook with his fury, the shaking leaves rattling like a viper's tail. Appropriate, he thought, snatching his hands back without releasing his tight grip. The move stripped leaves from branches and left skin from his palms hanging in their place. He hardly felt the stinging pain.

He swung away, fighting the urge to march into the water garden and kill them both. How could she do this? How could she turn her back on him one minute and laugh with that miserable Black Blade the next?

He paced, his breath coming hard and fast, his vision black around the edges. Habit had him clamping down on his link with his Bloodsworn while he struggled to bury this insult, this rage, deep inside his soul. It was hard. His soul was so full of rage already. Rage at the gods for condemning him to the life of a Blade. Rage at Karess, Strum, Fate, and the rest of the Tragar's sanctimonious Inner Decca for allowing the Black Blades to capture him. Rage at the Tragar for not rescuing him sooner, for not healing him properly. For expelling him from his hard-won place in the Outer Decca.

If not for his injury, he would have made the Inner Decca in a few more months. Instead, he'd gone from Seventeenth Blade to babysitter for an empty villa. Even that position had been taken from him by Cu-Laurian, a man who would forever be a Black Blade no matter the color of his sword. How could no one but him see that?

He smashed his fist against his injured thigh over and over in impotent fury, ignoring each burst of stabbing pain. If not for Camarie's damned warriors, he would have replaced Fate An-Derrith in another year or two. As First Blade to Avalyr's First Bloodsworn he would have had the status he deserved. No one would have dared cast a pitying gaze in his direction. No one would even think of disobeying his orders.

And Sheren would never have refused him.

That she had was just one more insult he intended to answer. But how? And who would pay his price? Sheren?

No, not her. He had to believe her innocent. Her sweet, trusting nature blinded her, made her susceptible to Cu-Laurian's deceit. She was being led astray, deceived, seduced—

His mind shied and his stomach churned at the

visions that word conjured.

He spun around, the urge to find out if the visions were true digging into him like spurs. A few yards from the garden entrance, he jerked to a stop. Faint, childish laughter drifted on the stiff breeze. It took him a moment to be sure, but yes, the sound came from the water garden. Tension drained from his body in a rush. Seth was with them. Good. The Blade could do nothing with the child present. Sheren was safe.

For now.

He turned around, cursing softly and grabbing the trunk of a nearby tree as his weak leg buckled. He hadn't given his leg a single thought the last few minutes and was paying for it now. Pain shot from hip to ankle, the stressed muscles throbbing, demanding his complete attention. Gritting his teeth, he waited for the worst of the pain to fade, then forced himself to move. He limped into a small garden containing a stone bench and dropped down onto it with a rush of relief.

He sat there, massaging his leg and allowing the tense muscles to relax while he planned. Somehow, some way, he needed to figure out how to keep Sheren safe from Bracca Cu-Laurian for good.

Chapter Twenty-Three

Avera congratulated herself. Almost a full twenty-four hours had passed and so far she'd been able to keep her mouth shut about Seth. It was hard though. Every time Devlin looked at her, a confession hovered on the tip of her tongue, begging to be spoken.

Yesterday hadn't been so bad. When he'd finally gated into her room late in the day, he looked so tired and drained it had scared her, drove every other thought clear out of her mind. Then they'd kissed, and it was as if he caught his second wind. Hell, his second, third, and fourth wind.

She was still blushing when she asked him to go riding with her early this morning. He'd accepted gladly, clearly pleased to know she took joy in the horses he'd given her. He didn't even ask why Bracca wasn't with them. She had a half-truth ready, but thankfully hadn't had to use it. Keeping secrets from him was bad enough. Lying, even a half-lie, felt too much like another betrayal.

He would not be pleased at all if he had any idea Bracca had stayed behind to give Seth a lesson in Blade Duties 101: How to Handle Your Sword. Or in Seth's case, How to Hide Your Flaming Dagger. She tried very hard not to let that knowledge spoil their ride.

Mid-morning came, and they were several miles from the villa, when a small rainstorm blew in. It swept over the eastern edge of the valley, blocking out the sun. She worried at first, but Devlin informed her there was no lightning in the storm.

Something about Bloodsworn being able to feel the presence of lightning before it manifested because the building energy affected the magic waves. They rode back to the villa with the wind at their backs, laughing together as the rain poured down. For some reason she couldn't name, she enjoyed every wet minute of the ride.

It wasn't until they cantered through the gate and into the side courtyard between the villa's main house and stable that she started to worry again. The Silver Blades who'd shadowed her and Devlin turned toward the stable while Devlin motioned her to follow him to a wide, covered area just off the side of the villa. As soon as they were out of the rain, she jumped off her horse, falling back a little as her hand slipped off the saddle's wet pommel. Devlin caught her, swinging her around and pulling her into a tight hug complete with a long, wet kiss.

"Good catch," she said smiling up at him. She expected him to come back with some witty remark or at least let her go. He just stared down at her, his eyes the same cloudy shade as the rainy sky—a mixture of dark blue and gray with hints of sunshine on the edges. The world around them seemed to stop.

"I'll never let you come to harm, my lady love."

She traced his lips with her finger. "I know." She lifted her head for another kiss. The heat from his body seeped into her through their wet clothes and she pressed herself closer, wanting to feel every hot inch of him.

"Lady Avera, I've started a bath for—oh, forgive me."

Avera started at Sheren's voice and felt her cheeks flush. She tried to pull out of their intimate embrace. "Let me go," she whispered urgently.

Plastered against him as she was, Avera felt Devlin's silent chuckle vibrate in his chest. "Never," he whispered back.

Exasperated, but not really upset—it was extremely flattering to know he didn't care who knew how much he wanted her—Avera looked over her shoulder at Sheren. "A hot bath sounds wonderful, Sheren, thank you. I'll be up in a moment." Her new friend bobbed a quick curtsey, trying without success to hide her grin, and left hurriedly.

Avera turned back to Devlin just as a breeze swept through the open porch. The wind hit her wet clothing, making her shiver. Devlin frowned and released her at once. "You should go inside."

"Oh, now you let me go." She felt the absence of his warmth keenly.

Devlin began gathering the horses' reins. "It would be selfish of me to keep you here any longer. Go and get dry. I'll join you shortly." He reached up to adjust the halter around his horse's ears. She started to turn away only to have her gaze snag on the outline of his body revealed by his wet clothes. Memory flashed, calling up an image of him in the hall outside her apartment back home on Earth. His wet, cola-soaked shirt had clung to him like a second skin, outlining every delicious muscle.

Just like now.

She licked her lips. Cold, wet fabric shifted against her body as she took a step toward him, cooling some of the heat building inside her. She grimaced and plucked at the front of her wet blouse. "You know, with all that magic at your disposal, one would think you could solve this soggy little problem for me."

He glanced at her, then stopped fiddling with the halter to face her fully. His gaze traveled slowly down the length of her body. She knew her blouse clung to her breasts, outlining her cold, peaked nipples by the way his gaze lingered on her chest.

231

His smile turned absolutely wicked. "I could, but where would be the fun in that?"

Heat coursed through her, settling with a flutter in the pit of her stomach. So, he wanted to play, did he? Holding back her own smile, she sauntered up to him. With their gazes locked, she reached out and lightly ran the tips of her fingers down his chest, making sure one of her nails grazed over his hard male nipple. "You like keeping me wet," she said, her voice low, suggestive.

Power flared in his eyes, a sign she was coming to understand meant a slip in his control. "Yes," he growled.

Her hand drifted lower, blazing a trail down his hard thigh and back up to his crotch. She cupped him, saw blue fire kindle in his eyes as he grew in her hand, long, thick, and oh so very hard. She squeezed.

"Avera."

Her name came out in a deep, growly voice, sending another wave of heat through her. She placed her other hand on his chest and leaned toward him, urging him back between the two horses. His eyes never left hers as he moved for her, retreating until his shoulders pressed against one of the porch's columns.

Smiling, enjoying the fact he was letting her play, she squeezed him once more before sliding her hand beneath the edge of his tunic until she found the top of his wet breeches. She slipped her index finger inside the supple material, enjoying the feel of his hot skin. Slowly, she inched her way along until the tip of her finger brushed against the velvet smooth head of his erection. He shuddered.

She didn't, *couldn't*, move for a moment, feeling the pulse of his hard shaft pushing against her hand, begging for her touch. Slick moisture bathed her fingertip, prompting an answering flood of warm wet heat between her legs. She circled his shaft with her finger, spreading the moisture around the large head. Circled it again, lower, grazing just under the flared edge with her fingernail. Another shudder went through him, hips thrusting toward her just the tiniest bit. The fire in his eyes dared her to continue.

Avera tightened her grip on his shirt and stood on her toes to whisper in his ear. "You're shaking. If you're cold, I know where there's a hot bath you can warm up in."

His hands gripped her waist and jerked her tightly against him. The hard length of him pushed urgently against her lower stomach. "If I join you, you will need no bath to warm you, *me`surrasie*, that I promise you."

"Maybe, but baths can be a lot of fun. All that hot water and slick soap." She wiggled enough to get all of her hand inside so she could grip his shaft. His answering growl sent a shock of excitement through her. She tried to push lower, fingertips brushing his sack. He grabbed her exploring hand and pulled it free.

"You're point is made. A bath will be just the thing to warm us both up. Let me take the horses to the stable and I'll join you."

She couldn't resist getting in the last word as he hurriedly gathered the horses' reins. "Oh, Devlin?" When he turned to look at her, she gave him what she hoped was a sultry smile and brought her still damp finger to her mouth. "Don't be too long." She closed her lips around her finger then drew it out slowly. His eyes flared bright.

"Luma's bloody hell," he muttered, before setting off at a run through the driving rain.

Laughing, her heart pounding with anticipation, Avera turned and ran for the stairs.

****

Leaving the Blade's barracks, Bracca dashed through the rain, intent on reaching the villa and finding Avera. Allowing her to leave without him this morning had been an obvious, if difficult choice. He understood the necessity of ceding her protection to her Starmate at times, but he didn't have to like it. He wanted to see her in person, make sure the Tragar had done his job. He also needed to report on Seth's progress.

Just inside one of the villa's archways, he paused to shake the rain from his hair. With a chuckle, he stamped his feet to clean his boots. When he, Seth, and Sheren had returned to the villa, she'd warned them about tracking in mud. As if her fierce expression wasn't enough, Bracca's little blade brother had added his own warning.

"Don't forget," Seth had advised, "or mama will have you scrubbing hallways for a week."

"A dire punishment, indeed," Bracca agreed, darting a glance at the boy's mother. "With such a threat, I will be certain to remember to wipe my feet."

Giving his boots an extra hard stomp, he chuckled again at the memory of the pretty blush that had painted Sheren's cheeks.

The sudden shortness of breath came out of nowhere, catching him in mid chuckle. He coughed and drew in a deep breath. His chest tightened. He sucked in another breath. More tightness. It was as if his face was covered by several layers of thick cloth. No matter how deeply he inhaled, he couldn't seem to get enough air. The heaviness in his chest increased. Something was terribly wrong.

Just as he reached for his link with Avera a crushing wave of emotions spilled over him. Panic, fear, desperation. The weight of them all hitting at once drove him to his knees. He braced himself up with one hand, coughing, trying to breathe past the vice now clamped around his throat. He couldn't get enough air. He was dying. This had to be an attack from Camarie. He had to warn—

A single sweet, presence touched his mind, driving back everything, including that horrible choking feeling. A presence laced with sadness and longing and regret. A presence he knew. *Sheren!*

Recognizing her seemed to remove that terrible suffocating feeling. Bracca sucked in a deep breath as he surged up and sprinted down the hallway. He knew what was happening now. He even had a direction. Upstairs. Sheren was upstairs. And she was dying!

He pushed himself faster, flew around a corner, and almost collided with Avera at the foot of the stairs. The wide smile on her face flattened.

"What's wrong?" she demanded. Her side of their link snapped open. *Is it Seth?*

Bracca shook his head and headed up the stairs, taking them two at a time. *No. I don't know. Sheren—* He broke off and shoved his memories at Avera, hoping she would forgive his disrespect. She seemed to snatch his tumbled recollections mid-link.

Hurry! she called, *Sheren said she was drawing me a bath. I'll get Devlin.*

He couldn't answer. The sense of urgency swamping him was so strong he was sick with it.

A warrior stepped in front of him. Bracca knocked whoever it was aside without stopping. He had to reach Sheren.

He reached Avera's room and shoved the door open, running through the sitting room and bed chamber. Steam wafted out of the bathing room through the half open door. He slammed the door fully open to find the large room filled from ceiling to floor by a thick cloud of blue-tinged mist. His first breath burned his nose and sent a bitterness to the back of his throat. This was more than just steam.

"Sheren!" He dived into the winter-like fog, arms out, feeling his way with his feet. Two steps and he felt as if his throat was closing. He dropped to his knees where the mist seemed thinner. Here he could make out vague outlines through the dense haze; a small chest, an urn of flowers. To his right, an indistinct form hugged the floor. He crawled toward it.

Sheren's flesh was cold when he touched her. He turned her over, gathered her close. Windows banged open, mist swirled.

Devlin's clearing the room, Bracca. Are you all right? Did you find Sheren?

For once, Avera's voice in his head gave him no comfort. All he could think about was how still Sheren lay in his arms. He wasn't even sure she was breathing.

He laid her on the floor again as the air around them shifted, carrying the poisonous mist to the open windows. He felt for her pulse, the rise of her chest, found neither, and began to panic. She couldn't die! Leaning over her, he tilted her head back and covered her mouth with his own. If she needed air, she could have his.

He exhaled, pushing air and need into her starved lungs.

Someone grabbed his shoulders, jerking him roughly back.

"Get your mouth off her, you filthy beast!"

He ducked the blow Nerrilik aimed at him. Twisting free of the man's grasp, he shot his fist up, catching Nerrilik squarely under the jaw. The Silver Blade fell back, shaking his head.

"You fool," Bracca snarled, crawling to Sheren. "She's not breathing." Avera knelt beside him as he sent another desperate puff of air into Sheren's mouth. He wanted to roar, to scream, to cut and slash with his sword, but all he could do was breathe.

"There," Avera said, halting him as he lifted his head to draw in more air. "She's back. Her chest is rising on its own." Avera's fingers pressed against Sheren's neck. "Her pulse is faint, but it's there."

Bracca sagged in relief just as a large, male hand closed over his arm. Thinking it was Nerrilik again, he growled and swung his fist before really looking. Lord Devlin caught his wrist in a vice-like grip.

"Easy," his Bloodsworn's mate said. "We need to get Sheren to Healer Latessa at Bloodsworn Hall. She'll know what to do."

Bracca nodded sharply and gathered Sheren into his arms.

"I'll carry her," Nerrilik said stepping forward.

Bracca bared his teeth in a silent snarl, his hold tightening. The only way he'd release Sheren right now would be if Avera ordered him to. Even then he wasn't sure he could obey. He'd never felt such possessiveness over a woman before.

"No, Nerrilik," Lord Devlin said, waving a gate into being. "I want you to stay here and go through the room. See if you can find whatever it is Sheren used in the bath water."

Nerrilik's hands clenched and fell to his sides. "As you wish, my Bloodsworn." The look he shot Bracca as he bowed his head was full of venom.

"Wait until the mist dissipates," Avera warned. "As long as you can smell the odor of bitter almonds, stay out."

Her words gave Bracca hope. If she recognized this deadly poison it would save time.

Emerging on the other side of the gate, he found himself in the heart of an infirmary. Voices came from an adjoining room.

"Latessa!" Lord Devlin called. "Latessa, we need you."

"Over here," Avera said, pulling the sheet back on one of the cots. "Hurry, Bracca, help me undress her. The poison has saturated her clothes."

Gods above, she was still being poisoned? He laid Sheren down gently and reached for his knife. Motioning Avera back, he cut ties and seams with quick, efficient strokes. He turned his head and lifted the sheet over her as Avera removed the shredded clothing.

"First Bloodsworn?" Three women entered, two in gray robes, one in blue.

Lord Devlin indicated Sheren. "Poisoned air, Latessa."

Bracca smoothed Sheren's hair back from her face, noting worriedly that the almost white locks were now darker than her skin. An unhealthy blue tinged her lips and shadowed her eyes. He raised his head and found the healer's calm eyes as she approached, not caring if she saw the panic in his.

"Help her. Please!"

"Of course. Natcha. Pelinn." She motioned the other two women forward. "Attend to her breathing and circulation. You know the procedures."

"Yes, ma'am."

Bracca moved to the foot of the bed as the gray robed women took his place. Avera and Lord Devlin joined him. Minutes passed with nothing more than the sound of breathing filling the room. Healer Latessa finally opened her eyes and sighed, her expression one of curious concern.

"What is it?" Lord Devlin asked.

"Something very subtle, I fear. I've leached what I can from her blood and tissue, but the effects linger. Can you tell me anything about this poison?"

"I can," Avera said. "From the smell I'd say it's some form of Cyanide. It's a chemical poison that prevents the body from using oxygen by attacking the heart, lungs, and nervous system. We counter the effects with the use of sodium nitrate or sodium thiosulfate. Not sure what you call those here."

"Ah," Latessa said. "The names are unfamiliar, but I believe I know the poison you speak of. We have a root in the southern realms called *sava*. Uncooked, it is deadly, striking first at a victim's breathing."

"Do you know the cure?" Bracca asked, unable to stay silent any longer.

"I believe I do." She turned to one of the women in gray. "Go to the supply room, please. Bring me two measures of saltpeter and a bowl of water. We shall soon have the lady well."

Avera slipped her hand into his. "Bracca needs to be checked, too. He was in that mist long enough to get a good dose."

Healer Latessa smiled apologetically. "I'm afraid that is something only you can do, my Lady Bloodsworn. He is your Blade."

Her hand tightened on his. He caught a hint of her panic before she locked it away behind a wall of determination. "All right."

Bracca sat on the cot next to the one holding Sheren. Avera sat beside him, still holding his hand. He paid no attention as the Tragar murmured instructions in her ear. With the first rush of pleasure from Avera's magic-laced mental touch he shuddered, his gaze shooting to his lady Bloodsworn. Her eyes were closed, her face lined with concentration. Lord Devlin stood over her, the warning in his eyes easy to read. Bracca had best keep his lust to himself.

Nodding to the prince in acknowledgement, Bracca turned his gaze back to Sheren. Holding the lust at bay was no problem at the moment. All he could think about was how fragile Sheren looked lying on the cot. Pain that had nothing to do with poisoned mist stabbed his heart with her every breath.

He'd learned not to feel anything during his years as Camarie's Blade. He was only beginning to cope with the respect, gratitude, and yes, love, he felt for his Lady Bloodsworn. A love that went deep into his soul, the emotion far beyond a Blade's appreciation for his Bloodsworn. She was his family. A sister in all but blood.

Now whatever he felt for Sheren also crowded into his heart. The raw emotion threatened to overwhelm him with its ferocity. There was no way to fight it. No way to dig it out. It was a part of him, fully entrenched. He could no more deny his feelings for Sheren than he could deny his link to Avera.

Worse, seeing Sheren's pale face and limp body had driven home the fact that he no longer wanted to deny what he felt for her. He wanted to embrace it.

Luma help him, he wanted to embrace *her* and never let her go. And that, he told himself, was the ultimate in foolishness.

No First Blade could live long with his heart divided. Even divided by two completely different kinds of love.

Sooner or later, he would have to choose.

Chapter Twenty-Four

Avera came awake slowly. She was warm, the bed soft, and Devlin's scent surrounded her.

So did his body.

She felt the strength of his arms—the one pillowing her head and the one wrapped around her. Felt his chest press rhythmically against her shoulders as he breathed. Felt his hip nestled against her backside, his thighs cupping her, one leg wedged warm and comforting between both of hers. She nestled back against him, content just to be alive.

Until that thought brought memories crashing down on her. Sheren had almost died.

Devlin's arms tightened around her protectively. "Peace, Avera, all is well, love."

She turned, trying to pierce the darkness to see his face. On the bedside table, a candle sprang to life. The intensity of his blue eyes took her breath. He touched her face gently.

"It could have been you."

She knew what he meant. If Sheren had not been so thoughtful, Avera would have drawn her own bath. Devlin might have found her passed out on the floor, or worse, in the tub of water, drowned.

"I might have recognized the odor in time. Figured out what it was. Sheren had no clue."

His finger moved to her lips. "Do not blame yourself. There was no reason for you to suspect an attack in your own home."

"An attack?" She pushed herself up until she was sitting beside him. "No, Devlin, it was an

241

accident. Sheren said the mist started when she used the scented bath salts she got from your mother. Even I know your mother wouldn't try to kill me. She probably just used a new plant, like the *sava* Latessa mentioned. Without proper testing, she couldn't have known it would react like that."

He shook his head. "What happened was no accident. Fate told me Mother helped him and Karess track down every other bottle of salts from the same batch. They checked each one. None of the others produced the gas that almost killed Sheren."

Avera rolled out of bed and started pacing. He had to be wrong. "Maybe you didn't follow the same procedure. Did you use water from the same faucet? The water could have leached a mineral from the pipes it flows through. Or Sheren might have added something else to the bath water that acted as a catalyst. We need to ask her. We should reproduce the same effect with the original bottle of salts as a control test. Then we can—"

"The original bottle is gone."

She stumbled to a halt. "What? You mean it's been thrown out?"

His jaw tightened as he got out of bed and came to her. His large, warm hands settled on her shoulders. "No, Avera, I mean the bottle has been taken."

"But, that would mean—"

"It was taken by someone here in the villa. That means we have a traitor in our midst."

At first, she didn't know what to say. Someone in the villa, someone she probably saw every day, was trying to kill her. Cold dread poured into her followed by hot anger. Every damn time she turned around she faced death. A sword, a bullet, a knife. Now poison. What method would they try next?

Devlin pulled her into his arms. "I'm sorry, *me`surrasie.*"

Shaking off her morbid thoughts, she pushed back a little so she could stretch up to kiss him softly. "This wasn't your fault, Devlin. There's no way you could have known someone would spike my bath salts. I'll just have to be more careful."

"That isn't what I'm apologizing for." An uncompromising light entered his eyes that instantly put her on alert. This wasn't going to be good. "I'm moving you back to the palace, to my apartments—"

"No."

"—to keep you safe until I can find the traitor."

Her anger escalated. "And just how are you going to find him if you put me out of his reach? He'll have no way to try again. He'll go into hiding and disappear."

He shook her. *He actually shook her*! "I won't risk your life. I won't use you as bait in a trap so full of holes as to be non-existent. Camarie's getting too sly. He has to be behind this, meaning there's no question that whoever he's controlling will try again. This latest attack was more subtle than the others. We might not be so lucky next time. Moving you out of harm's reach is the only way to keep you safe."

"But we're on guard now. There has to be some way you can protect me without taking me out of the equation altogether."

"I can't protect you from what I can't see coming."

"Then teach me to protect myself. Teach me to use magic."

****

Her words froze Devlin mid-anger. Teach her to use her magic? Why hadn't he thought of that before? She was Bloodsworn. There was no reason she couldn't tap into the magic for her own use. Her demonstration at the Council proved she had access to more than enough magic to power a shield. Not that a shield would protect her from something as subtle as poison, but if the traitor tried a more direct attack he would not find Avera such an easy target.

"Very well."

Excitement sparkled in her green eyes. "You'll teach me?"

"Yes. I promised to do so, if you recall, and I always keep my promises. However, do not think that just because you can call a shield I'll allow you to put yourself in danger. I still want you back at the palace."

She made a face. "And I'll still try to talk you out of it. But let's save that scintillating discussion for later. Right now, I'd really like to get a handle on this magic stuff. What do I do first?"

Trying not to smile at her eagerness, Devlin sent out a pulse of magic, summoning clothes for them both. She glanced from his silk tunic and sleep pants to the bulky, shapeless robe he'd chosen for her, and scowled at him.

He grinned back. "I was having trouble concentrating."

"Well I'm not standing around looking like a frump." When she started to untie the belt at her waist he held up a finger.

"Remove that, and your magic lesson will have to wait." He let the ever present desire he felt for her bleed into his eyes. "It is the middle of the night, we are within six feet of a bed, and I did not get the play I was promised earlier." He'd expected more than play after she rid Cu-Laurian's body of the poison. But for some reason, she hadn't been affected by her Blade's deep-healing lust this time. A situation he fully intended to investigate later.

With a cocky half-grin, Avera tugged the belt tight again. "All right." She dropped her hands to her sides. "Now what?"

"Close your eyes."

She did. He moved closer to her, circling to stop at her back. "Think about the magic. Find the place in your mind where it sleeps. Let me know when you've found it."

She answered quickly. "Okay, I see it."

"Now touch it lightly, just lightly."

She jumped as if startled. "Sensitive stuff."

"Yes." He leaned around to see if her eyes were still closed. They were. A frown of concentration wrinkled her brow and she was biting her bottom lip. She looked so utterly adorable he had to fight not to kiss her.

"Now," he said. "I want you to step back from the magic just a moment and picture yourself in your head. Do you remember the shield I put around you in the stable when the horse tried to kick you? How it hazed the air, made it look thicker?"

"Yes, I remember."

"Good. I want you to take that picture of yourself and place a haze around it, just like—"

He broke off and stumbled back as a shield popped into place around her. Damn, she was a quick student. He hadn't even finished instructing her.

Silently, he walked around her, examining the barrier for weak spots. There were none he could see.

"Well, what's next?" she asked, sounding impatient.

"Open your eyes."

She obeyed, and her eyes widened. She reached out a hand, hesitated, then gently touched the barrier. Lips curving into a smile, she flattened her palm against the haze. He could see the muscles of her arm flex as she pushed. The barrier held. Her bemused gaze shot to him. "Are you doing this?"

He laid his hand against the barrier opposite hers. "No, this is all you." He leaned into her shield to test its strength. For a second, he made headway, forcing his way through the first layer. Avera gasped.

He was about to reassure her when the barrier flexed, like a muscle contracting, then sprang out sharply, shoving him away. He fell back, landing hard on the thick rug beside the bed. She was beside him in an instant, the barrier gone.

"Oh, Devlin, I'm so sorry. Are you all right?"

Stunned more by the knowledge of what had happened than the fall, he lay there looking up at her. Never had he heard of a shield being used as a weapon. Her hands fluttered over him anxiously. In the over-sized robe, she looked more like an innocent child than a powerful Bloodsworn. But there was no denying she had more power than a Bloodsworn with only two Blades should command. Of course, he'd known she was special the moment he'd seen her driver license's picture.

He grinned suddenly, grabbed her, and rolled her beneath him.

She grinned back at him. "I guess this means you aren't hurt."

In answer, he lowered his head and kissed her, savoring her taste, the feel of her soft lips molded to his. She wrapped her arms around him, pulling him closer. He deepened the kiss as her hands glided down his back, leaving trails of fiery heat in their wake. She tipped her head back, breaking the kiss.

"I take it the magic lesson is over," she gasped, her voice breathless.

"For now." Straddling her, he sat up, knees on either side of her thighs. "I think another lesson in mutual pleasure is long over-due." He reached for the tie at her waist, watching as lustful heat surged in her eyes. Slowly, he tugged the belt loose. Just as slowly, he peeled the edges of the robe aside to reveal her naked body. Fingers spread wide, he held a possessive hand over her belly, close, but not touching her skin.

"I feel as if I haven't touched you in years instead of minutes," he said hoarsely.

"Then by all means," she said, arching her back slowly until her hot skin pressed against his palm, "touch me now."

Chapter Twenty-Five

Bracca stood at Sheren's door, staring at the smooth, dark wood while the sounds of the night whispered around him.

She lived.

He'd helped her to her room himself a few hours ago. She'd smiled at him, thanked him in a breathless voice, and he'd left her alone with her son. Healer Latessa had promised him she would be fine after a day of rest. He should turn around. He should go next door to his own bed and sleep.

Sleep? With the female he craved like he craved essence a mere wall away? He almost laughed at the impossible thought.

He ran a hand over his face and stepped back. Nothing good could come of this obsession. His life was already committed to his Bloodsworn, the sister of his heart. The one woman he couldn't live without.

No, that was wrong. He wasn't sure he could live without Sheren, either. Not anymore. She wasn't just his heart's desire. He was beginning to suspect she was his *karia*, his whole heart. Never in his life had he wanted a female as he wanted her.

Which would not be a problem if Avera had more Blades besides a half-grown boy and a child.

He didn't dare leave her well-being in the hands of Devlin Tragar's Silver Blades. They weren't bound to her. They didn't love her as he did. Despite whatever command Devlin might give them, faced with a choice between their own Bloodsworn and Avera, she would come second. With Camarie still hunting her, she needed a warrior at her side who thought of no one else but her.

That isn't you anymore.

The truth of that thought shamed him. He couldn't afford to let his feelings for Sheren weaken him. He had to be strong for Avera. They were family now. He knew from their link how much that meant to her, and it meant just as much to him. He had no choice but to turn his back on his heart. At least, for now.

He turned away just as Sheren's door opened.

"Bracca?"

Her soft voice went through him like a sharp blade. Turning back, he kept his eyes lowered, afraid she would see the longing for her he could no longer deny. "Forgive me. I did not mean to disturb you."

"You didn't. I woke up and felt like I needed some air. Would you...will you walk with me?"

He had to look at her then. Poised in the doorway, one hand clutching the frame, the other holding a shawl around her shoulders, she didn't look strong enough to stand, much less walk. He swallowed an instinctive urge to order her back to bed, and bowed. "I would be honored, my lady."

They walked in silence for a little while, passing soundlessly through the darkness of the courtyard. Side by side they skirted urns of flowers and potted trees, close, but never touching one another. He made sure of that. When they reached the fountain, Sheren stopped. Her body swayed. She put one hand on the fountain's edge.

Bracca started to reach for her and caught himself. "Are you all right?" Gods, but he wished he had the right to touch her.

"I'm fine, just a little dizzy."

"You should return to your room."

She shook her head. "Not just yet. I think..." She took a deep breath and let it out. A faint smile graced her lips as she looked at him. "I think if you help me, I can make it to the swing." In a slow, graceful gesture, she held out her hand to him.

Bracca stared at her trembling fingers, wishing he was stronger. But he wasn't. The need to touch her was too great. Carefully, he closed his fingers around hers. He would have to be blind to miss the shiver that went through her. Swearing silently, he tried to release her at once. Causing her discomfort of any kind was the absolute last thing he wanted to do.

She wouldn't let him go. Not only did her grip tighten, but her other hand closed over the top of his, effectively caging him. She closed her eyes and stood still, simply breathing and holding his hand. Feeling as if he were dreaming, Bracca watched her smile widen slowly into one of true pleasure. He almost asked her what she was thinking about, but held his peace. As long as he didn't know for sure, he could imagine it was him.

She opened her eyes. Still holding his hand, she wrapped the other around his arm. He led her to the swing situated beneath the shelter of a vine-covered arch. She settled onto the cushion with a sigh. He started to move away.

"Sit with me. Please?"

He hesitated. She didn't know what she asked. If he didn't move away, put distance between them, he'd be on that swing with her in his lap.

"Please," she said again, tugging gently on his hand.

What else could he do?

"That's better," she said, lacing her fingers with his after he'd settled beside her.

Bracca wasn't so sure. The urge to put his arms around her burned inside him. He wanted to touch her, soothe away her pain. She looked pale and fragile. And so very, very beautiful.

He swallowed back a rush of desire. "Are you

250

sure you don't wish to return to your room? Healer Latessa did say that you should rest."

She shook her head. "Perhaps I am trying to hurry things a bit, but I just couldn't stay inside any longer." Her free hand pressed against her chest. "I woke up and felt as if I couldn't catch my breath. I think...I think maybe my body remembers dying."

Her words sent denial racing through him. "You did not die."

She met his gaze squarely. "I was told I had stopped breathing, Bracca."

"You did not die," he repeated firmly. He was sure he would have felt it in his soul if she had.

"Only because of you," she whispered.

Light from the twin moons filtered through the tangle of vines overhead, bathing her upturned face. Her lavender eyes, wet with unshed tears, glittered like amethysts. Staring into them, Bracca carefully tucked a lock of hair the color of moonbeams behind her ear. "I couldn't let you die."

She took his hand, pressed it to her cheek, and closed her eyes as if savoring his touch. The simple gesture shook him too his very soul. Then her sweet lips brushed against his palm.

Bracca was lost. He could only sit there and savor the pleasure her velvet touch brought him. He drew in a deep breath, her scent filling every empty place inside him, causing every cell of his body to beg for more, for everything. Things he'd be a fool to ask for.

Vet, he had to stop her before it was too late.

"Sheren."

"Hold me, Bracca. Please. I need to feel alive tonight."

Her words shattered him. He had nothing left to fight with. Her request slipped right into his all too willing heart, taking it over. Part of him realized the battle had been lost the moment he'd seen her on the balcony overlooking the training grounds.

Slowly, with far more restraint than he felt, Bracca drew her into his arms. Burying his face in her hair, he breathed in her sweet scent again. He'd be content to sit like this until the next moon change.

Sheren, however, seemed to feel differently. She made a small impatient sound. Lifting her head, she cupped his face in both hands. "Perhaps I didn't make myself plain. I said I need to feel alive."

She leaned forward and kissed him. Hard.

Bracca tasted desperation in the swipe of her tongue against his lips, felt her hunger for him in the nip of her teeth. The potent combination sent him spinning over the edge of sanity. He took possession of the kiss, of her, pressing her back against the swing's cushions. Gods, she tasted sweet. Beyond sweet. And the way she returned his kiss, the urgency, the need, hit him like a delicious rush of essence. Never had he felt such desire. Nothing could make this moment better.

Then her roving hand caressed his crotch.

Sweet Luma's blessings!

He broke their embrace, bolting up as if dodging a slashing sword. His sharp movement set the swing into wild motion. Breathing hard, he backed away, unable to take his eyes off the pure temptation lying sprawled back against the cushions. Kissing her was one thing. He could almost justify snatching at the piece of Heaven she offered. He couldn't allow himself to take more. Not when she was so clearly vulnerable.

She reached for the ground with one foot, stopping the wild swinging, and sat up, her gaze still full of heated desire. He clenched both hands into tight fists. It took everything he had not to crush her into those cushion again. His body cried out for him to take her here, now. *Take everything she offers.*

He'd never wanted anything more in his life.

"You should return to your room," he ground out, aware how desperate he sounded. "You need to rest. You will feel better in the morning." *And you'll feel differently about me.* He was sure of it. She couldn't possibly want him like this in the light of day. If he gave in to her desires now, she might hate him for it forever.

"It's all right," she said, rising slowly from the swing. "You don't have to be afraid. I'm not going to change my mind."

If only he could be certain of that. But even if it were true, he was afraid he couldn't be the gentle lover she needed and deserved. He wanted her too much.

"I know you won't hurt me. I want this, Bracca, so very much." She reached for him, slipping her arms up around his neck.

With a groan Bracca surrendered to her demands, pulling her tight against him. He couldn't walk away from this, *from her*. He had to try to be gentle. For her, he'd somehow find the strength.

****

The emotions singing softly in Sheren's mind swelled to a grand chorus as their bodies pressed together. She embraced each element of the seductive song, the desire, the respect, the resolve, even the fear, making them her own.

Bracca swept her up in his arms. She held onto him, their gazes locked together, as he strode quickly through the darkness. When they came to her door she whispered, "Your room."

His arms tightened. A few more steps brought them to his door. She was the one to reach for the handle, push the door open. He closed it with a shove of his hip, leaned against it for a moment.

No light, natural or magic, softened the blackness filling his room. Without being able to see him, Sheren concentrated on her other senses.

She breathed in, his male scent filling her head and making her mouth water. Tension made his arms and chest feel like smooth, sun warmed rock. The roughness of his harsh breathing sent chill bumps down her arms. The way his hands gripped her possessively, one on her thigh, the other near her breast, sent flutters through her stomach. Bracca was a man holding himself in check by a thread, and she meant to cut that thread.

She ran a hand around the side of his neck, tangling her fingers in his dark hair. Using that grip, she pulled herself up until she could kiss his throat. A hard swallow rippled the muscles beneath her lips. She pressed another kiss just below his jaw, a third to the side of his neck, nestling a fourth just below his ear. She flicked his earlobe with her tongue. He groaned roughly and shoved away from the door. The feral sound pleased her, sending shivers up her spine and butterflies swarming in her stomach. She sensed the thread of his control stretching thinner and thinner.

"Wait here." He set her on her feet and stepped away from her.

She heard him moving in the darkness. Part of her realized he was deliberately making noise—footsteps, shifting clothing—just for her. A moment later, the soft, steady glow of an essence globe, a sphere of glass filled with Avalyr's magic, pushed back the darkness. She turned toward the glow as Bracca set the globe in a stand next to a bed.

His bed.

He straightened and faced her.

Feeling nervous for the first time, Sheren slowly slipped her shawl from her shoulders and laid it across the back of a chair. His gaze followed her every move, smoldering with a dark, inner fire.

He reached for his sword belt. Fingers flicked

the buckle open. He drew the belt from around his waist and let it fall to the floor near the bed. The move surprised her. Sayjan had always removed his sword with a sense of reluctance, caressing and petting it like a lover before setting it aside. He never would have left it on the floor.

Bracca had just tossed his sword aside without a second thought, as if all his focus was truly centered on her. The thought made her knees weak.

Reaching for the hem of his tunic, Bracca took a step toward her. The tunic flew off into a dark corner at his next step. Sheren could only stare at the expanse of his bare chest and hard, flat stomach as he approached. Fresh desire swirled inside her. She could no longer tell if it was his emotion or hers. Nor did she want to.

He ran a calloused finger along the edge of her jaw. "Tell me again that you want this."

"I want you."

"There are other men more suitable." The muscle of his jaw flexed. "Nerrilik—"

"Is not suitable." She stroked his cheek, felt the tightness in his jaw loosen. "I want *you*, Bracca Cu-Laurian. You, and no other."

The thread of his control snapped.

His mouth came down on hers, hard, demanding, desperate. Joy filled her. This was exactly what she needed. She kissed him back with all the longing in her heart. Her hands slid up his arms, squeezed the bare skin of his shoulders, before sliding around his neck. She clung to him, unable to do anything but feel.

His hands brushed down her back, finding the simple tie of her dress. When the tie knotted, he didn't bother trying to undo it. A jerk of his hands broke the small straps free.

She hadn't donned an under dress when she'd risen from bed and his hot palms pressed against her bare skin. His fingers flexed, then splayed, reaching, as if trying to touch her everywhere at once. Her mind spun as his hands slipped lower, dipping beneath her dress to knead and caress the cheeks of her bottom. Tingles raced over her skin. Need spiraled through her with the speed of a whirlwind, touching down in the place between her legs, making her throb. Moaning, she responded to the pressure of his hands by rubbing her hips against him, seeking the hard length of flesh she could feel behind a simple barrier of leather.

With a curse, he broke their kiss. He gripped her hips, holding her still as his lips moved to her cheek, her jaw, the tender flesh of her neck. Like his hands, his lips seemed to be everywhere at once.

He slid a hand up her side, skimming the side of her breast, to grip the sleeve of her dress. He tugged. "Off. Now. Or I'll rip it more."

He kept up the assault on her neck as she let her arms drop. The dress slipped from her body. Then she was on his bed, his weight settling on top of her. She pulled his face to her, kissing him with a hunger she didn't think she'd ever known. Never could she remember feeling this desperate for Sayjan's touch. Never. This was something else. This driving, out of control emotion was not one she would ever forget. And she wanted more.

"Beautiful," he whispered against her lips. "You are so beautiful." His hand closed over her breast.

Chill bumps raced over her as he found her nipple, plucking it to rapid attention. And when he bent his head to take her raised nipple into his mouth, she felt the world come apart. Emotions swirled, spun, threatened to drag her under.

And still she wanted more.

"Bracca, please." She wanted him to kiss her again. Wanted him to touch her, to fill her. Gods, she'd felt so empty for so very long. She wanted him inside her, wanted to feel him deep inside. She just...wanted.

His mouth moved to her other breast. Unable to stay still, she moved beneath his assault, her body in constant motion. One hand fisted in his long dark hair while the other skimmed his bare back until she reached the waistband of his leathers. Feeling cheated by the material between her and his skin, she gripped the soft leather and tugged. When he showed no sign he noticed, she tugged again, harder. He finally raised his head. The intensity of his gaze almost made her forget what she wanted.

"These. Off. Now. Or I'll rip them." Not that she actually could, but his own words seemed to convey her urgency perfectly.

Without saying a word he rolled to the side, fingers flying, fumbling at the fastenings of his leather breeches. She heard his boots hit the floor one after the other. His wadded leathers followed. Then he was back, drawing a gasp from her as his hot skin slid against hers. She shifted her legs, opening them so he could settle between them. His weight felt glorious.

He kissed her again, all but devouring her. The tip of his shaft nudged at her wet entrance, dipped inside once, twice.

"Now," she breathed into his mouth.

He surged into her with one fluid stroke, burying himself deep inside. His groan of pure pleasure coupled with the wave of sensual delight flooding her, sent her body into a convulsion of ecstasy. Part of her was sane enough to be grateful his mouth slammed over hers in time to swallow the scream she couldn't hold back.

On and on, the pleasure rolled, each stroke of his hard length prolonging the moment until tears leaked from her eyes at the beauty of what she felt. The euphoria singing through him every time he moved in and out of her sang through her as well. She sensed him revel in the way her body accepted him, caressed him, squeezed him.

"Again," he commanded harshly as he began to move faster. "Come for me again, my *karia*."

Wanting nothing more than to obey him, she wrapped her legs around his thighs, raising her hips to meet each powerful thrust. He'd called her his *heart*. Right then, she felt as if that were true. She felt a part of him, and he a part of her.

He slipped his hands beneath her shoulders, gripping her, holding her in place as he took his pleasure from her body and gave it back to her tenfold.

She felt the approach of her second release, knew his was close as well. When they hit at nearly the same time, intense pleasure inundated her body and mind. She splintered into a thousand pieces, her body straining against Bracca's as her inner muscles clenched and milked his hard length. Once again Bracca sealed his mouth over hers. This time his shout mixed with her scream as his body clenched and jerked until he'd spent himself inside her.

****

Struggling to catch his breath, Bracca gloried in the feel of Sheren shuddering beneath him. For years he'd only been with a female when driven by the lust from an occasional deep-healing. He'd never met a woman he truly desired. Never felt the need to pleasure her simply for the joy of feeling her come in his arms. Not until Sheren. Being with her, sharing her pleasure, was a gift beyond measure.

He buried his face in her neck and gave her sheath a slow, languid stroke with his softening shaft. By Luma, he wanted to stay inside her forever. The sensation of her silky muscles gliding against his sensitive skin was almost painful, yet it was a pain he welcomed. He still found it hard to believe she really wanted him.

He nuzzled her, trailing his lips over her sweet smelling skin until he found cool, salty moisture. Jerking his head up, he searched her face, heart stuttering at the sight of tears leaking steadily from her closed eyes. Gods, he'd hurt her. Taken her without a thought to her care. What kind of black-hearted monster was he?

Her eyes popped opened. "Shhh," she whispered, raising a finger to his lips though he knew he hadn't spoken a word. "These are tears of happiness, not pain." She smiled and stroked his face. "I am not used to such pleasure as you have shared with me."

He couldn't help the tiny surge of satisfaction her words brought him. Still, he studied her closer to be sure. Her lashes were spiky, wet with tears, but her beautiful lavender irises held nothing but joy and wonder. The fear in his heart melted under the warm glow of her smile.

"You are truly all right?"

In answer, she raised her head and brushed a kiss over his lips. "Truly," she whispered. "Though I would be even better if we could do this again."

Still inside her, he felt himself growing hard again at her words. Amazement and desire shot through him. He vowed to go slow this time, savor her body. He would need the memories later. Just because she accepted him this night did not mean she would do so ever again. He understood her need to feel alive after her close brush with death. He shared that need with her. To feel her alive and breathing in his arms was an imperative he couldn't deny. Though after tonight, he might never feel alive again without her.

"It will be my pleasure to grant your request, my *karia.*"

He set about pleasuring her, showing her with his body just how precious she was to him. He couldn't help hoping that if he pleased her enough, she might realize she needed him, too.

Later, too sated to move, much less get up to extinguish the light, Bracca tucked an already drowsing Sheren close to his side and closed his eyes. He lay there counting her breaths, trying to imprint the moment into his heart until sleep claimed him.

****

A burst of adrenaline jerked Bracca out of a deep sleep. Gasping, he bolted upright in bed, his heart pounding as if it would come apart in his chest. His first thought was that Avera needed him. He slammed open his link, reaching for her as he sprang from the bed. He realized three things at once.

Avera's link was tightly closed in a way he'd come to recognize as her request for complete privacy when she was with her Starmate; Sheren was no longer in bed with him; and his shaft was harder than it had ever been in his life.

"I'm sorry, I'm so sorry." The horror in Sheren's frantically whispered words jerked him around. She trembled near the bed, naked, her bundled dress clutched over her lovely breasts. Her wide lavender eyes regarded him in alarm. "It was under my dress. I didn't know. I touched it by mistake. I'm so sorry." She looked down.

It took him a hand-full of heartbeats to recognize the tangle of leather lying at her feet. When he did, a wealth of self-disgust joined the jumble of emotions churning in his gut. Over a decca of years he'd been a Blade. He knew better than to leave his weapon lying around like a discarded piece of clothing. Hadn't he just drummed that first Blade lesson—the care of one's sword—into Seth yesterday? Yet right now he couldn't even remember taking his sword off much less leaving it on the floor.

Bracca bent and snatched up his weapon, freezing when Sheren cringed and stepped away from him. He stared at her, noting her hunched shoulders and white knuckles. "Sheren?"

She wouldn't meet his gaze.

"It's all right, Sheren," he said gently. "No harm is done." He placed his sword on a nearby table.

She lifted her head, squaring her shoulders and raising her chin as if preparing to meet some dire punishment. "It will not happen again. I promise."

"I told you, it's all right. You didn't hurt me."

She shook her dress out with a snap of her wrists, then paused to examine the torn tie. "Don't lie to me, Bracca. I saw the way you came off the bed."

Anger stirred in his blood, adding a bitterness to the thrill of lust holding him in its tight grip. "Look at me. If I were in pain would I have this?" He waved a hand at his demanding erection.

The moment she looked at him her hands stilled. Her confused expression almost drew a laugh from him. When her eyes kindled with interest, his shaft jerked with impatience.

He wanted to take her back to bed, but wasn't sure if he should even move. She still seemed poised on the edge of flight. What had her husband done to put such fear in her eyes for accidentally touching his sword?

She wet her lips and his shaft jerked again. *Vet.*

"I need to go see about Seth. He'll be up soon. I don't want him to...I need to be there when he wakes up."

Her decision to hide the fact she'd been with him shouldn't bother him. He'd known there would be no repeat of this glorious night. That didn't stop the stab of pain in his heart.

"Of course." He moved to his dresser and came back with a pin. He waited until she'd pulled the dress over her head then pinned the back together. She ran her fingers through her hair, arranging it into a semblance of order. Then he draped her shawl around her shoulders.

Wrapping the ends over her breasts, she looked up at him. "Thank you."

"Before you go, I want you to do something." He needed to prove to her she had nothing to fear from him.

"What?"

He reached for her hand and led her to the table. Before she understood what he wanted, he pressed her hand to the hilt of his sword. The contact was extremely, exquisitely brief.

She gave a sharp cry and jerked her hand back. "Are you mad? Why would you do such a thing?

He couldn't answer her. As soon as her fingers had grazed the hilt, every muscle in his body locked. His throat tightened. His skin burned. His heart actually jumped in his chest. Blood surged in his veins and pounded in his aching groin.

"Bracca?"

Her hand closed around his arm. He drew in a deep breath, held it, then expelled it slowly. As he did, his muscles relaxed.

He met her anxious gaze. Tears glimmered in her eyes. "Why did you do that?"

"To prove to you that your touch can never cause me pain."

Her questioning gaze darted down to his throbbing shaft.

He had to smile at her look of doubt. "Yes," he admitted, "that is painful. But you know it's not the kind of pain I refer to."

"I don't understand. When I touched Sayjan's silver sword, even sheathed, he said it caused him extreme discomfort."

"In truth, I do not understand, either." He

cupped her face. "All I know is that your touch affects my body like a flood of essence."

Amazement lit her eyes. Then her cheek flared hot beneath his hand, the scarlet blush visible between his fingers.

"Doesn't your Bloodsworn know what you feel when someone else touches your sword? Does she feel—"

"Any other touch, yes. But I've checked, and both sides of our link are still locked down tight. Your touch affects only me."

"How is that possible?"

He shrugged. "I have no sure answer. Perhaps it has something to do with you being Seth's mother. It is possible the Tragar may have more knowledge. We can ask or not as you will."

"Don't you want to know?"

"The reason doesn't really matter."

"Well, I think it does. I think we should ask him. Or Karess. He might know."

"He might," Bracca agreed. "I'll speak with him first."

They heard a rooster crow outside.

"I have to go."

He kissed her hand. "Will you come with Seth to his morning training session? Avera will be there as well. The Tragar has business at the palace this morning."

"Yes, I'll come."

"Good."

He cracked open his door to check for early morning risers. Nothing stirred within his hearing or sight. The night still held the villa's residents in its sleepy grip. He opened the door wider for her. She paused.

"I hate leaving you like this." Her hand brushed his erection, sending a burst of pure lust rocketing through his body. "It doesn't seem fair," she whispered. Her fingers closed around him. He bit back a groan.

"I will survive," he assured her. Though he would not survive long if she continued to touch him. He attempted to remove her hand.

Instead of releasing him, her fingers tightened. "No."

"You need to return to Seth," he said, his voice sounding strangled even to him.

"In a moment."

Before he realized what she intended, she'd closed the door and urged him to lean against it.

"What—"

The question died in his throat as she dropped to her knees. Her warm breath bathed his aching flesh. He thought he heard her whisper something that sounded like, "I have always wanted to know what this was like." Then her lips closed around him.

Air shot out of his lungs, his head snapped back into the door, and his knees threatened to buckle. Squeezing his eyes tightly shut, he stayed upright by sheer force of will, not wanting anything to disturb Sheren's sensual exploration of his body.

For a few long, ecstasy-filled minutes nothing else mattered but the feel of her soft lips, the flick of her eager tongue, and the grazing nips of her teeth. Nothing else in the world mattered, but Sheren.

Chapter Twenty-Six

"Can I go now?" Seth begged.

Sheren made a show of examining his breakfast plate. She and Seth sat at a table in the small courtyard where the warriors and servants ate their meals. All but two of the other tables were empty. Nerrilik and two other Silver Blades sat at one, discussing guard assignments. Bracca sat alone at another.

Her eyes had sought the Amber Blade out the moment she and Seth entered the courtyard. Their gazes had met, his head nodded in greeting, and he'd returned his attention to a pile of leather on the table in front of him. If not for the flash of heat that shot through her shield, she might have thought the previous night nothing but a dream.

"Mama?"

Seth's impatient whine drew her attention. She smiled and gave his hair a brief caress. "Yes, sweetling, you may go."

He shot off the chair. Throwing his arms around her waist, he placed a wet kiss against her cheek. "You're coming, right," he whispered in her ear.

She cupped a hand around his ear and whispered back, "Lady Avera and I will join you soon. Behave for Bracca. No falling in the water."

"No falling," he promised. Before she could include jumping in on purpose, he was gone, sprinting toward Bracca at a dead run. The warrior had already gathered the leather, part of which, she knew hid her son's amber dagger.

She watched them leave, Seth skipping along

beside the man she'd made love to last night. And yes, she was wise enough to admit love had been in that bed with them despite the brief time they'd known each other. What else could have made her set aside her vow not to become involved with a Blade ever again?

She heard someone come up behind her and tensed, recognizing the uneven walk. "Good morning, Nerrilik." She glanced over her shoulder, her usual polite smile in place, to find him scowling. But not at her. His gaze, too, was fixed on Seth and Bracca.

"I advise you not to let Seth get too friendly with Cu-Laurian, Sheren."

She bristled at the wealth of loathing in his voice. "Why shouldn't Seth be friends with Bracca?"

Something dark flashed in Nerrilik's eyes when he looked at her. "Bracca, is it?"

She stood and started gathering empty dishes. "Yes. He saved my life yesterday, Nerrilik, and has been nothing but respectful to me and kind to my son. My friendship and the freedom of first names are little enough to offer him in return."

He grunted. "As long as that is all you offer him."

Ordering herself not to blush, Sheren met his gaze coolly. "What I choose to offer him is none of your concern."

The muscles of his jaw ticked as his gaze hardened. He grabbed her arm before she could even think to move away. His grip hurt. "We've gone over this before. As your protector, everything you do is my concern. You know how I feel about you."

She refused to let him intimidate her. Silver Blades might see Nerrilik's possessiveness as his right, but she knew of an Amber Blade who would not. "And you know I don't return those feelings," she snapped. "We will never be more than friends,

Nerrilik, and you are straining the boundaries of that."

"There you are."

Nerrilik released her and stepped away as Avera came toward them. Sheren could sense something bubbling beneath the woman's calm exterior.

"Good morning, Nerrilik," Avera said. Her sharp, green gaze went from Nerrilik's hand to Sheren's arm before she turned her full attention to Sheren. "Almost ready for our walk?"

"Almost. Just let me take these to the kitchen."

"All right. I'll meet you outside." She nodded slowly to Nerrilik, a warning in her gaze, and left.

Sheren took a step and felt Nerrilik catch her arm again. She should have known he wouldn't give up so easily.

The wave of dark emotions clawing at the barrier in her mind came out of nowhere. She gasped and tried to pull away.

"No, Sheren, please, you must listen to me." Nerrilik took the dishes from her and set them back on the table. Then he took her hands in his. She couldn't stop him, too shocked by the depth of loathing and hatred she felt coming from him.

"You and Seth need to stay away from Lady St. John and her Blade. Far away. It's not safe."

"What do you mean it's not safe?"

"The fire, the poison mist, those were not accidents."

She knew her face paled. Not accidents? The possibility had worried her, but to have it confirmed...

"The Tragar believes there is a traitor," Nerrilik continued. "Someone here at the villa. They are trying to kill Lady St. John, or Cu-Laurian, or both."

She shook her head, the thought of either one of her new friends coming to harm—Bracca especially—making her limbs feel weak. "You have to be wrong. Lord Devlin would never leave Lady Avera here if she were in danger."

Nerrilik snorted in disapproval. "He says she is stubborn. She wants to catch the assassin. He's a fool to give in to her, but that is the reason she remains here. We're watching her and Cu-Laurian very closely, but that is no guarantee we'll catch whoever it is before they strike. I don't want you or Seth to come to harm by whatever they plan next."

Silver Blades were watching Bracca and Avera? Closely?

She looked toward the courtyard exit. She had to get to them, warn them. Whoever was watching Avera and Bracca would follow them to the garden. They'd see Seth with his dagger.

"I'm sorry, Nerrilik, I have to go. Lady Avera is waiting."

His hands gripped her arms and he shook her. "Didn't you hear a word I said? You have to stay away from them."

"No, I won't. I can't. They're my friends."

"Your friends?" His laugh was a hard, sharp cough of derision. "She is from another world and he is a Black Blade. Don't trick yourself into believing either of them care about what happens to any of us."

"Avera cares. She has a good heart, Nerrilik. And Bracca's sword is amber, not black." She wanted to shout that she knew his heart was good as well but didn't dare.

"A change of sword color does not change who he really is. Ten years of service to the Dark Bloodsworn is enough to mark any man, Cu-Laurian included."

She stared at him, convinced she'd misunderstood what he was saying. It simply wasn't possible. Bracca couldn't have been a Black Blade.

Black Blades were ruthless to the point of being sadistic. Most were known to have no conscience to speak of, much less a heart. The ones who'd killed her husband and captured Nerrilik had tortured the warrior for days in an effort to cripple his Bloodsworn by proxy.

Nerrilik slapped a hand against his damaged leg, the sound making her jump. "Perhaps you can forget what the Black Blades took from you, Sheren, but I cannot. I have good reason not to welcome one of Camarie's Outer Decca with open arms."

Not just a Black Blade, but one with status? It could not be true.

Nerrilik looked at her strangely. He reached up to touch her cheek. "Are you all right?"

"Yes, of course I am." She brushed his hand aside, not blaming him for his concern. She could imagine how strange she must look with her face frozen in shock. "Now tell me how you know Bracca was a Black Blade." Did Lord Devlin know? Did Karess?

"It is no secret. Camarie sent Cu-Laurian to Earth with orders to kill Lady St. John. Fate stopped him by breaking the bastard's sword. He would be dead now if that stupid female had not meddled. Why do you look so surprised? I mentioned this the first time Karess forced Cu-Laurian's presence on us at the palace."

"I suppose I forgot." She fought to reconcile what Nerrilik was telling her to what she knew. Nothing made sense. "Are you sure there wasn't a mistake? Perhaps Bracca was there to help Lady St. John."

"There is no mistake. He was supposed to kill her to negate the Seventh Prophecy. He failed to obey his Bloodsworn. Then he added to that betrayal by linking with the woman."

He almost spat the words, so thick was the disgust in his voice. Sheren couldn't respond. She felt numb with disbelief. Why hadn't anyone told her? Lord Devlin should have. He knew the pain she carried. Or Karess. Yet it was Karess who'd left her in the care of a former Black Blade not once, but twice. Why would he do such a thing?

Because Bracca was no longer a Black Blade. He was an Amber Blade, and Karess trusted him. So did Avera, so did Lord Devlin, and, more importantly, so did she.

The realization hit her like a jolt of lightning. No matter how many years he'd been tied to the dark Bloodsworn, she'd read Bracca's soul last night. She'd all but held his essence in her hands while they'd pleasured one another. The stains on his soul were many and dark, but none so black she considered him unredeemable. His sins were no worse, she imagined, than Nerrilik's.

Was this the reason the Amber Blade had held back from her even when the longing for her burned inside him so hot she could feel it? Was this the cause of that sense of desperation she'd felt in him last night? A fear that she wanted him just for one time only and not forever? She'd said as much, hadn't she? "I need to feel alive *tonight.*"

"I need to go find…Seth." Bracca. She needed to find Bracca. She had to make sure he knew his past didn't matter to her.

"I'll go with you."

"No. That is, I'm sure you have other duties. I won't be long, I promise. Seth and I will return shortly." With Silver Blades watching their every move, Seth's Blade training would have to wait.

Nerrilik looked like he wanted to stop her, but finally he said, "Good, see that you do."

She nodded and left, hurrying through the villa's halls to the outside. She saw Avera immediately, the other woman strolling past the beds of flowers marking the entrance to the gardens.

"Avera! Lady Avera," she corrected herself. The woman looked up and smiled. A true smile of friendship. At that moment, Sheren wanted nothing more than to link arms with her friend and walk into the garden in search of Bracca and Seth. But she could feel eyes on her. More than one set, she was sure. Perhaps even Nerrilik. She had to make him think she was taking his warning seriously else he might follow her.

"I'm sorry, but I can't join you as we planned."

Avera's brows arched. "Oh? Is something wrong?"

"No, no, nothing is wrong. I just remembered a chore I'd forgotten. I hope you understand." She whispered quickly. "Did you know you are being watched?"

"Not a problem. I'd still like to take a walk, though. Before you leave, could you show me the path you told me about yesterday?"

Sheren nodded. "Of course. It's this way."

As soon as they were out of sight of the courtyard Avera whispered, "Yes, I know. I was going to warn you about that. I thought there were a few too many Silver Blades hanging around this morning."

"Do you know they are watching Bracca, too?"

A frown wrinkled Avera's forehead. "No. Who told you that?"

"Nerrilik."

Avera snorted softly. "I don't think that warrior likes me very much. He's always scowling when I see him."

"He does not approve of your status as Bloodsworn, I think."

"He's got plenty of company."

Sheren stopped at the intersection of two paths. "Do you want me to try and distract the Blades?"

"No. I don't like all this sneaking around. I'm

going to tell Devlin about Seth just as soon as he gets back."

"We need to warn Bracca."

Avera waved a dismissing hand. "I've already warned him and Seth not to go waving that dagger around."

It took a moment for Sheren to understand that Avera had used her links. "Oh. That's good."

"Bracca says they'll meet us in the garden where I first ran into you and Seth. If we can't shake our watchers by then, we'll call it a day and wait for Devlin."

Sheren hesitated. Losing their watchers did not sound like a good idea. But then, these were Silver Blades, well trained in their warrior craft. She didn't think they could be lost that easily. She also needed to hurry back so Nerrilik would not get suspicious. A quick glance around assured her Nerrilik himself was nowhere to be seen. She finally nodded. "All right."

They walked quickly through the various small gardens. Avera seemed to have a good idea of where she was going, surprising Sheren by her knowledge of the little known gates and paths she chose. By the time they reached the play garden with its lush grass and shady trees, Sheren couldn't tell if they were being followed or not.

Avera led the way to one of the stone benches. Sitting down, she took a deep breath and said, "Well, that was fun. I think we lost most of them when we ducked out of that little jungle garden."

"How did you know about the gate behind the vines?" Sheren asked.

Avera tapped her temple. "Seth told me. He told me about the loose bar on the locked gate three gardens back, too. I think that's where we lost my last two watchdogs."

Sheren felt a sudden tiny spurt of jealousy at

Avera's reminder that she and Seth could speak to each other through their link. An emotion she quickly crushed into oblivion. Without this kind woman, Seth would be dead. As long as he thrived, she could share his affections with Avera St. John. She wasn't as sure about sharing Bracca's affections.

"Bracca told me last night that you consider him family." Avera's quick smile made Sheren realize how possessive she sounded. She hadn't intended to let anyone know how close she and Bracca were. Not yet. There were still things they needed to work out. Things that might make any kind of a relationship impossible. The last thing she wanted was for her feelings for him to cause problems between him and his Bloodsworn. That didn't mean she intended to back down now that Avera knew how she felt. She held the other woman's gaze, refusing to feel embarrassed.

"That's right," Avera said. "He's my big brother and Tyr is my little brother. And Seth is, well, Seth."

"Did Bracca give you my message about Seth?"

Avera nodded. "Yes, he did. Thanks. My mothering skills are practically nil. Practicing on Seth should be a real adventure."

"How did you and Bracca meet? I know it was on Earth, but no one has mentioned the details."

"Ah," Avera said with a little laugh. "Now there's a good story to pass the time."

"Did he really try to kill you?"

Avera jerked back with a look of mild horror. "Good gracious, no! Where did you hear that?"

Sheren fought back a relieved smile. "I'm sorry. Perhaps I misunderstood. Maybe you could tell me what really happened."

"Well, it's true he was *sent* to Earth to kill me. But that's as far as it went. According to him, the moment he saw me, he knew I was the Bloodsworn he was supposed to be linked to." She held up two fingers. "He saved my life twice by killing other Black Blades. I wasn't about to let Fate and his crew hurt him after that. So, I decided he had to come with us.

"We tried to get back to Devlin, but that didn't work out. Camarie kept using Bracca's sword to hone in on us and send in more warriors. Bracca took it upon himself to break his sword and with it, his link to Camarie."

Sheren's hand went to her throat. Bracca had broken his sword, not Fate. Nerrilik had so much of the story wrong. "How did you know you could link with him?"

"I didn't. But I couldn't just sit there and watch him die. He'd told me a little about the whole Bloodsworn/Blade thing earlier, including how a blood-link was formed. That was the only thing I could think of to try." She grinned. "Imagine my relief when it actually worked."

"And surprise as well, I would imagine."

"Yeah, that, too." Some of her grin faded. "Needless to say, Devlin wasn't happy when he caught up to us. I wasn't too happy with him at the time either, but that's another story."

"You both seem happy now."

Avera shrugged. "Happiness is transient. It comes and goes. All two people can do is cherish the moments when they have it and stick together through the rough times when they don't. I'm expecting one of those rough times to crop up this afternoon, but hopefully it won't last long."

Hurried footsteps called their attention to one of the entrances. Sheren breathed a sigh of relief when Bracca appeared, Seth by his side. Her son ran to her, lips poked out into a pout. She hugged him and kissed the top of his head. "What's wrong?"

"Bracca and Lady Avera say I can't practice with my dagger because of the Silver Blades. I want to practice, mama."

"I know, sweetling, but you must be patient. Your Bloodsworn and blade-brother are only trying to protect you. We will have this sorted out soon."

"I hope so," he said, leaning heavily against her.

She looked up at Bracca, needing reassurance as much as her son. A wave of carnal hunger surged through her the moment their eyes met. His, hers, theirs. It diminished between one heartbeat and the next, as if half—*his half*—was suddenly locked away. With an effort, she locked hers away as well.

A muscle flexed in his jaw just as his gaze swung to Avera. His dark eyes narrowed. Sheren knew from experience he was speaking to Avera.

"If you are discussing something important, I would like to be included, please."

"Sorry," Avera said instantly. She looked meaningfully at Seth. "Just trying to keep things calm."

Her arms around her son, Sheren looked at the other woman pointedly. "Rule number one. Protecting children from the world leaves them vulnerable to the world. They need to be aware when danger threatens."

"Not every danger, surely? And not when they're so—"

Sheren stared in horror as a bright light engulfed Avera, causing her to stiffen, then collapse to the ground. Bracca started to swing around, his hand on his sword, then he, too, was hit with the same light.

"Bracca!" Seth cried. He twisted out of her arms and dropped to his knees next to Bracca. Sheren wanted to run to him, too, but she went to Avera instead. Frantically, she felt for a pulse. The strong beat made her sag in relief.

"No, my dear, they're not dead."

Sheren whirled at the unfamiliar voice coming

from behind her. Fear grew as several men entered the garden. The first were Blades, but definitely not any Silver Blades she knew. The man in their midst, arrogantly strutting in shiny boots and swirling blue cloak, had to be their Bloodsworn. She didn't recognize him, either. She did, however, recognize the man walking with a slight limp just behind him.

"Nerrilik?"

The Silver Blade shot a glance at the strange Bloodsworn before coming to her quickly. She ignored the offer of his hand as she rose. This was all wrong, and she knew by the guilt she felt coming from Nerrilik that he was somehow involved. Color darkened his face and his hand dropped into a clenched fist.

"Everything is fine, Sheren, don't worry."

She nodded, hoping he meant he'd called his Bloodsworn. Seconds passed with no new gate winking into existence.

"Where is Lord Devlin, Nerrilik? Didn't you call him? Why isn't he here?"

"Lord Devlin isn't coming," the strange Bloodsworn said, every word ringing with smugness. "Is he, Nerrilik?"

Nerrilik didn't answer. Sheren stared at him a long moment, anger quickly replacing her disbelief that he would betray his Bloodsworn. His gaze slid away from the accusation blazing from her eyes. Deep inside, she began to tremble.

Bracca moaned. She swung around to go to him, only to have Nerrilik stop her.

"Leave him be. He is a Black Blade, Sheren."

She jerked her arm out of his grasp. She was getting very tired of him putting his hands on her. "Why do you keep saying that?" she said angrily. "You know his Bloodsworn is Lady Avera, not Camarie."

"Now, perhaps," the strange Bloodsworn

drawled. "But I assure you his sword was as black as a moonless night before he linked with the Earth woman. Cu-Laurian was one of Camarie's elite. I'll wager he has killed more men, women, and yes, children, too, than all of the Tragar's precious Silver Blades combined."

Now that, she knew, was wrong. Bracca had killed, yes, but only when he was forced to. And never had he taken the life of a woman or child. That kind of guilt she would have noticed immediately. Instead of bothering to refute the ridiculous accusation, she asked, "Who are you? What do you want here?"

He swept her a mocking bow. "My name is Kapatree Du-Farishi, Bloodsworn to sixty-two Blades. As to what I want?" He shrugged. "There are several things, actually. Shall I list them for you?"

"I would rather you list them for the Tragar." She took a step in Bracca's direction. She had to wake him, and knew of only one thing that might work.

Kapatree chuckled. "I'm afraid the Tragar is occupied with Bloodsworn council business at the moment. Timing is everything, don't you agree? So, back to my list. At the top is Avera St. John." He languidly pointed at Avera's still form. Sheren took another step toward Bracca. "And at the bottom of the list is your lovely self. But don't feel slighted, my dear. You are at the bottom of my list of desires, not Nerrilik's."

Her gaze shot to the man she'd once called friend. The blatant hunger in his eyes made her skin crawl.

"Nerrilik, what have you done?" she whispered.

His face flushed. "I have done only what Sayjan would expect of me."

"Sayjan would never have wanted you to betray your Bloodsworn." She could see the glint of sunlight off Bracca's sword hilt from the corner of her eye.

"You think not?" Nerrilik growled. "You think he wouldn't want me to take revenge for his death?"

"Lord Devlin didn't kill Sayjan—"

"He killed him just as surely as if he'd plunged a sword into him with his own hand. Sayjan wasn't ready to fight. He was still just a novice. He shouldn't have been anywhere near that battle. But the Tragar didn't care. Why should he? The man has Blades to spare, Sheren. Losing Sayjan was nothing to him, just like leaving me in the hands of those thrice-damned Black Blades was nothing."

Fury burned in her at the bitterness and self-pity coating his words. "You are a fool. You would be dead long ago if not for Lord Devlin. Dead again four years ago if he had not searched for you until he found you. He could have sundered your link with a mere thought. Instead, he searched for you, rescued you. He gave you back your life."

Nerrilik's face twisted into a snarl. "You have no idea what you're talking about. You think I should be grateful to him? The only reason I was tortured was because of my link to the Tragar. I begged him to sever the link, to let me die, but he refused. Hang on, he said. I'll find you, he said." Sarcasm and hatred thickened his voice, making it almost unrecognizable.

Sheren suppressed a shiver. "He did find you—"

"Not until after the damage was already done," he shouted, striking his injured leg with a fist. "I'm nothing more than a cripple now. He deserves to pay, Sheren. For Sayjan's life. For the life he took from me. He will pay with the one thing he values most."

Terror surged through Sheren. They meant to kill Avera. Perhaps not here and now, but she knew without a doubt that was what Nerrilik meant. *If Avera died, so would Seth and Bracca!*

Just the thought of losing even one of them brought debilitating pain welling up inside her. Such a loss would be unbearable. Such a loss could not be allowed.

Protective anger surged, blocking out the pain and fear and flooding her with strength. Her hand shot out, catching Nerrilik square on the cheek with a slap hard enough to knock him back a step.

"If you try to harm Bracca, Seth, or Lady Avera," she said, her voice shaking with rage, "I swear I'll kill you myself."

Chapter Twenty-Seven

Devlin's gaze shifted from the disturbing news in his hand to Jerran standing near the fireplace, and finally to Caveon seated across from him. "Do you trust this information?" he demanded. Expecting a firm assent, he was surprised when Caveon hesitated. The elder Bloodsworn was not one to act on anything other than fact.

Caveon cleared his throat before answering. "The information was provided by one of our own council members who lost a Blade in obtaining it."

"That is not an answer to my question. You're asking me to hare off to the other side of the world to chase Camarie. I'm asking for proof that this isn't a trick to get me out of gate's reach of Avera. Exactly who told you my uncle is hiding in Realm Senyah?" The island realm was situated far off the western coast. Half a world away from Realm Hedaud where he was supposed to be pursuing Churian.

"As I said, one of the council members."

"Not good enough. We both know the council is not as trust-worthy as it once was."

Caveon drew himself up. "That is a serious accusation, Lord Tragar. You would do well to remember that Luma herself approves each council member."

"And just how many candidates has she not approved over the years, Caveon?" He knew the answer as well as Caveon did. Luma always approved a proposed candidate because she didn't care who was chosen. She depended on her First Bloodsworn—a person she chose personally—to police the rest of Avalyr's Bloodsworn, not the Council.

Before Caveon could answer, Jerran said, "It was Kapatree, Devlin, and before you start swearing, I went to Senyah and did some checking of my own."

Caveon started, twisting around in his chair. "You did what? On whose authority?"

"My own. Sorry Grandfather." His tone was not the least apologetic. "But I don't trust Kapatree any further than a Blade can gate him." He moved closer to Devlin's desk, motioning to the message scroll. "Camarie's presence in the village checked out. I didn't see him in person, but I saw enough Black Blades and heard enough from the locals to believe he is there."

"*Was* there," Caveon corrected, his tone thick with disgust. "Or did you think no one would notice a Bloodsworn with a decca of Blades and not pass on the information to him? Only a fool shows his hand before the game's even begun, boy." He shook his head. "My apologies for taking up your time, First Bloodsworn. It appears we will have to resume our search for the Dark Bloodsworn."

Jerran made a disgusted sound of his own. "Do give me a little more credit, Grandfather. Even I know better than to take a decca of Blades on a reconnaissance mission."

Caveon froze in the act of rising from his chair. Devlin noted the glint in Jerran's eyes and the stubborn tilt of his chin. Oh, this was going to be good. He sat back, his concerns over the validity of the information momentarily set aside.

"Half decca then," Caveon snapped.

"Try none."

The veins on Caveon's neck stood out. "You went alone? Luma's bloody hell, what were you thinking?"

"I was thinking one man, properly disguised,

could sneak into an enemy's camp un-noticed, gather information, and sneak out again without arousing suspicion."

"*Vet,* boy, you could have been captured. What then of the lives you hold in trust, not to mention your own?" Devlin's lips twitched as Caveon's rant picked up speed. "I swear I'll gate your First and Second to the top of Mystia's frigid plateau and leave them there. What were they thinking to allow you to do something so reckless? The useless fools."

Jerran held his arms out to his sides. "Peace, Grandfather, I am un-harmed, as you can plainly see. And Talon and Drell can hardly be held accountable for my actions. You may forever see me as the boy who clung to your tunic and hung on your every word, but I am no longer an infant Bloodsworn. Besides," he flashed a look of chagrin to Devlin, "I didn't tell my Blades about my plans until after I'd returned."

Devlin shook with silent laughter. Jerran had indeed been an infant Bloodsworn. He'd linked with Talon, his First Blade, mere days after celebrating his fifteenth year. Drell, his Second Blade, followed barely a month later. Both men were older than their young Bloodsworn by a decca of years, and both had come to view Jerran as a younger brother, perhaps even a son. Even Fate's and Karess' overprotective tendencies paled in comparison. "I'm surprised they've let you out of their sight long enough for you to attend this meeting, my friend."

Jerran snorted and tapped his temple. "Who said I'm out of their sight? Anyway, it won't be easy to get to Camarie. Besides his Blades, he has hired several bands of mercenaries."

Devlin held up the message. "What of this village, Brancornick? How fortified is it?"

"Not very, but you can't be proposing an outright attack. Camarie's a coward. He'll gate away at the first sign of one of our Blades, and we'll be right back where we started."

"A Blade, yes, but would he leave if those attacking were just another pack of nameless mercenaries?"

Caveon sat forward. "No, he would not. He may be a coward, but he is an arrogant coward. He would defend his bolt hole from anyone he viewed as ordinary rabble. Such a diversion should keep his own mercenaries and Blades busy while we close the trap around him. Excellent."

"We'll still need to find out exactly where Camarie has his lair beforehand," Jerran said, pacing between the fireplace and Devlin's desk. "No sense ransacking the entire village. There's a mill situated just outside the south wall. I've already been inside, so I can use it as a point of entry—" He jerked to a stop mid-step and winced, one hand going to his head. "*Vet!* All right, all right. *We* can use it as a point of entry. Are you sure you two are Blades? You act more like a pair of mother hens." He looked over and winked at Devlin.

Devlin grinned back. Dealing with over-protective Blades was a never-ending job. They never seemed to understand the fact their Bloodsworn sometimes needed to fight his own battles. An extremely difficult task with a pack of men he considered as close as brothers breathing down his neck. Something Churian had angrily pointed out to him on more than one occasion.

His smile faded as concern for his brother surfaced. The mere possibility of Churian being at the mercy of Camarie's twisted whims had him feeling something close to panic. He needed to contact Shan and Valcon immediately, have them intensify their search.

A ripple of unease went through him, settling in the vicinity of his chest. At first he thought it part of his fear for his brother. But the unease grew, spreading like a stain through his body until his skin prickled. Something was wrong.

Quickly, he ruffled through his links, searching for the problem. All seemed well, yet the uncomfortable feeling persisted. He searched deeper, gasping when he brushed against his mate-bond with Avera. His connection to her usually sat like a tiny jewel in the heart of his mind, glowing with life and love. Now the jewel flickered frantically, as if struggling to stay alive. Adrenaline flooded his body. He stood so fast his chair fell over with a crash.

Fate, Karess, gather whoever is dressed for battle and come to me. He ran for the door, sweeping it open with a thought.

"What is it?" Jerran demanded.

Who threatens you? Fate snarled.

"I don't know," Devlin said to Jerran. *The threat is not to me,* he said to Fate. "Avera is in danger," he told them both, and broke into a run in the hall.

Chapter Twenty-Eight

Kapatree laughed. "Ah, Nerrilik, I see now why you want her so much. She has spirit. I am almost tempted to take her for myself."

Nerrilik stopped rubbing his cheek. "That is not part of our deal," he growled.

Sheren felt the tension thicken the air. Every one of Kapatree's Blades suddenly focused on Nerrilik.

Now, she thought.

She dove for Bracca's sword, giving Seth a push toward the hedge as she passed him. "Run Seth, bunny hole." She didn't wait to see if he was able to wiggle his way into the small hole in the hedge, but a curse from Kapatree told her he had. She also glimpsed two of his Blades running out of the garden. Terror for her child filled her as she wrapped her fingers firmly around the hilt of Bracca's sword. *Please, please, let him feel my touch like he did this morning.*

With a gasp, Bracca sat straight up, nearly knocking her over. The relief flooding her was short lived.

Kapatree's delighted laugh filled the garden. "Amazing. You didn't tell me how talented your woman is, Nerrilik. Her touch can awaken an unconscious Blade. Very interesting, indeed. Too bad such a valiant effort is wasted."

Kapatree raised his arm, magic swirling around his hand, and pointed at Bracca. Without thinking, Sheren threw herself between them.

****

"No!" Bracca tried to move, to knock Sheren out of the way, but his body refused to cooperate. He barely got a hand on her skirt as the blast hit her, knocking her back. Somehow he managed to get under her before she hit the ground. She sprawled over him, limp and un-moving. Agony ripped through him as he gathered her close. He made sure she was still breathing before lifting his head to glare at Kapatree. That was when he noticed Nerrilik. The Silver Blade stood at Kapatree's side.

"I swear I will kill you both for this."

"Foolish words coming from a man with no magic," Kapatree sneered, raising his hand again.

Nerrilik knocked Kapatree's arm down. "No, you'll hit Sheren."

Magic shimmered in the air around Kapatree, its presence causing Nerrilik to stumble back. "Careful Silver Blade," Kapatree warned sharply. You wouldn't want me to renegotiate our agreement at this stage. It would take but a whisper of rumor to reveal your part in all this. What do you think your precious Bloodsworn would do if he found out you were responsible for the poisoned air that should have taken his Starmate's life, hmmm? Which death do you think he'd grant you, slow or quick?"

"You swore if I helped you, you would take over my link and allow me and Sheren to live in peace on your lands. You gave me your word, Kapatree."

"I told you I would *try* to link with you. These things are never certain, Silver Blade. As for the woman, I wish you luck. Females with a little spirit are always such a delight to break, but if you are man enough to tame yours, I will be very surprised.

"I myself will be far too busy to assist you." Kapatree's hungry gaze settled on Avera. "Camarie never said she had to die immediately, just that I take her if the opportunity presented itself. So take her I shall, most pleasurably. Lady St. John and I have a long-overdue appointment."

White hot rage shook Bracca to the core of his being. He would not allow these men to take away the two most precious things in his life. Never before, not even in the darkest recesses of his mind, had he thirsted for the powers of a Bloodsworn. Now, he would give the last breath of his life to be able to wrap Avera and Sheren in glowing shields while piercing the heart of every man in the garden with a spear of pure magic.

But he wasn't Bloodsworn. He was nothing more than a warrior, a Blade honed in the fires of pain and suffering. All he had to fight with was the sword of his Bloodsworn. Carefully, while everyone's attention seemed to be elsewhere, he eased Sheren onto the thick grass and slowly drew his sword. Stealthily, he moved a step toward the crazed Bloodsworn.

****

Seth scooted out of the bunny hole, scrambled to his feet, and ran. Help. He had to get help. Silver Blades would be good. Lord Devlin would be better. He could use magic to stop the bad men.

Heavy steps pounded behind him. He glanced back at the two warriors chasing him. Both men carried ugly, dark blue swords. The sight made his heart pound harder in his chest. He sprinted down the path and swung around a short stone wall. If he could just get to the water garden on the other side, he knew he could get away. The men wouldn't be able to slip between the bars of the gate over the stream like he could.

One of the men flew through the air and landed in front of him. Seth stumbled to a halt. How had he done that? Then the other man jumped from the top of the stone wall, and he knew. They were bigger than him, so they'd climbed the wall instead of going around it, and cut him off. He should have stayed to the gardens with the tall hedges. Too late now.

Seth backed away, his gaze darting back and forth between the dark swords. The men had the exits blocked. There was nowhere to run. Snatching up a rock, he cocked back his arm. "Stay back."

The warriors paused. One of them grinned nastily. "Think yourself a warrior, lad? Going to fight off our swords with a puny pebble?"

The other twirled his dark sword. "We don't have time to play with you, child. Drop the rock and we won't hurt you."

Seth's heart pounded as he watched the deadly spinning sword. He wanted to swallow, but his mouth was too dry. He wanted to cry, but knew he couldn't do that either. He had to get away. He had to find help for his mother and Bracca and Lady Avera. If only Bracca had let him carry his dagger.

One of the men made a disgusted noise. "Enough of this," he said. "Kapatree didn't say we had to bring him back in one piece." His sword flashed out.

****

Devlin stepped through the gate into Villa Porenmagie's courtyard with two decca of Silver Blades, plus five Sapphire Blades and another five of Bronze. He hadn't quibbled when Jerran and Caveon insisted on joining him.

Instead of wasting time by searching the villa, Devlin grabbed the first servant he saw.

"Where is Lady St. John?"

The man trembled at the sight of the small army invading the courtyard. "She...she's in the gardens, my lord."

"Where in the gardens?" They were vast, and he didn't want to waste time searching them one by one. He'd always enjoyed his grandmother's intricate, maze-like gardens, but right now all he wanted to do was blast every hedge to ash and crumble every wall to dust until he found Avera.

"I do not know, my lord. Maybe the water garden?"

Devlin cursed. He didn't have time for guessing games. The unease in his chest burned, stirring his magic to a frenzy. Quickly, he snapped open every one of his links to the Silver Blades assigned to the villa. One or more of them should be guarding Avera regardless of where she was. But as each responded to his hail, his dread grew. Most, alerted to his presence, were already in the courtyard. The rest were scurrying to join them. None were in the gardens with Avera.

At least that's what he thought at first.

Nerrilik was the only one who didn't answer his summons. Devlin closed his eyes and sought the Silver Blade through the connection to Nerrilik's sword. There. He alone was in the garden. Devlin tried reaching him again, but their link stayed tightly closed. Why wouldn't the man answer?

He threw out a hand, opening a gate to the water garden. He sensed Nerrilik's sword in that direction. It was as good a place as any to begin searching. Choosing ten warriors at random to stay behind and guard the villa, he ordered the rest to follow him.

Karess physically held Devlin back while Fate slipped through the gate first. In retaliation, Devlin sent a pulse of magic through his skin to remind his friend of his powers.

Karess hissed, jerking back and shaking his hand to relieve the sting. "*Vet*, Dev."

"Don't get in my way again, Karess."

"Don't be an idiot, and I won't have to. Getting yourself killed won't help your Starmate."

Devlin didn't bother with a reply. He knew Karess was right. He also knew that if a Bloodsworn, say, Camarie for instance, had been waiting on the other side of the gate, Fate would be the one dead.

The surrounding garden seemed empty when Devlin stepped through the gate, quiet but for the gurgle of water tumbling over small waterfalls and bubbling up in fountains. *Anything?* he asked Fate.

The tall warrior stood near one of the entrances to the garden, his head tilted as if listening to something. He put a finger to his lips. *Voices on the other side. Two men, a boy.*

Devlin eased up beside him, hearing a man's deep voice.

"Enough of this. Kapatree didn't say we had to bring him back in one piece."

All caution left Devlin. He burst into the next garden, sending out a wave of magic ahead of him to shove the two Blades away from Seth. They staggered and spun to face him. He recognized their blue-black swords, if not the men themselves. What were Kapatree's Blades doing here, and why were they threatening Sheren's son?

One of the men lunged toward Seth. Devlin threw out a hand, releasing a bolt of magic that knocked the man off his feet. He grabbed the other man in a magic vice just shy of deadly. He needed answers after all.

"Seth?"

The boy ran up and grabbed Devlin's free hand. "You have to come. Lady Avera's in trouble. A bad Bloodsworn came and knocked her and Bracca down. I ran when mama told me to, but she's still there. And there are more men with ugly swords. They might hurt her and Bracca and Lady Avera. We have to hurry. Come on, come on, this way."

****

Bracca saw the moment Kapatree noticed him, or perhaps one of his Blades warned him. Kapatree's eyes lit with dark amusement, and his hand rose almost languidly. Magic erupted in a flash of light, shooting straight at Bracca. He squinted, throwing up his sword in reflex, knowing it would do no good. He would die, and the two women who meant more to him than life, would suffer for his failure.

He felt the heat of magic when it hit his amber sword. Felt it wash over him, *around* him, the tingling essence passing harmlessly to either side as if sliced in two. He blinked, taking in Kapatree's astonished expression.

"Impossible!" The Bloodsworn raised his hand again. Another flash blinded Bracca for an instant. Again he held his sworn in front of him. Again the heat of magic seared the air around him. The hilt of his sword warmed in his hand then returned to normal in the next breath.

"How?" Kapatree shouted. "How are you doing that? No one can deflect magic except another Bloodsworn. You're nothing but a worthless Blade."

Bracca could only look from his sword to an unconscious Avera and back again with a sense of awe. The amber-colored metal glowed with more than the usual telling light that indicated a blood-linked weapon. His sword pulsed with life, the presence of Avera's essence so strong it was as if she stood beside him. No, in front of him!

Even unconscious, she somehow managed to imbue his weapon with her power. He looked up at the dumbfounded men facing him and grinned. "Apparently my Lady Bloodsworn does not consider me worthless."

"No matter," Kapatree snapped. He motioned sharply to his men. "Take both females. Disarm the traitorous Blade any way you wish, but don't kill him. Camarie wants him alive."

"Yes, my Bloodsworn." One of the Indigo Blades—probably Kapatree's First—moved forward. He motioned the others to spread out.

Bracca had no choice but to let the enemy surround him. He couldn't leave Avera and Sheren unprotected. Nor did he have any illusions that he would be able to hold off almost a decca of trained Blades. He might manage to take two, maybe even three, but the others would eventually overwhelm him. As soon as one got close enough to hold a sword to Sheren's or Avera's throat, he would have no choice but to surrender. But until then...

He spun, catching the dark edge of a sword and twisting it away. His backswing slashed through leather and flesh, biting deep into the chest of another opponent. He carried through the swing, blocking the first sword again and knocking back the man wielding it with a sharp kick to the groin. He grabbed a third man's wrist, holding on long enough to drive his amber sword into the man's side.

Four more took their places. They kept their distance, prodding him, trying to herd him away from the women. He set his feet, refusing to move. They would have to kill him to get to Sheren and Avera.

They rushed him all at the same time. The air seemed filled with the deadly arcs of blue-black swords. Far too many for him to turn every blow.

Pain ripped into his left side. He twisted away, stabbing blind, his sword finding its mark with a spray of blood. More swords flew at him like a flock of deadly ravens. He knocked back each one in quick succession, feeling his strength slipping away. Another sword bit into his back. A third sank deep into his thigh. He staggered, fighting the wall of pain rushing toward him.

The link in his mind shuddered awake.

Bracca?

Avera. Sister! Forgive me.

Pain exploded in the back of his head, driving him into darkness.

Chapter Twenty-Nine

The quick flash of intense pain coming from Bracca jolted Avera into full consciousness. She opened her eyes just in time to see him hit the ground. Several warriors carrying dark blue swords surrounded him.

"Well done. Now hurry, gather them up. Someone might have heard that little exchange."

She knew that voice. Looking around, she found Kapatree walking toward her, his dark blue cloak flapping around his ankles.

"What are you doing here?" she demanded. One of the warriors heaved Bracca's unconscious form over his shoulder. "Leave him alone!"

"Now, now, my dear, no need for hysterics. I merely wish to renew our acquaintance. Remember your offer of a one-on-one engagement? I've thought of nothing else." He stroked his crotch suggestively.

She used the nearby bench to push herself up. Whatever had knocked her unconscious—and she was thinking it must have been a shot of Kapatree's magic—still lingered, making her feel dizzy. "You sick bastard. If Devlin doesn't kill you this time, I will."

Kapatree chuckled. "Assuming the lowly Tiger ever discovers the truth, he is welcome to try. As for you killing me, I'm afraid the chances of that are very slim indeed. I am far stronger than you. There is nothing you can do either as a female or a Bloodsworn that I cannot counter."

He stepped closer, one hand already reaching for her. She didn't know if it was that grasping hand or the sick, perverted hunger in his eyes that made her reach for her magic. The barrier popped into place around her so suddenly it took Kapatree completely by surprise. He yelped and jerked his hand back as if he'd just been bitten.

"You filthy bitch," he snarled, rubbing his fist. Maybe her barrier did have a bite to it. The possibility made her smile. That is, until she saw the man carrying Bracca step through the gate.

"No! Bring him back!" Another man stepped around her carrying Sheren. "Nerrilik?" The Silver Blade held Sheren's limp body with great care. "Nerrilik, what's going on, what's wrong with Sheren? Where's Devlin?" The warrior kept walking as if he didn't hear her. He paused when he reached the gate where one of Kapatree's men blocked his path.

"Remember our bargain," Kapatree called. A vicious smile curled his lips. "Since you have your hands full, Gillare will do the honors if you like."

"I'll get it myself," Nerrilik snarled. He shifted Sheren to one shoulder. At first, Avera thought he was drawing his sword to take on Kapatree's warrior. She gasped when all he did was toss the weapon aside. It landed in the grass a few feet away, silver bright against the dark green.

Alarm shot through her as the Indigo Blade moved aside, and Nerrilik stepped through the gate with Sheren. What the hell had happened while she was unconscious? Had her whole world turned upside-down again?

A flash of light made her flinch as bright magic splashed against her shield. The air around her thickened, absorbing the released essence like a sponge, then resumed its steady haze.

Kapatree's brows rose. "Extraordinary." He held his hand out, palm up, his expression one of intense concentration. Magic appeared, suffusing his skin in a shimmering glove. The essence thickened, swirling and coalescing into a bright ball hovering just above his palm. When it filled his hand, he casually flicked the glowing sphere in her direction.

She felt the resulting explosion of concentrated magic all the way to the depths of her mind. It sent her cringing away, mentally and physically. Automatically she reached for her links, shutting them down as tight as possible. She didn't want any of this to bleed over and hurt Bracca, Tyr, or Seth.

Seth. Where was Seth?

She hadn't seen hide or precious hair of the child since she'd awakened. Was he hiding, or had they already caught him and taken him through the gate? Cautiously, she reached for him. His little voice rang in her head as soon as she opened her side of their link.

I'm coming, I'm coming. I'm bringing Lord Devlin, and Fate, and Karess, and Strum, and Kiel, and—"

That's good, Seth, very good. Tell Lord Devlin to hurry, okay? Kapatree's leaving. He has Bracca and... She stopped herself before mentioning Seth's mother was already gone. The child didn't need to know that yet.

Just beyond her barrier Kapatree paced and cursed. Damn, she wished she knew how to throw those balls of magic. She'd make him wish he'd never set eyes on her.

Only one warrior remained standing near the gate. His gaze shifted nervously to the two entrances to the garden. "My Bloodsworn, we must go."

"Not without her. I want *her.*" He stabbed a finger in her direction.

"We will have to get her another time, my Bloodsworn. Please, come away now."

"Another time, another time," Kapatree muttered. "Always it's another time." He walked directly up to her and placed both hands against the barrier. Fingers dug into the thick air. "You have ruined everything. Leaving you behind to identify me means I will have to go into hiding. Not that I haven't planned for such a contingency, but you have upset my time-table."

"Glad I could help. By the way, if you harm Bracca or Sheren, there's not a hiding place deep enough that I won't find you."

He started backing away, that lascivious grin returning to his face. "Perhaps one day, if you look hard enough, I'll *let* you find me." He gave her a mocking bow. "Until then." His blue cloak swirled through the air as he turned and stepped into the gate. His Blade followed him just as Devlin and a host of Silver Blades ran into the garden.

One of the Silver Blades sprinted ahead of the rest toward the barrier.

"Kiel, stop," someone bellowed. The young warrior came to an abrupt halt half a step from diving through the gate, his body frozen like a statue. Kapatree's laugh drifted back through the shining oval just before it winked out of existence.

"You idiot," Strum shouted, marching up and snagging Kiel by the back of his neck as he un-froze. "Did you think Kapatree was just going to leave the gate open for the rest of us?"

"But, Lady Avera—"

"Is over there with our Bloodsworn if you bothered to use your eyes. Luma save me from rash young fools."

Then all she could see was Devlin. He stood before her, his beautiful blue eyes sweeping over her body anxiously. She released her hold on the barrier and fell into his arms.

The tears caught her by surprise.

"He took them, he took both of them." She could barely get the words out between sobs. Part of her tears sprang from pure impotent rage. She hadn't been able to protect anyone but herself. What kind of person only protected herself? "I couldn't stop them."

"I know, *me`surrasie*, I know. We will find them."

"I still cannot believe Kapatree would do such a thing."

She wiped her eyes and focused on Caveon. "Oh, it was him all right. Blond hair, perpetual sneer, and a shitty superior attitude all wrapped up in a dark blue cloak the same shade as his Blade's swords. The man's an evil prick. He and Nerrilik both."

"Nerrilik? What does he have to do with this? Where is he?" Devlin looked around.

"His sword is here, my lord."

The sea of Blades parted and Avera saw Fate standing over Nerrilik's sword.

"He was taken as well?" Devlin asked.

"No, he wasn't taken. I'm sorry Devlin, but Nerrilik is the traitor. He made some kind of deal with Kapatree to help him either kill or capture me."

Anger suffused Devlin's face. "And what could he possibly get in return that would be worth betraying his Bloodsworn?"

"Sheren. Kapatree apparently promised he could have Sheren. That's why he took her, too."

"My mama's gone?"

Avera swore to herself. She'd forgotten Seth was even in the garden. She looked for him amid the sea of tall men, finally finding him standing a few feet away holding Bracca's sword.

Everyone else seemed to notice him, or at least what he held, at the same time. Caveon's deep voice boomed out over the gasps filling the air. "Drop that weapon this instant, child." His horrified gaze, as well as everyone else's shot to her. She didn't understand why at first, then remembered no one here knew Seth was Bracca's blade-brother. A situation she knew she needed to correct.

Tears welled in Seth's eyes, quickly spilling over. Instead of obeying Caveon's order, he shook his head and clutched the weapon tighter. Afraid he was going to cut himself, Avera pried herself from Devlin's grip and hurried over to him, sinking to her knees.

"It's all right, Seth. We'll get Bracca and your mama back. I promise. Can I hold Bracca's sword for a little while?"

Seth sniffled and nodded. A collective sigh of relief spun through the garden as soon as his fingers left Bracca's sword. Avera ignored them for a moment and hugged Seth tightly.

"Avera, are you all right?" Devlin asked.

She stood and faced him, keeping a hand on her small Third Blade. The suspicion in Devlin's eyes as he looked from her to Seth cut through her like a knife. She wished they were alone. Telling him this, especially with Caveon and Jerran present was not going to be easy. Taking a deep breath, she decided now wasn't the time to beat around the bush. They had to start looking for Kapatree.

"Two days ago, I formed a blood-link with Seth. That's why it doesn't hurt me when he holds Bracca's sword. Seth is my Third Blade."

Stunned silence met her announcement. She focused on Devlin's face, trying to read the emotions. Shock, disbelief, fear, doubt, anger, everything she'd expected and more.

"How?" he finally asked.

"He was sick. I felt called to him just like I was to Tyr. Only I didn't have to cut myself on a knife beforehand. When I realized what was happening, I asked Sheren's permission to try and form a link, and she said yes. I used Bracca's dagger, and the magic, as I've been told often enough, did the rest."

"Impossible," Caveon sputtered. "Children do

not get the blade-illness. There has to be some other explanation."

Devlin's gaze bore into hers. "I do not want to believe it any more than you do, Caveon."

She knew he wasn't talking just about Seth's new status. "I'm sorry," she said softly. "I should have told you sooner. I was going to tell you today, but…" She shrugged weakly.

Caveon huffed. "The Council will want proof."

The thick barrier snapped into place around her and Seth before she'd even completed the thought. She pinned a withering gaze on the elder Bloodsworn. "No one is going to lay one finger on Seth's dagger just to see if he's really a Blade. Anyone tries, and I don't care if I have to practice until doomsday, I will learn how to throw magic fireballs and make whoever hurts him regret they were ever born. Do I make myself clear?"

The shield flexed once in Caveon's direction. He stepped back quickly, eyes widening before narrowing in anger. She intercepted a few glares from the warriors standing near him. His grandson, however, chuckled.

"You should have seen that coming, Grandfather, she is female after all." Lord Jerran swept her an elegant bow. "Forgive him, my lady, I beg you. He is an irascible fellow at best, but my grandmother loves him so he must have some redeeming qualities." His teasing expression shifted to one of solemn promise. "I assure you, no one will harm your young Blade. There are other ways to confirm a mind-link, are there not, Devlin?"

"Yes, but later. Avera, please…" His hand rested against the barrier. The pain in his eyes struck her as she realized she'd shut him out along with everyone else. She shoved the magic back into the box in her mind. The air around her quickly returned to normal. With a sigh of relief, she stepped into Devlin's waiting arms.

"She has ignored the Council's edict," Caveon pointed out. "There will be repercussions."

Lord Jerran snorted. "What are you going to do, Grandfather, break a link with a child? I think the repercussions of a five-year-old becoming blade-sick would be of far more concern to the Council. You know what this means, don't you?"

Avera answered the rhetorical question. "The blade-illness has mutated. There's no telling who it will strike or when. It might even have crossed the gender barrier."

Caveon's "Luma forbid." was joined by a host of different swear words. Not a single man there would wish the blade-illness on an empathic female.

I can't find my dagger, Lady Avera. Do you know where it is?

Avera looked around, sensing Seth, but not seeing him right away. "No Seth, I don't remember seeing it. Did you leave it in the water garden?"

"What is it?" Devlin asked.

"Seth says he can't find his dagger. Where are you, baby?"

Devlin pointed behind her. "He's over there."

"No," she said, stepping in the opposite direction from where he pointed. "He should be over here somewhere. Seth?"

"Yes, Lady Avera?"

She spun around as Seth ran to her. He had been behind her after all. How was that possible? She thought she'd been getting better at sensing where her Blades were. It had worked pretty well with Bracca anyway. She could even feel Tyr in the general direction of the palace. Why hadn't she felt Seth?

She stopped breathing as the answer came to her. She should have thought of it before. *Avera, you can be so slow sometimes.*

Quickly, she knelt down in front of the child. "Seth, sweetie, do you remember the last time you saw your dagger? Did Bracca have it?"

The boy's head bobbed excitedly. "I remember now. He was getting ready to show me the different ways to hold it when you called to tell us about the Silver Blades. He wrapped it up quick in some leather and tucked it back here under his tunic." He reached around and patted his back.

Standing, Avera smiled at Devlin in relief. "Bracca has Seth's dagger with him. We can use that to find them."

She didn't understand the shear horror of his expression or why he swooped Seth into his arms. Twin gates appeared at the same time.

Caveon stepped forward holding out his arms. "I've got him. I'll make sure he's safe. You and Jerran go after Kapatree. Take my First Blade with you. When you find him, make sure you call me."

"Hurry," Devlin urged as the bewildered boy change hands. "Hurry, Caveon!"

I'm scared.

It's okay, baby, she assured him, though her worry spiked as Caveon and his men disappeared through the gate at a run. "What is it, what's wrong?"

"Seth's dagger," Devlin said, grasping her shoulders. "They'll search Bracca and find Seth's dagger. They'll take it."

The horror of his words sank in, bringing time to a stand-still. "No," she whispered. Bracca's sword slipped from her fingers. Devlin gathered her into his arms just as she felt the first twinge of pain. The next wave came hard enough to buckle her knees.

Devlin picked her up. He moved to the stone bench, trying to settle her in his lap. She couldn't stay still. Something twisted inside her, boring into her like a drill. Deep in her mind she heard a scream, high pitched, thin, the despairing cry of a child in agony. She screamed, too.

Then her link to Seth shuddered and went terrifyingly still.

"Seth," she gasped. "Seth!" Tears streamed down her face. "Oh, Devlin, they broke his dagger. They've killed him!"

Soothing hands brushed her face. "Avera, stop crying, please, beloved. Check for his link. Is it gone completely, or just silent? Do you feel it at all?"

She gulped and pulled herself together long enough to search her mind. Relief left her trembling inside and out. His link was there, right where it should be. But it was different. Weaker somehow. Blocked maybe? Shielded? Yes, that felt right. Somehow the link was shielded so tightly that it felt no more substantial than a memory. But it was there.

She gulped. "Yes, I feel it. How did you know it would still be there?"

"Caveon took Seth to Latessa. She can't heal a Blade, but she can use her ability to put him into a deep sleep. She's also been experimenting with placing a shield around a Blade's mind."

"Yes, I can feel that, too."

"Good. It won't hold forever, but should last long enough for us to get his dagger back."

"What if they decide to break the dagger before we find them?" Stupid question. She knew the answer. Seth would die.

Jerran dropped to one knee in front of her. "My grandfather may be resistant to change, but he will not allow a child to die for the sake of his stubbornness. He'll try to link with Seth. We all will if necessary. On that you have my word."

"Thank you," she said. She slipped her arms around Devlin's neck. "And thank you, too. I'm very sorry for not telling you about Seth sooner. If I had, maybe none of this would have happened."

"If you had, we might not have discovered the traitor, and his next attempt on your life might have succeeded. Not that I would wish to trade Sheren's or Seth's life for yours. Cu-Laurian's I would have to think about."

"Beast." She kissed him once.

"If we're going after Kapatree, I, or rather Talon and Drell," Jerran said dryly, "would like to gate home and pick up a few of their blade-brothers."

She sighed and wiggled out of Devlin's lap. "We better get going then. Think you can find me a scabbard for this while we're there," she said, picking up Bracca's sword. "I want to take it with me."

"You are not going." The note of finality in Devlin's voice didn't even slow her down.

"And just how do you expect to find Kapatree without a compass?" She tapped her head. "Shielded or not, I can still feel Seth's dagger when I reach for it."

She heard Devlin's teeth grind together. "I don't want you anywhere near Kapatree."

"If you insist on leaving me behind, I guess I'll just have to play with my magic until I figure out how to cast my own gate and follow you."

Both Devlin and Jerran paled at her words.

"Um, Devlin, I think she means it."

"I know she does," Devlin snarled. He grabbed her by the arm and jerked her to his side, capturing her chin with his other hand. "You will stay as close to me as this at all times. No wandering off on your own, understand?"

She snuggled in closer, wrapping an arm tightly around his waist. "Perfectly."

"Very well. We go to Jerran's home first. Then you may point us in the right direction. Do not get your hopes up that we'll find them on your first few tries, Avera. Tracking down a Blade over a long distance by trying to sense his sword takes time."

The oval gate that appeared was larger than she was used to. The room visible on the other side was long, lined on both sides by a row of columns. The ceiling looked as if it was made of glass. She could easily see a broad slice of cloudless blue sky. Avera glanced up at the sky above the villa, noting the clouds spread from horizon to horizon.

"Wait," she said, an idea coming to her. She turned to Jerran. "Just where do you live in relation to here?"

"A thousand miles or so east," he said. "Why?"

"If I take a reading on the dagger from here, and again at your place, and then at a third position, we can mark the directions on a map and narrow down the search area. What do you think?"

Every man there looked at her with an odd expression. She didn't realized what it was until she glanced at Fate. As their eyes met, he inclined his head, his normally grim lips twitching up to form a small smile of approval.

"I think, my lady Starmate," Devlin said, looking at her with pride, "that Kapatree does not have a fireball's chance in Luma's frozen hell of hiding from us."

"And I think I'm jealous," Jerran said, grinning at Devlin. "I've changed my mind. I would very much like to be you."

Devlin shot her a look of pure possession. "Too bad."

Chapter Thirty

Bracca woke to cold and pain. So much pain he could not, at first, begin to take stock of his injuries. His head pounded in time to his heartbeat as he lay still trying to recall what had happened to him. Something painful, certainly. A battle?

Memories of his past crowded in, taunting him. Times when he'd been hurt fighting in some conflict of Camarie's making and been forced to wait until his evil Bloodsworn finally got around to healing him. Sometimes he'd lain in pain for days, delirious, expecting death to claim him at any moment. Sometimes, he'd almost wished for it. Almost.

He'd never sought to take his own life as some men did who ended up in the dark Bloodsworn's service. Where there was life, there was hope. His link with Avera proved that.

Assuming he really did have a blood-link with a woman from another world.

The possibility that the time with her was nothing more than a product of his fevered imagination had his heart racing. He couldn't still be a Black Blade, could he? The very idea nauseated him. Avera St. John had to exist. And Sheren—ah, gods, his precious Sheren—had to be more than a wistful, erotic dream conjured by his desperate mind. She had to be real.

He started to reach for his link and thought better of it. His sword. He wanted to see his sword first. He felt at his side for his scabbard. He always slept with the hilt of his weapon under his hand. His searching fingers found nothing.

He opened his eyes—or tried to. The lids felt sticky, gritty, as if they'd been closed a long time. He blinked several times to clear them, and looked around. Torchlight flickered through the small barred window of the room's door, giving him enough light to make out his surrounds. Carefully, he turned his aching head. A cell, maybe even a dungeon considering the chill. So far, not very encouraging.

He slowly rolled to his side, then levered himself upright. The room tilted and spun a few times before finally settling down. He tossed back the coarse blanket covering him to examine his injuries.

Someone had stripped him. Or perhaps he had undressed himself. He couldn't recall. Regardless, he was naked except for a few white bandages. The one around his thigh looked relatively clean with only a small reddish-brown stain. The bandage tied around his middle featured a larger area of dried blood. He pressed on it a little, trying to determine how long it had been there, and hissed at the instant pain. Not long, he decided, noting the fresh blood creating a dark red halo around the older stain.

He couldn't see the wound on his back just under his shoulder, but it had to be bad since whoever had bandaged him had tied his left arm to his side. A fourth bandage wound around his head. He fingered it gingerly, finding an area of stiff material covering a tender, fair-sized knot just behind his ear.

He dropped his hand and gripped the side of the cot. "*Vet*," he swore softly. Locked in a dark cell with nothing but a hard cot and a slop bucket, battle wounds no more than a day old, and his sword missing. What else did he need to tell him he'd been taken prisoner?

But taken prisoner by whom?

Deep in his mind, his link stirred, telling him

his Bloodsworn was trying to reach him. For a moment, he was afraid to open his side. Afraid he'd find Camarie on the other end and not Avera St. John. Steeling himself for disappointment, he opened the mental door.

Bracca! Thank God!

He closed his eyes, savoring the sweetness of his heart-sister's voice.

Bracca, can you hear me? Please answer!

I am here, my lady Bloodsworn, though I do not know where here *is.*

You're somewhere inside a bloody mountain fortress, my friend. We've been looking for you and Sheren since yesterday. Sorry it took so long. Kapatree is really good at hiding. Are you two all right?

The surrounding cold seemed to seep into his bones. *Sheren was taken as well?*

Yes. She's not with you?

No, she is not. A vision of a garden popped up suddenly in his mind. Sheren, Avera, and...Seth. Yes, he was beginning to remember.

Well, vet! We don't want to storm the place without at least having an idea of where you and Sheren are located. Kapatree might try to cut his losses and kill you both if he realizes he's under attack by an army of Blades and their pissed off Bloodsworn.

Can you not open a gate to me here?

I wish. Unfortunately, not only do I still not know how to call a gate, even if I did, it's Seth's dagger I'm honing in on, not you.

The bottom fell out of Bracca's stomach. He'd had Seth's dagger on him when he was knocked unconscious. Whoever had taken it from him might not know it for what it was, but they would have handled it. And Seth... Gods above, he was only a child. He had no defenses, no training. And whatever he felt would go straight to Avera, completely uncensored.

Bracca?

He blinked, coming out of his waking nightmare. She did not sound as if she were in agony. *Forgive me, my lady, but you are correct. I do not have Seth's dagger. Nor do I know where it is. How fares my youngest blade-brother?*

Sleeping and shielded, thanks to Healer Latessa. Remind me to send that woman some flowers and a big thank-you card when all this is over. Right now, Devlin wants a better idea of your location.

A dungeon would be my guess. A very cold dungeon. He could see wisps of his breath when he exhaled. He pulled the blanket around his shoulders to ward off the chill. *The walls, floor, and ceiling look as if they are carved out of solid rock. The stone is a dark color, blue or black more than gray. No windows. The only door has a small, barred opening.*

Can you get to it?

They left me unchained. Give me a moment.

He forced himself to stand, then walk forward. With each step, his stiff body complained about the blood loss and lack of food. And lack of water, he realized, hearing a steady trickle of liquid as he neared the door. His mouth suddenly felt as dry as a Hedauden sand pit.

The chamber beyond was much larger than his cell. A rough table and two chairs occupied the center, the table empty but for a discarded pile of rags. In the wall opposite him were three doors, just like his. In the wall to his right was another door, this one solid and banded with metal. On the left he could see stairs carved into the stone wall, leading up, out of sight. He bent down, but could not see where they led.

He described everything to Avera.

Wait a minute. Jerran just sent what you

described to his Grandfather through one of his Bronze Blades, and his Grandfather thinks he knows this place. Hang on, Bracca. We may have a plan yet.

Bracca didn't answer. His gaze had gone back to the pile of rags on the table. Something about them looked familiar. He couldn't see the colors very well in the muted light, but some of the rags looked white. An odd color to find in a dungeon. Of course, his bandages were white, too. As white as a lady's underdress.

Chills swept his body. He turned his head and lifted a bit of the fabric running over his shoulder to his nose. He sniffed, then closed his eyes and drew in a much deeper breath.

Sheren. She had been the one to bind his wounds. Her feminine scent still clung to the scraps of cloth that had once lain close to her skin.

His gaze shot back to the table. Not a pile of rags at all, but Sheren's clothing. *All* of her clothing. He finally recognized the cloth of the dress she'd been wearing the morning after they'd made love. The violet shade had brought out the lavender in her eyes. "Sheren," he whispered, a new ache forming in his heart.

Was she locked in one of those other rooms, stripped bare, a prisoner as he was?

"Sheren?" he called. "Sheren!"

Echoes bounced back to him, her name repeated over and over in his voice, mocking him. He rested his forehead on the metal bars as the last echo died. He didn't know if he should be glad or not that she hadn't answered. If she had, it would mean she was in this dark place with him. He needed her, needed to feel the warmth of her body, the soft touch of her hand. But more than that, he needed to know she was alive and well.

The creak of a door echoed down to him from above. Someone was coming to check on him. Likely they'd been sent to shut him up. Jailers rarely appreciated a noisy prisoner.

Several footsteps. More than one visitor then. Many more. Voices drifted down to him. Bracca held his breath, listening. Someone laughed, a mellow, cultured sound with an edge to it that he easily recognized. Some types of madness can never be completely hidden.

****

The fire wouldn't catch. The sullen servant who had brought the wet wood laughed when Sheren pointed out its condition. All she'd been able to coax from the damp logs were a few smoldering flames and a lot of smoke. She generated more heat pacing in front of the useless fireplace than the fire did.

Several times Sheren glanced at the locked door of the room she'd been left in. Thank Luma Nerrilik had decided to leave her alone for a while. After he'd shown her Seth's amber dagger and threatened to tell Kapatree what it represented, she would have agreed to anything. Her willing cooperation in a binding ceremony was little enough price to pay.

Of course, Nerrilik had only been guessing about the dagger. She hadn't known that at the time. Her horrified reaction to his threat had been enough to confirm his suspicion and place her in his power. Still, she didn't think she'd be able to hold on to her pretense of accepting him if he tried to touch her again.

A sound at the door froze her in place and sent her heart racing. The lock clicked and the door opened. Lord Kapatree entered first, followed by Nerrilik and a decca of Kapatree's Blades. She couldn't keep from glancing at the sheathed dagger at Nerrilik's waist. The amber hilt of her son's weapon was hidden beneath a leather wrapping, one she'd put on herself. Nerrilik could have hidden the entire dagger, but she thought he preferred to have it where she could see it. A reminder that he held her son's very life in his hands, a warning to ensure she obeyed his every word.

She bit her tongue to keep from asking about Bracca. Lord Kapatree had allowed her to clean the warrior's wounds and stop the bleeding, but only so he wouldn't die before Camarie arrived. They'd simply left him in that cold, dark place below. She knew he was alive, could feel the dull edge of his pain in her mind, but that was all.

Unless they were found soon, she feared both she and Bracca would become victims of their separate demons. He would be taken, tortured, and eventually killed, by Camarie. A part of her would surely die with him, making her own future twice as hard to bear. She would live on, tortured every day by the touch of a man she despised and the hold he had over her child.

The shiver that shook her from head to toe had nothing to do with the cold permeating Kapatree's fortress. Still, she pulled her borrowed cloak tighter around her. The sky-blue gown Nerrilik had forced her to change into was thin and silky, clinging to her every curve and doing nothing to ward off the chill.

"Cold, my dear?" Lord Kapatree's voice oozed with concern. "You must forgive me. This is not one of my major residencies and as a result the amenities are quite lacking." He flicked a hand in the direction of the fireplace. A narrow stream of magic shot through the air, engulfing the smoking logs with a loud whoomp. White hot flames filled the fireplace to overflowing, sending out a wave of heated air. Sheren threw up her hand to shield her face as she took several hasty steps back from the greedy blaze.

She glared at the smug grin on Kapatree's face. The arrogant Bloodsworn moved closer to the fireplace after the flames settled down to something less than a conflagration. He held his hands out, then rubbed them together. "That's better. Not that we will be here much longer. Camarie has arrived to claim his property. Once he leaves, we'll all be off to a new location."

Sheren felt the blood drain from her face. The dark Bloodsworn was here? Already? Nerrilik caught her arm as she swayed.

"Are you all right?"

"Yes. Yes, I'm fine." But Bracca would soon be anything but fine. He would be dead.

A sense of crippling loss hit her, bringing tears to her eyes and making her tremble. How could she lose him so soon? She'd only just found him.

A sly glance from Kapatree had her blinking rapidly, forcing the tears back. If begging would save his life, she would drop to her knees in an instant and weep rivers of tears over Kapatree's boots. But she would not add to the Bloodsworn's sick satisfaction by pleading when she knew it would do no good. He had no intention of allowing her or Bracca to go free.

Nerrilik took her hand, which was still trembling, and kissed it. She wanted to hit him again, but didn't dare. "Do not worry. None of Camarie's Black Blades will come anywhere near you, *me`surrasie*. You'll be safe with me." He tucked her hand possessively into the crook of his arm. She tried to ease away only to have him pull her tighter to his side. Pressing his lips to her hair he whispered, "Remember our bargain, Sheren. I'm very fond of Seth. Don't force me to hurt him."

Sheren bit her lip to hold back the hysterical laugh at his choice of words. Bargain? More like an ultimatum. Do or say whatever he wished or Seth would suffer. Such a threat was not one she would likely forget.

****

Bracca gripped the bars of his prison and watched Camarie's arrival with mixed emotions. He wanted the man's blood for the long years of torture and hunger he'd had to endure. At the same time, a part of him was terrified that somehow, some way, Camarie would get him back. Steeling himself, he met the gaze of the last man he ever wanted to see again.

"Hello, my Blade." Camarie smiled, his voice warm, as if greeting an old friend.

"Former Blade."

Some of the warmth left his expression. "Yes, so Sardis informed me. I was quite surprised to hear you still lived after I felt your link shatter. Even more surprised to learn your new Bloodsworn is Devlin's little Earth female. Quite a feisty little package, I must say. I don't know who I'm more envious of. Devlin, for being inside her body, or you, for being inside her mind."

Bracca didn't rise to the bait. There was no way Camarie could know of Avera first hand.

"You're wondering if I've actually seen her. She has the most vivid green eyes, wouldn't you agree? Very striking with her golden skin and midnight black hair."

"You've seen her in your Blades' memories."

"I've seen her in person." His smile slid wider. "I've touched her. *Recently*."

Impossible. The Tragar would never allow Camarie to get that close.

An oily chuckle. "I see you don't believe me. I assure you, it's true. I've become quite the chameleon. It's very hard to kill someone if you don't know where to look for them. I've learned to be...unpredictable."

That much was true. Camarie had indeed changed over the past two years. He'd taken to disappearing for days at a time with only Sardis and one or two others for protection. Each time he returned, he seemed different in some way. A little stranger. A little less...stable.

Camarie's eyes glittered, the madness more pronounced than Bracca had ever noticed. "One might even say I've learned to slip beneath the most stringent of noses." He pulled a bottle from a pocket and set it on the table. It took Bracca a moment to place where he'd last seen the bottle.

He met Camarie's self-satisfied gaze with a bored expression. "Are you trying to tell me you are the one who poisoned Avera's bath salts?" The possibility of Camarie having that kind of freedom inside the villa made his blood run cold.

A frown flickered across Camarie's face, quickly replaced by another sly smile. "Technically, no. I provided the poison to taint the bath salts, but one of Devlin's own did the deed. Apparently he holds a grudge against my Blades for an incident several years ago and insists on taking it out on you. No Lady Bloodsworn, no Bracca Cu-Laurian. The logic of a simple mind astounds me."

Bracca cursed silently. "Nerrilik would never work for you."

"Then it's good he doesn't know I'm the one in charge."

Nerrilik must think he worked for Kapatree alone. The fool. "And the fire?"

The frown settled in this time. Camarie tapped his chin. "The fire. Yes, that was Nerrilik's work as well. I really must discuss his level of usefulness with Kapatree. Now that his duplicity is revealed, he'll no longer have access to Villa Porenmagie. If Devlin doesn't handle the situation himself, there may be an unfortunate accident in Nerrilik's future. We'll simply have to wait and see. Kapatree said he promised the Silver Blade a reward for helping to capture you, and insists on keeping his word. A minor flaw in my old friend's otherwise delightfully devious character."

"What kind of reward?"

"The woman, of course. What is her name?" He snapped his fingers. "Ah, yes, Sheren. Pretty enough, I suppose. If she had dark hair instead of blonde, I might even want her for myself, though I think Kapatree already has plans for her."

Rage kindled in Bracca's belly. He wanted nothing more in that moment than to be three feet away from Camarie with his amber sword in his hand. He'd gut the dark Bloodsworn first, then go after Kapatree. The Silver Blade would be last. If he had any say in the matter at all, Nerrilik's death would be slow and extremely painful.

Camarie chuckled. "Ah, poor Bracca. Does the lady's fate bother you that much? Perhaps I can convince Kapatree to hold the binding ceremony down here before we leave. I don't believe Nerrilik would mind if he knew how much you cared.

Bracca gathered himself, swallowing his rage and stuffing his feelings for Sheren as deep as possible. He didn't have a choice. This man wanted to torture him. If he really knew what Sheren meant to him, he would do more than hold a ceremony in front of him that bound her to another man. He would physically torture her, knowing Bracca would die a little with each cut or lash to her skin. He could not even beg Camarie to spare her.

"The woman is friend to my Bloodsworn, nothing more."

"Really? I'm told she threw a fit when she awoke and was told you'd been taken as well. She demanded to see you. Nerrilik refused, but Kapatree over-ruled him and allowed her to treat your wounds so you wouldn't die too soon. He told me her touch on your sword jerked you out of unconsciousness. He also said she took a blast of magic for you." He leaned toward Bracca's cell, held a hand to the side of his mouth and whispered loudly. "I think she is more than just a friend."

"She knows Avera cares for me."

"Perhaps. Perhaps after the binding ceremony I'll insist she stay and watch our first session together. It will be interesting, I think, to see just how far she'll go to save her friend's Blade."

Bracca?

Here.

Are you alone?

No. Camarie is with me.

Excellent! An extremely short pause. *Devlin wants to know how many Blades he has with him.*

A full decca. His gaze darted to Sardis standing just beyond Camarie, then away. The Black Blade must have been watching him far closer than he thought because he immediately stiffened. A second later, Camarie spun around, all traces of his easy arrogance gone. In his place was the man Bracca had seen many times over the years. Sharply perceptive, coldly sadistic, and without an ounce of mercy.

"Sardis thinks you are talking to your little female Bloodsworn."

"Sardis should leave thinking to those of us with brains larger than a grape. I am actually trying to decide on the best way to kill him. I've imagined so many ways over the years the choice is difficult."

Camarie's eyes narrowed. "Truth, and not truth. I think—"

He broke off, spinning around again to face a corner of the chamber just as light from a gate flooded the room. He backed away. Black Blades rushed in between him and the gate.

Bracca strained to see who came through the gate first. Hopefully, it would not be Avera. He didn't think the Tragar was foolish enough to allow her to place herself in danger, but he knew his heart-sister. She would not be content with waiting safely back at the villa. Oh, no, she would insist on being in on the rescue.

Thankfully, it was three Silver Blades who came through first, followed by three warriors holding swords of sapphire blue. A seventh man stepped through the gate, magic glowing in the hand not holding a sword. Bracca recognized Jerran Ti-Peregrine an instant before the Bloodsworn fired the ball of lethal essence straight at Camarie. The dark Bloodsworn threw up a barrier and lobbed his own attack. The shot sent Ti-Peregrine diving sideways while behind him more Blades poured through the gate—Silver, Sapphire, Bronze, Emerald.

Bracca looked at Camarie and grinned. "It appears you have lost."

A snarl twisted Camarie's features. "Not everything." He threw out his hand, sending a blinding ball of magic directly into Bracca's face.

Chapter Thirty-One

Bracca had just enough time to spin aside before the blast of magic turned the door into thousands of deadly splinters. Pain ripped into his back, joining the agony that flared from his wounds at his rapid movement. He fell to his knees, gasping, barely keeping himself off the floor with the brace of his hand. He didn't know why he bothered except that he expected Camarie to come through the doorway any moment to finish what he started and he didn't want to die lying helpless on the ground.

A roar of pure frustration rose over the sounds of battle. Bracca looked over his shoulder to see the dark Bloodsworn beating his fists against the barrier of magic filling the open doorway.

"No one defies me," Camarie screamed. "No one leaves my service unless by my will. You are mine, Cu-Laurian. Mine to destroy. Your death will become legend among Blades."

With each blow, the essence comprising the barrier flared into a brilliant, cheerful rainbow, as if mocking his efforts. Bracca rolled sideways until he could sit somewhat comfortably on one hip. Straightening his injured leg and bending his other, he rested his arm on his knee and watched his former Bloodsworn's impotent fury. By the time Sardis appeared and grabbed his shoulder, Camarie's civilized façade had cracked completely, leaving him a wild-eyed mad-man with spittle running down his chin. The image was one Bracca readily burned into his memory.

"My Bloodsworn," Sardis begged, "we must go.

There are too many." Clearly reluctant, Camarie allowed himself to be drawn away. Every other step he hurled a blast of magic at the barrier. Twice he had to fend off another Bloodsworn's magic. All the while Sardis kept up a steady stream of words Bracca couldn't hear.

Finally, a gate appeared near the two men. At its edge, Camarie stopped to glare at him. Bracca couldn't resist the urge to smile and wave. He decided that watching Sardis wrestle his raving Bloodsworn through the gate was almost worth the pain of a few splinters.

It was only a few minutes later when things began to quiet down in the chamber outside. Bracca used a nearby wall to pull himself to his feet. He still had to find Sheren. He could sense her above, somewhere up the stairs. She was frightened, but he couldn't get a clear sense of why.

He reached the doorway just as the magic dissipated. Stepping out of his cell he was surprised to see the Bloodsworn waiting for him. He carefully inclined his head. "Lord Caveon."

"Amber Blade."

A low whistle came from behind him. He turned and met Karess' cheerful gaze. "*Vet*, Bracca, you look like a naked porcupine. It's going to take hours to pull out all those splinters."

A tingle of magic rushed over Bracca's skin from head to toe, making him shiver.

Karess raised a brow. He bowed low to Caveon. "I stand corrected, my lord, and thank you for your kind assistance to my friend."

"I thank you as well," Bracca said. He inclined his head once more since his injuries wouldn't let him bow.

Caveon harrumphed. "Yes, well, he could hardly wear clothes with all that wood sticking out of him."

Bracca gritted his teeth as another wave of

magic settled clothes on his wounded body.

Lord Jerran walked up. "I know you're uncomfortable, Bracca, but we have no time to worry about bandages right now."

Bracca nodded and looked around the room. The two Black Blades not dead stood surrounded by a small army of warriors with grim faces. He recognized the two men as part of Camarie's Inner Decca. Another Bloodsworn stood nearby, one Bracca had seen at the Council, but didn't know. Of Avera and her Starmate, there was no sign.

"Where is my Bloodsworn?"

"She and Devlin went after Seth's dagger," Lord Jerran said. "It's upstairs somewhere."

A scream filled the chamber, followed quickly by another. Everyone focused on Camarie's two men who had collapsed and now lay writhing in pain on the floor.

"*Vet! Vet!* Camarie's sundering their links." Karess paced back and forth in agitation.

Lord Jerran winced as another piercing scream rent the air. "I hate to see that happen to any man. Do you think we can save them, grandfather?"

"Do not bother," Bracca said coldly.

"Why not?" Caveon snapped. "Do you think you are the only one deserving of a second chance?"

Bracca forced himself to watch the dying men. "Kilth and Lichas are Camarie's Fifth and Seventh Blades for a reason. They enjoy causing pain and suffering as much as he does. They would not welcome a second life where they could not indulge their perverted whims. Trust me, had these two been brought before the Council and their crimes revealed, you would think this punishment not harsh enough."

The frown didn't leave his face, but Lord Caveon heaved a sigh. "I would prefer to bring their Bloodsworn to justice. It is unfortunate that he escaped."

"Devlin is not going to be pleased," Lord Jerran said.

Karess snorted. "Devlin? I'm worried about Lady Avera. I have never seen a female so thirsty for blood. If she gets her hands on Kapatree or Nerrilik—"

Bracca shoved past him, ignoring the various stings and stabs of pain. Avera was too impulsive for her own good. She would see Kapatree and go after him without pausing to remember he was a powerful Bloodsworn. She could not protect herself from that kind of magic.

Five steps up the stairway, he realized he would never make it. Or if he did, it would be on one hand and one knee. The pain in his thigh and back was excruciating.

Light flashed. A gate suddenly appeared on the next step up. Through it, he could see a landing with some stairs leading down. He didn't bother to ask which Bloodsworn had called the gate, though something told him it was Lord Caveon. Never would he have thought to be so indebted to the elder Bloodsworn.

He stepped through the gate onto the landing at the top of the stairs. He moved to the door standing slightly ajar, only to have Karess dodge around him, sword in his hand. "You're worse than Devlin," the Silver Blade whispered harshly. He ducked his head through the opening, paused, then nudged the door wider and slipped through.

Bracca started to slip through after him, only to have Lord Jerran hold him back. He barely kept his impatience in check as two Sapphire Blades moved silently into the hallway beyond. A long moment passed before Lord Jerran tapped his shoulder and nodded once to signal the way was clear.

Limping down the long hallway, Bracca reached

for Avera through their link. He could feel her nearby, could probably track her if she didn't answer, but that would take time they didn't have. He needed to get to her now. More than that—and he was acutely aware of how much more—he needed to get to Sheren.

Chapter Thirty-Two

Sheren couldn't stop herself from shaking. Something bad was happening. She could feel it.

"Come," Nerrilik said, putting his arm around her. She was too upset to even protest. "There's no need for you to be afraid, *me`surrasie*."

"Of course not," Kapatree said, sounding impatient. "No one here wants to harm you."

"I'm not afraid." No, she was more than afraid. She was terrified. Whatever was happening, she knew somehow that Bracca was in the center of it.

He'd been unconscious the last time she'd seen him. Injured, defenseless. What was Camarie doing to him?

She swayed as several unbidden images sprang to mind just as Kapatree said, "Look on the bright side, my dear. At least now, you no longer have to worry about Nerrilik inadvertently killing you."

His strange words succeeded in pulling her out of her near-frantic state. "What?"

"That was not my fault," Nerrilik complained. "Sheren was not supposed to draw the woman's bath. She is chatelaine of the villa, not a maid."

Kapatree snickered. "You must learn to take credit for your failures, Nerrilik. Though failing to kill Cu-Laurian in that shed fire might not be considered a failure since Camarie would have skinned you alive, slowly and with great relish, if you had succeeded. He wants the pleasure of his former Blade's death for himself."

Sheren could hardly believe what she was hearing. She'd known there was something wrong

323

with Nerrilik, but this? She managed to jerk out of his grasp, her agreement with him momentarily lost in the face of her rage. "You set the fire that almost killed Bracca and Seth!"

Nerrilik ran both hands through his hair. "I was not trying to kill Seth, Sheren, just Cu-Laurian. He is a Black Blade. His very presence at the villa defiles Sayjan's memory. I had to do something."

"Don't!" She held up a hand to ward him off. "You are never to speak of my husband again. Can't you see what you are doing? You are letting what happened four years ago dictate how you live your life. You're letting it ruin you."

Blood suffused his face. "I was already ruined the day the Tragar left me to those Black Blades!"

The door burst open, admitting an agitated servant. "My lord, there is a disturbance in the dungeon."

Kapatree waved a dismissing hand and turned back to the fireplace. "Of course there is. Ignore it."

"But—"

"I said ignore whatever sounds you might hear coming from below. Lord Camarie would not be pleased to be interrupted."

"Even the sounds of battle, my lord?"

Kapatree spun away from the fireplace. "What sounds?"

The servant gulped. "Besides the usual screaming, I heard the sound of sword fighting, and what sounded like the detonation of several magic blasts."

Kapatree's alarmed gaze sought and found one of his men. "Go see what is happening and let me know at once. And, for the sake of us all, keep out of Camarie's sight. If this is nothing but the Dark Bloodsworn playing with his present, I don't want him to think I'm spying on him. Go!"

When the warrior sprinted from the room,

Nerrilik shifted beside Sheren, clearly uneasy. "We should leave now."

"Not until we know for sure what is happening."

Kapatree started pacing.

Curious, Sheren cut a slit in her shields so she could read him. The ability was becoming easier each time she used it. What she found swirling through the Bloodsworn's aura did not surprise her.

"You fear Camarie."

His head jerked in her direction. He gave a short, brittle laugh. "Of course. Any sane person would be a fool not to fear him. He has three times the blood-links I do. Three times the power."

"No one has that many links," Nerrilik said. "Not even the First Bloodsworn."

"So the Council would have everyone think. However, it is very difficult to keep count of Camarie's Blades since he doesn't report them."

"How many does he actually have?" Sheren asked.

Still pacing anxiously, Kapatree answered absentmindedly. "Close to two hundred, perhaps more. The number rises daily. He has recently figured out how to track down men with the seed of the blade-illness in them. He captures them and keeps them imprisoned until it manifests. When it does, they have no choice but to choose him as their Bloodsworn."

"I've heard some men would rather die."

A brief, humorless chuckle escaped from Kapatree. "I'm quite sure that's true. However, he has also become very good at forcing a link on an un-willing man."

He stopped pacing and shot them a wicked glance. "I have seen his methods. Not a very pretty sight, I assure you. Interesting though. I do wish he would tell me how he—" He broke off suddenly, eyes flickering.

Sheren held her breath for the short time it took for his expression to alter. His lips flattened. His eyes turned cold and hard. Every Indigo Blade in the room suddenly snapped to alert. Some moved to leave, running quickly out the door. Others hovered closer to their Bloodsworn, sharp gazes darting around the room as if expecting an attack any moment.

Hope stirred to life within Sheren. Perhaps Avera had finally been able to trace Seth's dagger. Perhaps she and Devlin were even now rescuing Bracca. She glanced at Nerrilik, wondering if she dare snatch her son's weapon and run. Better not. At least not until she knew in which direction help lay. Running into more Indigo Blades, or worse, Black Blades, would gain her nothing.

Even as she hesitated, Nerrilik's hand dropped to the dagger's covered hilt as if preparing to draw the weapon. With a rush of horror, Sheren realized it was the only blade he wore. He'd told her he left his silver sword in the garden. Kapatree hadn't provided him with another. If he used the amber dagger to fight and kill someone, what would it do to her son?

"What is wrong?" Nerrilik demanded of Kapatree.

"We have unexpected company."

Nerrilik's face paled. "The Tragar?"

"Not yet, but I would not be surprised if he is not already here somewhere. What I don't understand is how they could have found us so quickly." His speculative gaze settled first on her, then Nerrilik.

Nerrilik shifted uneasily. "If we're under attack, why are we still here?"

"Because Camarie brought only a decca of Blades and may need help. I know better than to run out on him. He will expect my men to back him if need be, and unlike him, I do not have so many Blades that I can leave some behind to fend for themselves."

"I have no loyalty to Camarie or his Black Blades. I am taking Sheren out of here now. Open a gate."

Kapatree's eyes glinted. "Do you think to command me, Silver Blade?"

Two warriors stepped forward, their swords pointed at Sheren and Nerrilik. "Are you going back on your word?" he asked accusingly.

"Don't insult me," Kapatree snapped. "I never break my word. I promised to take you with me if you helped capture Cu-Laurian and the Tragar's Starmate, and I did, even though the bargain was only half satisfied." He motioned toward her. "I even gave you your woman. Whether you are able to keep her remains to be seen."

Nerrilik's grip on her arm tightened painfully. "Sheren is mine. She has always been mine."

"By the look on her face, I think Sheren disagrees with you."

Sheren gasped in relief at the sound of Avera's disapproving voice. The doors of the room flew wide, allowing several people to pour into the room. She caught sight of Avera's determined face through the sea of warriors surrounding her just as the first flash of magic left Kapatree's hands. A wide barrier sprang up, shielding Avera and the men with her.

"Damn you, Tragar," Kapatree shouted.

Lord Devlin forced his way through his Blades to stand in front of them. His smile was enough to send a shiver down the bravest man's spine as he held his hands out to his side. "You should never have allied yourself with my uncle, Kapatree." His head lowered, and so did his voice. "And you damn well should never have attacked my Starmate." His arms began to close. As they did, the barrier that kept Kapatree's magic at bay flexed and curved, closing inexorably around Kapatree and his men.

327

The backwash of magic from Kapatree's frantic blasts flared uselessly against the strong shield. He stopped when the backwash rebounded, striking one of his men and killing him instantly.

Nerrilik staggered back as Silver Blades engaged those of Kapatree's men not trapped with him. When he snatched Seth's dagger free, Sheren threw herself on him, trying to wrench the small weapon from his grasp. She couldn't let him use it.

Avera's voice rose above the noise of battle. "*That* belongs to Seth."

Sheren sobbed in relief as the dagger flew out of Nerrilik's hand and sailed across the room to Avera. She tried to push herself away from him only to have him jerk her back. He bent down swiftly, hand fumbling at his boot, and came up with a small thin-bladed knife he held to her throat.

Gasping, she leaned back against him away from the blade. "What are you doing?"

"Don't fight me, Sheren. You have to see this is the only way for us to escape and be together. Don't make me hurt you."

She swallowed, feeling the press of the sharp blade against her throat. Her gaze sought and found Avera's. The other woman stood not far away, closely flanked by Devlin and the dark-skinned Fate. Young Kiel hovered directly at her back, eyes blazing in anger. Beside him stood a hard-eyed Strum and several Blades she didn't know. It seemed ridiculous that Nerrilik did not realize the futility of his situation. He would be captured, possibly killed in the process. The only question was whether or not she was going to die with him.

****

Careful, Avera sent to Bracca as he approached the room she was in. *Nerrilik has a knife at Sheren's throat.*

White hot rage filled his veins. He wanted to

rush into that room and slam his fist into Nerrilik's chest and rip out his heart.

A surge of calm flooded his link with Avera, leaching away the blinding anger until he could think again. *Easy*, she said, *I don't think he wants to hurt her, but he's desperate. We have to time this just right.*

She sent him a plan. One he realized must have come from the Tragar when she revealed the part where Bracca was allowed to kill Nerrilik. A much quicker death than a Blade who had betrayed his Bloodsworn deserved, but Bracca was not about to complain. He wanted Nerrilik's blood.

He crept to the edge of the open doors, aware Karess and the others had dropped back. They wouldn't interfere. Even wounded, limping, his clothes wet with blood, they recognized his need to do this.

A body lay near the doorway just inside the room. Bracca recognized one of Kapatree's Indigo Blades from his fight in the garden. The sight of the man's dead sword lying near his hand made Bracca's palm itch for his own.

It'll be in your hand, soon. I brought it with me.

Satisfaction poured through him at Avera's words. Then his prey came into sight. Peeking around the corner, Bracca froze, his gaze fastening on the knife poised at Sheren's throat.

"Stay back," Nerrilik said, dragging Sheren with him another step. One step closer to Bracca.

Devlin Tragar walked into view, a hard, resigned look on his face. He took several more steps before stopping, forcing Nerrilik to turn so that his back was to Bracca at the perfect angle. "You know I can no longer maintain our link, Nerrilik. Not after everything you've done."

"You can. You should! You owe me that much!" His hand shook. Bracca leaned forward.

Wait, Avera cautioned. She moved into his sight. She didn't make the mistake of looking past Nerrilik to him, but kept her gaze fastened on the Silver Blade.

Nerrilik took another step back, his voice desperate. "Besides, you need me. You can't afford to lose the magic from our link. Kapatree told us Camarie has over two hundred Blades. Soon, not even the whole Council will be able to stand against him. Just let us leave, and you'll never have to see us again. You can keep the magic."

Devlin shook his head. "I think not."

Now!

Nerrilik stiffened.

Bracca surged forward. He snaked an arm around Nerrilik's throat and grabbed his wrist at the same time, forcing the knife away from Sheren. Nerrilik thrust Sheren away and drove his elbow back, directly into Bracca's injured side. Pain took his vision and his breath. He held on, squeezing Nerrilik's wrist until he felt bones grind together.

A second blow doubled him over. Gasping for air, he shoved Nerrilik in the direction of the dead body, hoping he'd trip and fall. He did, but recovered fast. Bracca was still shaking the pain out of his head when Nerrilik came after him.

Then suddenly, the pain was gone. Bracca recognized Sheren's sweet warmth shielding his mind as he braced himself on his injured leg and kicked the Silver Blade back once more.

Pulling himself up a second time, Nerrilik shot an agonized look in Sheren's direction. Bracca fought the urge to look as well, keeping his gaze on his prey. He already knew Avera had Sheren safely at her side.

Nerrilik stole a glance toward the door. Bracca smiled at the dismay on the traitor's face when he found the doorway solidly blocked by a wall of grim warriors. The soon to be dead Silver Blade spun back around, snarling and dropping into a deadly crouch.

"You think you've won. You think you'll have her. But I refuse to let her be tainted by a Black Blade."

The unexpected attack came too quick for Bracca to stop, much less intercept. He tracked the flight of the dagger, his heart stopping as he realized it flew straight at the woman he loved. It never reached its target. Four walls of magic sprang up, shielding Sheren and Avera both.

Avera grinned at him. *I think I can safely say we've got Sheren covered. Now take that traitor down so we can go home.* She held up something. Bracca had just enough time to recognize his sword before the amber weapon flew into his outstretched hand.

His multitude of aches and pains receded as strength poured into him. With a twist of his wrist, he spun the blade in a wide circle, welcoming it back with a wave of fierce possession.

Inside his mind, the barrier created by Sheren's presence shivered, but held firm. His gaze flew to her. She stared at him, fear and worry easy to read in her lavender eyes. He knew part of her fear was because he was a warrior, a man steeped in violence. As gently as possible, he pushed the touch of her mind away from his. It was bad enough she had to see him fight. He didn't want her to feel his intense satisfaction when he took Nerrilik's life. He wasn't usually so bloodthirsty, but the Silver Blade had threatened everything Bracca held dear in his world. Killing him would be a pleasure. Never would he inflict that part of himself on his gentle Sheren.

Reluctantly, she acceded to his wishes, her comforting presence withdrawing from his mind. Her understanding, her acceptance of him, violence and all, lingered, soft as a dream, yet more real than anything he'd ever felt in his life. Gods knew he

331

would never be worthy of her, but he swore in that moment he would never stop trying.

He turned back to Nerrilik to find the desperate man armed with the dead Blade's sword. Well enough. With Sheren watching, a fair fight would be better than a slaughter, though the end would be the same.

This won't take long, my lady Bloodsworn.

Chapter Thirty-Three

Bracca had been true to his word, Avera thought, watching Nerrilik's body disappear through the gate. One, two, three strikes, and it was over. Thank God. And here she'd thought working with experimental chemical compounds was stressful. Ha!

Devlin came up beside her. "Are you ready to go home?"

"More than ready. Tell me this kind of stuff doesn't happen very often. I don't think I can handle the stress."

He drew her into his arms. "Maybe not this particular scenario, but stressful things do happen on occasion. Fortunately, we Feyune have discovered an excellent stress reliever."

"Oh, yeah? What's that?"

Devlin leaned down and nuzzled her ear. "Perhaps a practical demonstration would be better."

His warm breath made her shiver. She was tired of being cold. She wanted the warmth of her villa, or better yet, the warmth of her very own biological space heater, preferably naked. "I'm always up for a little demonstration. It might have to wait just a little while, though."

Avera nodded toward Bracca and Sheren. After being assured that her son was safe, the petite blonde successfully bullied the big, bad Amber Blade into taking off his bloody shirt so she could see to his new wounds. A waste of time, actually, since Avera intended to heal every nick and scratch once they got home.

Please, he said before she could point that out to

Sheren. *She needs this, as do I.*

What's a Bloodsworn to say to that?

"I'm going to be a little busy when we get back," Avera reminded Devlin.

Blue fire lit his eyes. "So you will. I think we should re-schedule my demonstration for another time."

"Oh, no you don't—"

"Because you will not have the patience for it after you heal your Blade."

"I'll not have the pa..." Her cheeks, hell, her whole body flushed as she caught his meaning. The magic of their Starmate bond *and* deep-healing lust? Just the thought of what that meant made her even more anxious to get back to the villa.

"Lady St. John?"

She turned to find Caveon, Jerran, and three other Bloodsworn Council members she'd been quickly introduced to earlier as Toryn, Niall, and Mikael, standing in a group. Every one of them, Jerran included, had a solemn air about them. Devlin tensed and took a half step that put him partly in front of her.

Uh-oh, must be judgment time.

She wasn't aware Bracca had moved until he also took a step in front of her. What's more, Sheren stood at his side, a fierce look on her beautiful face that reminded Avera of an angry mother bear.

Then Kiel was there, followed quickly by Strum, Karess, and, knock her down with a feather, Fate.

Every Silver Blade who'd come with Devlin stood protectively in front, beside, or behind her. What's more, she didn't think Devlin had ordered them to.

Some of the other Bloodsworn's Blades started joining the party, lining up to face them. After only a short moment every one of them backed off, clearly unhappy.

Avera forced her way to the front, literally squeezing between rock hard biceps and triceps. She glared at Devlin and Bracca until they moved apart enough so she could stand between them. Then she faced Caveon's heavy gaze, expecting to see stern disapproval. Instead, she'd swear his sharp eyes held a twinkle of amusement. "I believe you had a question, Lord Caveon?"

"More in the nature of some relevant information."

"Such as?"

"It is permissible for a Bloodsworn to request a second hearing concerning a Council ruling once subsequent information has been…revealed."

She let the words sink in. "I see. Thank you for the information."

A few seconds of silence passed.

"Grandfather." Jerran said pointedly.

Lord Caveon heaved a sigh. "Oh, very well. It is usual for the Bloodsworn to make a request for the hearing several days in advance during a formal audience at Bloodsworn Hall. However, since we have a majority present here…" He dangled the end of the sentence like bait on a hook.

Wary of biting without knowing the rules, she glanced up at Devlin. "Any special protocol I need to follow here?"

He slipped an arm around her. "No. Merely state your request."

"Right." She faced the waiting Bloodsworn. "I, Avera St. John, hereby request another hearing on the subject of whether or not I'm a proper Bloodsworn."

"You are a proper Bloodsworn," Bracca growled.

"Yes, but the Council's ruling says I don't have the same rights as everyone else."

"Nonsense," Toryn said.

"Don't nonsense me." She pointed at the

Bloodsworn in the spiffy leathers. "You know what I mean. I bet no one put a leash on you when you became a Bloodsworn."

Devlin's arms tightened. "Does the Council recognize Lady St. John's request?"

"We do," Jerran said quickly. He grinned and stepped around his grandfather. "You are most certainly a proper Bloodsworn, lovely lady, don't let anyone tell you otherwise. As to our unusual methods, I'm sure Devlin would have remembered about the second hearing clause in a day or two. I just thought it best to hurry things along considering the nature of the new information. Speaking of which." He turned to Sheren. "If you will allow me, I would be happy to look after Seth for a day or two."

"Why can't he come home now?" Sheren turned worriedly to Avera. "You said he was safe. Is something wrong with him?"

Avera arched a brow at Caveon. "Well, answer the lady. You know I can't feel my Third Blade from this far away."

The older man managed to wince and look offended at the same time. "The child is in my care. Of course he is fine. I received a message from Latessa a few minutes ago via my Blades saying he is awake and doing well. No lingering effects from having his...weapon, in the wrong hands."

Smiling slightly, Avera inclined her head to him in thanks. She touched the amber dagger safely secured at her waist, and turned back to Sheren. "It's up to you if you'd like to go get Seth now. No, Bracca, you can't go with her," she said, cutting her Blade off as he opened his mouth. "In case you haven't noticed, you're still bleeding. I need to take care of all those wounds."

He snapped his mouth shut. Sheren stared at him a moment before meeting Avera's gaze. "You will deep-heal him?"

"Yes." She leaned toward Sheren and whispered. "You do know what that means, right?"

Sheren nodded slowly, her gaze returning to lock with Bracca's. The look in her eyes as she stared up at him made Avera certain her Blade would not be needing the services of a *shetha* later.

"Lord Jerran," Sheren said. "If you would bring Seth home in one—"

"Two," Bracca said quickly, making Avera bite her lip to keep from laughing.

"Two days," Sheren agreed, her cheeks blushing bright red. "We would be most grateful."

"As you wish, my lady."

"Right," Avera said briskly, "let's go then." Anticipation slammed into her, doubling her heart rate and making her stomach quiver. She couldn't take her eyes off Devlin. He looked so good to her she was surprised she wasn't drooling.

Several shining gates appeared around the room in quick succession. She kept her wistful sigh to herself. It would be great to have the power to open gates. If only that power didn't come with such a steep price.

Part of her wanted the right to link with more Blades and part of her didn't. That small, scared part of her wanted to crawl into a hole and pretend this whole Bloodsworn-Blade thing didn't exist. Better yet, she wanted men like Bracca, Fate, and Karess, and children like Tyr and Seth, to not need a Bloodsworn at all.

If the reason they couldn't touch Avalyr's magical essence was an illness, there had to be a cure, right? Not something that magically appeared after ten successful prophecies, but an actual scientific cure. Her thoughts scattered as Devlin suddenly swept her off her feet and into his arms.

"What in the world of Avalyr are you doing?"

"Carrying you so you are not too tired to heal

Bracca when we reach the villa."

His quick response made her laugh. "Your concern is touching, but something tells me Bracca's health isn't your main focus here."

"No," he said, settling those deep-water blue eyes of his on her. "You are."

Chapter Thirty-Four

For the first time in his life, Bracca never wanted the lust from a deep-healing to end. Freshly healed, he and Sheren barely made it to his room. They collapsed onto his bed in a flurry of torn clothing and desperate kisses. He was sure he'd died and ascended to Paradise when she took him in her hand and guided him into her body. Never had he felt this way about any woman in his life. The way she touched him, accepted him, sent his heart soaring.

Panting, fighting for control, he slid effortlessly inside her, amazed again at how well they fit together. She had to have been made just for him. He pulled back and pushed his way inside again, groaning as pleasure zinged through his entire body. Slick, snug muscles caressed every inch of him as he slid inside, and milked him like a tight fist when he withdrew. He wanted to hold back, to bring her to pleasure first, but it only took a few heated strokes to bring his release boiling to the surface.

He groaned as his seed gushed into her in hot, violent streams, making her passage even slicker than before. Not once did he stop moving, could not have stopped even if he wanted to. Instead of his release calming some of the lust, it only seemed to make it worse. Just the thought of his essence joining the cream of her desire sent him into a frenzy of need.

He kissed her, licked her, sucked and nipped at every inch of skin he could reach. He wanted to pleasure her in every way possible, bring her to orgasm again and again. With a growl of possession, he settled his mouth on one of her breasts and suckled hard, flicking her nipple with his tongue.

"Bracca!" She arched into his mouth, her legs tightening around his waist as he pounded into her at a frantic pace. She clutched his head to her breast and came, her body jerking against him, her strangled cries music to his ears. Again, he never stopped moving, never stopped claiming her, but he slowed, burying his face in the white silk of her hair long enough to drink in her sweet scent while she caught her breath.

Then he drove her up again, allowing himself to join her at the peak this time. Hard spasms racked his body as they came together, making him feel as if his bones might break. Making him feel loved.

A long time later, the lust returned. Not as strong, but still persistent enough to wake him with an ache in his balls and blood throbbing in his hard shaft. Beside him, Sheren stirred. She stretched, moaning slightly. He rolled over instantly, checking her, needing to know what was wrong.

"What is it?" *Vet!* If he'd hurt her, he would never touch her again. At least not when he was caught in the throes of a lust he couldn't control.

Her hand reached up and flowed down his back in a long caress, stirring his desire to a fever pitch. He pushed the urges back, worried he'd done too much all ready.

"Don't," she whispered.

"Don't what?"

"Don't hold back what you feel. I want your desire. I need it."

Her words sent that very desire spiraling up even as they froze him to stillness. She felt his emotions? Is that what she'd meant when she told him she could feel him? Did that mean she knew the power of the love that had broken his battered soul wide open to her shining light? Did she love him in return?

He gazed into her dark, lavender eyes, searching for answers. She stroked his face.

"I see you, Bracca Cu-Laurian. From your first touch, I've seen into your soul."

He flinched and looked away, shame eating up his desire.

"Stop that." She took his face in both hands, forcing him to look at her. "You have nothing to be ashamed of. The stains of whatever black deeds Camarie forced on you are his to bear, not yours." Her fingers smoothed back a lock of his hair. Wonder took over her gaze. "Your soul, the part of you that holds your honor, shines so bright I can hardly bare to look upon it. And when I do, I never want to look away. I love you."

Her words healed his heart, even those places Avera hadn't been able reach. He leaned down and kissed her, savoring her taste, drawing the very essence of her more firmly inside him. She was there, a part of him now. Would always be a part of him no matter what the fates, or the gods, or even the Ultimate Power, made of his future. Sheren would always and forever be his.

Her lips smiled beneath his. "I like that."

"What?"

"You're feeling very possessive of me right now. I like how it makes me feel."

"And just how does it make you feel?"

"Loved."

His heart swelled. That was exactly how he felt every time she looked at him the way she was doing now. He swore right then he would do anything to keep that look in her eyes.

A splinter of doubt immediately struck at his confidence. Would he be able to keep that vow? He was still Avera's First Blade, her first protector. His duty and honor demanded her life came before all others.

Sheren ran her finger over his brows. "You're worrying again. Stop it. Whatever it is, we'll face it together."

He never wanted anything to come between them. Not a half-truth, not a misunderstanding. Everything had to be out in the open.

"Sheren, I am Avera's First Blade. She has demanded a review of the Council's edict because of Seth, but they still may not allow her any more Blades. Until Tyr is much older, there is no one who can take my place. Her protection must be my first priority."

"And so it shall," Sheren said firmly. "I'm not blind to the truth, Bracca. I know keeping Avera safe is the same as keeping you and Seth safe. That part of Sayjan's link with the Tragar never bothered me. It was the headless zeal with which he performed his duties. He put himself into danger when he wasn't ready. He was focused so much on gaining status as a Blade that he cut Seth and me out of his life entirely. He cared for us, but he would have been just as happy without us. I can't live that way again."

"I don't want you to. Status means nothing to me. Avera will always be the sister of my heart, but I would give up my position as her First Blade without hesitation if there were someone else. You know this."

"Yes, I do. And as long as you don't take foolish chances with your life, and never forget Seth and I need your love and care, too, I can live with you putting Avera first until she finds a new First Blade."

"That may not happen for a long time. Tyr will not have the level of skill required for several years."

She drew him down for a long kiss, then

scattered others over his face and neck, making him shudder. "Something tells me Lady St. John is not the type of female to allow a group of males to dictate to her heart. If her heart tells her to help another blade-sick man, she will do so, and worry about the consequences later."

Bracca chuckled, his body stirring at the feel of her lips sliding across his skin. "Indeed. She is quite fearless. Though I am in no position to bemoan her impulsive behavior, I am grateful she has someone like the Tragar to help me watch over her. When she is with him, I can turn my attention to far more important matters." He slipped a hand down to press firmly between her legs.

"Mmm." Sheren moaned in agreement. "I feel your lust rising again." Her lithe body moved seductively against his. "I need you, Bracca."

"As I need you, my *karia,* my heart. Always and forever." With a deep kiss, he settled his body into the warm, welcoming cradle of hers.

Epilogue

Devlin woke to the feel of soft, female wetness sliding over him in a tight, hot sheath. Eyes still closed, he savored the moment. Being on the receiving end of his adorable Starmate's deep-healing lust was something he could easily get used to. If he wasn't careful, he might even find himself searching for ways to sink a sword between Bracca's ribs. An accident on the training field, perhaps?

"I know you're awake. You're smiling again."

He opened his eyes. Avera rose up on her knees above him. The smile she wore turned sultry as she slowly pressed down again, taking him deep inside her. She leaned forward, hands on his chest, and repeated the move several more times. Her slender fingers began to knead the muscles of his chest like a cat, and he swore he could almost hear her purr.

For a long time he said nothing, content to watch as she took her pleasure from his body. Every time she came down on him, her eyelids almost closed and a little moan slipped from between her lips. To do that to her, give her that much pleasure, made him feel more powerful than the entire Concourse.

Reaching up, he cupped her breasts. She leaned into his touch until he could feel her hard nipples bore into the center of his palms in erotic little circles. He tightened his grip, then moved to squeeze each pert nipple between his fingers.

She moaned and began to ride him faster.

When she started to lose rhythm, Devlin slipped his hands down her body to settle on her hips. He slowed her down, holding her to a lazy tempo until a soft whimper of distress slipped from her. He chuckled.

"Is this what you want?"

He began to raise his hips each time she came down, adding a sharp thrust to the meeting of their flesh. She sighed appreciably.

"Yeeeessss."

He still kept the pace measured, driving her up slowly, letting the urgency build and build until she was fighting him for control.

She finally snarled at him. "Damn it, Devlin, stop playing around!"

He gave her his most wicked grin. "As you wish, my lady."

He gripped her hips, holding her tight to him as he rolled them both over. Hooking her legs over his arms, he used the long, hard thrusts that never failed to send her spiraling out of control. She came apart quickly, screaming his name, calling him her beloved. Only then did he let go, finding his own pleasure in a release so powerful it left his fingers and toes tingling. Collapsing next to her, he kissed her and tucked her into the shelter of his body before allowing sleep to claim him once more.

****

Avera lay snuggled next to Devlin's side for a long time, watching him sleep. *Poor baby*. She'd worn him out. Not that she thought he'd do any serious complaining when he woke up. Even in sleep, he had a slight smile on his face. It did her heart good to know she'd put it there.

Taking a deep, contented breath, she did something she thought she'd never do. She closed her eyes and whispered, "Thank you, God, for putting my name in that stupid prophecy." Without it, she never would have known this wonderful, loving man. Devlin had given her everything she'd ever wanted out of life. A home, a family, and his deep abiding, totally unconditional, love. Nothing could make her new life better.

A chill breeze brushed her shoulders, bringing with it the faint scent of evergreens and raising goose bumps. Avera sat up cautiously and looked around. She must be imagining things. For a minute there, she'd swear she heard a woman's faint, tinkling laugh.

Shaking her head at the absurd notion, she reached down and flicked the covers over them both. Then she snuggled back into Devlin's warmth, and drifted off to sleep.

A word about the author...

Kathy Lane was born and raised in central Florida. She grew up running wild through orange groves and swamps, tagging after her older brothers when possible or creating her own imaginary adventures. Writing fiction has always been a passion for her, so it's a mystery how she ended up working as an accountant.

When her sons grew up and moved out, she filled her empty nest with a computer and began writing again. She is a member of RWA and her local chapter, Tampa Area Romance Authors. She is also a member of the Florida Writers Association and Infinite World of Fantasy Authors.

Kathy still lives in Florida, where she gets frequent visits from her two sons, Joe and Jon, and her wonderful niece, Darelle.

Thank you for purchasing
this Wild Rose Press publication.
For other wonderful stories of romance,
please visit our on-line bookstore at
www.thewildrosepress.com

For questions or more information,
contact us at
info@thewildrosepress.com

The Wild Rose Press
www.TheWildRosePress.com

To visit with authors of The Wild Rose Press
join our yahoo loop at
http://groups.yahoo.com/group/thewildrosepress/